THE LAND OF
NOD

THE LAND OF
NOD

A NOVEL BY

MARK A. CLEMENTS

DONALD I. FINE, INC.
New York

$8.95

To Nancy Voris, with all my thanks and love.

Library of Congress Catalogue Card Number: 94-061905
ISBN: 1-55611-442-7

Manufactured in the United States of America

10 9 8 7 6 5 4 3 2 1

Designed by Irving Perkins Associates, Inc.

This novel is a work of fiction. Names, characters, places and incidents are either the product of the author's imagination or are used fictitiously. Any resemblance to actual events, locales, organizations or persons, living or dead, is entirely coincidental and beyond the intent of either the author or publisher.

ACKNOWLEDGMENTS

Thanks to the family—Mom, Dad, Leslie, Patty, Neal, and Nancy —for a childhood that's the envy of everyone I know. And thanks to the buds—Joe Miller, Freak, Newt, Troll, Keebs, Sumo, Sue, and Sprout, for helping me grow up . . . a little. Oh, and thanks to Katie Mellen, for proof.

PART

I

MAYBERRY LOST

CHAPTER ONE

THANKS FOR THE MEMORIES

First came the roar. Then the scream. Then the wild gunfire echoing from boulder to boulder to boulder. Corporal Dittimore, crouching deep in the bushes, counted silently. He reached only *two* when the shooting stopped.

Which meant another of his men had died. The third one. He was alone.

Almost alone. *It* was here somewhere: the shadow beast.

Gripping his MP-80 submachine gun, Dittimore imitated a rock and considered his options. They were few. "Shadow beasts are the meanest, fastest creatures anyone's ever seen," Commander Kegler had said during the premission briefing. "And remember, their hide is so tough, you've got to keep shooting for at least three seconds to kill one."

The beast had leaped on Fred McMillan first, clawing out his throat and then vanishing before the rest of the squad could bring weapons to bear. The survivors had split up to hunt the creature. Dittimore's decision. Obviously a bad one.

But he intended to live to regret it. He'd chosen an ambush site of his own: thick bushes on either side, sheer rock wall behind, canyon floor in front. That was where the shadow beast would have to pass if it wanted him.

The key now was to stay motionless and alert. Spot the beast first. Make sure he had those three vital seconds.

The silence, broken only by the rasping drone of insects, stretched out even as shadows shortened. Sweat oozed like melted solder into Dittimore's eyes, but he ignored it. Mustn't move. The shadow beast might be nearby, equally still, waiting.

From time to time the corporal did move his eyes, looking up through the parted lips of the canyon to where half the sky was hidden by a dark, towering storm cloud. Except it wasn't a cloud. It was a tree. The Tree of Death, so huge the path of its shadow created a wasteland a hundred miles long.

Exploring the Tree of Death had long been a goal of Commander Kegler's. Dittimore knew that if he, himself, survived this mission he'd just be sent back later with a new squad. Which was idiotic. The Tree of Death spawned many horrors, including shadow beasts. Who knew what lived *closer* to the tree? He ought to tell Kegler to shove—

Insubordination. The upswell of guilt was immediate. But why should he feel guilty about not wanting to go on more pointless missions? He and his buddy, Mike, had been considering leaving the service entirely. He knew Gail would be pleased if he did. *Childish games,* she called these assignments.

Dittimore made up his mind. Tomorrow Gail would be returning from a long trip, and he'd give her a present: He'd tell her his days as a Federation scout were over—

Something rattled overhead. Gasping, Dittimore jerked the MP-80 up. Scanned the cliff's edge. No movement. A rock must have fallen. Wiping his brow, he turned back toward the canyon floor.

The shadow beast was twenty feet away and closing fast, claws and teeth extended. It might have been a human being dipped in purple-black paint and studded with fangs. It burst into a sprint, roaring.

Dittimore gasped, jolted to his feet and pulled the MP-80's trigger. A rattling cough shredded across the rocky landscape: *KAKAKAKAKAKAKAKAKAKAKAKAKKKKKK!* As bloody chunks of the shadow beast exploded backward, Dittimore counted silently, *One-Mississippi . . . two-Mississippi . . . three-Mississi—*

"Killed you!" he shrieked even as the creature's talons closed around his neck. "You're dead!"

"Am not!"

"Are too! Three seconds, I counted three seconds!"

"You didn't even hit me!" The shadow beast backed away angrily, Red Ball Fliers thumping up dust. "Missed me by a *mile!*"

"No way! I blasted you right in the head!"

"Did not! You were aiming clear over—"

From behind Dittimore came a sharp, sliding thump. A rectangular opening appeared in the cliff face. "Jeffry and Timmy," a woman's voice said from the darkness. "If you boys can't play without arguing, maybe you'd better find something else to do."

"Sorry, Mom," Jeff Dittimore said, hanging his head.

"We'll be quiet," Timmy Kegler added.

The window slid shut again.

"Way to go, idiot," Jeff snarled.

"It's not *my* fault! You're the one who—"

"Timmy," said another voice, "you just can't *stand* being killed, can you?" It was Mike Norris, walking around the corner of the house with the other two dead soldiers behind him. All three carried weapons—an electron blaster for Mike, a laser rifle for Fred, and a brace of zap pistols for Abe. Wood and nails and pieces of model airplanes. Only Jeff's MP-80, which he'd gotten for his twelfth birthday, looked like a *real* gun. It sounded like one, too, if you triggered a spring-loaded knob. But Jeff preferred to create his own vocal sound effects so he could vary the volume and add the whine of ricochets if he wanted to.

"I blew you away," he insisted in a voice raw from machine-gun noises and puberty.

"Did not." Timmy's Brylcreemed hair looked like a collage of Things You Find In The Yard—twigs, leaves, even a ladybug struggling weakly. His pinched face was flushed, his fingers still curled into shadow beast talons. "I got you first. You're a dead man."

"Uh-uh," Dittimore said, and poked Timmy in the chest with the muzzle of the MP-80. *"You're* the one who's—"

"—dead."

I sat up, eyes wide, and the image of Timmy Kegler plunged into a well a quarter-century deep. Despite the air conditioning, sweat trickled down my brow. Had I really been talking in my sleep?

Wind breathed heavily outside the window—a Santa Ana wind blowing desert dryness across San Juan Capistrano. Violent crime rates soared during Santa Anas, I'd heard. Wives stabbed husbands. Fathers strangled children. Policemen shot without thinking. Arsonists torched cities.

I flopped back on the bed, conscious of the empty space around me. Sulphurous yellow streetlight and leaf-shadows from the eucalyptus tree in the front yard tumbled against the curtains. Back when I was a boy, there had been no man-made light outside my bedroom window. My room had faced a cultivated field in Indiana, and the night sky had been disturbed only by stars, the moon—and, in the distance, the Big Tree.

The Big Tree. Jesus, what a vivid dream. The Big Tree had been an oak. Not one of the stunted species common to Southern California, nor of course the monstrosity of my dream—but certainly enormous, visible from almost anywhere in my neighborhood. Always lurking in the corner of the eye, like the castle of a child-eating ogre.

My friends and I had had such stories about that tree. Me, Timmy Kegler, Mike Norris, Fred McMillan and—

Suddenly I knew why I'd had this particular dream. Just yesterday, as I was leaving the office for lunch with a client, a boy had ridden past on a bicycle. I only glimpsed him as a reflection in the windows of the office building; still, my first thought was, *That's Abe Perry.*

Which was absurd. For one thing, Abe Perry had disappeared in 1965. He'd either run away or been kidnapped, and had never been seen again as far as I knew. Even more obviously, if he were still alive he'd be in his early forties, like me. No, it was just that the boy on the bike had worn thick glasses like Abe, and had a similar body shape.

Still, the incident must have stuck with me enough that my subconscious had built a dream around it. No . . . conjured up a memory. I had even viewed myself from the outside, as we often do when looking into the past. Skinny and sunburned, my hair clipped tennis-ball short except for a tuft in front—the trendy Hollywood Burr. Playing Space Explorers. Space Explorers! My friends and I must have played some version of that game five times a day during a typical summer. Others, too: Caveman, Dinosaurs, Army, a dozen more. Exciting games Timmy Kegler had dreamt up or modified, and for which he dictated the rules and the roles. Timmy would probably be a movie director now.

In the dream we boys had looked to be about twelve or thirteen years old. Norman Rockwell kids, scabbed at elbow and knee, wearing jeans or cut-off shorts, canvas tennis shoes and whatever shirts we felt provided good camouflage for exploring the dangerous alien planet of Middlefield, Indiana. Wringing the last drop of fun out of the summer before another school year began. Wait, not just any school year . . . in the dream, hadn't I been thinking about seeing Gail Rohr again after a long absence? Yes. That would have made the year 1965. The very year Abe and Timmy disappeared.

The wind blasted against the side of the house with a dry, rattling cough so strong it seemed to dim the light outside the curtains. I glanced over, then jerked back so hard my head banged against the wall.

A human silhouette shivered against the curtains.

It's amazing how much you can discern from a mere silhouette. This one had narrow shoulders, a round Charlie Brown head, the hint of eyeglass frames extending to either side. Abe Perry again. Except he would have to be twenty feet tall to peer in through the bedroom window.

Even as I thought this, the wind faded and the silhouette dissolved in a swirl. I let out a long breath, slumped back onto the mattress. Jesus. Eucalyptus-leaf shadows, that was all I'd seen. That and the residue of a silly dream.

Groping my reading glasses off the nightstand, I peered at the alarm clock. Two A.M. Damn. I'd only been asleep for half an hour. Amazing how large this bed was without Janice in it. How empty. I'd gotten used to having her here, usually already asleep by the time I got home from work. What a way to think of it: *I'd gotten used to having her here.* Seventeen years of marriage.

Extending my arms to the sides, I pushed down on the mattress, as if to subdue something. Ugly fantasies longed to seep up. Janice in this bed, afternoon sunlight exploding through the window. Janice in this bed with the pool-cleaning man, with the postman, with the neighbor's sixteen-year-old boy . . . fantasies in detail only.

"No girls in our club," Timmy had always said. "They're troublemakers."

I glanced at the clock again. Still 2:00 A.M. A couple of hours ago, lying here wide awake, I'd contemplated swallowing one of the prescription sleeping pills Janice had left behind. Now I found myself thinking about it again. But despite the fact I needed my rest for an important meeting tomorrow—no, today—I pushed the notion aside. That could too easily be step one of a trip to the Betty

Ford Clinic. Something which had happened to several of my colleagues over the years.

Colleagues. Funny, the word *friends* didn't come to mind anymore. Not like it used to.

Timmy and Mike had been part of my life from the beginning. Together we had endured Sunday services at Middlefield Methodist Church, learned to swim at the YMCA, entered nursery school. Mike had lived on a farm outside town, Timmy in a small house near the railroad tracks. Being halfway between, my home was our headquarters. On weekends Mom always set two extra plates at the lunch table without even asking. She had a nickname for us— the Three Stooges? The Three Musketeers? Something like that.

The other members of our group, Fred and Abe, had moved onto Oak Lane when we were all about seven, Fred next door, Abe across the street. I still remembered the first time the whole group got together.

"Do you believe in ghosts?" Timmy had asked the newcomers.

"Yes," they said sincerely.

"Do you like dinosaurs?"

"Sure."

"What about girls?"

"Uggggggh."

"Let's go play."

Summers in the fields and dry ravines. Winters in snowy yards, sledding, building forts, constructing grotesque white sculptures.

"You talk like you grew up in Mayberry," Janice had groaned once, when I mentioned that some problem our daughter faced hadn't existed when *I* was a kid. "Everything has a downside."

Which was true, of course. Opie had never been a bed wetter the way I used to be. Beaver Cleaver hadn't suffered from nightmares like mine. Christ, how many times had Mom or Dad snapped on my bedroom light in the middle of the night, then trudged from closet to bedskirt, showing me there were no demons or monsters lying in wait? "You have to get control of your imagination, Jeff," Dad would say patiently on the nights he drew the duty. On alternating nights, Mom would wipe my brow and sigh, "Timmy's been telling ghost stories again, hasn't he?"

Still, in the big picture of life all that was pretty tame. My buddies and I had never had crack cocaine thrust in our faces, or been arbitrarily gunned down along the side of the road, or feared to open our trick-or-treat bags to strangers. The bullies in our neigh-borhood terrorized us with rubber-band guns, not Uzis.

Of course, that was a long time ago. Adulthood is a coy hunter, catching us while appearing to flee. I remembered when I was a sophomore at USC, studying prelaw. One of Mike Norris's infre-quent letters had arrived. It said he'd just returned to Middlefield after Vietnam, where he'd served half a tour before his parents became ill and turned the farm over to him. After they died he stayed, although, as I recall, he'd always hated farming.

Then, late in 1971, he sent me an obituary notice from the Mid-dlefield *Monitor*. The photo had depicted a young man with a square jaw, military haircut and, on his forehead, a half-inch scar shaped like a bird in flight. According to the article, Fred McMil-lan had also made the round trip to Vietnam—but he returned full of bullet holes and was hospitalized for months, only to die in his parents' home from a brain embolism. A hero's ceremony was to be held at Shady Acres Cemetery on the weekend. Mike had scrawled a note across the bottom of the clipping: *Remember how we all ran around Shady Acres that one Halloween when we were ten? Remember how Fred always hurt himself when we played Army, but never let it bother him? Think it bothers him now?* The paper had reeked of pot. I'd never bothered to write back, I re-called, and that was the last letter Mike ever sent.

I'd received a letter from Gail Rohr once, too. An invitation, actually. To her wedding. There had been no personal message in-side, and I'd thrown it away.

Thrown it away . . .

The wind grumbled fitfully, and shadows swirled through the room. I glanced at the window. Gasped. Another silhouette hung there. This time it was that of a large, full-grown man, his hands raised as if to push open the window—then he was just shadows of leaves whirling away. I wiped my face with my palms. That damned eucalyptus. It would surely lose some limbs before the night was over. Janice would have to call the gardener.

No, she wouldn't. In her own way, Janice had vanished into the past, just as all my old friends had done. And if there was one thing I'd learned in my life, it was that the only direction you could move was forward.

Turning away from the window, I punched up my pillow and

tried to relax. Something warm and wet trickled down my face. What the hell, what the hell, nobody could see. For the first time since the final divorce papers had arrived at my office two weeks ago, I wept.

CHAPTER TWO

SPILLED INK

Four hours later I sat in my car on I-5, waiting impatiently for traffic to move. San Juan Capistrano, where I lived, and Santa Ana, where I worked, are among those L.A. satellite communities that are in reality about as independent of their huge neighbor as one drop of the ocean is from another. Over the course of the day, traffic surges in and out of the metroplex like a tide. Knowing that, I had long ago made a habit of leaving for work at least an hour early and returning well after 7:00 P.M. As I'd told Janice on the rare occasions she'd complained about eating dinner with no one but our daughter for company—they *had* been rare occasions, hadn't they?—it made more sense to spend the extra time at the office than to join commuter lemmings in freeway gridlock. But maybe she hadn't understood that. Maybe she'd honestly never equated my work habits with the lifestyle she enjoyed. The house, the Mercedes, the country club. The free time.

If so, it was still no excuse. I'd never stopped her from getting a job if she wanted one, or completing her education, or doing anything she chose to do to fulfill herself.

Of course, she'd never consulted me about the type of fulfillment she *did* choose . . .

That's enough.

This morning I was trapped in traffic by the ironic fact that after all the trouble I'd had sleeping last night I ended up snoozing right through my alarm.

The traffic in the next lane began to creep forward. "Come on, come on, come on," I muttered at the pickup truck in front of me,

11

then glanced at my cellular phone. But I didn't pick it up. Not yet. That would be admitting I was going to be late for the single most important meeting of my professional life.

The traffic in the next lane halted again. A Mercedes stretch limousine, its windows almost as black as its paint, now idled beside me. I felt a certain wry satisfaction in knowing its occupant was stuck out here just like everybody else. Of course, he or she was probably also sipping mimosas while watching CNN on TV.

The limo's tinted windows made fine mirrors, reflecting part of my car's roof and the sky beyond. Like polarized sunglasses, the glass even clarified the shapes of the clouds that swept in from the coast to dissolve like breaking waves against the smoggy inland air. The "marine layer," as TV weatherpeople liked to call it, rarely extended this far from the ocean. I gazed at the shifting forms of the clouds with remote fascination. As kids, my friends and I used to lie on our backs on the grass, watching corn-fed Midwestern clouds tower against the ocean-blue sky. *I see a pirate ship!* Mike would shout. *There's a lion's head!* from Fred. *I see a horse!* from Abe. *Spaceship!* from me. And from Timmy: *There are two dragons fighting. See them? Watch, one's tearing the other one apart. Rrrrrrarrrrrrgh . . . RRRRRRRRRAAARRRRRRRGH!* . . . *see?* And we usually would. Or say we did.

Now, as I stared at the clouds surging across the car window, I saw nothing recognizable. That irked me. Last night, I'd done better with the shadows on the bedroom curtain. Did I have to be half asleep to accomplish what used to be automatic? If someone showed me a stack of Rorschach blots, would I say, "Looks like spilled ink" to every one?

I started as an ambulance whooped down the median, lights batting against the center divider. Oh, great, this gridlock must have been caused by an accident up ahead. If so, there was no telling when we'd start to move again. Sighing, I grabbed the phone and pressed the speed-dialer.

"Warrick, Jackson and Kline, attorneys at law," a voice said.

"Shauna, it's Mr. Dittimore. Please tell Mr. Warrick I'll be late for our eight o'clock meeting."

A pause, no doubt while the receptionist assimilated the idea of Mr. Dittimore being late *twice* in half a month. The other time had been the day after the preliminary divorce papers arrived.

"Are you talking about the Sinclair meeting?" she asked.

I ground my teeth, a habit I'd developed years ago in place of smoking. "Yes. Is Mr. Sinclair there yet?"

"He just went into the conference room with Mr. Warrick and Mr. Jackson."

I felt my blood pressure rising—the only moving thing in the vicinity. Sinclair Synthetics, Inc., was one of the firm's biggest and oldest clients; Mr. Warrick had personally handled their account since roughly the last ice age. But Warrick was easing toward retirement now, and he'd been grooming me as his successor on this client. It was an honor as well as a professional vehicle. And now here I sat, helpless. Because of a dream.

"What would you like me to tell them?" Shauna asked with a suspicious shade of pity in her voice. I recognized the tone—she knew about my marital problems. *Poor Mr. Dittimore. No wonder he can't keep his schedule straight.*

"Tell them my car blew up and I was burned beyond recognition," I said.

Silence. *He's losing it,* she was probably thinking now. I rubbed my forehead. If only I'd gotten more sleep last night, and less nostalgia. "Just tell Mr. Warrick I'll be there as soon as I can," I said, and hung up.

In the next lane, the limo crept forward a couple of inches, and I glanced at it again. Its windows swarmed with clouds. Suddenly something took shape in them. Dark gaps here, lighter areas there . . . a face. It eddied, coalesced—and for a moment, it looked like a *real* face, not on the window but inside the car, peering out at me. The face of a boy with small blunt features, burr-cut hair, and eyes quivering behind thick-lensed glasses.

My breath died in my chest. Abe Perry. He looked exactly like he had in the school photo they'd used on the front page of the Middlefield *Monitor* dated November 1, 1965. A second photo had depicted a boy with a narrow, seal-like face, dark eyes, and slicked-back hair. He wore a plaid shirt with a torn collar and the top button missing. The caption of that photo read TIMOTHY KEGLER. Above was an enormous headline:

MIDDLEFIELD YOUTHS MISSING

KIDNAPPING FEARED

The Mercedes's rear window slid down, shredding Abe's face into haze. No, it wasn't Abe at all. A palsied old man stared through the opening, gestured at me. Mechanically, I rolled down my window. "Excuse me," the man wheezed. "Would you happen to have any Grey Poupon?"

It took me a moment to recognize the line from a stupid mustard commercial. The old man burst into wheezy laughter and disappeared again behind the rising window. Swirls of cloud reappeared and began to congeal . . . I looked away. My heart raked against my rib cage like a lump of cloth on a washboard.

I took a deep breath, let it out. Damn last night's dream. Today of all days, I had to get control of my nerves.

Far ahead, sirens whooped. My lane moved forward a few feet, then stopped again. I sighed.

Only in California.

"Mr. Sinclair left twenty minutes ago," Shauna said the moment I walked into the reception area. She gave me the sort of doe-eyed look usually bestowed upon starving Somali children. "Um . . . Mr. Warrick would like to see you in his office right away."

I nodded, showing nothing of what I felt—lawyer's armor—and walked briskly past her.

Naturally, Warrick's office was located in the corner of the building with the best view. The decor was exactly what clients expected: dark paneling, bookcases full of leather-bound volumes, walls displaying framed degrees, certificates, awards. One enormous window faced south and another east; from here, twenty stories up, I could see that traffic was still barely creeping along I-5. There was little consolation in that.

Mr. Warrick looked up. At the age of fifty-seven, he could have been a cover model for *Forbes* magazine—the kind of small man who always photographed like a giant. His body was kept toned in the office weight room, his suntan preserved at a local salon. As always, his perfectly tailored suit exuded understated prosperity. Some people said he'd had hair implants to maintain his gray coif, but if so the implants were perfect.

As he leaned back his reflection slid like a skater across the polished mahogany of his desk. He said nothing.

I'd thought up plenty of lies during the last hour, but instead of using them, I just said, "There was an accident on the freeway. I got caught in the traffic. I'm sorry."

His gaze never left my face. "You realize how important it was for you to be here?"

"Yes, of course. I'm sorry." My mouth wanted to keep going, offering to shine his shoes and mow his lawn, but I clamped it shut. Warrick wasn't an unreasonable man, but he was absolutely merciless with the weak. Friend or foe, it didn't matter. My recognition of this trait had enabled me to move up in the firm as others tumbled down.

"Bob Sinclair was sorry he didn't get to meet you," Warrick said. "And I was embarrassed. I'd already told him how dependable you are." His hands opened in a gesture of inquiry. Not for the first time, I noticed that his nails, though buffed, were so short they had to have been trimmed with his teeth.

"I'm sorry," I said again.

His gaze roved toward a photo on his desk. Although its back was turned toward me, I knew it featured Warrick, his wife, their four grown children. All the kids were Stanford graduates, lawyers or doctors. "I understand your wife left you recently," he said.

The air froze in my lungs. I wasn't surprised that he knew—he might not hang out around the coffee machine all day, but nothing in the office got past him. It was just the words, the facts themselves, hitting me again like blunt arrows.

Finally I nodded. "We actually split up three months ago. Irreconcilable differences."

"Is that germane to your missing the meeting? Are you having trouble concentrating on your work?"

"No to the second. To the first . . . I'm not sure."

"Have you considered counseling?"

"Marriage counseling?" I hid a stab of anger. *No, but I've considered beating one or two of Janice's boyfriends to a pulp.*

"Either that," he said, "or individual counseling. Whatever's needed for you to get on an even keel again. We have some excellent therapists as clients, you know."

"Yes, I know."

"Please sit down, Jeffry."

Jeffry. He'd never used my given name before. Was that good or bad?

I eased into one of the visitors' chairs and gazed at him across a maroon pond.

"I'm not going to beat around the bush," he said. "You've been with us for twelve years. You're an experienced professional; I know you understand that private and professional life must remain separate. At least, I always assumed you understood that. Was I wrong?"

"No."

"A lot of people depend on us being here, being available and responsible. Correct?"

"Of course. I—"

"As you know, I'm retiring soon. Jackson won't be long after. We're counting on strong, stable leaders like you to move up and keep this firm strong." According to some article I'd once read, it takes six muscles to produce a smile. Warrick now used about three. "After all," he said, "there has to be income to pay into my pension fund, right?"

I felt my lips curl up at the corners, too, although a knife of pain stabbed deep above my left eye. I was forty-two years old, and he was treating me like a child. Of course, I'd behaved like one all day. Crying like a baby? Sleeping through my alarm? Jumping at cloud shadows?

"I understand," I said. Leaning forward, I clasped my hands on the desktop. "Any chance of setting up another meeting with Mr. Sinclair soon?"

"That's more like it." He used all six smile muscles. "To be honest, things didn't go that badly this morning; I just told Bob you'd been called to court for a deposition." I managed a smile, too; we both knew the firm's practice involved virtually no trial work. Then his facial muscles gave up, exhausted. "But I thought you needed a little scare—something to remind you of your priorities. No matter what else in your life goes wrong, your career is always under *your* control. Understand?"

"Yes, sir."

My office was a smaller version of Warrick's. It had only one window, but the view was a good one of the freeway and, when the smog wasn't too bad, the Newport Beach skyline. On the wall across from my desk hung a variety of framed documents: my diploma from the University of Southern California, my license, certificates indicating I'd passed various forms of Continuing Professional Education, and plaques from community-service organizations: The United Way, the Santa Ana YMCA, Habitat for the Homeless, a dozen more. I'd served on boards of directors, taken charge of fund-raising operations, acted as secretary and treasurer. *Business contacts. Honey. Part of the job.* Beneath the plaques were photos of me and assorted colleagues at one or another charitable *soirée*, grinning at the camera through booze-flushed faces above tight bow ties. The Old Boys Club. I stared at these for a moment, feeling a swell of pride, then sat behind my desk, my anchor. Next to the telephone stood a framed photo of Terri, looking quite elegant in her eighth-grade graduation dress and fancy hairdo. As I looked at it, I felt prouder than ever. She was turning out to be a terrific young woman, very much her own person. Opening a bottom desk drawer, I removed the photo of Janice that used to stand next to Terri's. Compared them. Remarkable similarity. I looked at the static grins on the wall again. Unlike Warrick, I didn't own a single group photo of my family, the three of us together. It was one of those things I'd always intended . . .

Never mind. There would never be such a picture now; that was reality. So be it.

I tossed Janice's picture into the trash, frame and all. Yesterday's *Wall Street Journal* landed on top of it. I shifted Terri's photo to a more central position on my desk, where I could see it at a glance.

Then I got to work.

CHAPTER THREE

SHADOWS AND WHISPERS

Traffic was no problem on the way home. Even in the Los Angeles area, the freeways pretty much turn into open racetracks by 8:00 P.M. As I steered onto my street, I stared at the house. It was the mirror image of the one across the street, which was identical to the one three doors down: two stories of cream-colored stucco and terra-cotta tile, a single palm tree in front, privacy fence in back. The tiny front lawn was getting bushy. Before Janice left, it had always been as flat as green sand. I had let it go. Every time I looked at it, I wondered how many muscular, sweaty landscapers Janice had invited in for a beer . . .

Enough.

The avocado tree in the backyard was just visible from here, its underside lashed with blue whips of light from the swimming pool. The pool lamps came on automatically at dusk, to prevent the heirs of any potential burglar who fell into the water and drowned from winning a wrongful death lawsuit. In contrast, the house itself was completely dark. Stupid. If I was going to continue working this late, I'd better start leaving a few lights burning while I was gone.

Parking in the garage, I deactivated the house alarm and entered through the kitchen. As the banks of fluorescents flashed on, I noticed that the counters were cluttered with coffee filters, old newspapers, donut boxes. Janice had fired our maid the same day she'd left the house; no doubt as a not-so-subtle dig at me: *Fend for yourself for a while. See how you like it.* I hadn't found the time to look for a new maid yet.

The only sound in the house was the trapped-hornet hum of the fluorescents. No wife yelling that the leftover roast was in the microwave, no loud music from Terri's room . . . I hadn't called my daughter for a couple of days. Too long. Not because I didn't want to talk to her but because Janice refused to let her have a private line, and I was afraid that if Janice answered the phone I'd have another sleepless night.

Suddenly the disarray in the kitchen infuriated me. I hadn't been this sloppy since I was a child. I tidied up quickly, and switched on the dishwasher although it was only half-full. At least it made some noise.

Next I opened the fridge. I wasn't really hungry, but I hadn't eaten all day. There was nothing in there that didn't look like it belonged in a petri dish. I sighed. I must have driven past a dozen grocery stores on the way home. There were a lot of habits I was going to have to relearn.

Maybe Janice will apologize and come back.

I was surprised and shamed by the longing in the thought. I'd thrown her picture away today, and been glad to do it. Surely this didn't mean she was right about me after all. Had I really taken her for granted as maidservant and mother?

I slammed the refrigerator door. If only I'd caught her with a lover, just once. Come home early and walked into that archetypal confrontation so beloved by *Playboy* cartoonists. But no. I'd found out I'd been cuckolded only after she *told* me, leaving the news in a note by the side of the bed. "Other men make me feel special," she'd written. Not "the other man," but "other *men*." At first I'd assumed there had been no lovers at all, that she was lying, being vicious. Then I thought about things I'd noticed only in passing during the past year—comments overheard, new bed linens bought; and once, God help me, I'd found an unfamiliar pair of shorts in my dresser that Janice said were a birthday gift she'd forgotten to give me—and I'd *believed* her—the thought made me so sick I just about couldn't stand it.

Even though that note would have made potent ammunition in court, I'd torn it up. As Janice had no doubt known I would, or maybe she hadn't; it was useless trying to understand her now.

Now, according to Terri, Janice was dating a born-again Christian. Going to church every Sunday morning and Wednesday evening, with Bible study classes twice a week. Janice Dittimore,

washing the guilt from her adulterous soul with words—a goddamned spiritual laundromat.

I stalked back to the family room.

There was no need to turn on a lamp. The swimming pool was
just outside wide glass doors, and its sinuous light guided me to
the bar. I opened the first bottle I came to, poured a shot, drank—
tequila. Fine. I poured another. Fire roared in my stomach, and the
buzz hit me immediately. Good. This type of meal was nothing to
make a habit of, but after a day like today, surely I was entitled—

Outside, something moved abruptly. I looked up as a dark figure
sprinted along the back fence, turned and raced toward the house.
I staggered back, terror jerking through me like an electrical
shock. The figure shimmered, elongated, and burst apart against
the light from the swimming pool. Christ, a shadow. Another goddamned shadow.

Shakily, I raised the glass of tequila to my lips.

"Nod," a voice whispered.

I choked, barely caught the glass as my numb fingers released it.
My heart wrenched sideways in my chest so hard I thought I heard
it tear. I looked around. Everything in the room appeared alien and
wavery in the blue light, as if resting on the bottom of the ocean.

A boy's shadow shimmered against the far wall.

This time I wasn't fooled. It looked fairly realistic, the shadow.
Short, slender, with an incongruous round head. One hand raised
as if in greeting. Abe Perry. Abe Perry again . . . But this time I
stayed perfectly calm. Traced the source of the shadow with my
eyes. There. The alignment of the end table and floor lamp would
do it. As always, a simple explanation.

When I looked back, the shadow had changed. Now it had no
head at all.

My hand snapped toward the nearest light switch. But at the last
instant I stopped. Took a deep breath. "Fuck you," I said to the
shadow through the darkness. I was starting to feel a little dizzy.
The headless shadow stayed there, hand raised, quivering and billowing as if blown by a wind I couldn't feel. I stalked around the
bar, over to the end table. My shadow appeared on the wall, approached the smaller one. I stopped. Odd, from this angle it was
difficult to see how the lamp and end table could create the shape
of a boy, headless or otherwise. But *something* was doing it.

As I raised an arm, my shadow reached toward the shadow boy. I remembered Timmy Kegler again, how he would make monster shadows with his hands and bite at the rest of us with them. "Gotcha!" he'd cry gleefully. "Gotcha!"

My shadow finger slowly approached the boy's shoulder. For some reason I began to tense, as if—

"Nod," a voice whispered in my ear. I let out a whistling shriek and whirled. One hand slapped the floor lamp. It cartwheeled over the couch, base over top, shade flying away. The bulb popped.

There was no one behind me, beside me, near me. I staggered backward into the sliding doors, eyelids fluttering, and wondered how long I'd be in the hospital from my heart attack.

But my pulse quickly eased. "Okay," I muttered out loud. "Okay, Goddamnit, that's enough." I allowed myself a little laugh. The only shadow on the wall now was mine, and a bit of the end table's. No lamp now, of course. And no headless boy. No nothing.

I returned to the bar and gulped down two more shots of tequila. The booze was really kicking in now. I felt detached from myself, mind humming like a motor hooked to nothing. Perfect. I picked up the fragments of broken lightbulb and set the lamp up again. Glanced back at the wall. My own shadow, standing by itself, looked back at me. "Those are really shadow people," Timmy had always said. "They follow us around. In the daylight they're flat, but at night . . . in the dark . . . that's when they try to get you. They want to be real and make you live on the other side."

"Jesus, Dittimore," I muttered. "Go to bed."

As I left the room, I found myself listening to the darkness behind me. For what? A whisper? A stealthy footstep? I heard a hissing rush, and was reminded of wind blowing through the leaves of a huge tree, making them dance and quiver . . . But it was just the sound of the dishwasher in the kitchen.

Only that, and nothing more.

"But why?" Jeff asked.

"Because we haven't been out there for years." Timmy had wet his sweaty head under the garden hose and smeared back his hair; now it reflected the sky in glossy blue stripes.

"So?" Mike asked, setting his homemade electron blaster aside. As always, a faded engineer's cap like the one his father wore in the fields was pulled so low over his forehead you could barely see his eyes. "It's *boring* at the Big Tree."

The gang sat on Jeff's back porch in the shade of the rose trellis, each boy with a tall glass of cherry Kool-Aid at hand. On the lawn, a sprinkler waved a slow fan of coolness over the parched grass. Beyond that, through rainbows of mist, Jeff could see the Big Tree rising like a gray-green volcano above the cornfield.

"How would you know if it's boring or not?" Timmy demanded. "You just said we haven't been out there for years."

"Well, it always *was* boring," Mike grunted. "There's nothing to do out there."

"This time there will be. You'll see."

Jeff cleared his throat. "I thought you hated the Big Tree. I thought you said it was *evil*."

Cupping his chin in one hand, Timmy gazed into the field. "I've been thinking about that. I don't think it's evil anymore. I think it's . . . I'll show you, if you'll come out there with me."

"This isn't like the time we were supposed to go to Venus, is it?" Fred asked suspiciously, his broad jaw tilting sideways. "That time in the furnace room?"

Everybody looked at Timmy. Two years ago, he had for some reason become convinced the chief janitor of the Middlefield Methodist Church was from Venus. Timmy claimed that one Sunday before church he'd followed the janitor into the basement furnace room. The guy had walked up to a complicated control panel, fiddled around with a bunch of dials, then stepped into some kind of booth—and disappeared. Obviously, Timmy said, what looked like a furnace was actually a matter-transporting device like in the movie *The Fly*. Nobody had even thought to ask why Timmy was so sure Venus was the janitor's destination.

"Do you think we're being *invaded?*" Abe had whispered, his eyes as round as his face behind thick glasses. Abe attended St. Malachi Catholic Church in Brownsburg. Fred was a Baptist or something. Neither of them had ever seen the janitor before.

Timmy shook his head. "Naw, it's always the same guy going back and forth. And he's pretty nice. I think he's just, like, studying us." Then he leaned forward. "But what if *we* went to *Venus?*"

Jeff, who had just finished reading *The Wonderful Flight to the Mushroom Planet* for the tenth time, had been enthralled. "You mean use the transporter ourselves?"

"Sure. I saw how it worked; I could do it."

They entered the church on Saturday. The choir was practicing and had left one of the back doors unlocked. To Jeff, the almost unoccupied building felt eerie with its empty hallways and the singing echoing from the sanctuary. He shivered with excitement, fear, dread. What the gang was doing wasn't exactly *wrong*—the door was unlocked, after all—but he knew his parents would be upset if they found out he'd snuck into the church on a Saturday. Unless, of course, he went to Venus and back. Who could get mad at a kid who visited another planet?

They reached the door to the basement unchallenged. But the sanctuary was only a room away, the singing much louder, and none of the gang relaxed until they were huddled together at the top of the basement steps with the door closed behind them. It was very gloomy here, but they didn't dare switch on a light.

At the bottom of the stairs they found a large room stuffed with folding chairs and tables, old choir robes, hand-painted signs for fund-raising events gone by. A door marked FURNACE stood in the shadows on the far wall.

The gang approached the door as a single many-legged organism, Timmy and Jeff in the lead. Somewhat to Jeff's surprise, the door was unlocked. Beyond, the only light came through a narrow, dusty window near the ceiling. The room was only about the size of Jeff's living room back home. The floor was smooth concrete, the walls cement block with hardened concrete oozing like old toothpaste from the joints. Overhead ran a tangle of ducts, conduits and pipes, in a pattern so confusing it *had* to be of alien origin.

"There," Timmy whispered, pointing.

The furnace wasn't being used now, in June. Jeff knew the equipment had been installed only a year or so ago—he'd heard his dad talking about raising money for it—and in its modern, hard-angled way, it *did* look more like a transporter than a heater. Probably it did both things, so nobody would get suspicious.

Jeff realized he hadn't been breathing much, and opened his throat to the air. But he couldn't shake a growing feeling of unease. What if Timmy was wrong about Venusians being nice? "Are you sure the janitor's gone?" he whispered.

Timmy gave him a scornful look. "Only farmers work on Saturdays."

On the front of the furnace was a panel covered with gauges, switches and dials. Timmy walked confidently up to it. "Okay," he said in a low voice. "Okay, you guys go stand in there." He pointed at a narrow gap between the furnace and one wall.

Jeff blinked. That was supposed to be the "booth" Timmy had mentioned? It was just an alcove plunging into darkness. Conduits wound above and around it, making it look like a . . . well, a mouth. A cobwebby mummy's mouth.

"In *there?*" Abe whispered loudly. As always, his clothes were spotless.

"Yes, in there," Teddy said impatiently. "That's where the janitor disappeared. Now hurry up while I set these dials."

Jeff moved first, trying not to appear scared as he walked stiffly into the alcove. To his relief it wasn't very deep. He turned his back to the rough concrete of the wall. Everyone but Timmy squeezed in in front of him, forming a black screen. As he shifted around, he felt something feathery-stiff brush his cheek. *A spider!* Claustrophobia turned into near panic. He barely subdued the urge to scream and swat wildly at the spider before he realized it was just the corner of a magazine sticking out from between two pipes.

Timmy was hard at work at the transporter controls. Peeking between two silhouetted heads, Jeff couldn't see exactly what Timmy was doing, but he recognized the rapt expression of concentration on his friend's thin face. This was how Timmy looked when they played with plastic army men, setting up epic battles. The *whapping* sound of big switches turning echoed through the room.

Jeff jumped as a heavy *thump* erupted on all sides. The ducts around the alcove began vibrating. The magazine tickled his cheek again. A powerful hum grew in the air.

Timmy backed away from the control panel, his eyes wide with awe, then turned and sprinted across the floor, skidding into the alcove so hard he rammed Fred into Mike, who backed into Jeff with a thud. "Stand quiet!" Timmy whispered. "Here we go! Here we go!"

The transporter was cycling up and up, its breathy drone now amplified by a deeper thunder. The air in the alcove shivered. Jeff felt his body tightening with anticipation . . . and fear. What if this didn't work? Or what if it didn't work *right?* In the movie *The Fly*, a guy got his disassembled body parts mixed up with those of a passing housefly. What if he, Jeff, ended up with Fred's head and Mike's feet, or Abe's bad eyes and Timmy's brain? Or what if they couldn't live on Venus when they got there? Or what if they could live there but the Venusians wouldn't let them come *back?*

For the first time, the full magnitude of what they were doing struck him, and he had to choke down a second, even worse surge of panic. It was too late to back out now. The rumble of the transporter had grown very loud; they were going to Venus any second now, and—

They all screamed as a brilliant flare of light dissolved the world —but when Jeff's eyes adjusted, he found himself still staring into the basement of the Middlefield Methodist Church. Bright now. Standing in the doorway was the head janitor, wearing his gray coveralls. There were white paint spatters on his hand where it rested on the light switch. "What are you kids *doing?*" He stormed into the room. "Didjoo turn the furnace on? That's *dangerous.* All right, come out of there right now."

One by one, sheepishly, the gang complied. Jeff, waiting his turn, wished he could sink between the pipes in the alcove and disappear. He felt the tickling on his cheek again, and looked over in annoyance. His eyes widened. In this light, he could see at least a dozen magazines crammed in between the conduits beside him. The one that kept touching him had fallen halfway out. *For Gents* was the title on the cover. Beneath that . . . Jeff gaped. A picture of a woman, naked from the waist up, her enormous titties thrusting out like nuclear missiles.

Timmy's voice jerked him back to the back porch and the present: "The janitor tricked us that time. Did you notice he disappeared for good right after that? Hey, I still say he was from Venus and we could have made it there if he hadn't shut off the transporter. It doesn't matter. There are better ways to travel the universe, anyway. I'll show you. But you gotta come out to the Big Tree with me."

Jeff found his gaze drawn across the fields again, toward the Big Tree. The sight roused unpleasant memories. Nights of no sleep and urine-drenched sheets, of panic and shame. The Big Tree projecting its darkness through his bedroom window.

"Timmy," Abe said, "I'd like to go out there and everything, but it takes a long time. What if we don't get back in time for dinner?"

Timmy turned on him, eyes glinting like those of a hawk spotting prey. "What's the matter, Abe-o, afraid your *mommy* might get mad?"

Abe's round face reddened. "Well, I don't want her to worry is all." He took off his glasses, produced a handkerchief from his back pocket, wiped the lenses carefully. Jeff watched with interest. He didn't know anyone else who carried a snot rag all the time, not that Abe ever actually blew his nose into it. He only used it to polish those glasses.

Fred, his long, knobby frame half-reclining on the steps, said impatiently, "Well, let's make up our minds. Are we going to hike out there or not?"

Jeff knew *he* didn't really want to go all the way out to the Big Tree, least of all today, the last day of summer. His thoughts were already focused on tomorrow, the first day of school . . . on seeing Gail Rohr again. Private, secret thoughts.

Still, Timmy was right about one thing: this *was* the last chance the whole gang would have to go out to the Big Tree. In fact, it was probably their last chance to do much of anything together for a while. Another secret, this one shared with Mike.

He jumped to his feet. "Okay, let's hit the trail."

Timmy grinned. "I knew I could count on you, *Kemo Sabe.*"

CHAPTER FOUR

OPEN DOORS, CLOSED DOORS

Kemo Sabe . . .

I opened my eyes.

The Santa Ana winds were blowing again, a broom of dry desert air sweeping everything out to sea. Shaking the eucalyptus tree in the front yard.

I looked at the curtains. No weird shadows tonight. Still, my body was as rigid as Styrofoam. I made myself relax. There was nothing to—

Whock whock whock. I stiffened again. That had come from downstairs. Who would be knocking at the door at—I put on my glasses and looked at the clock—2:00 A.M.? And why weren't they using the doorbell?

The sound wasn't repeated. Maybe it hadn't been a knock at all. Something else—a branch rapping against the porch.

Still, I found it hard to relax again. Which was annoying. It wasn't like me to jump at shadows or odd noises. Those days were long gone . . .

"Son," Dad said in his level, rumbling voice, "you're almost twelve years old. That's too old to be scared of a tree, don't you think?" Dad was in Jeff's room for the sixth time that month. "And why is it that you're only afraid of it at night? Doesn't that tell you something?"

How could Dad, who seemed so wise, not understand that night and day had nothing in common? How could he not know that the moment he left the room, the Big Tree would transform back into

27

its real shape: an enormous human head perched on a thin neck? If Jeff stared at it long enough—and he never seemed to be able not to—he would even see its scowling face. Sometimes he could hear its voice as well, a sinister whisper stirring the cornfield: *I know where you live, boy, and sooner or later I'll get you.*

Mom was just as dense. During one of her mercy visits, she had asked him why he didn't just close the curtain if the Big Tree scared him so much. She hadn't understood that you could *never* let Bad Things out of your sight. If you did they would sneak up and grab you—or send their slaves to do it.

The Big Tree couldn't leave its field, of course—at least, Jeff didn't think it could—but it had many such helpers. The shadow people who lived in Jeff's closet. The slimy creatures under the bed. The troll-like beast crouching in the hallway, waiting patiently for a little boy to make a break for the bathroom.

"If you turn your back on them," Timmy had warned, "you'll never be seen again."

Although Dad had laid down the law about Jeff's night light two years ago, removing the strongest weapon against the bad things, Jeff still possessed a grab bag of defensive talismans: prayer; carefully arranged covers; open bedroom doors; closed closet doors. As a member of Timmy Kegler's gang, he also knew the Indian sign for warding off evil, which Timmy had taught them. The Indian sign could fend off most dangers if you dared reach your hand out from under your blankets to make it.

Of course, Jeff didn't need such defenses when Dad was there. Dad was stronger than any shadow person or hallway troll that ever lived.

"Jeff, listen," Dad said, his work-toughened hands rasping over his chin in the darkness. "Every town has something like the Big Tree—a place where there are supposed to be ghosts, or UFOs, or foo-lights. It's what they call a collective myth. Do you understand that?"

Jeff nodded. For eleven years he had nodded during those nocturnal lectures, just to keep Dad in the room and talking. But this time it felt different. Dad had never used a phrase like "collective myth" before. Why would he do it now unless he thought Jeff was old enough, *mature* enough, to understand?

"You mean like the Haunted Bridge out by Avon?" Jeff asked. "I've heard big kids talking about it. They say some lady threw her baby off there one night, then jumped off herself. Now her ghost walks around at night, crying."

Dad nodded. "There are at least two other stories about that bridge. That's my point—people *want* to believe in ghosts. Like Timmy. And that's okay, it's even fun sometimes, but *it's not real*. The Haunted Bridge is just a bridge and the Big Tree is just a tree, nothing more. Wood and leaves and bark. If you don't believe it can hurt you, then it can't. Understand?"

Jeff nodded. He had to admit, for all the time he'd been scared of the Big Tree, it had never actually *done* anything to him. *Wood and leaves and bark*. Why be afraid of wood and leaves and bark? After all, the frame of his bed was made of wood, right? So were the doors on his closet, and he'd always depended on those to keep the shadow people from escaping . . .

Whock whock whock.

I jerked up in bed, ears straining against the howl of the Santa Ana. The inside of the room was brighter, thanks to the streetlight outside, than my childhood bedroom had been even with the night light burning.

Funny how clearly I could suddenly remember all that stuff about the Big Tree and my night terrors, especially considering how seldom I reminisced about my life back in Indiana. My own child, Terri, had certainly never suffered from such bad dreams. Her occasional nightmares usually featured the boogeyman from a silly horror movie—Freddy Krueger, the Queen Alien, the Stepfather. Pretty tame stuff compared to the bladder-bursting horrors I'd manufactured for myself as a kid, with Timmy Kegler's help. I couldn't help but laugh.

Timmy. He'd thought up more demons and monsters than—

WHOCK WHOCK WHOCK.

I jerked violently. Damn it, someone *was* pounding on the front door. This better not be some kid's idea of a joke. Throwing back the covers, I pulled on a robe and stumbled downstairs.

I was reaching for the doorknob when the sound came again, so loud I jumped away: *WHOCK WHOCK WHOCK!*

That was when I realized I'd actually been about to open my door to an unknown person in the middle of the night—in Orange County, the Serial Murder Capital of the World. Had I gone crazy?

Switching on the porch light, I peered though one of the little windows in the front door.

No one was outside, not on the porch and not on the street. I scowled and turned away.

WHOCK WHOCK WHOCK! I whirled instantly, deactivating the alarm system even as I jerked the door open.

No one was there. The Santa Ana stirred a flurry of blood-colored bougainvillea blossoms around my feet.

Then I saw two plastic garbage cans lying empty in the street. I must have heard them banging together.

Shaking my head, I walked out to the street and stacked the cans one inside the other, then placed them upside down on the lawn. As I walked back toward the house, I was struck by how abandoned and lonely the neighborhood seemed at this hour, with the Santa Ana hooting through the surrounding canyons.

My shadow, doubled by the streetlights behind me, flowed up the porch steps and into the foyer. The darker half disappeared inside. At the same moment the door started to swing shut. Shit! It would lock itself! I lunged forward and thrust my forearm into the gap just in time. The door crunched against muscle and bone with agonizing force, then rebounded. I cursed and jammed the edge of my foot against the bottom of the door. Damned Santa Anas!

Back in the bedroom, I draped my robe over the chair by Janice's dressing table and climbed into bed. As I settled onto the pillows, I realized the closet doors were open. Had I left them that way? I didn't usually.

The closet doors were of the sliding type that reveal only half the interior at a time. The door nearest the bed was pushed all the way back. I could see my suits receding into perfect darkness rank by rank, like paper soldiers.

When I was a kid, I had *never* left the closet door open at night. If I were a kid now I'd be terrified, convinced that a shadow person or other deadly creature had slipped into the house while I was outside and now lurked in the closet; the next time I groped in there for a shirt or pair of shoes, cold hands would—

"Booga booga," I murmured out loud, and smiled sardonically at myself. *You can't let your imagination run away with you*—Dad's favorite quote. I wished I could tell him about this, how I'd gotten myself spooked, however briefly, by an open closet door. Just like in the old days. But of course Dad didn't remember the old days anymore. Or the new days, or the last two minutes.

"Booga booga," I said again, and turned my back on the closet.

"Knock, knock."

I looked up from a batch of bank statements so fast my neck popped. I winced.

"Jeez, Dad, I'm sorry." My daughter stood just outside my office door. "I didn't mean to scare you."

Smiling, I got to my feet and held out my arms. "Come on in, honey, it's all right." We embraced, and I wondered how long she'd been this tall. I also wondered when she'd dyed her hair. It certainly hadn't been this black the last time I saw her. A week and a half ago? Two weeks? "Have a seat."

She took one of the client chairs across from the desk and crossed her legs. God, her skirt was short. She had Janice's sleek hair and slender, leggy beauty, and my pale brown eyes. But her hair was cut in some kind of asymmetrical fiasco that made me think of the crop circles in England—shaved here, long there, sticking up on the other side. Style, of course. I had to remind myself I'd been just as concerned about peer pressure when I was fifteen.

"You look tired, Dad," she said. Her lipstick was the color of raw steak. She never used to wear lipstick.

"I'm okay." I rubbed the back of my neck. "How did you get here, anyway?" She had her learner's permit, which meant she couldn't drive solo. As for public transport, she wouldn't have any more idea how to use the Orange County bus system than I would.

Her mouth twitched back and forth. "Uh . . . Mom brought me."

"Oh. Is she in the lobby?"

"No, she stayed in the car. We were doing some back-to-school shopping, you know, and I'm all, 'Mom, I want to stop by and say hi to Dad.' And she said okay." More mouth-twitches, as if her lips were trying to decide which ear they wanted to hide under.

"I'm glad you came. Too bad you can't stay awhile, though. We could have lunch at Perrine's."

Twitch. Not long ago, our precious moments together hadn't been this awkward. But I kept wondering what Janice might have told Terri about the reasons for our divorce. Not the truth, of course. Or at least not all of it.

"Do you need money or anything?" I asked. "For clothes or school stuff?"

She shook her head. Her left ear was pierced three times. I glanced at her photo on my desk, just to make sure. One earring on both sides. I couldn't believe Janice was letting her get away with this.

"Looking forward to school starting?" I asked. It would be a new school for her now, a Long Beach school.

A shrug. "Kind of."

"Hey, you'll make new friends. And you can always visit your old ones on weekends. You'll be able to drive wherever you want to pretty soon, anyway."

"I know. Dad . . ."

"Yes?"

"I miss you."

It was like a kiss with a slap attached. I felt fire building behind my eyes. "Hey, I miss you, too, honey."

"Can I come and visit you sometimes?"

"Well, of course, but remember there are certain schedules . . . under the divorce arrangement . . ."

"Oh."

"Listen, I don't think Janice would stop you from seeing me anytime you wanted to. And you know I'd love it." I leaned across my desk. "Honey, is something wrong?"

"No, not really, it's just . . ." Her voice faded; she started looking around my office as if she'd never seen bookshelves before. Then she sighed, "Mom wanted me to give you these." Opening a purse not much bigger than her fist, she extracted a bunch of pamphlets and held them across the desk without looking at them, or me.

I took them, glanced at the titles. *God's Intention for Your Life. Are You Ready to Face Eternity? The End of the World is Nigh.* I looked up. "You've got to be kidding."

She shook her head. "That's not why I wanted to see you, though. Mom just gave those to me in the parking garage. She was all, 'Your father needs these.' "

I dropped the tracts on the desk. "She doesn't try to make you go to church, does she? I mean, unless you want to?"

Terri finally looked at me. "No, she doesn't make me, but she's all, 'You'll come to Jesus when the time is right.'"

I rubbed my eyes. "This is amazing."

"Dad, she doesn't like my friends anymore, even my old ones. She doesn't like my clothes, or the stuff I put in my room, or the way I talk, or *anything*. She's all freaked out. It makes me mad. Can't I come stay with you?"

I kept the surprise off my face. And the anger, because suddenly I understood why Janice hadn't minded bringing Terri to see me, and to deliver those tracts. Janice wanted me to know that our daughter was becoming . . . something neither of us had intended. And it wasn't her, Janice's, fault. No, it must be mine, for not being there enough during Terri's adolescence, for not providing firm guidance. Bullshit. When I spoke, I did so in my most reassuring lawyer voice: "I'm afraid not, Terri. The court is granting custody to your mom, and that's all right, because, well, you know what my work hours are like. You're better off with her for now. It's only for a couple more years, anyway. Then you'll be in college, and—"

"Okay. Just thought I'd ask." Her slender fingers dipped into her purse and pulled out a cigarette. It was halfway to her lips before a look of horror and dismay passed over her face and she looked at me. Blushing furiously even as her mouth pulled itself into a defiant bow, she stuffed the cigarette out of sight again.

I shook my head in disbelief, but knew better than to get huffy or bossy. "Terri . . . I know all this has been tough on you. It's been tough on all of us. But don't go hurting yourself because of it. Don't . . . lose control. Okay?"

She bit her lip. One foot jiggled nervously on the end of a long leg.

"Terri?"

She looked up. Tears magnified her eyes. My eyes.

"Listen," I said. "You know you can call me anytime. I mean that. I'll help you all I can. As for this stuff—" I picked up the religious tracts and dropped them ceremoniously into the trash can. "You don't have to put up with it. Just hang in there for a while. Okay?"

"You don't know what it's like," she snorted through her tears. "Mom goes to church *every single night* now, and plays these preacher tapes all day and even in the car. And she brings these *nerds* over to meet me. I mean, even if they aren't nerds, they're like totally brainwashed, you know? I want to pick my *own* boy-friends, Dad."

I held my hand across the desk. "All right, I'll talk to her. I'll see what I can do."

She clutched my hand. "Thanks."

"When the time is right," I added.

CHAPTER FIVE

TAKE A HIKE

The cavemen tramped across the plain under a sky like blue fever. They carried flint-tipped spears and bone knives. Their heads and shoulders bobbed in a line above the leafy plants that surrounded them. Eyes shifted alertly, watching for danger: saber-toothed tigers, dire wolves, cave bears—and, worst of all, the half-animal, half-human creatures called Bikkids.

Far ahead loomed their goal, the Mountain of the Gods. The journey there would take days of constant vigilance. Legend had it that evil things lived on the mountain.

"Saber-tooth!" A harsh whisper from Hawkeye, the chief. Everyone fell into a half-crouch. Hawkeye glanced around. "Wolf, take Urrgh and circle to the right. We'll attack from both sides."

Wolf hesitated. "What's the matter?" Hawkeye demanded.

"Nothing." Wolf moved off through the plants, Urrgh at his heels. Leaves sawed dully at their bare arms.

After a minute, Wolf glanced back to see how far they'd gotten from the rest of the tribe, then halted. "This is stupid. I said I'd go to the Big Tree, but why do we have to play this dumb game, too?"

"Don't worry about it, Jeffo," Mike said, taking off his engineer's cap and wiping his brow. "Nobody can see us except the rest of the gang."

"I still feel stupid." Nevertheless, Jeff continued on through the half-grown corn until he and Mike were in position. He waved his spear, and Timmy waved back. With a wild shriek, Timmy leaped up and swung his arm. His spear scratched white against the sky, arced down, stood quivering in the corn. A swarm of other spears plunged after it. Jeff's struck closest.

"It's only wounded!" Timmy shouted, pulling his knife out of his waistband. "Attack!" Howling, he charged through the corn.

Jeff didn't move. He glanced at Mike, who shrugged.

Timmy was racing headlong toward the spot where the spears had fallen. His skinny, suntanned limbs gleamed with sweat. Fred followed gamely, while Abe trudged along in the rear.

Jeff automatically analyzed distances and angles, and realized he could get to the spears first if he hurried. Whooping, he burst into a sprint. He heard Mike thumping hard behind him.

Timmy recognized Jeff's intentions, and his teeth showed in a grimace as he sped up. Jeff put his head down and lunged through the corn, knees pumping high, the way he'd seen varsity football players do in practice. Now he was sure he'd beat Timmy to—

One of his feet turned on a loose dirt clod. He stumbled, tripped over a tangle of corn leaves, almost fell. By the time he caught his balance, it was too late. Timmy was triumphantly stabbing his spear into the earth again and again, attacking the saber-toothed tiger with such fervor Jeff could almost picture the great cat there, struggling.

Everybody joined in, except Abe . . . Trogg. As always, he stood a discreet distance away, watching for predators. Keeping clean.

It became a killing frenzy. Dirt and leaves flew. Bearclaw and Urrgh were hurled aside by the cat's raking paws, but bounded back immediately, hacking away. When the beast lay dead, the cavemen clustered around it in a bowl of crushed foliage. Except for Trogg, they were all gasping, and sweat carved snail tracks through the dust on their chests. Finally Hawkeye straightened and turned toward the mountain. "All right, let's move on before any Bikkids show up. We've still got a ways to go."

He headed off in a crouching run, Bearclaw and Trogg behind him.

But Jeff and Mike hung back. Jeff hefted his spear. Spear? It was nothing but the stalk and carrot-shaped root of a reedlike plant that grew in the gullies behind Fred's house. Jeff snapped it in half over his knee. "This is *stupid*," he said.

"One more day." Mike paused. "Have you told Timmy what you and me are going to do tomorrow?"

Jeff glanced at the trio of backs receding through the corn. "Not yet."

"What do you think he'll say?"

"He'll say football's for jerks and sissies, like baseball and basketball."

"And what will you say?"

"I'll say 'No it's not, Timmy. You just don't want us to do anything *you* don't like to do.' "

"What do you think he'll say about that?"

"Who cares?" Jeff stomped on his spear, breaking it yet again, grabbing the resulting knives. He looked at Mike critically. "You're not gonna chicken out on me, are you?"

"No . . . I just hope we both make the team. They've already started practicing."

"We'll make it. Coach *asked* us to try out, remember?"

"That was last year, in PE class."

"So? He'll still want us. We'll just tell him we were gone on vacation all summer." *Like Gail,* he thought.

"Like Gail?" Mike asked, as if he were a mind reader. He examined the point of his caveman knife. "Do you think she's back from Arizona yet?"

"Oh, probably." Jeff tried to sound casual.

"I'll bet she got you a present."

"Why?"

"Because she *likes* you, you dork."

"She does not." Jeff scowled to cover the smile that threatened his face. *Did* she like him . . . *that way?* Was it so clear even Mike had noticed? "Come on, let's get moving before the others get too far ahead." He took off at a sprint. Suddenly he felt like he could run forever. *Because she likes you, you dork.*

They caught up with the rest of the gang. No one spoke. Sharp-edged corn leaves whipped at their arms and sides.

Ahead reared the Big Tree.

The boys all had their theories as to why this lone tree had been spared by whatever long-dead farmer had originally cleared the field. Abe said that in the old days, settlers always tried to keep at least one shade tree handy in each field. Mike, whose family tilled a modest spread, said that the Big Tree had probably already been huge back when the land was cleared, and it was easier to plow around it than try to remove it. Timmy's version went back even farther: He stated flatly that the Big Tree had once been used by Indians for magic rituals, and a curse would fall on anyone who chopped it down. "There are spirits out there," he said. "And if you don't know what you're doing, they'll get you even during the day. That's why we always have to make the Indian sign of protection before we walk under the tree."

From here, the Big Tree rose like a vast shimmering cloud. Jeff glanced over his shoulder. The town had sunk from sight into a tide of corn; only the water tower, painted white with big black letters spelling MIDDLEFIELD, was visible. If you ignored that, you could almost imagine you were alone in a vast, prehistoric killing field.

"Pteranodon!" Hawkeye shouted, and before Jeff even thought about it he had hurled himself sideways into the adjacent furrow, vanishing under the leaves like a marlin plunging back into the ocean. He was encased in a shadowy tunnel, its roof a loose green wickerwork of leaves and its floor as hard as concrete. The smell of dirt and watery sap sank into his nostrils.

He wondered what would happen in real life if the farmer caught them out here. They'd crushed more than a few corn plants, after all. Would they get hauled before their parents? Grounded? Be made to pay the farmer? How much did a corn plant cost, anyway?

He visualized the farmer coming along on his tractor, spotting a bunch of kids lying out here pretending to be cavemen. More and more often lately, Jeff had experienced this exterior perspective on himself and his friends. They weren't cavemen, and they weren't spacemen, although Jeff hoped to be a real astronaut someday. They certainly weren't wild animals or dinosaurs. What they were was eighth graders; at least, they would be tomorrow. The oldest kids in junior high. What would Gail think if she knew they were doing this? Knew *he* was?

Lying in the cool green world under the corn, he tried to imagine how Gail would look tomorrow as they walked to school together —not just the two of them, of course; all the gang except Mike took the same route to school. Gail would be wearing a skirt instead of her usual jeans or shorts, and her long brown hair would be brushed back and held in place by a comb. Her breasts would nudge the front of her blouse. He'd noticed the presence of these unexpected bumps early in the summer and been surprised, almost shocked; he'd also thought about them ever since. Gail just *had* to be placed in his class section this year, so they'd share the same teachers all day. She *had* to.

The ground seemed to have developed a sharp ridge directly beneath his pelvis. He rolled onto his side and saw Abe a couple of rows away, crouching as low as he could get without actually putting his hands, knees or rear end on the ground. Unlike everyone else in the gang, who wore only Bermuda shorts and sneakers, Abe was dressed in a white T-shirt and jeans with sharply ironed creases. Abe's mother always gave him holy heck if he came home dirty, never mind with torn jeans. She would take him to the bathroom and put him in the tub and scrub him *herself*, and man, he was almost thirteen years old.

Behind black horn-rimmed glasses, Abe's blunt face was sweaty but clean. As Jeff watched, he raised one wrist and looked at his watch. Something about that watch was sissy, the way the clean white handkerchief was sissy.

Jeff couldn't help feeling sorry for Abe. School never treated him well. People would ask him things like "How's your log cabin?" all the time, and make fun of the fussy way he moved and talked. Then there was the fact that his mother actually expected him to play *flute* in the school band. And he'd do it, too.

Jeff turned his head. Fred lay on his belly in the next row, his blunt jaw pressed into the earth, eyes squeezed tight in concentration. A V-shaped cut on his forehead streamed an alarming amount of blood; he must have dived headlong into a rock. As Jeff watched, Fred scrubbed a palmful of dirt into the wound. Fred believed that "clean" dirt was good for cuts, and since he was always getting sliced and scuffed yet never had to go to the doctor, maybe he was right. He'd have a dandy scar on his head, though. It occurred to Jeff that Coach Reynolds might be able to use a tough guy like Fred on the football team. If coach was interested, maybe Fred—

Timmy's whisper crept out of nowhere, as breathy and disembodied as the rustle of the corn: "Keep still, men, keep still . . . it's going over now."

Oh, grow up, Jeff thought. This just got stupider and stupider. For one thing, pteranodons went extinct long before cavemen existed, and Timmy knew that—but then, when did facts ever interfere with a Timmy Kegler game? If only he'd apply all that energy to something *other* people liked to play, he'd be a good receiver, a good shortstop, a good—

Then Jeff heard the sound, a breathy whickering overhead: *whup-whup-whup*. And suddenly he could see the pteranodon quite vividly in his mind, its wings like vein-threaded sails as it swooped low over the corn, searching for human flesh . . . Looking up, he saw a small airplane, its engine barely ticking as it coasted out of the sky toward Middlefield Airport. But through the flickering shadows of the corn leaves, the flying object could also be a pteranodon, with talons and hungry eyes . . .

"Get it!" Timmy shouted, except he was Hawkeye again and Jeff was Wolf, bounding to his feet with a big lump of summer-hardened earth clutched in his hand. Spears and dirt clods showered after the distant airplane.

"Got it!" Hawkeye cried. "It's going down! Come on!"

Wolf sprinted at top speed, gaining on Hawkeye, passing him. Throwing back his head, Wolf howled with primitive glee.

I awakened sitting up again, mouth stretched wide in a manic grin, and for a moment I could still feel the hot, pollen-heavy air rushing past my face.

Then I let out my breath, and the yodeling voices faded down an echoing tunnel to wherever children play forever. I listened for the wind, but the Santa Ana had evidently expired. All was quiet, outside and in.

I squinted at the clock. Four-fifteen. I flopped onto my stomach. *Get some sleep.*

I could smell Janice on the pillowcase. A faint scent, not quite perfume, not quite sweat. *Her.* Hadn't I bought new pillowcases, too? Maybe I should go downstairs and sleep on the couch. No, forget that; why let her abuse me even when she wasn't here? Think about something else.

Funny, I could picture Gail Rohr much more clearly than I could Janice. And smell her, too—cut grass and dandelions. Gail had been a real beauty in her unadorned, tomboyish way. Lord knew what she looked like these days, though. She'd probably wrung a whole litter of children through her once-nubile body by now.

It seemed I should know her married name. Hadn't her husband been a Brownsburg Bulldogs football player? That seemed right—a linebacker, like me. Bill Jones or something, an innocuous WASPy name.

I wondered if he and Gail were still married. Did they live in Middlefield? Did Gail ever think about me? Did I ever pass through *her* dreams?

She had had gray-green eyes. She could run faster than any boy I knew. And she was strong—she'd once given Jerry Wagner a black eye, and Jerry was the meanest of a whole family of juvenile delinquents. She could kiss, too. Fervent, searching adolescent lips and tongue . . .

I rolled onto my side. *Jesus, Dittimore, grow up!*

On the curtains hovered a man's shadow. Suddenly it was moving, oozing through the window, onto the wall. It rippled across Janice's dressing table, and for a moment I thought I saw *something* in the mirror, a large figure dressed in pajamas flashing white, and then there was just the shadow again. It leaped to the closet and vanished through the open doorway. Had I left the door open again? Inside the closet the half-visible shapes of my suits and shirts seemed to move, to reach out to the shadow and pull it in a gesture that was half welcoming and half capturing, and then it was gone.

And I was sitting up in bed. Pinching my arm, wincing at the pain, even as I realized the shadow had been cast by a car passing by on the street outside, a common enough occurrence—so why was I so sure the shadow had been Fred McMillan's, Fred McMillan who had died in 1970?

Because I was still half asleep, that was why. Half dreaming. No big deal.

Lying down again, I pulled the sheets around my neck until there were no gaps.

And stared at the open closet.

CHAPTER SIX

WOOD AND LEAVES AND BARK

First Jeff noticed the sound: a crackling rumble like a bonfire, although it was actually millions of leaves rustling in the wind. Next he noticed that the corn was getting shorter and shorter with every step he took, sinking to his waist, his knees, gone.

He looked up.

The Big Tree filled half the world. Its trunk, eight feet across at the base, was a black column rising from a lake of shadow. Above, foliage soared into the sky in tiers of dark green shimmering with silver overtones.

"We're here." Timmy looked around, then walked under the tree with Abe, Fred and Mike at his heels. Each of them raised a fist, pinky finger extended—the Indian sign of protection—before the Big Tree's shadow swallowed them.

Jeff stayed where he was, the sunlight on his face.

He hadn't been this close to the Big Tree in a couple of years. Now, as he stood at the edge of its shadow, he waited for the old fear to strike.

It didn't. He saw exactly what Dad had described to him: wood and leaves and bark. No huge, sinister face. No shadowy figures. He heard nothing but the wind, the electric buzz of cicadas, the sawing of crickets. No whispering voices.

If you don't believe it can hurt you, then it can't.

Timmy's voice shot out of the gloom: "Hey, Wolf, you gonna stand out there all day?"

"Hold your horses," Jeff said, and marched forward. He didn't make the Indian sign, either.

The shade felt wonderful, like a cool pond closing over him. He blinked as his eyes adjusted. Under here, the ground was root-heaved and as hard as winter, littered with jawbreaker-sized acorns. He spotted a tuft of grass near Mike and Fred, and flopped down on it. Timmy was already perched on the raised knee of an exposed root; Abe sat gingerly near Timmy's feet.

Jeff looked around. Overhead, the canopy of leaves closed out the sky, while on all sides the corn formed a shimmering wall. There was no sign of Middlefield, not even the water tower. But Jeff still wasn't scared. This place wasn't frightening at all. It was like being inside a huge green tent.

He suddenly realized how dry his throat was. "I can't believe we came out here without food and water," he said. "We should have at least brought our canteens."

Timmy snorted. "Cavemen didn't have canteens."

"No wonder they're all dead."

There was a little laughter, then Abe said, "I've got some gum. That'll get our spit running." He passed around a slightly crumpled pack of Juicy Fruit. For all Jeff knew, it was left over from last Halloween. Abe never spent his own money on candy, comic books or anything else for that matter—but if he had goodies on him, he always shared.

"Indians used to march across the desert for days without water," Timmy said, jaw working busily. "It was part of becoming a brave. It gave them visions."

"Where did you hear that?" Mike asked. Everybody knew Timmy made things up, then pretended they were facts. He also sometimes read something interesting or saw it on TV, then pretended he'd made it up.

"I read it in a book on Indians," Timmy said. Tilting his head back, he stared up into the green cloud of the tree. "Did you know the Indians used to sacrifice people here?"

"No way," Jeff said.

"Yeah, they worshipped big trees like this one. So sometimes they'd bring a prisoner out here and sacrifice him. That way they could get the spirits in the other world to help them do things, kill their enemies and stuff." He pointed between his feet, where two roots made a deep, purse-shaped pocket in the earth. "They'd bury part of their sacrifice down in the roots, and put the rest up in the branches, so both halves of the tree would be fed."

"Come on," Jeff sneered.

Timmy's eyes narrowed. With his tanned skin and his greased hair standing out in all directions, he looked a bit like a crazed Indian himself. "Did you hear about the Big Kids who came out here on Halloween twenty years ago? They were supposed to be at the Fall Festival, you know, but they came out here instead, and—"

"That happens all the time," Mike said. "Big Kids come out here every Halloween."

"This was different. This time, one of the Big Kids accidentally cut his hand on a bottle and bled on the ground under here. Nobody will say exactly what happened next, but when the Big Kids got back to town the next morning, all their hair had turned white."

Jeff had never heard this particular story before, which made him suspicious of it. Also, he wasn't sure it was *possible* for a person's hair to turn white overnight.

"What did they see?" Abe asked in a hushed voice that contained no doubt at all. Abe was the only member of the gang, besides Timmy, who still believed they'd almost gone to Venus that time.

"Nobody knows," Timmy said. "Because when they walked into town, they couldn't talk, either."

Jeff's laugh, a flat bugle blast, startled even him. "Who told you that one?"

"My dad."

The laughter halted. You didn't make fun of Timmy's dad, not *ever*. Everyone in the gang had seen the thick leather strap Mr. Kegler kept hanging by the back door.

Fred had been picking casually at the fresh scab on his forehead. A trickle of blood ran to the corner of his mouth; he licked it absently. "Well," he said, "there aren't any Indians here now, and this isn't a desert, and I'm dying of thirst."

Timmy looked at him as if he were something your mom would tell you to scrape off your shoe before you came into the house. "What a sissy. This is the first time we've been out here in centuries, and all you can do is complain."

"*I'm* glad we came," Abe piped.

"Why *did* we come out here, anyway?" Mike asked. "You said you were going to show us something."

Timmy hesitated. One hand rose and absently caressed the bark of the tree. His fingers were long and slender, but the nails were ragged nubs with bloody edges. "I told you, this is a magic place. We were always scared of it before because we didn't understand it."

Wood and leaves and bark, Jeff thought. "Changing your tune?" he asked.

"I just understand more now. And I think the Big Tree can help us."

"Help us what?" Mike asked.

"Oh . . . do lots of things. Like make school better."

Abe winced at the word *school.* "How?"

Timmy crossed one foot over the other, mirroring the configuration of the roots beneath him. "You know it's going to be really bad this year, in eighth grade. For one thing, they'll divide us up into different class sections. We won't all be together."

"Different sections?" Abe cried.

"Yeah," Mike said. "Like, say you're in Section One. You'll have the same home room and lunch hour as everybody else in that section, and a lot of the same classes and stuff. But you won't be in any classes with people from other sections."

Abe looked horrified. "But . . . what if *none* of us are together?"

"Oh, that won't happen," Mike said. "There are only four sections."

"But still . . ." Abe brushed nervously at his pants. "Even if they split us up, we'll do stuff together on weekends, right? Play games and stuff?"

"After your flute lesson, you mean," Fred snorted.

"So?" Abe's eyes narrowed. "What's wrong with that?"

"Nothing." Timmy pinned Fred with his stare until Fred looked away. "Besides, stupid class sections aren't the big problem. The big problem is even *getting* to school."

"Huh?" Abe's eyes widened again.

"I'm talking about Big Kids. They're the worst things around here, and they'll be coming after us—right, Jeff?"

Jeff said nothing, dug at the ground with his fake caveman knife.

"They'll come after us?" Abe prodded.

"Yeah, because we have to walk right past the high school to get to junior high."

"We had to do that last year, too," Mike said.

"Yeah, but this year we'll be *eighth graders*. Big Kids hate eighth graders more than anything. They'll be waiting for us to set foot on high school property, and then—*bam!*" He smacked a fist into his palm. Abe jumped.

"High school kids don't care about us," Jeff said, less firmly than he would have liked.

"Unless they catch us taking the shortcut. Don't you remember that time when we were nine, Jeff?"

Jeff shrugged. "That was a long time ago. Besides . . . I'm not so sure those guys were really after us."

Timmy regarded him silently for a moment, brows slowly drawing together. He uncrossed his feet. "Right," he said. "Big Kids are cool. None of them would ever beat you up. Or stomp on your jack-o'-lantern on Halloween. Or throw iceballs at you in winter. Or shoot you in the back with a rubber-band gun. Come on. You know how they get when they're that old."

"We're almost that old, Timmy," Fred said in a reasonable voice as he pressed a piece of dry moss against his bleeding forehead.

"Yeah, but we're different."

"You're different," Jeff said, trying to lighten things up. "You're nutty as a fruitcake." Mike and Fred laughed.

Timmy's expression hadn't changed. "I guess you *want* to be like Big Kids, huh, Jeff?"

Jeff stopped smiling. Maybe this was the time to tell Timmy about football practice.

But before he could speak, Timmy began leaping from one exposed root to another, all shins and elbows, yet agile as a mountain goat. "Big Kids are a bunch of jerks," he said. "Trying to be cool. A bunch of jerks."

"You can't help growing up," Jeff said. "Some things happen whether you want them to or not."

Timmy halted, weight balanced on one dirty Red Ball Flier. "Like what?"

Jeff opened his mouth, closed it again. "I don't know. Like getting hair on your dick?"

Everyone had a good laugh at that one; Timmy giggled so hard he almost fell off his perch. Fred snickered, "Your mom would wash your mouth out with soap if she heard you say 'dick,' Jeff."

"You're right. Dick, dick, dick." They all laughed some more.

"That's not what I'm talking about," Timmy said at last. "I

mean we don't have to do all the stupid stuff Big Kids do—work on cars, play sports, talk about girls all the time. Do you think Big Kids ever do the stuff *we* do? Do you think any of them would come out here like this?"

"Every Halloween," Mike said. "You said so your—"

"Yeah, but they come here to *drink*." Timmy's voice gushed scorn. "To get drunk and act like idiots. Not to *explore*."

"Yeah," Abe piped. "We're *explorers*."

Jeff couldn't stand it. "This is just a *tree*," he said, waving an arm overhead. "We're only a mile from home. Maybe not even that far."

"Oh, yeah?" Timmy's eyebrows rose. "You're sure? Can you see your house from here?"

"Well, not with the *corn*. But I know where it is."

"Are you sure? Maybe it's gone. Maybe it disappeared while we were coming out here. You don't *know*."

"Oh, sure, my house disappeared." Despite himself, Jeff imagined it—and felt a chill. The wind gusted, and the surrounding leaves made a sound like the applause of a distant crowd. Jeff became overwhelmingly aware of the bulk of the Big Tree, the sheer mass of the wood and vegetation looming above him.

"Want to find out?" Timmy turned and placed his palms against the Big Tree's trunk. His face was red under the dust, the sweat, the summer tan. "Want to climb up and see?"

Everybody stared at him. Climbing the Big Tree was pointless; on top of that, it wasn't even fun. There were no branches to grab for the first eight or nine feet, and even if you got boosted up to a perch, you still couldn't see Middlefield because of all the leaves. And after that, forget climbing. The trunk divided into two equal portions that extended up another twenty or thirty feet without any branches along the way. The upper levels of the tree had never been explored, so far as any of them knew.

But before Jeff could point this out, Timmy turned and pounced onto the trunk of the tree, his fingers locking around thick scales of bark, his toes digging into fissures. Slowly, he began to climb. It wouldn't last long, and they all knew it. Not even Mike with his strong farmer's hands could get clear up to the fork without a boost. Any second now, Timmy would fall, then say something like, "The soles of my shoes are too slick."

Five seconds passed, then ten. Timmy was still going. Grunting, gasping, sweat pouring into his grimacing mouth. Hands reaching, Red Ball Fliers jabbing. "I'm a mandrill baboon!" he cried shrilly. "One of the meanest, toughest animals in the world!" He was almost four feet off the ground when one of his feet slipped. He cycled it wildly through the air, somehow keeping his handhold until he was able to dig the toe back in. He climbed higher. Higher.

Jeff was still waiting for the fall when Timmy hauled himself into the crotch of the tree.

Abe shot to his feet. "Way to go, Timmy!" The rest of them stared at one another in disbelief. Up in the tree, Timmy got to his feet and braced himself in the fork like ammunition in a slingshot. His naked chest and stomach were scraped raw. "Come on, you bunch of wimps," he gasped. "Or are you too *mature* to climb trees anymore?"

Glances shot around again, then Jeff, Mike and Fred leaped at the tree. Only Abe hung back. He wasn't allowed to climb, of course.

The others attacked the trunk from different angles. Jeff couldn't see anyone else, and didn't try to. He concentrated all his attention on his own grip, the placement of his toes. But before he had gone three feet, the muscles of both his hands locked in agony and he dropped to the ground, stumbling over the exposed roots. Mike and Fred plummeted down a moment later, almost in unison. Fred now sported a wide skid mark on his chin to go with the scabby cut on his forehead.

"The bottoms of my shoes are too slick," Jeff said, scuffing a sole in the dirt. "No traction."

"Mine, too," Fred said.

"Mine, too," said Mike.

"Look!" Abe shouted.

The rest of them followed his pointing finger, and their mouths dropped open. Timmy was no longer in the crotch of the tree. He was climbing again.

A cramp in my hand woke me up. I raised my head, realized I was in my office at work, and that my fingers had locked around the edge of my desk. I jerked them free, got up and walked to the window.

The sun had just gone down. On the freeway, many of the cars had their headlights on.

I flexed my fingers. I never fell asleep at my desk. Never had before. Of course, I hadn't exactly had a restful night recently, had I?

The twentieth floor was unoccupied except for me. Warrick had stuck his head into my office at about seven, but luckily I'd been on the telephone. He'd eyeballed me for a moment, then raised one hand in ambiguous salute and left. Since then, even the janitors had come and gone. But I still didn't want to leave. Go back to that empty house.

In the west, the sky had turned a scorched orange. The coastal clouds looked like they were blazing.

Suddenly I was aware of the picture I must make to any driver who glanced up: a solitary silhouette staring wistfully into the sunset. An executive who hadn't figured out that the era of the Yuppie was over and oh, by the way, you can't be forty-two and still be a Yuppie anyway.

I focused on my reflection in the window. Tailored suit, tailored hair. And beyond that, the impressive office for which I had worked so long and so hard, for which I had sacrificed so much.

Just then a man walked into the reflected room. He wore white pajamas and leather slippers. His shoulders were wide, yet the pj shirt hung in limp folds as if there were no flesh beneath. His skin gleamed gray white except for the purplish, V-shaped scar on his forehead. Under one arm he cradled a human head wearing black-framed glasses. Abe Perry's head. Moving past the desk, they stepped toward me, and Fred reached out as if to—

—tremble and dissolve into the shape of an airplane sinking out of the sky outside, its landing lights a blur across the tinted glass.

Air hissed through my lips. Turning, I strode to my desk and dropped shakily into the chair. I would *not* look into the hallway. Not because I was afraid of seeing Abe and Fred there, in whole or in part, but because checking would mean I *expected* to see them. Which was crazy.

"Goddamn it," I said, and was dismayed by the quaver in my voice. What was happening to me?

I pushed some papers around on my desk. My gaze, confined to this limited space, lit on the telephone. I hesitated, then picked up the receiver and punched a speed-dial button.

Two rings. "Dittimore residence," a woman's voice said, cheerful as usual.

"Hi, Mom."

"Jeff! Why, how nice." Her voice perked up even more, although she sounded surprised as well as pleased. I usually only called on Sunday afternoons.

"How's everything going?" I asked.

"Oh, fine. I've just been sitting here reading to your father."

"Oh."

"You should see him, Jeff. I really think he's beginning to *understand* things. Yesterday I was reading him Dave Barry's column from the *Sun,* and he actually smiled. You should have seen it."

"That's great, Mom," I said around the rock in my throat.

"He'll beat this. I pray for him every day."

"I'm sure that helps." *God's Intention for Your Life,* I thought.

"Honey, you sound kind of down. Are you all right?"

I pictured Dad in his wheelchair, in his prison body and his prison mind, or what the stroke had left of them. *Where Will You Face Eternity?*

And here I was, feeling sorry for myself because I'd had a few bad dreams. "I'm fine," I said. "Just having a little trouble sleeping lately. How's the weather?"

"Fine, just fine."

I knew it was roasting out there this time of year. Mom and Dad had moved to Phoenix only because the cost of living there had been lower at the time, and I'd been able to sell their California house for a huge profit in the early 1980s real-estate boom. They needed those funds to get by, even with Medicare and a stipend from me. What they really needed was a live-in nurse, but Mom wouldn't have that.

"You should come out for a visit," Mom said. "We'd love to see you."

"I wish I could. But . . . well, now's not a good time. You know." I hated to use the word *divorce.* It wasn't one she liked much.

"No wonder you can't sleep," she said. "It's got to be very difficult. And you've always had trouble getting a good night's rest anyway."

"Funny you'd mention that," I said. "You'll never guess what I've been dreaming about lately."

"What?"

"I keep dreaming I'm a kid again, running around with my old friends. Mike Norris and Fred McMillan and Abe Perry and Timmy Kegler. Remember those guys?"

"Why, of course. You were quite a crew, you boys. Especially you, Mike and Timmy. I used to call you Wynken, Blynken and Nod."

I shivered. *Wynken, Blynken and Nod.* That was it. Not the Three Stooges or the Three Musketeers—Wynken, Blynken and Nod. I even remembered Timmy's reaction the first time she'd said it. "I'm Nod!" he'd cried in the same peremptory tone he used when he proclaimed, "I'm a tyrannosaurus!" or "I'm a puma!" in the games we played.

But that wasn't all of it. Nod had also been the name of something else . . .

"You used to have the most terrible nightmares when you were a boy," Mom said. "Remember?"

"You and Dad had to come into my room almost every night, I remember that."

"Timmy was always getting you riled up with those stories of his. My, what an imagination that boy had. Although you were nearly as bad all by yourself."

"I wonder if Timmy ever turned up again," I said in what I hoped was a casual tone.

"I don't know, honey. We sort of fell out of touch with everyone in Middlefield over the years . . . It's best to forget about things you can't change, anyway."

I thought about Dad again. *I pray for him every day.*

"It wasn't all bad," I said.

"Middlefield? Oh, no, of course not. That's not what I meant. It's just . . . After those poor friends of your disappeared, well, that sort of thing can scar a young mind."

Not just a young mind. I remembered that for months after that Halloween of 1965, every mind in Middlefield had picked at scabs. Two boys were missing; evidence indicated that at least one of them, Abe Perry, had tramped off into the waste ground where Lincoln Avenue dead-ended near the cornfield. No one knew why. Because the other missing boy, Timothy Kegler, had been Abe's best friend, it was logical to assume that was where he'd gone, too.

But then what? Were the boys runaways, or had something more sinister happened out there in the darkness? Possibilities were traded like baseball cards. The attitudes and demeanors of the missing boys' parents were privately observed and publicly dissected. Abe's parents had wandered through town with their faces turned away from everyone until May, when they had moved. As for Mr. Kegler, on the first anniversary of Timmy's disappearance, he had made an eye-to-eye arrangement with a shotgun.

On the following Halloween, the Big Tree had gone up in flames. Luckily the weather had been wet and the crop that year was low-growing soybeans, so the fire hadn't spread far despite the fact the Middlefield Fire Department couldn't get to it. In the end, all that had remained of the Big Tree was a blackened stump protruding from the earth like a rotten tooth. Ashes and coals and dust.

"Honey," Mom said, "I think I'd better put your father to bed. Would you like to talk to him first?"

I winced. "Sure."

A moment later, the breathing started. Slow, shallow, even. I pictured Mom standing behind the wheelchair, holding the receiver to Dad's ear. Waiting. I knew she could hear my voice, or lack of it.

"Hi, Dad," I said. "How are you? Everything's good here. I'm looking forward to seeing you in the fall. Terri is too. Love you."

The breathing never changed pitch or cadence. Dad, his eyes fixed on nothing. As they had been for the last eight years, ever since the stroke knocked him to the ground while he was mowing the lawn. He had lain there in the baking Southern California sun for almost a half-hour, staring at the world from his new and limited perspective, before Mom saw him and called the paramedics. By then, Dad had become a thing to be tended, himself.

Please die, Dad, I thought over the phone, trembling at the triple impact of love, guilt and fury. *Please please die soon.*

The breathing went on for several seconds, as insensate as a ticking clock. Then Mom came back on the line. "We're really glad you called, honey."

After I hung up I sat quietly for a while, reflecting on how unevenly life hands out its parcels of fortune, both good and bad. Where was I in the receiving line?

Then I realized someone was standing in the doorway of my office, watching me. I shot to my feet and shouted, "Leave me *alone!*"

Mr. Warrick staggered back so fast he almost fell.

CHAPTER SEVEN

VIEW FROM THE TOP

It was impossible. Yet Timmy was shinnying up one of the main forks of the Big Tree, his arms and legs sprawled precariously around its girth as he inched along with wormlike contractions of his torso. There was no resting place above him for what seemed like a mile, and nothing below to break his fall if he slipped. "Come on, you bunch of sissies!" he shouted.

Nobody moved. After a moment Jeff got the feeling the rest of the guys were watching him from the corners of their eyes. He wheeled toward Abe. "Boost me up."

Abe sighed. "Okay." He always got this job. "But remember, don't mess up my pants or Mom will kill me."

A few seconds later Jeff made the rushing, convulsive leap from Abe's cupped hands toward the crotch of the tree, and grabbed hold of a protruding ridge of bark. Now came the tense, exciting moment of clinging by his fingertips while trying to get traction with feet and legs; now the straining chin-up; and finally the awkward slither into the fork of the tree. He sprawled there on his belly, legs dangling, the crushed-cardboard smell of bark in his nose. The ground looked like a brown and green carpet draped over bowling balls. It looked that solid, too.

"Get out of the way before I knock you out of there!" Mike shouted. He'd turned his cap around backward on his head.

"Oh, shut up," Jeff muttered, twisting into a sitting position. Far above, Timmy's legs receded steadily. Jeff peered up the other fork. It was almost identical to the one Timmy was on, with a steep incline and no real handholds for what looked like the height of the Middlefield water tower. Jeff licked his lips.

Just then Timmy's voice squalled through the tree in another eerie ape-scream imitation. Jeff looked around, but his friend had disappeared. Nothing was visible overhead except a patchwork of foliage and branches. "Woosie-woosie-woosie!" Timmy's disembodied voice mingled with the rush of the wind. "Whatsamatter, *afraid?*"

"Come *on*, Jeff," Mike pleaded. "Move!"

Scrambling to his feet, Jeff shouted into the canopy, "Coming after you, monkey face!"

"Ha! See you at the top!"

Reaching as high as he could on his chosen fork, Jeff clutched scales of bark and jump-pulled himself up, bare knees swinging high to clamp the tree. Staring straight at the bark, he extended his arms again and pulled himself up another notch.

By the fourth repetition, he knew this was a mistake. Traction was minimal, his grip the same. The bark raked the insides of his arms and thighs like dull saw blades. And the fall . . . If Timmy hadn't already somehow made this climb, Jeff would forget about it right now. And no harm done. No one would think he was a sissy. If Timmy hadn't already done it.

He kept climbing. Inches at a time.

The bark formed mountains and canyons beneath his focused gaze. He concentrated on that, trying not to think about the sprained ankle that awaited him if he lost his grip. Or the broken leg. He'd have to kiss football goodbye. And he already had his positions picked out: wide receiver on offense and linebacker on defense. He wondered if he'd be able to hear individual fans shouting from the stands. Mom and Dad, for example. Gail Rohr . . .

He paused, shoulders burning, arms shuddering wildly. Looked down. Mike clung not far below him on the trunk, shinnying up slowly, eyes crunched closed. Farther down, Fred had just grunted his way into the crotch of the tree. And below that . . . oh, God. The ground looked smooth now, a distant map.

Then Jeff looked up, and shock made his grip even weaker. Had the branches somehow gotten *higher?* He knew he couldn't make it, but he couldn't back down, either, not with Mike there. Taking a deep breath, he forced himself upward again.

The trunk seemed to get steadily steeper in his arms, as if it were straightening even as he climbed. Yet he kept going. *You're just making it worse for when you do fall,* a voice whispered in his head. A breathy, insinuating voice, the one that used to float across the fields at night.

He glanced down, hoping Mike had already retreated. No such luck. The engineer's cap was still there, if farther behind. Fred was about five feet up on the other fork. Even as Jeff watched, Fred slipped, caught himself, then slipped again. Then, to Jeff's horror, he spun around to the wrong side of the trunk, nothing but fingertips showing. Abe, standing directly below, let out a bleat of horror and ran. A moment later Fred plummeted earthward, feet first. He hit with a "WHOOP!" Jeff heard plainly, then flopped onto his side. For a moment he lay perfectly still, and Jeff felt a slimy-cold wave of dread wash over him. *He's dead. Oh, man, he's . . .* Then Fred stirred and sat up. He shook his head, shoved Abe away and got unsteadily to his feet. Walked around a moment, dropped onto a root.

"He's okay!" Abe shouted. "He's okay!"

From above sailed Timmy's voice: "Nice try, Fred the Sled! I'm on my way to the top! All the way! The first person to reach the top of the Big Tree!" He let out another ape shriek.

"Man oh man," Jeff muttered, resisting the urge to brush away an ant that had parked itself on the back of his hand. Sweat burned like acid in his eyes. *All the way to the top? He's really serious? He's gonna beat me.*

Looking up, Jeff pictured Gail clinging to the lowest branch. She wore only the shredded remnants of a dress, like Jane in the Tarzan books. Her long naked legs dangled in space. Her eyes brimmed with helpless terror. *Help!* she wept. *Help me, Jeff! I'm scared!*

Jeff's lips peeled back. Locking his arms around the tree, he planted his toes hard in the fissured bark. Jerked his body upward. Did it again. And again. In his mind, his body was draped in the skins of the mighty lion, Simba.

And the jungle was his home.

I awoke straining against the pull of the dream the way I'd strained against gravity while in the dream. Shaking it off was difficult. Last night I'd broken down and swallowed one of Janice's sleeping pills.

But it seemed to have helped. The alarm was buzzing. I rolled over, hit the button. I felt woozy, but otherwise pretty good as I looked around in the gray predawn gloom. I'd reached a new day without another . . . hallucination.

Last night at the office, Warrick had obviously been tempted to call the men in the white coats after I'd screamed at him. But I'd made up a story, told him my wife's lawyers had been sending process servers out to harass me, making me jumpy. He'd seemed to accept that, even suggested getting a restraining order. I'd said I'd take care of it. But he'd also mentioned, again, that I might want to consider "getting some help" for my nerves.

It was kind of him to be concerned, but the only help I needed was rest, a couple more nights of uninterrupted—

"*Pssssssssssssst.*"

I sat up fast enough to make the bed groan. Looked wildly around the room. *I heard that. I heard that.* But no one was there.

"*Pssssssssssssst. Jeff.*"

The closet door stood halfway open. Last night, I'd made myself leave it like that . . . hadn't I? Inside hung dark, uncertain shapes. Of course, I knew what they were: suits, coats, ties, shoes in a neat row underneath. Normal objects.

My gaze traversed the room. There was the bureau, Terri's picture on top of it. There, the window. There, Janice's dressing table.

And a man sitting in front of it.

My breath hooked inside my throat like tangles of barbed wire.

Nothing moved. I was aware of my heartbeat, of the distant rush of highway traffic, of the clock's hum.

Nothing moved.

"Dittimore," I blurted, "you're an idiot." Now I remembered—I'd draped my robe over the back of that chair when I got into bed. As I had last night, and the night before . . .

"You look good, Jeff," the silhouette murmured.

My head rapped against the wall. But to my surprise, after the immediate tidal wave of terror surged past, what I felt was flat relief. This was *real*. Someone was actually in the room. My commanding legal voice shot out: "Who the hell are you and what do you want?"

The man shook his head. He wore something white and shapeless, like sheets off a line. "Your mom would wash your mouth out with soap for saying 'hell,' Jeffy," he said. "And I can't believe you don't recognize me. Don't you know an old friend when you see one?"

"Old friend?" I whispered. The voice *did* sound familiar . . .

"Buddy. Pal. Don't you remember?"

The lamp on the bedside table. It was solid brass. If I got a good grip and swung hard enough, I might be able to—

"It seems like yesterday to me," the man said. "You remember yesterday, don't you? All our troubles seemed so far away." The room had grown lighter, painting details onto the man. His garments consisted of an overlarge pajama shirt and pants; bony ankles showed between the pantcuffs and the slippers beneath. Gaunt cheeks, sunken eyes. Someone who had been hurt. Someone who had spent time in a hospital. On his forehead, a V-shaped scar . . .

My flesh contracted. *"Freddy?"* I whispered.

He leaned forward. "In spirit only, man. I'm here to deliver a message. Like Marley's ghost. Remember *A Christmas Carol?* It was one of Nod's favorite stories, remember?"

I stiffened. "Nod?"

"He wants to see you, Jeff. Have a little get-together, talk about old times."

"Fred, I—"

"Listen, and then do what I say—otherwise there's worse to come, man." He rose to his feet. "You have to go back. Don't waste time, Jeffy. Go back now. You're *needed.*"

Almost without thinking, I grabbed a fold of skin on my forearm and squeezed hard. The pain made me wince . . . and when my vision cleared, there was no one at the window.

"Christ," I said weakly, and groped for my glasses again. I slipped them on and, sure enough, saw nothing by the dressing table but my discarded robe draped over the chair. I sank back slowly, like a deflating balloon. Most of the room was clearly visible now. Dressing table. Bureau. Closet—still dark in there. But I could see into it a little bit. My suits all had hands and feet, and grim, angular faces. The largest figure wore pajamas and slippers.

"I should never have let you talk me into joining the football team, Jeff," Fred said. "Now you have to go back and set things right." Around him, the other figures stirred, sliding away into greater darkness. Their hands clutched at Fred, pulling him along.

"Make it right, Jeff," he said. "Make it right. That's what friends do . . ."

By the time Jeff reached the first branch he was panting like the old air compressor at Stan's Sinclair station. But he didn't mind; the feel of a more or less horizontal surface under his grasping hand made him want to weep with relief. He hoisted his body up, straddled the branch and clutched the trunk with all his might. Closed his eyes.

Did it did it did it . . .

Awareness of his surroundings crept back bit by bit. Beneath him, the branch swayed like the deck of a ship. He heard the vast rush of leaves, and birds calling. And—

"Yoo-hoo! Jeffy!" Timmy hooted from somewhere overhead. "I *seeeeeeee yooooooooooooooou.* Come and get me if you can!"

Jeff opened his eyes. He was surrounded by masses of leaves through which branches ran like big, unsteady pipes. He looked down. The layers of foliage did funny things. Leaves blocked his view of Mike, but Abe's tiny upturned face was visible through a gap, shouting, "Be careful, you guys!"

Jeff grinned, let go of the tree trunk with one arm and waved. Now that he was actually here, safe and sound, what he'd done was cool. It was something. It was an *accomplishment*.

Mike's tight voice rose from below: "Jeff, you there? You there, man?" He didn't sound as close as he should be.

"Yeah!" Jeff tried unsuccessfully to spot his friend. "Keep on coming."

"I can't . . . I can't make it. I have to go back."

Jeff was surprised. Mike was used to tossing around bales of hay, digging postholes, lugging sacks of feed. He couldn't be that tired, could he? "That's okay," Jeff called. "Fred already gave up."

"But I—I can't—I can't see behind me. To go down." Mike's voice was high-pitched and craggy, a tone Jeff had never heard in it before.

"Don't worry." Jeff kept his own voice calm. "Just let yourself slide a little bit at a time, nice and slow."

"Okay," Mike gasped. "Okay. Okay, I'm doing it."

"Nice and slow. See you at the bottom, later."

"Okay. Okay."

After a minute had passed without any bloodcurdling screams, Jeff bent his head back and searched the branches above him. They dwindled in size and increased in quantity, an ascending wooden scaffold. In places, splashes of sunlight brightened the canopy. He couldn't see Timmy, but clearly heard him yell, "Last one to the top's a rotten banana!"

"No fair!" Jeff bellowed back. "You got a head start!"

"Wah, wah, cry like a baby!"

"Bet I get higher than you do!"

"Bet you don't!"

Clutching the trunk, Jeff pulled his feet under him and started to climb.

It was much easier going now, one limb leading smoothly to the next. Soon any hint of the ground disappeared. Jeff concentrated on what was above him, moving from handhold to handhold, easing into a rhythm. Overhead, flecks of blue sky materialized like glittering stars, then joined into constellations, galaxies. Now there was a branch everywhere he put a hand or foot. When he finally stopped, it was only because the limbs had gotten so small they bent noticeably under his weight. The trunk itself had dwindled to the width of a gutterpipe, and rocked gently back and forth. He figured he could still go a bit higher if he really wanted to, but reminded himself that just because he couldn't see the ground, that didn't mean it wasn't there.

Where was Timmy? He looked around, although he doubted that even Timmy, who was smaller than he was, could climb much higher than this.

No one was in sight. He listened. As before, the only sounds were the bright rush of the wind, the chitter-chatter of birds, and the electric buzz of summer cicadas. The trunk rocked gently back and forth like a giant metronome.

I did it, he thought. *I'm in the top of the Big Tree.*

A flash of sunlight struck his shoulder. He turned his head and gasped.

Timmy had been wrong; Jeff's house still existed. He could see it plainly, if in miniature, from its shingled roof to its light brown siding. As he watched, the back door opened and his mother, flea-sized, came out carrying a laundry basket under her arm. She bustled around the clothesline, unaware she was being watched from the sky. From here she looked terribly insignificant, fragile.

Past his house lay dozens more of similar size and shape, a tidy mosaic of roofs. Toward Main Street, older, taller houses rose up. Gail lived in one of those, although Jeff couldn't be sure which one. He pictured her at home right now, brushing summer vacation out of her hair, thinking about school. Maybe thinking about *him*.

To the north was the high school complex. The gymnasium looked like a giant loaf of bread, its top burned black, and the classroom building like the pan it had been baked in. He could see that the parking lot held only a dozen or so cars this afternoon, although that would, of course, change tomorrow. In the adjacent practice fields, moving helmets glittered in the sun. Varsity players, running drills. He looked at the football stadium itself, with its bleachers and goalposts, its pristine rectangle of white-striped grass.

He tried to spot the junior high building beyond the high school, in the older part of town. It was barely visible from here, a red brick cube buried in masses of trees. Tomorrow, he'd start a new year there. A new life. It felt that way.

How would the world look from even higher up? he wondered. He began to climb again, slowly and carefully, keeping the swaying to a minimum. The next gap in the foliage faced away from town. Jeff got comfortable and peered through.

This view was even more spectacular than the first: an assembled jigsaw puzzle of fields expanding toward the horizon, shades of green and brown fading into milky blue. He saw roads, houses, farms, a tractor chugging through a distant field. Enormous cloud shadows pitted the ground like cobalt-blue lakes. He saw . . . *everything*.

He looked up again. Maybe he could climb higher still. Grabbing the next branch, he tested it for strength.

A fanged, roaring face lunged out of the leaves. Jeff screamed and jerked back, hands flying up. He heard a crisp *snap*. And suddenly he was falling, falling . . .

CHAPTER EIGHT

MILES TO GO BEFORE I SLEEP

"You look tired," my wife said.

I blinked at her. It was lunchtime and we were at Perrine's, a restaurant across the street from my office building. Janice had called me at work at nine o'clock and said, "We need to talk about Terri."

So here we were. Perrine's was a large, glass-walled establishment, the gaps between tables crammed with so many plants you half-expected a monkey to reach out and snatch away your Skinless Breast of Chicken with Roasted Asparagus Tips. I conducted a lot of business here.

What had Janice just said? I looked tired?

"I'm fine," I said. Just looking at her made me angry.

Still, in a way, her asking to meet me today was fortuitous. It would be a good time to tell her I intended to sell the house. This morning I'd awakened on the bedroom floor, a band of sunlight burning on my face. On the floor! Getting out of that house was obviously critical. Cutting entirely free of the past, that was the key.

Grudgingly, I had to admit it had worked for Janice. She looked prettier than she had in years. Not so skinny. After giving birth to Terri, she'd gone on a fanatical diet-and-exercise program that had never ended. At times I'd wondered if she might be anorexic. But right now she looked fit and healthy in a simple blue dress I'd never seen before. An equally simple cross hung around her neck from a web-thin gold chain. I wanted to choke her with it, I admit.

We'd both ordered preluncheon drinks: Calistoga sparkling water for her, a martini for me. Let her frown in disapproval. Except she didn't. She looked sad instead, which really aggravated me. I remember when she used to gulp gin like it was Kool-Aid.

"Okay," I said after the drinks arrived. "You called this meeting. What's wrong?"

She stared into her glass, then up at me with the big, crystal-gray eyes that had mesmerized me so many years ago. "How have you been?"

"I thought you wanted to talk about Terri."

"I do. But . . . You really look worn out, Jeff. It bothers me. Believe it or not, I still care about you."

"Yeah? Wanna have an affair?" I grinned. The expression felt so damned strange on my face I wasn't surprised to see her lean away.

"I'm . . . it's not like that," she said. "Things have changed."

"Sorry, I don't believe anything I don't read in a note by the side of the bed. Must be the lawyer in me coming out."

For a flash, a familiar gravity pulled at her face, making it look bitter and shrewish. Then she sighed, closed her eyes, and the scowl melted away. *Did you just pray for strength, Janice?* I thought, and felt an almost overpowering urge to hurl her water in her face.

Her eyes opened again, fixed on me steadily. "I can't tell you how sorry I am. About everything."

I said nothing.

"You have every reason to be angry with me," she said, "but I've changed. It's over between us, but I've still changed."

"Hmph." I felt the grin tugging at my face again, and suddenly remembered a movie I saw a long time ago on *Nightmare Theater* —Timmy's favorite TV show. *Mr. Sardonicus*, it was called. A superstitious peasant, digging up his father's grave to retrieve a winning lottery ticket, is so horrified by the rictus on the corpse's face that his own features get locked into the same hideous grin. "Now you're going to tell me you're born again, right?" I asked.

Her face remained placid. "Yes."

"How perfect for you. You cheat on me for years, then wipe it out with one dunk in an indoor swimming pool."

She closed her eyes. "I wish you'd try to understand. I wish you'd try to find the peace in the Lord that I—"

"Stop." I slugged down the rest of the martini; for a moment it felt like the olive had gotten stuck in my throat. "Don't even start. You know how I feel about that crap." I looked around for a waiter, not that I was hungry. Instead, I saw Mr. Warrick, just entering the restaurant with a client. Great.

"It's not God's fault your father had a stroke, Jeff," Janice said sadly.

"You're right. It's not God's fault my father had a stroke, or that there's war in Bosnia, or that babies are born with AIDS. Shit happens. That's exactly right. That's exactly the point."

The pitying look wafted over her face again. "You're not even trying to understand. You've strayed so far. Sometimes I think if we'd kept going to church after what happened to your father, we . . ." She glanced into my eyes, then quickly down. "That's not why I'm here, anyway. I'm here because Terri's worried about you."

Funny, I thought, *I got the impression she was worried about you.* "What do you mean?"

"She had a nightmare last night. It was terrible. She woke up screaming. I ran into her room, and she was staring at the wall and shrieking her head off. She said she dreamt you killed yourself."

My mouth was dry. Where was that damned waiter?

"Well, that would be ESP. Wouldn't it?"

Janice was not amused. "She saw you standing on a cliff somewhere, looking out at the ocean. There was a little boy with you. He was holding your hand real tight. She said she wasn't sure if he was trying to pull you back or push you. But finally you jerked your hand away and said, 'I'm too old for this, Jimmy,' and jumped off the cliff."

"Jimmy? She said *Jimmy?*"

"Something like that. She wasn't very coherent. Why?"

"Nothing. No reason. If that waiter doesn't show up in a minute, I swear to God I'm going to kill him."

Janice didn't respond to either the blasphemy or the threat. Just kept those gray eyes boring in at me. "Jeff, you're not . . . you really are okay, aren't you?"

"If you mean am I suicidal, no," I snarled. "I'm just tired. Come on, Janice, it was just a dream. After all Terri's been through in the last few months, I'd be amazed if she didn't have a nightmare or two."

"Yes, but she only had this one after she visited you the other day. And now that *I've* seen you—oh, hi, Justin."

I looked up to find Warrick standing at my shoulder, smiling pleasantly. "My client went to the ladies' room," he said, "so I thought I'd just jump over and say hello. Janice, Jeff didn't tell me he'd be having lunch with you today. It's nice to see you again."

As they chatted I said nothing, just smiled noncommittally and let my gaze wander. Behind Janice stood a terra-cotta planter three feet high, full of black earth and great tufts of what looked like grass, except they grew taller than a man. Suddenly I noticed that the dirt was moving, as if something was trying to push to the surface from beneath. A bug of some kind? A worm? Claude Perrine would have a heart attack.

"—Jeff?" Warrick said.

I looked up. "Pardon?"

"I said, would you stop by my table and say hello to Ms. Underwood before you leave?"

"I'd be delighted." I watched him return to his table. It wasn't far away, and offered him a clear view of me between potted plants. Terrific. I turned back to Janice, and found a young man with a ponytail standing beside the table, pencil poised. "Good afternoon. My name's Jeremy; I'll be your waiter today. Our specials are—"

"I'm not hungry, thank you," Janice said.

"Jeremy, I'll have the Caesar salad with blackened chicken," I said. "Hold the bugs."

"Pardon?"

"Never mind. Another martini, too, please, Jeremy."

The waiter nodded uncertainly and left.

Janice was staring hard at me again. "Jeff, are you sure you're all right?"

"How many times are you going to ask me that?"

She didn't back down. "It's just that I know you. You weren't this stressed-out when you were waiting to be offered a partnership at the firm."

"I was younger then. And I had a supportive wife at home."

At last, a flash of genuine pain in her eyes. "That's not fair."

"Janice, you once put another man's underwear in my dresser. Please don't use words you don't understand, like 'fair.' "

She averted her face, but I didn't get as much satisfaction from her shame as I'd expected to.

Behind her, the dirt in the planter stirred again. Not in just one place, but several, as if a family of worms was boring its way up. I didn't really want to see them, but I kept staring.

"Terri tried to call you last night," Janice said softly.

"Huh?"

"After her dream, she tried to call you. She was just sure you were dead. I barely kept her from calling the police when you didn't answer."

"I was home," I said. "I guess I turned the phone down too far." I wasn't about to admit I'd knocked myself out with Janice's left-over sleeping pills. Despite myself, I looked back at the planter. Several pale knobs were pushing slowly from the earth. Big, fat grubs. My stomach recoiled. Christ, I was never coming here again. "I'll call Terri tonight," I said. "Set her mind at ease. Okay?"

"That would be good."

Her voice seemed far away. The grubs, their shiny heads sprinkled with crumbs of mulch, had burst well into sight now—three, four, five of them in a circle. Twitching, groping for the light. Except they weren't grubs. Grubs don't have fingernails.

I shot to my feet and stumbled back, almost tripping over my chair. Everybody stared at me. Janice said, "Jeff? Jeff?"

A small, pale hand rose from the dirt in the planter, fingers twitching as if to throw off the mulch. Around the wrist was fastened a kid's cheap Timex watch with a black leather band. *Takes a lickin' and keeps on tickin'.* I recognized it. I recognized it.

I stepped back again. Janice stared at me, unaware of the hand groping around behind her. I bumped into someone, spun. It was Fred McMillan with his gaunt cheeks and flapping pajamas. He held a serving dish on which rested Abe Perry's head, eyes fixed impassively on mine.

"Go home," Fred said sternly. *"Now. We'll do whatever it takes to make you go home."*

I lunged in the other direction, crashed into the table. Janice yelped. A vase of flowers fell over with a splashing bang. Faces snapped toward us from all directions.

In front of me, Jeremy the waiter held my Caesar salad in his hands and stared in embarrassed disbelief.

"I'm okay," I said. "I'm okay. I'm okay."

From the corner of my eye, I saw Mr. Warrick rise to his feet.

"Jeff?" Janice touched my shoulder. "Are you all right?"

I whirled toward her and roared, *"Stop treating me like a child!"*
And then everything went gray as I fell . . .

. . . through crackling masses of leaves, even as he realized that
the monstrous face above him was only Timmy's. Timmy playing
baboon, pretending to attack. Now, receding, that face looked not
horrible but horrified. Jeff thrashed his arms out for any branch
that might support him, felt them whipping past, breaking, bending. He fell faster, faster—started to scream—

And a stout limb whacked up squarely between his legs.

The world exploded into red-black clouds, but he had the presence of mind to throw his arms out in a hugging gesture, clutching
the trunk of the tree. The branch between his legs creaked alarm-
ingly, but did not break. Agony radiated like spears of lightning
from his groin. He heard a moan—that wasn't him, was it? How
could he moan when he couldn't even breathe?

Gradually, his vision cleared. Through dancing motes of light he
saw Timmy scrambling toward him in a frenzy of branches.
Timmy's face was as white as if he had cleaned chalk erasers on it.

The piercing pain between Jeff's legs dwindled to a pulpy, burning ache. Cheek resting against the tree trunk, he watched Timmy
find a perch nearby.

"Are you okay?" Timmy gasped.

Jeff tried to speak, couldn't.

"Are you okay? Man, are you *okay?*"

"Ungh."

Timmy slumped in relief. "Man, I thought you were gone."

"Jerrrrrrk," Jeff managed. He thought he might be drooling, but
didn't care. At the moment, he wasn't sure he even wanted to live.

"I didn't mean to scare you like that," Timmy said. "I thought
you knew I was there."

"I'll . . . bet."

Suddenly Timmy began to giggle, spastically, hiding his mouth
behind his shoulder. "You should have seen your face. You should
have seen your face, man."

"Ha, ha." Jeff felt well enough now to consider murdering
Timmy when they got back to the ground. But his relief at being
alive was stronger than his anger. He just hugged the tree and
rested.

"Let's call this a draw," Timmy said, serious again. "I mean, you got almost as high as I did."

"I would have gotten even higher if you hadn't jumped out at me," Jeff wheezed.

"Yeah, well . . . let's just call it a draw."

Jeff nodded. The pain was tolerable now. He spotted something over Timmy's shoulder, and pointed with his chin. "Look."

Timmy twisted around, and stiffened at the view of Middlefield. "Wow. *Wow.* I'll bet you can see a hundred miles!" His expression grew dreamy. "If I could be any animal in the world, I'd be a hawk. Then I could just jump out of this tree and fly over town, look down at everybody." This was pure Timmy Kegler, Jeff thought. After they watched *Sea Hunt* on TV, he wanted to be a shark. After *Wild Kingdom,* it was a black panther or a wolverine.

Jamming his right foot against the base of a branch, Timmy gripped the slender trunk of the tree with one hand and leaned out, swinging his upper body over the green void. He looked like he was really thinking about flying. "What kind of animal would you like to be?" he asked.

"Quit bending the tree," Jeff said nervously. "I don't know. I'm never going to be an animal, so why worry about it?"

"Come on."

"Well . . ." He glanced toward the football field. "A wolf, I guess."

"Yeah, that would be cool. You'd be a wolf and I'd be a hawk, and we'd go to the Rockies and live in the woods. We'd never have to go to school again, or go back home."

Jeff blinked, surprised. He couldn't imagine not wanting to *ever* go home. Sure, he'd run away once or twice, but never long enough that his parents even noticed. Maybe Timmy felt differently because his mom had left a long time ago—either died or walked out, depending on who was doing the gossiping. Timmy never talked about her at all.

"How come you hate school so much, anyway?" Jeff asked. "You always get good grades—"

"—except in math," they finished in unison. Timmy smiled briefly. "Good grades are easy to get. That's no problem. It's just . . . you know, there are so many jerks at school."

"I kind of like seeing the people I never saw all summer," Jeff said. He was thinking of Gail, but didn't say so.

"Not me. I'd rather just do this all the time. Go places, have adventures."

That was pretty funny, Jeff thought. Timmy never really went anywhere. His dad didn't take him on vacations; Timmy hadn't even gone to church camp in Ohio that one summer Mike and Jeff had gone.

Across the cornfield, sunlight brightened and dimmed with the passing of the clouds, making the earth seem to rise and fall like the surface of the ocean. Jeff thought Middlefield looked almost as pretty from here as one of his mother's paint-by-the-numbers pictures. "Mom took me to get my new school stuff yesterday," he said. "I got a notebook with a Gemini 3 capsule on the cover."

"A Gemini notebook?" A spike of interest from Timmy. Then it flattened. "I'll bet it was more expensive than the plain ones, though, right?"

"A little." Now Jeff was sorry he'd brought it up; he knew the Keglers were pretty poor. Mr. Kegler had been out of work since the gravel pit outside town closed. "But you can always draw something on yours," he went on quickly. "Your notebooks always have the coolest drawings."

Timmy shrugged, but Jeff could tell he was pleased. "I might be an artist someday, if I don't go to the Rockies and become a mountain man." To Jeff's relief Timmy pulled himself back toward the tree, slid down and straddled a branch. His naked chest and legs were scraped fluorescent pink; Big Tree tattoos. "This is the year teachers start asking us about what we want to be when we grow up, you know."

"I'm going to be an astronaut," Jeff said, although that was common knowledge. "I want to be the first man on Mars."

"If I don't get there first."

Jeff smirked. "You'll have to get better at math if you want to be an astronaut."

"I'm not going to be an *astronaut*. You don't have to be an *astronaut* to go to another planet. It all has to do with dimensions. Finding a door between dimensions and just going through."

"You saw that on *The Outer Limits*," Jeff said. So had he, actually. *The Outer Limits* used to be his favorite show, even though it had only added meat to his nightmares. "That's just made-up stuff. It's not *real*."

Timmy's eyebrows arched. "How do you know?"

"It's not scientific."

"Scientists don't know everything."

"No, but they know *that.*"

Timmy tilted his head back and stared up at the glints of sky flashing through the leaves, his eyes brimming with blue and green light. "Oh, yeah?" he said.

CHAPTER NINE

HAPPY LANDINGS

"Where you headed?" the young soldier in the next seat asked.

I started. *Nod*, I almost said. Instead I glanced at him without warmth, no invitation to chat. He wore a khaki uniform. His hair was almost shaved on the sides and back, marginally longer on top —the style that gave Marines the nickname "jarheads." His smile was a bit shaky, his hands clamped to the armrests of his seat. A Marine who was afraid to fly? He kept staring at me hopefully.

"I'm going to Indiana," I finally said. I didn't add that my route was by way of Phoenix, El Paso and Atlanta. That's what happens when you make reservations at the last minute.

He nodded as if my destination had great significance to him. "I'm from Michigan myself."

"Nice state." I turned deliberately away. Maybe it would be better to talk to him, to anybody, than to brood about my problems— or fall asleep again. But I didn't feel up to idle chatter.

What about Nod?

Nod. The land of Nod. The name resonated . . . but I didn't want to think about that, either. I wanted to keep my mind firmly on the reason I was going back to Middlefield.

It had nothing to do with ghosts, of course; at least not "real" ghosts, the spirits of the dearly departed. I hadn't believed in ghosts of that sort since Middlefield, or for that matter, in spirits of any kind—including the immortal soul—since my father had his stroke.

Nor did this trip have anything to do with Terri's odd nightmare about me. When people feel insecure, as Terri was at this moment, they're bound to have their misgivings cast back at them in the

71

mythic shape of dreams. Standing on a cliff, the fear of falling . . . these are universal symbols of anxiety.

That was why I was going back to Middlefield. Anxiety. When a man faints in a restaurant and awakens just in time to wave off a clutch of paramedics, he has to admit he's not coping with his own stress. And when the symbols of that stress come from a time much earlier in his life, then he's forced to acknowledge the solution might lie back then, too. I was returning to the source in the best way I knew. Despite Warrick's claims, I had little faith in therapy.

Warrick himself had driven me to the airport. "Don't you want to stop by your house and pack?" he'd asked on the way. Eyeing me.

"No time. My flight leaves in half an hour." A lie. But I hadn't wanted to go back to Capistrano even for a second, not even in broad daylight, not even with Warrick at my side. Daylight and companionship hadn't stopped me from hallucinating at Perrine's, had they?

I wondered if I'd have a job left when I returned. I'd told Warrick this trip would help me get back on my feet, emotionally; still, on the way to LAX his manner had been that of a father delivering his last favor to a disappointing son.

Below the plane, the cracked brown mountains around Palm Springs eased past, and the plane bucked as it surfed over the great waves of air they pushed up. I heard a gasp, and turned toward the Marine again. His hands, all cords and veins, clutched the armrests as if they were barbells and the world powerlifting championship was on the line.

I had to say something. "Nervous?"

He glanced at me sidelong and smiled ruefully. "Would you believe I'm a jet pilot? I know, I know, but it's not the flying that bothers me. It's being on an airliner with someone else at the stick. It's knowing I'm not in *control*. Can you follow that?"

"Yes," I said, turning back to the window. "I can follow that."

"Oh, yeah?" Timmy said. "What about the land of Nod?"

A long, steady gust of wind swept through the Big Tree, making the entire world rock first one way, then the other. A snatch of an old nursery rhyme rolled through Jeff's mind:

Wynken, Blynken, and Nod one night
sailed off in a wooden shoe—

"The land of Nod?" he said. "That's a fairy tale parents tell their kids—Dreamland or something."

"Not exactly," Timmy said. "It's the land where dreams come true. That's not the same thing."

Jeff didn't see the difference, but decided not to say so.

"And it's not a fairy tale," Timmy went on. "It's even in the Bible."

"Huh?"

"I didn't know that, either, until last Sunday. Remember the sermon?"

Jeff thought back. He seldom paid attention during church. He believed in God and Jesus—who didn't?—but church itself was boring. Timmy himself had once admitted that during sermons, he imagined the sanctuary was full of water and he was scuba diving above the congregation.

"What about it?" Jeff asked.

"Remember how the minister was talking about being your brother's keeper?"

"So?"

"So he read about Cain and Abel in the Bible. Cain killed Abel, remember?"

Jeff did, sort of. He'd been surprised that God had been so mean to Cain, rejecting his sacrifice. That didn't seem very Godlike. Maybe He'd just liked Abel better because Abel was younger. A lot of parents were like that. Jeff was glad he didn't have a brother.

"Afterward," Timmy went on, "God sent Cain someplace. Remember where?"

"No."

Timmy leaned forward, making the branch bow precariously. "The land of Nod."

"The land of . . . yeah, but come on, that's not the same place you're thinking about."

"Why not? Everything in the Bible is true, right?"

"Yeah, but—"

"The thing is," Timmy said urgently, "the thing is, Nod isn't a real country, like France or England."

Jeff had had a lot of weird conversations with Timmy, but this one was really losing him.

Timmy stared straight ahead. "See, nobody's ever found the land of Nod. So it can't be a real country, see? It's gotta be another dimension, like the Twilight Zone. *That's* why dreams come true there. God just sent Cain there to get him away from his family, that's all. It wasn't really punishment."

Jeff frowned. "That sounds like Purgatory. Abe says that's where souls go if they're only a little bit bad."

"That's Catholic," Timmy said dismissively. "Only Catholics believe that. I'm talking about a *real* place."

The boys were silent for a moment. Leaves rustled around them.

"Okay, if there's a *real* land of Nod, how come nobody's been there since Cain?" Jeff asked.

"Maybe they have. Other dimensions are all around us, we just don't see them. But there are doors. Remember the Roanoke Colony?"

"Sure. All the settlers disappeared."

"Without a trace."

"You think they went to the land of Nod?"

"Yeah. The Indians helped them. Remember, there was a word carved on a tree or something? A word nobody understood?"

"Sort of . . ."

"CROATOAN," Timmy said smugly. "That was the word. That's Indian. See, the settlers had the Indians to help them go to the land of Nod."

"Or they all just got scalped," Jeff said, casting about in his mind for a way to change the subject. To sports, maybe. Football, maybe.

"No way," Timmy said. "They disappeared *completely*. Wouldn't you want to do that? Get away from here if you could? Tonight, maybe."

Jeff shrugged. "Where to?"

"Anyplace you can dream of." Timmy smiled, eyes bright. "We *can* go to the land of Nod. *I* almost made it last night."

The words were delivered with such conviction that for a moment Jeff absolutely believed them. Then he remembered the Venus-transporter fiasco. "Get serious. You didn't really go to another dimension."

"I did too!" Timmy's shout sent unseen birds fluttering. "After I went to bed last night, I couldn't sleep. I was lying there in the dark, you know, half-awake. Then I heard voices. A long way off, like that time we heard the choir practicing in the church, you know? But not singing, *chanting*. And guess what they were chanting?"

"I don't know, Timmy."

Timmy's voice became oddly deep, sonorous: "Crooooo-aaaaaahhhhh-tohhhhh-aaaaahhhhhnnnnnnnn."

Jeff realized his heart was beating faster. He could almost hear Mom's voice: *Timmy's got you all worked up again, hasn't he?*

"It was coming from the Big Tree," Timmy said. "The voices were coming from here."

"How would you know? You can't even *see* the Big Tree from your house."

"Sure you can. Look." Timmy pointed at Middlefield, but Jeff couldn't pick out Timmy's neighborhood, far less a particular house. "I knew this was where the voices were coming from," Timmy said. "So I followed them here."

Jeff blinked. "You walked all the way out here last night?"

"Not walked. I sort of just . . . *came*. I thought about being here, and here I was. I mean, on the ground. Under the tree. It was pitch-dark. So I walked out . . ." His eyes fixed on Jeff's face. "And I wasn't in Middlefield anymore."

"Where were you?" Jeff asked, trying to sound scornful, and almost succeeding. "Oz?"

"The land of Nod."

"How do you know *that?*"

"Because that's where I wanted to *be*, Jeff," Timmy said. "The Big Tree is one of those dimensional doors, see? That's why the Indians used it, to call people from the other side and get what they wanted."

"That's bull. You don't know that."

"Yes I do. The Nodkin told me."

"What?"

"The Nodkin. The people on the other side. They were waiting for me when I came out from under the tree. We see them all the time, you know, except to us they're just shadows. I even used to think they were scary, but they're not. They're like the Big Tree, you just have to understand them. See, last night *I* was the shadow and *they* were real. Because I hadn't gotten all the way over, just my mind."

Suddenly Jeff was struck by a horrifying thought: What if Timmy talked like this at school? Blabbed about crossing between dimensions and visiting other worlds? Having shadow people calling his name out of an old tree? The kids would laugh at him. They'd say to Jeff, "He's *still your friend?*"

"Come on, Timmy," Jeff said. "Hey. You just dreamt that."

Timmy shook his head. "Let me finish. The Nodkin couldn't really see or hear me, because like I said, I was just a shadow to them. But they knew I was close. Jeff, they want me to come all the way over to their side!"

"It still sounds like a dream to me," Jeff said.

"*No.* Listen—I heard Dad calling, and the next thing I knew I was in front of my own house. I saw Dad standing in the driveway shouting for me to come and clean up a broken bottle. He couldn't see me, Jeff. Then I woke up."

Jeff made an annoyed buzzing noise through his lips. "So it *was* a dream."

"No." Timmy leaned forward, eyes glittering. "*No.* Because Dad *really was in the front yard, yelling at me to come out and clean up a broken bottle.*"

Jeff gave the tree trunk a violent shake, making leaves leap back and forth. "Look, man. This is just a tree, wood and leaves and bark. It can't make you go to another dimension."

The fire in Timmy's eyes shuttered down. "You really believe that?"

Jeff hesitated, suddenly uncomfortable as the focal point of that dark, narrow stare. "Yes."

"What if I prove it then, Jeff? What if I come and get you tonight? Will you go with me?"

Jeff couldn't help it, he made a hacking sound that was only partially a laugh. "Sure, Timmy. I'll be waiting."

Timmy looked at him a moment longer, then turned stiffly away. "Maybe Mike will go, then. 'Course, he couldn't even make it to the top of the Big Tree." He spun back. "Come on, Jeff. All three of us can go. You, me and Mike."

"Okay, then, what about Abe and Fred?"

It was a long time before Timmy replied. "Abe's okay, but he's . . . you know . . . kind of a sissy. And Fred mostly just follows along with whatever the rest of us are doing. No, it would be best if you, me and Mike went. Wynken, Blynken and Nod, traveling the universe. Come on, it'll be great."

Jeff wanted to make Timmy really think about what he was saying. "What if we couldn't get back again?" he asked.

Timmy blinked. "Why would we want to?"

"Because what?"

I straightened so suddenly my neck twanged like a harp string. The Marine was long gone. Beside me sat an elderly woman with a navy blue suit and a face as hard as a plank of maple. In the nest of her lap perched a paperback with a cover featuring grinning, capering skeletons. She had started the book when we boarded the plane in Atlanta. Now her finger marked a point near the middle.

I cleared my throat. "Pardon?"

"You said 'Because.' Kind of loud."

"Oh." I rubbed the back of my neck. "I was dreaming."

Small, meaningless smile. "Well, we're on our way down now. Maybe you can stay awake. You snore, too."

I wasn't sure if she was joking or just being rude, so I pretended I hadn't heard her. She returned to her book. *Nice old lady.* I looked out the window.

Far below spread a blue-gray carpet of clouds snagged here and there into tufts dyed silver by morning light. I didn't know when they had appeared.

The plane tilted, began to descend.

You don't think it's possible to travel between dimensions?

I rubbed my neck again.

The land of Nod. At last I'd remembered, and it was no big deal. Nod had simply been Timmy Kegler's version of Utopia—an amalgam of escapist fantasy, science fiction, half-baked Bible verses. Pure imagination. Timmy hadn't been satisfied with creating an imaginary friend, the way many children do. He'd had to fabricate a whole *dimension,* and populate it with people whose greatest wish was to have him visit them. Poor Timmy.

My ears popped and squealed as the clouds rose. I watched their ascent with wary excitement. As soon as we passed through them, I would see the land of my youth for the first time in a quarter of a century. A trip through time as well as space. *Wynken, Blynken and Nod, traveling the universe.*

The plane's shadow appeared, racing unevenly over the clouds. It grew steadily larger.

Home. The word blossomed in my mind again. It was, of course, inaccurate. I'd lived in Southern California for more than half my life. Southern California was *home.*

But I couldn't deny the fact that my heart never pounded this way when I flew into LAX.

The plane's wingtip skewered its own shadow. Tendrils of cloud gnawed their way up to my window until the view vanished in a sea of uniform gray.

The fog lightened, shredded, whipped away. Below sprawled a flat grid of squares, green on green on green in all directions. It was the same vista I'd been amazed by from the top of the Big Tree twenty-five years ago—only now I really *could* see a hundred miles, or close to it.

I relaxed again, forehead cool against the plastic window.

I'd already decided exactly how I was going to handle this visit: fast and hard, a nostalgic commando raid. Rent a car, drive to Middlefield, check out whatever old haunts remained. See if any of my school chums were still around. In other words, prove to my stubborn subconscious that the simpler, kinder days of my youth no longer existed. Then I'd leave again and get on with my real life. Shouldn't take more than a day or two.

Below, roads rose into view, a systematic grid of straight lines like the web of an anal-retentive spider. I remembered driving along those roads at night in my first car, a jacked-up 1960 Rambler. Pedal to the floor, suspension swaying like the hips of a belly dancer. Ditches and fences hurtling past, rabbits leaping panic-eyed into the surrounding fields. Gail sitting on the bench seat beside me, simultaneously laughing with glee and squealing in terror, her fingers clutching my thigh.

A half-hour later, I walked out of the jetway. A nearby newsstand was selling bright red Indiana University T-shirts and checkerboard Indianapolis 500 memorabilia.

Home. Indeed.

A slight tremor of uneasiness rolled through me. It had happened. Despite all my intentions, my rationalizations, I was here. Veering into a restroom, I splashed cold water on my face and winced at my reflection in the mirror. Wrinkled, baggy face. Wrinkled, baggy suit—had I lost weight in the past twenty-four hours? I resembled something the plane had dragged all the way from Atlanta.

At the Avis counter I arranged for a car, then just stood there with the keys in my hand. It wasn't too late. I could still turn around, get onto another plane, go someplace else. Anyplace else.

I got myself under control. I was only here to visit Middlefield for a day or two, that was all. To find out what, if anything, I'd left behind.

The automatic doors opened and I stepped out into a wall of thick, humid air.

CHAPTER TEN

SIGNS OF ARRIVAL

Back when I was in high school, courting couples often drove out to Indianapolis International Airport—then called Weir Cook—to park at the end of the main runway, drink beer and neck while planes screamed overhead and turned the car into a giant vibrator. I'd parked out there a few times myself. After Gail and I broke up.

After you ran her off, you mean.

The maze of roads I drove along now led to nothing familiar. There were no handy parking areas next to the runway, no empty fields anywhere. Just office buildings, long-term parking lots, industrial complexes. How in the world were modern teenaged girls getting pregnant, anyway?

Cars zoomed around me as I crept around a tangle of ramps, searching for familiar landmarks. Nothing. For some perverse reason, I had refused to buy a road map—surely I could find my way to Middlefield by memory.

I was beginning to really doubt it when I saw a sign bearing a familiar name: Girls School Road. Smiling, I pulled onto it and headed north.

There was no getting lost now. I crossed Highways 40 and 36, both major roads lined with shops and gas stations. Along the way I pulled into a discount department store and bought a couple of pairs of slacks, some pullover shirts and a pair of comfortable rubber-soled shoes. Disposable razor, shaving cream, toothpaste, toothbrush. A cheap bag to carry it all in. Next I stopped at a gas station and changed clothes in the restroom. Shaved and brushed my teeth. Better.

After driving along Girls School Road for another mile or so, I spotted a familiar intersection and turned west onto a narrow, two-lane road. Within minutes the surrounding housing developments segued into fields of corn and soybeans bordered with dense stands of trees. The surface of the road became a scabby mosaic of old and new pavement over which the car jolted and bumped like a boat on a choppy sea. It was hard to believe I used to hurtle down this road at seventy or eighty miles an hour. Rolling down the window, I drank in a rich soup of moist air, pollen, airborne dust, and the golden aroma of drying weeds. Overhead, the clouds were splitting apart like pack ice, bright blue sky splashing in the seams.

I was alone on the road. Straight-ahead pavement, no turns for miles. I kept on.

Rolling over, Jeff looked at his bedside clock. Groaned. Only 4:00 A.M. Was this night ever going to end? Despite his exhaustion after the day's long hike and tree-climb, he couldn't seem to stay asleep for more than fifteen minutes at a stretch. Pain was a big part of the problem, of course. The muscles in his legs quivered and twitched constantly, and the skin on his forearms and chest felt scalded. He had ground his body against the entire length of the Big Tree on his way back down.

But the biggest problem was that he couldn't stop thinking about tomorrow. Today, now. Eighth grade. Seeing school friends again. Gail.

But this train of thought pulled a swaying caboose: football practice. He still hadn't told Timmy about his plans. By the time the gang had finally gotten out of the cornfield, everybody had been too tired and hungry to stand around and chat. They'd just waved goodbye and split up.

Almost. At the last moment, Timmy had slipped close to Jeff and murmured, "See you tonight."

"Huh?"

"Tonight, remember? We're going to check out the land of Nod. Remember?"

"Oh. Yeah. Okay." All Jeff wanted to do was stumble into the house and drink a gallon of ice water.

"Be ready for the trip of your life," Timmy said.

Jeff mentioned the idea at the supper table that night.

"The land of Nod?" Mom had said. "You mean like Wynken, Blynken and Nod?"

"I was thinking of the place they talk about in the Bible. You know, with Cain and Abel. I was wondering where it's supposed to be."

Dad swallowed a bite of roast beef. "I'm not sure there ever was a *real* land of Nod, Jeff. The Bible's full of things like that —*allegories*, they're called."

"But I thought everything in the Bible was true."

"Well, some of the stories are just there to teach us lessons."

"Like the Tower of Babel," Mom said.

"That's right," Dad said. "I doubt there was ever really such a thing, but the story teaches us not to get too proud. See?"

"Mmm."

Now, Jeff rolled onto his back and looked around the semidarkness of his room. The open window allowed in a stripe of moonlight that folded and cut like a silver river through piles of clothes, books and half-built models. On either side of the river lay vague shadows and pale angles of reflected light. The only sounds were the sleepy percussion of insects and the hiss of the breeze in the corn.

No Timmy in sight, naturally.

Jeff looked out the window. There stood the Big Tree, the moon dissolving in its foliage like a giant Fizzie lozenge. In an hour or so, the sky would start to grow lighter in the east. Morning of a new day, everything fresh—

Jeffffffff . . .

His head snapped up. He listened. Crickets. Frogs shrilling in the gullies behind Fred's house. Cornstalks rustling. Normal night sounds.

Jeffffffff . . .

Last year, Mike had gotten a cheap transistor radio for his birthday. The gang liked to huddle around it as if it were a small fire in the wilderness. During the day it picked up two or three Indianapolis broadcasts, and the country music station in Danville, and that was it. But at night it was as if the little box reached to infinity, catching fragments of broadcasts from Chicago, Cincinnati, other distant places. The boys would gather close, teasing the knob, bypassing local stations, listening for the faintest murmur from the speaker. Catch a word here, a laugh there. Voices, music, strange sounds. Like transmissions from the stars. Like this.

Jeffffffffffffff . . .

The curtains stirred. The wind was brushing through the corn, through the pair of little trees Mom had planted in the backyard, through—

Jeffffffffffffff . . .

He stared out at the Big Tree, black and pewter against the moonlit sky. Swaying slightly in the breeze, or seeming to sway.

Jeffffffffffffffffff . . . *itssssss meeeeeeee* . . . Louder now. The radio tuning in.

"Timmy?" Jeff whispered. Some anger in it. To combat the fear in it. Then he realized: Timmy must be crouching below the window between the hedge and the house. Playing one of his stupid games.

Let'ssssssssssssss gooooooooo . . .

Jeff hurled back the covers. "I'm going to beat your brains in, Kegler," he stage-whispered, hoping Mom and Dad wouldn't hear. "You'd better be gone when I get to that window."

But he was already there. The wooden floor felt cool under his bare feet, as if the moonlight had coated it with frost. In contrast, through the window rolled a summery cachet of mown grass and dew. Morning birds were tuning up their voices, joining the chorus of crickets and frogs. Across the field, the moon hung directly behind the Big Tree.

The backyard was slashed with ebony shadows. Swingset, tee-ter-totter, the two small trees. Below the window grew an emaciated hedge. "It would get bigger if you boys would stop hiding in it for five minutes," Mom often sighed. No one was crouching there now.

Rrrrriiiiight herrrrrrrrre, Jeffffffff . . .

But Jeff saw no one. Then, Timmy, a thin figure standing at the back fence. No, directly in front of him, close enough to touch. No, distant, huge, towering against the sky, blotting out the moon.

No . . . not there at all. Jeff realized the head he'd seen was actually just the Big Tree, the moon behind it a flash of eyes. Below that, the merged shapes of the saplings pretended to be a torso. Limbs for arms, shadows for legs. Not Timmy at all. Just imagination.

Hurrrrrrrrrrrrrryyyyyyyyy . . .

Timmy's voice seemed to come from the Big Tree, though, blowing on the wind. And the tree *did* look like a head, a face. Moon eyes imploring. Mouth moving. Breath of wind:

. . . *rrrrrrrrrrrrrryyyyyy, Jeffffffffff* . . .

Jeff stared hard at the face. Stared until it shimmered, blurred, became a tree again. When he looked away slightly, it turned back into a face. Like the constellation Pleiades, playing hide-and-seek in the night sky. Something to do with the blind spot in the retina. Dad had told him about that.

He glared directly at the tree again. After a moment, Timmy's face vanished. Jeff kept staring, staring. *Wood and leaves and bark*, he thought. The whisper began to fade, to blow away . . .

. . . *ffffffffffffffffffff* . . .

Wood and leaves and bark.

. . . and was gone.

I awoke just in time to see a flat metal sign and a mass of trees rushing at me in a tidal wave of green.

Bellowing, I stood on the brake. Rubber squalled. The steering wheel twisted like a weasel. Traction broke. One front tire dropped off the pavement into loose gravel. The rear tire followed. Weeds slapped bodywork. Gravel chattered inside wheel wells. The car halted in a reek of burnt Goodyears and dust. Metal sign stanchions rose inches away from the front bumper.

"Shit!" I gasped, leaning my forehead against the wheel. Lucky nobody had been tailgating me.

After a moment I sat back again. The sign reflected in the hood of the car, upside down, but I had no trouble reading it:

WELCOME TO MIDDLEFIELD
A GREAT PLACE TO PLANT YOUR ROOTS!

ORGANIZED SPORTS

CHAPTER ELEVEN

SENIORS

The sign was pitted with the acne of innumerable .22 bullet and BB strikes. From its bottom edge dangled a beard of emblems representing churches and service organizations: Lions Club, Kiwanis, VFW Post 1129; Southern Baptist Church, United Methodist Church, Lutheran Church. The whole display rose from a mass of weeds. It looked exactly the way it had the last time I'd seen it, receding in the back window of the family station wagon.

A car cruised past on the road, faces staring at me curiously. I raised a hand; I'm okay. The car accelerated away.

My nerves still jangled like charms on a bracelet, but I felt more in control again. Putting the car into reverse, I backed up a few feet, then pulled onto the road and drove past the sign, under an arch of branches and leaves.

Something moved in my rearview mirror. I looked at it just as a blood-spattered man staggered into the road behind me and collapsed with the boneless impact of the unconscious or dead. Behind him, two vehicles lay tangled together in the ditch, all eight wheels spinning. Steam rising in clouds. Shattered windows stained scarlet. Torn metal. Red, twisted shapes in the grass.

Slamming on the brakes, I spun around in my seat.

There was no wreckage behind me, no body. I saw a whirl of shadows on pavement. A thick growth of blackberry bushes clutching the base of the tree. A couple of red and white Kentucky Fried Chicken buckets someone had pitched into the ditch.

"Holy shit," I muttered, facing forward again. I was *tired*. Shaking all over.

A car pulled up behind me, honking. I drove on.

Within a hundred yards, the aftereffects of fright were replaced by the realization that the venerable town sign veiled considerable change. I saw a McDonald's standing at the mouth of a brand-new strip mall. A housing development of large, undistinguished homes disconcertingly similar to those back in Orange County. The old train station, which had been abandoned back in my day —rich fodder for Timmy Kegler ghost stories—had been converted into a gardening store called the Whistle Stop. The street next to it, Railroad, was the one Timmy had lived on—the "bad" part of town. But I didn't turn there. Not yet.

I cruised past Middlefield Community Park, a huge grassy field surrounded on three sides by woods. No kids there at this hour on a school day.

Across the street was the entrance to Shady Acres Cemetery, permanent residence of Fred McMillan, war hero. The grounds were maybe two hundred yards long, but their depth could have been infinite, vanishing into the shadows of ancient walnut trees. Headstones clustered back there like pale toadstools of all shapes and sizes. It occurred to me that in sunny Southern California most cemeteries are hidden from the view of major streets this way.

Shady Acres was a place I'd have to visit before I left town, I supposed. Stand over Fred's grave and think about the past. Part of my penance.

Penance? Where had *that* come from? Fred wasn't dead because I'd convinced him to try out for the football team, for God's sake. He was dead because he'd been drafted by the Army and shipped to Southeast Asia, where he'd discovered that real warfare wasn't much like the Timmy Kegler variety.

Make it right, Jeff. Make it right. That's what friends do . . .

I realized I was going forty-five miles per hour, and quickly eased off the gas. If Middlefield's present-day police officers were anything like the old ones had been, they'd take their thirty-mile-per-hour speed limit seriously.

Like most Midwestern towns, Middlefield had grown outward from the intersection of two highways. As I approached the center, I observed evolution in reverse. Here were 1950s one-story homes of stone, brick or wood. Then came houses of pre-World War II vintage, mostly two-story wooden structures with pillared front porches and steep roofs. And finally, downtown Middlefield itself:

tall red brick buildings centered around the intersection of Main Street and the street I was on, called York Avenue within the town limits.

The light was red and I stopped, staring around. The old buildings looked pretty sad—crumbling mortar, missing bricks, cracked window frames. The names over most of the shop windows had changed. With particular regret I noted that Topp's Theater, where I'd watched such classic films as *The Three Stooges on Mars*, had become Bob's Lawn Mower Repair. Finney's Pharmacy was now Rexall Drugs. I tried, and failed, to peer past the displays in the front window to see if the soda fountain was still there. Not likely, with a McDonald's just down the street.

The light changed. I turned left onto Main Street. The shop at the end of the block used to be a five-and-ten-cent store called Vanover's. That was where we boys had bought our squirt guns and cap pistols, soap bubble fluid and rocket ships powered by water and compressed air. It was at Vanover's that I'd ogled the MP-80 submachine gun that eventually became the crown jewel of my twelfth birthday booty. Now the store's space had been divided into three small shops, ranging from MAUREEN'S SECOND-HAND CHILDREN'S ATTIRE to KOLLEKTABLE KOMIKS AND KARDS.

I drove on, turned right on Landrus Avenue, then left on School Street. When I saw the junior high building, I shook my head sadly. The structure I recalled had been an ancient gargoyle of red brick, drafty and stern, with concrete lions guarding the steps. Now, in its place stood a crate of stone and glass that would have looked right at home in an industrial park. The adjacent gymnasium, once also red brick and taller than it was long, had been replaced with a cantilevered composite box.

I drove around the corner onto Farr Way, a narrow residential street that formed the eastern boundary of the campus. In my youth, the area behind the school buildings had been a tree-shaded lake of pea gravel where impromptu games of catch and tag-the-girls had taken place at lunch. The gravel had vanished, and the shade trees. In their place was a grassy field outfitted with soccer goals and a softball diamond. Very pretty. Very tidy. Ideal for—

Organized sports.

The sneering voice in my head was so clear, I almost turned to see if Timmy was sitting in the back seat. Instead, I pulled to the curb and stopped.

Across the street I saw something that hadn't changed: a narrow dirt alley spilling out from between backyards. It looked almost like a tunnel, tree branches twisting heavily above it, vine-choked fences on either side. A pair of metal posts stood at its mouth to keep cars out. That alley, a footpath really, had been the shortest route between my neighborhood and the playground, not to mention downtown Middlefield. But it had not been a shortcut to take lightly. Because to get to it from the far side, a kid had first to cross the entire high school campus. Big Kid's domain.

Jeff Dittimore, nine years old, had had his own library card for three whole years, and had never once returned a book late. But now, with the library due to close any minute, he remembered that his copy of *The Wonderful Flight to the Mushroom Planet* was due. He'd forgotten because this had been the first really warm Saturday of spring and he'd been busy playing Dinosaurs in the backyard with the gang.

The threat of the four-cent-a-day fine wasn't what dismayed him; it was the idea of disappointing the librarian, Mrs. White. This was the fifth time he'd read *The Wonderful Flight to the Mushroom Planet*, which was about a pair of boys who built a make-believe rocket ship that was turned into a *real* rocket by a scientist who needed the boys to save the Mushroom Planet. The day after Jeff read the book for the first time, he and the gang had built a spaceship out of cardboard cartons in one of the gullies behind Fred's house. A hard rain had turned the whole thing to mush. But he was sure there was some hint in the book on how to make a real spaceship.

What if Mrs. White decided to teach him a lesson about responsibility by not letting him check *Mushroom Planet* out again?

Timmy was wating on the corner, looking casual. Timmy always brought his books back late, but was never asked to pay the fine. Timmy thought it was because the librarians were under his spell. Jeff thought it was because everybody knew Timmy's dad hadn't worked for a year.

"We gotta hurry," Jeff said, breaking into a dead run up Lincoln Avenue.

Timmy loped beside him, his greased hair standing up in a

smooth, petrified wave. "We're not gonna make it. Library closes in five minutes."

Jeff glanced at the high school building across the street. As he ran, body pumping up and down, the rows of windows rippled like waterfalls. No one seemed to be around. That wasn't surprising. Not even seniors would be at school on a glorious day like this.

"Let's take the shortcut," he said.

Timmy, toting a book on dinosaurs and two collections of ghost stories, looked at him sharply, then over at the high school. "You kidding? Somebody might be there, getting ready for graduation or something."

"That's not until next month. Come on. We'll be okay."

"I don't—"

"What's the matter—scared?"

Timmy's eyes narrowed. "Listen—you know what Big Kids do if they catch you over there."

Jeff had, indeed, heard. Timmy had told them all about it: This one kid ended up in the hospital. This other kid was found hanging by his toes from a basketball hoop. This other kid got used in some kind of chemistry experiment. And on and on.

"Well, *I'm* going," Jeff said, bounding into the street.

Technically, the far sidewalk wasn't high school property, and was therefore neutral territory. But beyond that point, the risk escalated. The broad front lawn of the campus was relatively safe because the people who lived on Lincoln Avenue could hear you if you screamed. The school buildings themselves were to be avoided at all costs, of course. Unfortunately the shortest route across campus passed through the breezeway that connected the classroom structure and the gymnasium. And beyond that lay the student parking lot, where all bets were off. The school buildings blocked the lot from casual observation from the street, while the other side was bordered by peoples' back fences. This meant an interloper faced a long sprint across an open desert of striped pavement, in full view of any Big Kid with time on his hands.

As Jeff set foot on the front lawn, he couldn't help slowing down a bit, every nerve stripped of insulation. He glanced over his shoulder. Timmy was just crossing Lincoln, eyes flicking back and forth as if he were fording an alligator-infested river. His fist was raised and the little finger extended in the Indian sign of protection—but he was coming.

Ahead, the high school building rose like a mesa from a smooth green desert. All those windows, two stories' worth gazing down at him. What if a bunch of delinquents stood behind one of them right now, angry about having to serve Saturday detention or something, looking down at these two little kids and grinning? Timmy said some of the Big Kids weren't even human, they were aliens disguised as people, sent from Alpha Centauri to infiltrate Earthly society. *Flesh-eating* aliens.

Jeff looked away from the windows. Behind him, Timmy's breathing and footsteps grew louder, and Jeff let his friend catch up. In another few seconds, side by side, they reached the breezeway. They stood together on the concrete, breathing hard. Every noise was loud and echoey. Jeff glanced both ways. Doors on either side, small windows set into them. A long hallway behind the glass to the left. To the right, in the foyer of the gymnasium, posters left over from basketball season proclaimed GO WOLFPACK!!!

No one was visible in either direction. Jeff relaxed slightly. But they had to keep moving.

He stepped into the parking lot, then jerked to a halt. Two cars, windshields glittering in the clear sunlight, sat out there in that ocean of pavement. One, painted a lurid Candy Apple Red, was jacked up and had wide tires and spinner hubcaps. Timmy saw it, too, and gasped. A Senior's car.

"Okay," Jeff said in a low, tight voice, glancing around warily. "Don't worry. We're almost there. Let's go." He strode into the parking lot, moving briskly but not running. There was definitely a chance they were under observation—and anybody who watched *Wild Kingdom* knew what happened when a potential victim bolted.

It wasn't easy to keep his sneakers under control, though. The mouth of the alley looked like it was a hundred miles away. Two steel posts stood in front of it to keep cars out. He focused on those. Goal number one. There were similar barricades at the far end of the alley; those were goal number two. Beyond that was Farr Way, and then the junior high playground, the third and final goal. The alley itself was the problem—a narrow dirt path maybe thirty yards long, flanked on either side by fences too snarled with sticker bushes to climb over. It was a terrible place to get trapped.

Jeff glanced over his shoulder. Timmy was a half-step behind him, looking around warily. Still no one else in sight. Jeff's heartbeat began to slow. Maybe the parked cars were Auto Shop projects awaiting Monday morning's school bell.

As he passed the hopped-up car, he glanced at it with uneasy fascination. He didn't know much about cars; he hadn't had much of a chance to learn about them because Timmy thought they were boring. But he thought this one looked kind of cool, even if up close the rust was visible, and the dents in the doors. The grillework reminded him of a set of big teeth.

They passed the car without mishap, and at last the mouth of the alley was in sight. Jeff relaxed a little more. In a few seconds they would be safe even if somebody spotted them from the school. They were both fast runners.

"We've got it made, *Kemo Sabe,*' said Timmy, striding into the lead.

"Told you," Jeff said, irritated.

That was when he heard a strange sound behind them, soft and rhythmic: *vvvvvvp-vvvvvvp-vvvvvvp.* He glanced back to see three Big Kids running toward them.

His feet took off even before he'd registered that the pursuers weren't just Big Kids, they were *Seniors.* It was easy to tell—all three wore sand-colored corduroy pants scrawled with penned slogans, signatures, cartoons. Senior Cords, they were called. It was an annual tradition at Middlefield and some other high schools in the area. Girls wore corduroy skirts. Either way, the graffiti-garnished fabric served as mobile billboards during the last few weeks of school, advertising academic survival.

The sound Jeff had heard was ribbed fabric rubbing briskly against ribbed fabric.

"Seniors!" Jeff shrieked as he flew past Timmy.

He heard Timmy's gasp, then the fluttering sound of sprinting feet. But above that rose the heavier thunder of the Seniors' footsteps and the electric singing of their cords, growing louder by the second. Jeff's stubby neck-hair sprang erect, and his sneakers moved so quickly they scarcely seemed to touch the ground.

He reached the opening into the alley and shot between the barricade poles, shoes skidding momentarily sideways on the dirt path. Risked a glance back. Timmy was just behind him, eyes wide with terror, library books threatening to spill from under his arm. But the Seniors were only twenty feet or so behind *him,* long legs churning with easy strength, doodles and slogans sweeping back and forth: CLASS OF '61 RULES, SENIORS FOREVER, WE'RE OUTA HERE. Cartoons of Kilroy and football helmets and cars, scrawled signatures, arcane symbols. Despite the blur of shadows sweeping across the Seniors' faces, Jeff could see all three were looking at him and laughing—a wolf pack closing in for the kill.

Were their teeth pointier than human teeth were supposed to be?

In his mind Jeff metamorphosed into a Saturn V rocket, the second stage kicking in. A million tons of thrust drove him forward, eyes vast and burning in his face, teeth bared like the grille of a '57 Chevy. He stared at the posts at the far end of the alley. How had they gotten so far away?

"We didn't touch it!" Timmy shrieked over his shoulder. "We didn't touch your car!" Jeff realized his friend was trying to buy their lives. The only response was a soft, three-toned chuckle.

—VEEEEEP-VEEEEEP-VEEEEEP—

At that moment the end of the alley swept toward Jeff, then past, a scarred yellow post flashing by on either hand. He hit Farr Way without even thinking about traffic, practically flew over the blacktop and through the open gateway into the junior high playground, Timmy a step behind him.

They were supposed to be safe here; the playground was neutral territory—but what if their pursuers didn't *care* about that? After all, they were Seniors, the epitome of Big Kids. Jeff hurled a glance over his shoulder. Slowed down. Skidded to a halt at the corner of the building. Timmy sprinted past him, then came back. He was gasping like a dog in August, eyes wild.

The Seniors weren't there. Jeff stared at the mouth of the alley, saw nothing but shadows. He looked up and down Farr Way. Empty. Of course, the Seniors could have disappeared in any number of different directions by now . . . but he couldn't shake the feeling they were still in the alley, arrested by Farr Way the way vampires are stopped by running water. Standing in the shadows, watching, laughing, waiting . . .

"That was close," Timmy wheezed. "Come on, let's keep moving."

"I can't," Jeff said, and looked down at his hands.

"Why not?"

"I lost my book!" Jeff cried, and crumpled into tears.

* * *

I sat up. Slapped myself briskly across the face. This was no place to fall asleep, parked alongside a kids' playground. *I was just taking a nap here, officer, honest.*

I rubbed the back of my neck, determined to stick to my schedule, get through this visit quickly.

I made a U-turn and pulled back onto School Street and continued east for a minute. Then slowed to walking speed. In the middle of the block stood a gray, two-story house, its veranda shaded by a pair of enormous maple trees. The Rohr home.

My heart beat faster, washing away the exhaustion. Did Gail's parents still live here? Should I ask about her? Surely they would remember me.

As I drew closer, I saw a sign in the yard: FOR SALE.

Pulling to the curb across the street, I sat and stared at the house for a while. No car in the driveway, no sign of activity. The porch sagged a bit more than I recalled; the concrete steps leaned this way and that. The grass was far longer than the Mr. Rohr I recalled would ever let it get. But the paint looked fresh, and purple irises sunned their pursed faces along the walkway.

Why not?

Half-amused by the churning tension in my stomach, I climbed out of the car. Straightened my shirt. Strode up the flagstone walkway as I had so many times in the past. My heels boomed across the porch. To one side hung the wooden swing where Gail and I had sat on many a hot evening, holding hands and watching fireflies sputter over the yard.

As I pushed the doorbell, I found myself recalling my first formal date with Gail. I hadn't been sure if I was going to wet my pants or throw up. I felt exactly the same way now.

The bell clanged tonelessly, but no one came to the door. Simultaneously disappointed and relieved, I pushed the button again. Waited. No response.

Cupping my face against the window in the door, I peered into the foyer. Oak floor, coat closet, banistered staircase rising beyond. A brass hat stand stood like a butler next to the stairs. And in one corner, an antique grandfather clock reached nearly to the ceiling. Its pendulum hung motionless. I smiled. That clock had never worked.

Maybe I'd come back later.

As I walked back to the car, I glanced up the street. The next corner marked the intersection of School Street and Lincoln Avenue. Lincoln went past the high school and dead-ended at Oak Lane, the street where I used to live. This had been our normal route to junior high—the route that circumvented the high school campus.

Instead of climbing into the car, I continued toward the corner on foot. Somehow it seemed wrong to approach the old homestead in a rental car. Walking, that was how we'd gotten around for most of my life in Middlefield . . .

CHAPTER TWELVE

HEARTLAND

Jeff stepped off the front porch, clutching a slippery stack of brand-new notebooks under his arm. As the morning sunlight slapped his face, he smiled. Despite all the tossing and turning last night, he felt great. Excited.

The first day of school.

Abe stood on the sidewalk, holding the hand of his little sister, Marla. Jeff sighed. Marla was only seven, but already wore glasses as thick as February ice. There was nothing wrong with her ears, though, or her vocal cords: she listened to everything anyone said and told it all to her mother. Timmy called her Marlboro Mouth. He was funny sometimes.

Abe stood as stiff as a fence post. The creases in his pants looked like they could slice bread, and a little triangle of white T-shirt winked through the opening at the top of his plaid shirt. Jeff knew of no other kid who actually wore T-shirts as undergarments. "I have to walk Marla to school," Abe said in a voice of intense composure.

"Every day?" Jeff asked. He'd hoped the escort-Marla-to-elementary-school tradition would end this year, now that they were eighth graders. Abe didn't say anything, just looked down at the toes of his black shoes, which were as shiny as a new car.

Jeff's irritation passed quickly. Trauma couldn't stick to him in his new cords, polo shirt, and squeaky leather shoes. He looked around. Lots of kids on the streets, riding bikes, running, walking; eddies of color and sound migrating toward the schools.

"Where's everybody else?" Jeff asked. "We're going to be late if we don't get moving."

"We'd better not be late." Marla frowned sternly at Abe. "This is the first day."

Abe's eyes rolled like blue guppies in matching fishbowls, but he didn't say anything. Abruptly Jeff wished Abe would go ahead and leave right now, so Jeff could arrive on his own.

Next door, the screen door banged open and Fred bounded into the yard, the heels of his new shoes clacking on summer-baked turf. "Well," he cried, "here we go!"

"I wish it was Saturday already," Abe said.

"You're squeezing my hand too hard," Marla wailed. "And I'll tell Mommy if we're late!"

Jeff looked around again. "Where the heck is Timmy? We have to get this show on the road."

"I'm right here, dummy," said a voice from nowhere, and they all jumped. Marla let out a little peep of shock.

"You blind or something?" Timmy rose from the bushes next to the porch. He wore jeans with earth-blackened knees, and a red pullover shirt torn at the collar. Evergreen needles clung to his Brylcreemed hair like candy sprinkles on a birthday cake. The notebooks under his arm were ragged and dirty, obviously left over from last year, their covers scrawled with doodles. His battered lunch box featured a pirate motif: old sailing ships firing cannons at one another on one side, and on the other, a shark cruising over a sunken treasure chest. A little kid's lunch box, Jeff thought.

"How long have you been there?" he demanded.

"About two seconds."

"No way. We would have seen you sneak up."

"Maybe I teleported."

Jeff sneered. "If you can do that, why didn't you just teleport on to school?"

"You know I like to walk with you losers."

"Losers?" Fred dropped his notebooks and lunch box. "I'll show you a loser, buddy."

The two of them wrestled for a moment, but when Timmy started making snarling noises and cuffing at Fred with curled hands, Jeff glanced around nervously to make sure no one was watching.

"*Abraham,*" Marla whined. "Let's go."

"Be cool, Abe-o," Timmy said between snarls. "Marlboro, if you don't shut up, a Nodkin will come and grab you out of your bed tonight and bite your head off, see?"

Jeff thought that was a strange thing to say. Timmy didn't usually share his fantasy people with outsiders. Marla gaped.

"Let's get going, Timmy," Jeff said, "or we'll have to take the shortcut." He was half ashamed at how quickly that settled everybody down. Even Marla, who had begun to cry, was quiet.

The group headed down the block, Jeff leading, Timmy at his side. As they made the turn onto Lincoln Avenue, Jeff glanced over at the high school. Teenagers were converging on it from all directions, some in groups, some alone. Seniors, the only students allowed to drive to school, cruised down Lincoln yelling at their less fortunate companions through open windows.

Jeff thought again about the day he and Timmy had fled from the Seniors. More and more, he doubted the Seniors had been chasing them. He had the feeling the Seniors hadn't even been running all that fast. In fact, he suspected that the big kids in their graffiti-splashed cords had just been jogging to Finney's to order Black Cows when the two goofy little kids in front of them had taken off, screaming. Must have been pretty hilarious.

"Hey, man," Timmy murmured in his ear. "I came over to get you last night."

"Huh?"

"I told you I'd be there. What was your problem?"

"What are you talking about?"

"I called your name a million times. I know you heard me. Why didn't you answer?"

"Timmy, I don't know what you're talking about."

Timmy glanced around. Abe scuffed along a few paces back, holding his sister's hand and staring morosely at the ground. Fred was trying to tightrope-walk on the curb, arms flailing for balance. "You were supposed to go to the land of *Nod* with me," Timmy said.

Jeff felt a chill slide down his neck, as if a raindrop had splashed out of the blue sky. "There's no such place as Nod. I asked my dad—"

"You asked your *dad?*"

"Yeah, why?"

"Hey—how would he know about it? He's just a *mechanic.*"

"He's a department foreman at Allison," Jeff said. At least he has a job, he thought.

"Well, still," Timmy said, "he wouldn't know about this. You and I are the only ones." Timmy stared hard at him for a moment. "That's why you should have gone to Mars with me last night. I flew there in my mind. Once you reach the land of Nod, you can go *anywhere.*"

Jeff tried to think of a reply. Couldn't. They were halfway down Lincoln Avenue now; in a minute they would make the turn onto School Street, and Gail's house would come into view. Would she be waiting for them? She always used to; Jeff realized he'd taken it for granted she'd be there today. What if she wasn't? His heart thumped painfully. At breakfast this morning, he'd rehearsed in his head what he would say to her. He'd be cool, casual, in charge. But in his mental practices, he hadn't considered the possibility of having Timmy clinging to him like a narrow shadow, whispering about going to Mars . . .

"I still say you were just dreaming," Jeff said sternly. "Hey— dreams can seem pretty real, I know."

Timmy's eyes tightened. "You don't believe me, do you? That I can travel places in my mind."

"How?"

"Well, I can prove it."

"Guess what Gail's wearing today."

"How would I know?"

"A blue skirt and a white blouse. Wait and see. And a blue ribbon in her hair. You'll see."

A car horn blared loudly. Fred slipped off the curb and sprawled onto the street in a spray of notepaper. A hopped-up red Chevy rumbled past, trailing smoke and laughter—not just *a* Chevy, *the* Chevy. There were two or three guys sitting in it. One of them was Chris Wagner, who didn't have any good reason to ride to school since he lived right across the street from the campus.

Grumbling and red-cheeked, Fred scooped up his papers. One of his knees was scraped clear through the fabric to the skin. Fresh blood winked brightly.

Amazingly, Timmy seemed oblivious of the commotion. "I went to Gail's house last night," he said. "Right after I got back from Mars. I just wanted to see . . . if I could. She was in her bedroom, putting her clothes out."

Jeff's eyes narrowed. "You went into her *room?*"

"Not *me*, just my mind," Timmy insisted. "I can't make my body go places yet. Gail couldn't see me or anything."

"But you watched her . . . changing clothes?"

Timmy's face grew even redder. "No. I told you, she was getting her stuff ready for today. That's how I know what she'll be wearing."

Alternating waves of cold and heat rushed through Jeff. Certainly, he'd visited Gail's room in his own head often enough. "You're a pervert."

"I thought you didn't believe I could do it."

"I *don't.*"

They turned the corner. Just down the block stood Gail's house. A woman stood on the porch, looking their way. Jeff slowed down, disappointed. Who was that? One of Mrs. Rohr's friends?

The woman smiled and stepped into the sun, and Jeff's eyelids climbed so high his eyeballs began to burn.

Gail. She was suntanned almost as dark as a walnut; her brown hair gleamed with rivers of gold. Just below the hemline of her blue pleated skirt flashed graceful calves; her hips flared out and in again, a set of matching curves. Above that was a waist as pinched as the middle of a figure eight, then a white blouse clinging deliciously to smooth round hills. In her hair gleamed a blue ribbon.

Jeff's head snapped toward Timmy. But Timmy's eyes were fixed on Gail.

So were Fred's. "Wow," he said softly, brushing off his pants.

Gail walked down to the sidewalk and stopped, feet together, books cradled under her breasts. Waiting for them. For *him*, Jeff thought. What was it he'd intended to say to her?

"Hi, Gail!" Timmy called, his voice rather shaky. He raked his fingers through his hair. Needles sprinkled out. Then he said the line Jeff had rehearsed all morning: "You look great."

"Thank you, Timmy." Her voice had deepened from oboe to alto sax. The sound of it made Jeff's knees weaken. He tried to think up a new greeting. Surely "hi" wasn't good enough.

She looked at him. "Hello, Jeff."

"Hi." He stopped in front of her. Two feet away. Stared into her eyes.

"Have a nice summer?" she asked.

"Sure . . . uh, you?"

"Great. Arizona was so great. I brought you something."

Jeff could hardly breathe. Mike's prediction had come true. *Because she likes you, you dork.*

As she fished around in her purse, Jeff noticed her bracelet, thick silver set with an opaque blue-green stone. The colors were striking against her brown skin. Fine hairs on her wrist glinted like cornsilk. Jeff was ashamed he hadn't thought to get her a welcome-back gift.

She held out a long, slender box wrapped in plain white paper. "I got this on an Indian reservation."

"An *Indian* reservation?" Timmy cried, leaning close.

When Jeff reached out to take the box, his fingers touched hers, and his arm jumped like a fitful cat. The box weighed almost nothing. "What is it?"

"Open it and see." Under the tanned surface, Gail's cheeks glowed like sunsets.

Jeff tore off the paper and removed the lid. Inside lay a piece of wood about ten inches long, shaped like a dagger blade. It was painted sky blue and decorated with geometric patterns in black and white. To the wider end was fastened a hank of cord.

He looked at Gail.

"It's called a bull-roarer," she said. "It's Hopi. Or Pueblo, I forget. Watch." She took the blade out of the box and let it dangle by the cord. It almost reached the sidewalk. "Stand back, you guys."

They did. Raising her arm over her head, she swung the bull-roarer around in a circle, as if preparing to throw a lasso. The blade of wood rose to the horizontal, orbiting Gail like a wire-controlled model airplane. Her arm accelerated until the blade formed a blue ring around her. Then a wonderful thing happened. The blade began to hum, and then to drone, and then to emit a loud, resonant roar. Up and down the block, kids stopped and stared.

"Wow," Timmy said.

Jeff nodded. He thought the bull-roarer was great, but he thought that Gail, swinging her arm, her whole upper body, was the real gift. Graceful, strong, beautiful. Her face was flushed, her eyes glittered in a fierce squint, the tip of her tongue slipped out from the corner of her mouth. The howl of the bull-roarer resounded deep in Jeff's skull.

Finally Gail slowed the swing of her arm. The bull-roarer fell silent. Gail caught it deftly and coiled the cord again. Sweat glistened on her brow.

"Thanks," Jeff said as he took the wooden blade back in his hand. It felt hot. He was thanking Gail for more than the bullroarer, though; his gratitude extended to things he couldn't even define. He put the gift reverently back in its box. "That is so cool."

"Wish *I* had one," Timmy said.

"I wish I'd had enough money to buy one for everybody," Gail said. "Maybe you could make one for yourself, though."

"Yeah," Jeff said. "You could probably do that, Timmy."

Timmy stared at the box. "Yeah, but that one's *Indian.*"

"*Abe,*" came Marla's whiny voice. "We've got to *hurry.* Everybody else is almost *there,* and you have to take me clear down to *my* school."

Jeff looked up. She was right; except for their group, the sidewalks were becoming deserted.

The group set off at a quick pace, Jeff walking close to Gail. Her strides matched his exactly. He tried to remember what else he'd planned to say.

"Hey, Jeff." Timmy came close again. "Could I see it for a second?"

Jeff hesitated, then handed over the box. "Don't take it out," he said. He turned toward Gail, and noticed she was his height. He'd finally remembered one of his better lines: "So, how was the Wild West?"

She smiled. "I loved it. I learned to ride horses."

"Wow." His mind overflowed with the image of Gail on a horse, her chest bouncing . . .

"Well," Gail said, "what did *you* do all summer?"

"Um . . ." *Played Spaceman and Caveman and argued about who killed who.* "Oh, you know—just messed around."

"Did you go out for football?"

"Football?" Jeff tried to glance around without appearing to. Timmy had fallen back out of sight, but that didn't mean he couldn't hear. "Uh . . . no, not yet."

To his shame, some of the light bled out of her eyes. "But you said—"

"I'm still going to. Me and Mike, maybe even Fred."

"But hasn't practice already started?" Gail asked.

"It's okay, we can still try out today, right after—"

He looked over his shoulder as a thunderous roar erupted behind him. For a moment he was certain the red Chevy had leaped the curb and was bearing down on them, engine revving—then Timmy galloped past, one hand raised in front of him as if clutching reins, the other extended over his head, whirling the bull-roarer. *"Yi-yi-yi-yi-yiiiiiii!"* he shrilled in his imitation of an attacking Apache. "Just like the braves in Arizona, right Gail? *Yi-yi-yi-yi-yi-yiiiiiiiii!"*

Jeff looked at Gail. She looked back.

"What a dork," Jeff said quietly. Gail laughed behind her hand, and Jeff knew everything had changed.

CHAPTER THIRTEEN

NO PLACE LIKE HOME

I blinked, stumbled. Had I been asleep again—on my feet this time?

Across the street, the high school complex rose in a jumble of boxes and curves. The classroom structure had sprouted a new wing; behind the gym hulked a large building I guessed housed a swimming pool. I could see a corner of the parking lot, sunlight glittering on chrome and glass. Seniors' cars. Not a '57 Chevy Bel Air in the bunch, I'd bet.

I continued down the block, gazing at the houses. Small and boxy, but with full-grown trees out front—suburbia matured. I listened. Soft scrape of shoe soles on pavement. Birds cackling. Dog barking. Comforting, small-town sounds—but for some reason I felt uneasy. When I realized why, I smiled at myself: I'd never walked down this street, at this hour, on a school day before. What I really felt was a truant's guilty independence.

The restorer in my mind stripped away twenty-five years of additions and renovations to the houses. They were still recognizable as the placed I'd passed every day on my way to school, with the exception of one: the Wagner home. The house I remembered had been replaced by a modern structure of aluminum siding and triple-glazed glass, with little trees in front. Jesus, the Wagners. They were the guys who put snowballs in the freezer in February and cracked you in the head with them in July; who built rubber-band guns as big as bazookas with ammo cut from truck inner tubes; who knocked your books into mud puddles and dared you to *do something about it.* As Timmy once said, all four Wagner boys had acted like Big Kids even when they were little. Maybe the police had had to dismantle their house to look for hidden corpses or stolen goods. Wouldn't surprise me.

A few doors down, almost on the corner, was the Mean Lady's house. I'd forgotten the Mean Lady's name, if I'd ever known it. I couldn't even recall her face—to us kids, she had mostly been an irritable voice shouting "You boys keep quiet out there!" through her screen door while a cocker spaniel with threadbare ginger fur barked monotonously at her feet. Except for that dog, the Mean Lady lived alone. Timmy opined that it hadn't always been that way; the Mean Lady had killed her husband years before and buried him in the basement, where her children were chained to iron rings in the walls.

Poor Mean Lady. Her yard had been the only one around marked with KEEP OFF THE GRASS signs, so of course it was perpetually bisected by a footpath six inches deep. Similarly, her habit of pretending to be away from home on Halloween had resulted in her spending every November First scraping paraffin scum off her windows and dried egg off her porch.

Still, in retrospect my overriding feeling for the Mean Lady was pity. When I was in the eighth grade, just a couple of weeks before that terrible Halloween of 1965, her dog had disappeared. I remembered her wandering around her front yard in her nightgown, calling in a pale, keening voice: *"Liiiiiiindy! Here, Lindy!"* Funny, I could remember the dog's name, but not the owner's. Everybody had assumed the Wagners took the cocker; the Wagners had denied it, of course.

In my day, Lincoln Avenue had dead-ended next to Fred's house. Beyond that had been the wasteland of shallow ravines where my friends and I had harvested our Caveman spears. Now I saw that the ravines were gone, filled-in and smoothed-over. Lincoln continued on into a large housing development. No more ravines. No more spears. No fields to explore. I shook my head. As a kid I'd done my share of TV watching, but when I played, I *played*; recreation and imagination had been inseparable. No more. Now video games captured the minds of children in traps designed by somebody else; as for exercise, the only options were—

"Organized sports."

This time the words so clear I did whirl around. But I was alone.

As I continued on to the corner, more and more of the new housing development came into view. As I'd half-expected, it stretched across what had once been the field behind my house. Even the scorched stump of the Big Tree was gone, then. Someone's living room probably stood over its rotting roots now. Did their children dream of nasty things scratching at the floorboards?

I had reached Oak Lane. For a moment I stood there as rigid as a lamppost, afraid to turn my head. Afraid to look at my old house.

But finally I did.

Whatever I expected to happen next, I was disappointed. No thunderclap, no surge of music, no sudden revelation: *There it is! The reason I came back!*

The house was box-shaped, painted eggshell white with blue trim. I remembered when it had been painted beige and brown. In the front yard stood a maple tree twice as tall as the house. I recalled the sapling my mother had planted and nurtured, despairing when we kids kept trying to climb it. A two-car garage sat at the top of the driveway where Dad had always wanted to build one, but never had. God, the place was small. As I moved toward it, it didn't seem to get any bigger. The front yard had once been as vast as the African veldt; now it was no larger than a badminton court.

Curtains blanked out the front windows.

Crossing the street, I strode up the walkway to the front porch, mounted the two concrete steps, and rang the doorbell. Why not? Maybe this was the real reason I'd come back—to peek once more into this tiny place. To remind myself of how enormous a gulf separated nostalgia and reality. Perhaps after seeing that the past was nothing like what I remembered, I'd be able to carry on in the present again.

No one answered the bell.

As with most Midwestern houses, this one had two doors: a screen door with an aluminum frame, and behind that a wooden door with a couple of small windows in it.

I rang the bell again, heard it ding-dong thickly, as if muffled by a pillow. There had been no doorbell when I was a kid. Visitors just pounded on the door.

No answer.

After a moment's hesitation, I pulled open the screen door and looked at the little windows in the wooden door. Hesitated again. So quiet. I felt a prickling sensation on the back of my neck, and visualized a bored housewife standing in one of the nearby houses, watching me. Steam iron in one hand, telephone in the other. *Hello, police?*

Still, I put an eye against one of the little windows. Beyond lay umber twilight. I saw a tiny entryway, a living room overfilled with couch, recliner and coffee table. Dust danced in narrow sunbeams slipping between the drapes.

Turning my head slightly, I tried to peer down the hallway that opened off the living room, tried to glimpse my old bedroom. But the hallway was as dark as the inside of a mine shaft. Raising my hands, I cupped my face tightly against the glass. Widened my eyes. That was better. Now I could see a pale line of light that marked the foot of a closed door. That would be it. That—

The bedroom door swung open and a silhouette stepped into the hallway.

I staggered back a step, apologies and excuses flying to my tongue. There was no sound inside the house. Then it occurred to me that the shadowy form I'd glimpsed had not been very tall—about the height of a young boy who ought to be in school.

Putting my eye back to the window, I cupped my hands around my face and—

"May I help you?" a voice asked behind me.

My heels left the ground. I whirled, the screen door ricocheting off my hip and slapping against the wall with a shivering bang. At the foot of the walk stood a woman.

"I'm sorry," I said, grabbing the door frame. "I just . . . I was wondering about this house."

The woman was about my own age, although her hairstyle—a mound of puffs and curls—made her look older. So did her tight, patterned pants, tent-shaped blouse and white sandals. Very dated garb, but why not? I understood that bell-bottoms were making a comeback, too. The expression on her face was modern enough: level and suspicious. In one hand she clutched a long strap of pink leather; for a weird moment I thought it was a whip. Then I realized it was a leash, the bright chrome clasp at the end winking in the sun, attached to nothing. I glanced around. No dog in sight.

"Do you *know* the owners?" the woman asked.

"No, no." I smiled as reassuringly as I could. "See, I used to live in this house when I was a boy."

"Well, the Millers won't be back for a while. They're on vacation."

"Are you sure they're gone? I thought I saw someone in there."

Her thinly plucked brows lowered. "It wasn't a little boy, was it?"

"I'm not—"

"Is the door unlocked?"

"I didn't check." Now I did. "No, it's locked."

"Well, I'll go have a look around back. Maybe one of the Wagner kids broke in there."

"Pardon? Did you say Wagner?"

"Kids can be so bad," she said. "You really have to watch them, or they get into all kinds of trouble." She looked at me searchingly. Her skin was covered with cosmetic powder, cracking on it like dried mud. "Are you a good boy?"

"Pardon?" It was an odd question, one an adult might ask a child. But there couldn't be two years between us. In fact, I had the horrible feeling that if I asked, she would turn out to be somebody I knew from the old days. Maybe even someone I'd dated.

She didn't answer me; that sharp stare never wavered. "Well," I said, "nice talking to you." I started to walk around her.

"Don't get me wrong," she said, stepping in front of me. "This is a good neighborhood, a good town. I did leave for a while one time, but I came back. Turned out everything I needed was right here after all." She wound the leash around one hand. "You say you used to live here?"

"A long time ago."

"Well, you never know." She twitched the handle of the leash, making the clasp skitter across the sidewalk. "You might decide to come back, like I did. A lot of people have done that in Middlefield. It's nice here."

I grunted. "Well, thanks again."

From the high school building by Lincoln Avenue came the muffled ringing of a bell. A moment later, the rumble of voices and footsteps swelled out into the thick air . . .

Rumbling. Shouting. Clattering. Laughter.

The junior high cafeteria was located in the basement of the building. Concrete-block walls painted pale green; scuffed tile floor; tangle of pipes overhead. The only windows were dusty slits near the ceiling. When full of rowdy, tray-clashing teenagers, the place was bedlam.

In the past, Jeff had always brought a sack lunch to school, but today Mom had given him lunch money. It made him feel like a proper eighth grader, even though he knew this was a luxury that wouldn't come often.

Carrying his tray of pizzaburgers, mashed potatoes, corn and a carton of milk, he wound through the crowd back to one of the long tables at the rear of the room.

"That looks like dog food," Mike commented with a grin as Jeff sat down.

"Beats peanut butter," Jeff said, and turned to the other side. "Gail, want one of my pizzaburgers?"

She smiled, thanked him, and helped herself. He watched her mouth open to take a bite. Her teeth were fascinatingly white. He wasn't sure what made him more dizzy—the fact she was so pretty, or that she wanted to sit here beside him.

Things had worked out great. At assembly this morning, the eighth graders had been divided into five sections. Jeff, Gail and Mike had all been assigned to Section 8–3. Timmy and Fred were in 8–5; Abe was alone in 8–2. Overall, Jeff felt pleased with the outcome. Which made him feel guilty, too. This arrangement was pretty much the one he would have chosen.

He still wasn't sure if Timmy had overheard his and Gail's earlier discussion about football practice. Timmy had ridden his imaginary Pinto around and around the group all the way to school, the bull-roarer bellowing and shrieking. But during assembly, he had been silent and still, and when his name was called he had walked off without so much as a glance at the rest of the gang, the bull-roarer in his shirt pocket. Jeff hadn't had the heart to ask for it back at the time.

"Here comes Timmy," Mike said.

Jeff looked up as a new group of kids poured into the cafeteria and the noise level rose another unbelievable notch. Timmy, at the back of the influx, wasn't contributing much to the commotion. Books clutched under his arm, he stood against the wall and scanned the room.

"He better have my bull-roarer," Jeff said.

Gail leaned close. "Maybe you should let him keep it. He really seemed to like it. Besides, I've got some other stuff from Arizona for you."

Mike snickered.

Jeff felt dizzy. "You do?"

"Yeah. I'll show it to you after you get done with football practice, if you can come over."

"Sure . . ."

Staring at Timmy, Jeff battled an internal war of emotions. Mostly, he was relieved that Timmy hadn't been placed in his class section—but at the same time, he felt a weird, slippery sense of loss, as if he really were responsible for the way the sections had been designed.

But overriding both these emotions was a desperate desire that there be no long-term repercussions. He didn't want Timmy to become his enemy, after all. But if Timmy couldn't keep up . . .

Jeff wondered how to make Gail lean close again.

Just then, Timmy's gaze found them. He walked over, ignoring the crowd, swinging his battered Sea Battles lunch box. He sat directly across from Gail.

Jeff cleared his throat. "Hey, Timmy. How's Section 8–5?"

A casual shrug. "Boring."

"Already?" Gail asked.

"You should see some of the geeks in there. I think 8–5 is the retard section."

"No way," Mike said. "Then Abe would be in it."

Everyone but Timmy laughed. Even he smiled a little. Jeff felt himself unwinding. "Do you still have my bull-roarer?" he asked.

Timmy hesitated, nodded.

"Well, you can keep it."

"I can?"

"Sure. Take it."

Timmy glanced at Gail again, frowning. "Thanks."

Jeff scanned the cafeteria. Fred and Abe should arrive soon; when they did, the whole gang would be here for the last fifteen minutes of the lunch break. Maybe they could get together like this every day. Maybe everything would work out after all. Maybe Timmy hadn't heard Gail ask about football practice.

"One good thing about my section, though," Timmy said, opening his lunch box. "At least nobody will notice if I Nod off in class." He looked straight at Jeff.

"You mean you're going to sleep in class?" Gail said, sounding both shocked and titillated. "On purpose?"

"No . . ." Timmy dumped a small, lumpy apple and some kind of sandwich wrapped in waxed paper out of his lunch box. Jeff knew he made his own lunches. "I mean I'm going to visit the land of Nod whenever I want."

"The land of what?" Gail asked.

"Hey, Timmy," Jeff said. "Mr. Largus told us there's a portable planetarium in the science lab. It projects stars onto the ceiling. Won't that be cool?"

"The land of what?" Gail said again.

"Never mind," Jeff said. "He's just kidding."

To his relief, Timmy didn't contradict him. "I don't have Mr. Largus for science. I have Mrs. Edelstein. She's a moron."

"All the science teachers use the same equipment, though," Jeff insisted.

Timmy shrugged. "They aren't *real* stars, anyway. Not like the ones you see from Mars. You wouldn't believe all the stars you can see from Mars at night."

Gail blinked. Even Mike looked puzzled. "Don't you like any of your classes yet?" Jeff quickly asked Timmy.

"Nope." Timmy took a bite of sandwich. "So, do you guys have football practice today or what?"

Jeff stiffened, saw Mike do the same. With an almost explosive sense of relief, Jeff said, "Yes. Yeah. Mike and me both."

"And maybe Fred," Mike blurted. "Fred might want to play, too."

Timmy's gaze flicked back and forth. "Figures." He bent over his sandwich, and his voice became almost inaudible. "I hope you have fun."

"You could try out, too," Jeff said hopefully.

Timmy snorted. "Right."

"Come on, it's fun," Mike said. "We could all play together."

"Wynken, Blynken and Nod?" Timmy mumbled. "Hey, you guys want to play football, play football. See if I care. Me and Abe have better things to do."

"We can still hang out together on weekends and things, though," Jeff said. "Right?"

Timmy suddenly grinned, a grimace so hard and brittle it made Jeff recoil. "I doubt it, *Kemo Sabe*. Next thing you know, you'll be

signing up for the basketball team. Then baseball. Then going out
for track. Maybe get in on the school play." A blizzard of bread
crumbs spewed from his mouth. "Join the Honor Society. Mop the
floor at Finney's after school. Buy a car. Rebuild engines. Wear a
screwy letterman's jacket." The crumbs speckled the cover of his
notebook like snowfall. For the first time, Jeff noticed a new drawing scrawled there amongst the dragons and gape-mouthed sharks.
At first it looked like a tree, all squiggles and cross-hatching. Then
he realized he was seeing it upside down. It was really the head of
a girl, her long hair swirling. It was a good likeness, too. Jeff recognized the face. It was Gail.

"You're just like everybody else, Jeff," Timmy said. "I can't believe it. You're just like everyone else." And his palm swung down
onto his notebook with a slap.

Tap tap tap. "Hello?"

Woman's voice. Was it that airplane lady again? Why was she in
the junior high school cafeteria?

Taptaptaptaptap.

"Excuse me, sir? Are you all right?"

I sat back, wincing at pangs in leg, spine, neck. My head
thumped into something padded. Car seat.

For a moment, eyes closed, I was sure I was still in Santa Ana,
sitting in my car in the parking garage.

I opened my eyes. Dust-hazed windshield, overhanging leaves
beyond. Hot, dead air smelling of old cigarettes and new disinfec-
tant. I turned my head. A woman's face and poised forefinger
hovered outside the window. She'd been tapping against the glass.
Her eyes, gray green, were tight with concern or suspicion, or
both. Then they flew wide.

So did mine.

Gail Rohr.

CHAPTER FOURTEEN

SEEMS LIKE OLD TIMES

She looked terrific. The few wrinkles on her face were clustered at the outside corners of her eyes: laugh lines, we in the over-forty club like to call them. Wires of silver wound through her hair, which had lost a foot of length. But the stormy-sea-colored eyes were absolutely the same, and the wide mouth. As she backed away, her lips opened in disbelief, revealing the straight white teeth. She wore pleated slacks, a lightweight blouse. Her figure was still trim.

She kept backing away, and a memory crashed on me. *I never want to see you again!* I could almost smell the upholstery of my Rambler, hear the hiss of satin on vinyl as Gail slid away from me, the skirts of her Junior Prom gown flowing after her like a receding wave. Tears in her eyes.

I'd laughed. *Laughed* at her retreating back. Couldn't lose my cool just because she had said "no" and meant it. No way, man. Never knew who might hear about it.

There were other girls, anyway . . .

Gail stopped backing away, stood there in the middle of the street. What exactly was the expression on her face? Shock? Dismay? Maybe I'd made a mistake parking here, wanting to see her, after all.

I peeled myself out of the car, trying not to wince at the stiffness of my muscles. How long had I been asleep? I couldn't even remember getting back in the car.

"Hi," I said, wiping my sweat-dampened brow. "Recognize me?"

"Jeff." She said it as if she hadn't met anyone with the same name since I left town.

"Yeah." I shrugged. "Somewhat the worse for wear."

"Well. It actually happened. I wasn't sure . . . I thought . . . I thought you might just . . ."

"Just what?"

She blinked. "Nothing. I guess I didn't really expect to see you again."

"I hope you don't mind."

"No, of course not." But she didn't come any closer, even when a car rumbled down the street toward us. Only after I hurried over to the sidewalk did she move. We assumed our relative positions, an arm's length of space between us.

Stared at one another. She looked like she was trying to smile, but couldn't quite remember how to make her mouth bend that way.

Up School Street, a bell rang dimly, kept ringing. That made the time at least three o'clock in the afternoon. Some little nap!

"You look terrific," I said.

"You, too."

"Thanks." *For the lie,* I thought. I wanted to reach out to her, give her a hug, bridge the gap of years with physical contact. But that would probably be the wrong thing to do. Especially since she was standing so stiffly, with her arms crossed over her breasts like armor and an expression on her face that seemed trapped somewhere between warmth and fear. I lamely said, "I just got here this morning."

She uncrossed her arms, toyed with the wedding ring on her finger. Large diamond there. "So what brings you back?"

I opened my mouth and it stayed that way. What was I supposed to say? Finally I shrugged. "Business, sort of. Think we could go inside your house and talk?"

"Better not. I . . . never know when the realtor's going to bring someone by."

"Your mom and dad . . . ?"

"Retired down south. I've been staying here for, well, the last few months."

I've been staying here, she'd said. Not *We've.* "Oh," I said. "Well then, how's about I buy you and your husband dinner? Kids, too, if you have any. You and I can bore everyone to death with stories about the good old days. Is Joseph's Steak House still around?"

She had lowered her eyes, clutched herself again.

"Gail?"

"My husband . . . my children . . ." She looked up. "They're . . . they've passed."

I took a half-step toward her. She didn't change position at all, or lower her arms. I didn't know what to say.

A couple of high school kids walked past, boy and girl, hands clasped, curiosity on their faces. Adults don't hang out on the sidewalk this way.

Gail briskly wiped her eyes, tried the smile again. "It's a little early for supper," she said, "but you could buy *me* a hamburger. If you want to."

I hoped my smile looked more real than hers did. "Deal." We climbed into the rental. "Where to?"

Her hands were folded in her lap and her head was bowed, as if she were praying. "Head for Main Street."

Pulling a U-turn, I drove past the junior high, then turned north on Landrus. Somehow, this was the strangest thing yet—cruising through Middlefield with Gail Rohr beside me again. She smelled of dandelions . . .

"Did you say you're here on business?" she asked, sounding serene now, her head held high. "What would bring an astronaut to Middlefield?"

I laughed. "Well, I never got to be an astronaut. My old football injury kept me out of the military, and back then astronauts had to be . . . well. Actually, I'm a lawyer."

She nodded as if not the least bit surprised. "And your firm sent you here?"

"You could say I was in the area. I got nostalgic."

For the first time she laughed, although it was more a snort than the shoulder-shaking Gail Rohr guffaw I remembered. "Come on. You're the least sentimental person I've ever known."

Unexpectedly, anger spurted through me. How dare she tell me what kind of person I was—especially a quarter century down the road? Then the anger died. I half sighed, half laughed. "You know, a few days ago I would have agreed with you. But lately . . . well, I've been thinking a lot about the past. Things I did, people I knew.

Timmy, Mike . . . you . . . the whole gang. Maybe I'm getting old, but I felt the urge to come back for a day or two."

She was silent.

"It's true," I said.

Silence. She'd never been a chatterer; I remembered how she could say nothing for an hour if she felt like it.

Finally I sighed. "Okay, that's not all. My life is going down the tubes. The usual executive crap. My wife left me, my daughter's starting to look like a stranger . . ." To my horror, tears began to rise like a tide of acid behind my eyes. "I—I guess I just wanted to get in touch with the good old days again."

"And have you?"

I considered the question while the urge to cry receded. "I don't know. So much has changed."

She barked another laugh. "You think so?"

"Sure. The stores, the houses . . . everything."

"So you haven't found what you're looking for?"

I glanced at her. So solemn and remote, yet clearly the same Gail Rohr I'd fallen in love with as a teenager. "How would I know?" I asked. "I'm not even sure what it is I want. By the way, where are we going?"

"To the place all the cool kids go," she said.

I blinked, and a smile crept over my face. "You don't mean Big Bopper?"

"Going to Big Bopper later?" Mike asked.

"Huh?" Jeff, sitting near the end of the bench, had been watching Gail's thighs as her cheerleading skirt parachuted and swished.

"Big Bopper. A bunch of guys are going after the game. You wanna go?"

Jeff started to say, "Mom and Dad wouldn't want me to," but stopped himself. His parents were playing bridge with the Wrights tonight. Jeff hadn't minded them missing this game; as he'd told them, if the Middlefield Wolfpack didn't wipe out the Avon Orioles in a record manner, he'd give up football for golf. The score was currently 36–0, Wolfpack—and the second quarter had barely begun. Jeff and the other starters had been holding down the bench for fifteen minutes now. Jeff wasn't used to that, but tonight it was okay, for a couple of reasons.

First, it meant Fred had a chance to play. Fred wasn't on the starting squad, at least not yet. Jeff could tell Coach liked Fred's gung-ho, get-hurt attitude; if Fred gained some weight, he'd probably be a starting lineman by next year. He'd been talking about going out for wrestling, too.

Another advantage of sitting on the bench was that Jeff got to watch the cheerleaders from close up. And get watched by them. Especially Gail.

He knew he looked good in his football uniform. Too bad it wasn't mud-caked today. That always helped. He'd scored three touchdowns himself without a single grass stain to show for it.

He glanced back at the field. The night was autumn perfection: cool enough to subdue mosquitoes but not people, scented with fallen leaves and drying grass. The crowd in the stands was a gumball machine of colorful jackets. Far overhead swarmed the silver bees of the Milky Way.

The field was all floodlit green, thundering feet, flashing numbers. And, to the side, the gyrating cheerleaders.

Jeff hadn't expected Gail to try out for cheerleader, but hadn't been surprised when she got it, either. She was the best, the most popular. He was half-excited and half-jealous that everybody got to see her little panties when her skirt flew up.

"Hello?" Mike waved his hand in front of Jeff's face mask. "Anybody home?"

"I'm thinking," Jeff said.

Big Bopper was a drive-in restaurant a half-mile outside town, plunked right at the edge of a beanfield. High school students hung out there a lot, as did the occasional family in a kid-packed station wagon. You got served at your car window, or you could order from the walk-up and sit at a picnic table out front.

"Who's driving?" Jeff asked. He didn't know too many parents who would be willing to stuff a bunch of grubby football players into their car.

"Nobody. We're going to walk."

"Walk?" Jeff hesitated. It was no big deal for Mike to hoof it out there and waste half the night; his parents were already in bed. But Jeff knew Mom and Dad wouldn't like him going all the way to Big Bopper on foot, especially unsupervised. And least of all on a Friday night, with high schoolers in jalopies roaring up and down the highway, rowdy on beer and sloe gin. Plus, a hamburger for Gail and himself would cost all his milk money for the next week.

He turned and peered down the bench. Several guys were looking at him. Waiting for his choice, his lead. If he was out too late, he thought, he could always tell Mom and Dad there had been a sock hop after the game. They wouldn't even check.

Guilt flashed through him. He hated to lie.

Beside him Gail leaped, kicked. Bounce of breasts, swish of hair. He saw himself sitting with her at Big Bopper like a high school junior or senior, eating a Bopper Burger and drinking a shake, maybe rubbing his ankle against hers under the picnic table . . .

"Pssssssssssssssst!" That didn't come from Mike. For some reason, Jeff looked toward the Big Tree. It was barely visible through the hazy glare of the field lights, a black head poised against the sky.

"Pssssssssssssssst!" Hey, Jeff. Jeff, back here."

Now Jeff recognized Timmy's voice. It wasn't one he'd heard much during the last few weeks. In the month and a half since school started, Timmy had gotten weirder and weirder. During lunch in the cafeteria, speaking loud enough for anyone to hear, he would say that last night he'd mentally shot himself right out of the galaxy, a bolt of faster-than-light energy. Or he'd projected himself to Washington, D.C., and seen President Johnson sitting in the Oval Office with his feet on the desk. Or he'd plunged to the bottom of the ocean, where miniature black volcanoes spewed mud and scalding water from inside the earth. According to Fred, Timmy had even stood up in science class and told Mrs. Edelstein that tyrannosaurs had not been slow-moving lizards at all, but aggressive hot-blooded monsters that streaked like giant ostriches around the Cretaceous landscape, hunting *herds* of triceratops. When asked where he'd gotten that preposterous idea, Timmy had haughtily replied, "I went back in time and saw it myself."

The kids in school were calling him "Captain Strange." Abe, his constant companion during lunch periods and after school, was "Mr. Weird."

A couple of weeks ago, Jeff had started wolfing down his lunch so he could hurry out to the playground before Section 8–5 arrived in the cafeteria. Timmy seemed to have gotten the hint; he'd even stopped showing up for the walk to school in the morning. Which was okay. Jeff had grown tired of hearing the latest tidbits about the land of Nod: "Nod is a lot like *here*, only better. The people are friendly. They want me to come over. I know I can do it. I know I can make it all the way. Hey—want to go with me?"

"*Psssssssssst! Jeff! Jeff!*"

Jeff tensed. In his head he pictured Timmy behind him, leaning over the bleacher railing. Abe, Mr. Weird, would be standing next to him, as usual. Jeff imagined all the kids in the stands staring, watching, whispering.

Maybe if he pretended he hadn't heard. Bounding to his feet, he cupped his hands around his mouth and shouted at the field: "Go, Fred! Hit 'em! Hit 'em! Yeah!"

"*Psssssssssst!* Jeff! Back here!"

It wasn't going to stop. Next, Timmy would probably roar like a lion to get his attention. Jeff whirled, hoping his anger was visible despite the helmet and padding. As he'd expected, Timmy stood with his belly pressed against the rail, leaning forward, his narrow torso floating in a huge, ragged corduroy jacket that must have belonged to his father. And Abe stood slightly to the side, head crunched down inside the upturned collar of his marching-band coat, his gaze locked on the playing field with the empty fixity of a headlight-blinded raccoon. He held his flute case in one hand.

Timmy gestured at Jeff urgently. "Come here, come here."

Jeff glanced around. Several of his teammates, including Mike, were staring at him. So were a lot of kids in the stands.

Puffing himself up, he marched to the railing. "Can't you see there's a game going on? I can't talk now."

"What are you doing later? And Mike? And Fred, if he wants to go."

"Go where?"

Timmy glanced from side to side, then leaned even farther forward, eyes glittering like sequins. "To the land of Nod."

"What?" Jeff had heard the words clearly enough; he just needed time to accept the idea that Timmy had come to a despised football game to harass him with *this*.

"It's time to go to Nod, man," Timmy said urgently. "All the way. Everything's almost ready."

From the roof of his vision Jeff could see Bev Waterhouse watching Timmy and him avidly and whispering to Joyce Ritchie. Bev and Joyce were two of the most popular girls in the eighth grade. What if Gail was watching all this, too? Jeff swallowed. "I can't go," he said abruptly, but at a low volume he hoped carried no farther than Timmy. "I've got plans."

Timmy's expression crystallized. "Didn't you hear me? I said we're going to the land of *Nod*. Tonight. Things are almost ready. This is your *chance.*"

Jeff felt as if a hard, straining knot had formed inside him, and was being hauled on from two directions. Sadness and regret on one side, embarrassment and scorn on the other. Caught in the middle, he tried one more time: "Timmy, you gotta give this up, man. This crap about Nod just makes people think you're a dodo."

Timmy blinked and recoiled, face hardening. His eyes slanted toward the swish and flash of pleated skirts on the sidelines. "It's that *girl*, isn't it?"

"No. It's *you*, man. You just—"

"My dad says women are only good for one thing. That's all. You can't trust them for anything else." Timmy didn't say what the *one thing* might be; Jeff had an idea he didn't know. Hell, *Jeff* wasn't exactly sure himself.

Behind him, out on the field, whistles trilled wildly and the PA announcer blared something about a turnover. "I've gotta get back to the game," he said again, and started to turn away.

"What about it?"

The knot inside Jeff abruptly released; the rope sprang into a rigid, angry line. "Timmy," Jeff said, "forget it. I'm not going to the Big Tree anymore, understand? Mike, either. And probably not Fred. Now I've got to get back to the game." He turned and started walking toward the bench.

"You're *crazy!*" Timmy's shout whacked like a hand against the back of his helmet; the words carried above all the noise in the stadium. But Jeff just kept moving, shoulder pads rising like a turtle's carapace, a bitter taste filling his mouth. His face burned.

"You're just like all the rest!" Timmy screamed. "You'll never go to Mars now, Jeff! Never!"

Jeff heard scattered laughter in the bleachers. He kept moving, acting deaf. How had the bench gotten so far away? His knees were shaking with humiliation and anger by the time he finally dropped onto his seat. From farther down the bench, someone leaned out and stage-whispered, "Hey, Dittimore, how *do* you get to Mars from here, anyway?" This was followed by a chorus of half-subdued chuckles.

"Be quiet," Coach snapped, striding back from the edge of the field. "We have a game to play here. Third team defense, get on the field." He gave Jeff a scowl, then stalked back to the sidelines. Jeff sighed.

"What was *that* all about?" Mike muttered from the corner of his mouth.

"Are Timmy and Abe still back there?" Jeff asked.

Mike glanced quickly over his shoulder. "I don't see them."

"Good." Jeff's shoulders dropped. "Holy moly. Timmy thinks he and Abe are going to the land of Nod tonight. He wanted us to go along."

"The land of . . . you mean, *really* going?"

"That's what he said."

"Do you believe him?" Mike's voice was almost too quiet to hear.

Jeff turned his head. "What, that he's going to the land of Nod? Don't be stupid."

"No, no, I don't mean *that*," Mike said, a bit too earnestly. "I mean, do you believe he wanted *us* to go out to the Big Tree *with* him?"

"He's flipped," Jeff said uncomfortably. He finally spotted Gail, who was looking over at Jeff with a mixture of curiosity and worry on her face. He gave her a half-smile. She'd always thought Timmy was a creep anyway.

Mike said, "Don't you feel kind of bad about him sometimes? We used to be such good friends, all of us."

"It's his own fault," Jeff said vehemently. "We asked him to try out for football, remember?"

"Yeah, but I still feel bad sometimes."

"Well, don't. All he has to do is join in on a little normal stuff."

"Maybe he'll go to the Fall Festival this year. That would be good."

Jeff found himself actually considering the possibility. The Fall Festival, a homegrown minicarnival, was held in the high school gym every Halloween night. Its real purpose was to give young people an alternative to trick-or-treating, to keep Halloween pranks to a minimum. There were booths sponsoring games like ring toss and darts, with prizes ranging from rubber mice to live goldfish in little glass bowls. There were attractions like kissing booths and palm readers, and tons of homemade food. The big entertainments were the cakewalk, the sock hop, and above all the costume contest. All in all, the event was kind of hokey, kind of cool.

Jeff had gone to the festival only once before, when a prolonged thunderstorm canceled trick-or-treating. To him, trick-or-treating —the chance to dress up in a scary costume and run wild through the wind-blown streets—had always made Halloween the best holiday of the year next to Christmas. But a lot of that appeal, he had to admit, had had to do with Timmy. Timmy really gloried in Halloween night. Unlike the rest of the gang, he didn't buy his costumes at Vanover's 5-and-10. He made them himself, with scraps of cloth and tempera and whatever it took, transforming himself into a vampire or zombie or alien. The gang would follow him around until their bags overflowed with candy.

But that was kid stuff. This year, the Fall Festival was definitely the way to go. Jeff planned to dress up as Robin Hood; Gail, of course, would be Maid Marian. Timmy would probably barf if he knew that. To Timmy, the point of Halloween was to become a monster, not something cute or funny.

"He wouldn't go, no matter what," Jeff said. "He thinks the Fall Festival's stupid. Besides, he probably hates us now, too."

Mike sighed. "Yeah, but—"

"You boys interested in this game or not?" a deep voice demanded, and they looked up sheepishly at Coach. "If not, I'm sure I can find somebody else to take your places."

"Sorry, Coach," Mike said.

"We're interested," Jeff said at the same time.

Next practice, Jeff knew, he'd be running wind sprints for an hour.

CHAPTER FIFTEEN

RITUALS

"Sorry. What did you say?"

"I said, 'A penny for your thoughts.' You looked like you were a million miles away."

"More like a million years." I glanced around. Gail and I were parked outside a local kid's hangout, all right—but it wasn't Big Bopper, which according to Gail had been demolished in 1970. This new establishment—McDonald's, of course—featured no waitresses, no menus mounted on poles by the parking slots. Outdoor tables, yes—but located inside a fenced area crowded with plastic playground equipment. At Gail's request, we'd gone through the drive-through, then parked in the back of the lot.

This was very different from Big Bopper, but the same, too. The people inside the restaurant were mostly after-school teenagers laughing, whispering in conspiracy, checking each other out, strutting from table to table. Other youngsters hung around outside, watching the continuous train of passing cars.

I'd already brought Gail up to date on my recent life, minus the grisly details about Janice's infidelity. In return Gail had volunteered nothing at all about her own experiences. I'd been afraid to ask.

"I was thinking about the Fall Festival," I said.

Gail smiled—a small smile, but a real one at last, deepening the lines at the corners of her eyes. "That was always fun . . . but they don't have it anymore."

"No? How come?"

She was holding a vanilla shake; her hands made a helpless gesture around the cup. "You know how it is; the Fall Festival was

124

too corny for modern kids. So things got out of hand. Fights, drinking in the parking lot, smoking dope in the restrooms, all that."

"God."

"Whatever happened to the good old days, right?"

I managed a wry smile. "We do tend to romanticize it, don't we?"

"Do we?" she asked softly.

"My wife—my ex-wife—once told me I talked like I grew up in Mayberry." I nodded toward the parade outside the restaurant: seal-slick girls in black leggings; boys with glittering metal studs in their ears and computer-designed, hundred-dollar athletic shoes on their feet. "Well, I don't see Opie or Goober, do you?"

Gail didn't respond. "What about your daughter?" she asked. "Do you think her childhood has been as good as ours was?"

I thought about that. Deserts and the ocean versus pastures and riverbanks. Smog and skin cancer versus the Milky Way and mosquitoes. Balmy winters and brushfire summers versus rain, slush and snow. Gang-bangers with automatic weapons versus the Wagner boys with frozen snowballs. "It's an entirely different world," I said.

"What about you? If you had the past to live over again, would you change anything?"

I doubted she was referring to anything as personal as Prom Night. In fact, for a moment I could almost believe we were sitting at Big Bopper, she in her cheerleading outfit and me in my after-football clothes. Breathing the ether of young love while we conducted one of those deeply sincere discussions about life, death and God, as innocent as we would ever be. "Sometimes," I said, "I wonder what my life would be like if I'd done some things differently. Even little things. It's like that Ray Bradbury story where the guy goes back in time and accidentally steps on a butterfly. When he returns to the future, all of history has changed. Who knows what little choices we make now will do to our lives later?"

She stared at me over the top of her milkshake cup. "Was that an answer? You really *are* a lawyer."

I couldn't tell if she was joking or not, but I laughed. "Sorry. Sure, there are things I'd like to change—but given the chance, how do I know I'd change the *right* things? I mean, say that instead of playing in the football game where I hurt my knee, I stayed home that night. Maybe I'd still have two good knees—but on the other hand, maybe the next day, instead of being in the hospital, I would have walked out in front of a car and gotten killed. Or joined the Army, like Freddy. See what I mean?"

Her gaze roved away, back toward the McDonald's crowd. "It sounds like you believe in fate," she said.

"If you mean something written in stone from the beginning of time, then no."

"You don't think things happen for a reason?"

"I think shit happens," I said bluntly. "People come up with the reasons *afterward.*"

"You really think that's all there is to it? You don't see any plan at all, any . . . destiny?"

Obviously she wanted reassurance on this subject. And it was no wonder, since she had lost her entire family to a calamity. But I answered honestly: "No, I don't see that there's a plan. I guess I really am as unsentimental as you said."

She put the straw in her mouth, removed it. "Tell me something —what are the odds that you and I would both happen to be here in Middlefield, together, after all these years?"

For a moment I was a bit taken aback. Then I laughed. "Listen, if we'd met by accident in Kuala Lumpur, *that* would be fate."

She smiled slightly. We sat quietly for a while. I watched cars cruise past: Toyota pickups, Nissan sedans, Geo compacts. Then I saw a real anachronism: a 1957 Chevy Bel Air, Candy Apple Red, with spinner hubcaps throwing off daggers of light.

I blinked. Was it possible that that same '57 Chevy was still running? As I watched, it pulled out of the queue of cruising vehicles and cruised to the farthest end of the lot. Stopped. Three guys climbed out and strode toward the McDonald's. All of them had short haircuts—a style leaving fashion back in my day, trendy again now. All wore letterman's jackets with the big M stitched on the front, as well as beige corduroy pants with slogans and drawings scrawled on them from cuff to beltline.

I smiled and turned toward Gail. "Isn't it a little early for senior cords?"

Gail raised her head. "Pardon?"

"Senior cords. I thought that wasn't supposed to start until March or April." I looked at the parking lot again. The Seniors were gone. So was the Chevy.

"Jeff?"

"Man, I'm tired. A second ago, I thought I saw three guys in senior cords out there. Walking across the lot."

She reached out as if to touch my arm, then pulled back. "Jeff, are you going to visit anyone else while you're here?"

"I thought I might. I was wondering . . . is Mike Norris still around?"

"Yes . . ."

"What's wrong?"

"He's changed. A lot."

"What do you mean, a *lot?*"

She shrugged. "For one thing, he's become a recluse. I'm not sure he'd welcome a visit, even from you."

"Mike, a recluse? Does he still live on the farm?"

"What's left of it. He never married, doesn't have any friends. He only comes into town every few weeks for supplies, or so I've heard."

"Wow. What happened?"

"Vietnam, I suppose. Delayed stress syndrome or whatever they call it." Her gaze met mine. "The last time I visited him, he acted very strange. Paranoid, really."

I shook my head. "I *have* been out of touch too long. He was always Mr. Mellow."

"Not anymore." A shadow flickered across her face. "If you see him, just remember he's not himself. He might say or do anything."

"Thanks, I'll remember." Despite myself, I let out a jaw-cracking yawn.

"You poor thing, you must be exhausted after all that travel."

"Who's exhausted?" I glanced at my watch, which now read just past 4:00 P.M. "Ordinarily I'd still be at work right now."

"Where are you staying, anyway?"

"Nowhere, yet. I wasn't even sure I'd still be in town tonight."

"And now?"

I looked at her. The stormy-sea eyes, the soft lips. The same Gail. "Maybe I'll hang around a day or two, do some visiting."

"Good." She turned away. "Remember the old motel on Highway 136?"

"Sure." I didn't mention, of course, that the Sleep-E-Rest Motel was where I'd lost my virginity with Bev Waterhouse exactly one week after the junior prom where Gail and I broke up. "It's still there?"

"Sure. It's not the Hilton, but at least you wouldn't have to commute back and forth to the city."

"Thanks, I'll check it out." I paused. "Gail . . . I don't want to impose, but do you think I could see you again while I'm here?"

"I'd like that."

I was rewarded by another shadow of her real smile. "It really is good to see you again, Jeff. Maybe that old saying is wrong."

"What old saying?"

" 'You can't go home again.' "

Jeff hurried home from Gail's house under the spilled flour of the Milky Way. His feet navigated on their own because his mind was turned backward, reviewing everything that had happened in the last few hours.

Considering the way the football game had gone, with Timmy showing up, Jeff had almost decided to cut his losses and back out of going to Big Bopper. Now he was superstitiously glad he'd changed his mind. To his surprise, Gail had agreed to go to Bopper's with him, even though it meant fibbing to her parents, too. They'd walked side by side at the rear of a regular parade of eighth graders, wrapped together in a sense of shared adventure and guilt. Once at the restaurant, they'd split a burger and fries at one of the picnic tables while exchanging longer and longer stares. Wandering the gray-green oceans of Gail's eyes, Jeff hadn't even minded taking some razzing about Timmy's little freak show at the game. He'd minded it even less after the quarterback of the varsity team stopped by and said, "You played a good game tonight, man." The *varsity* QB!

As Jeff walked Gail home, their hands brushed together time and again, sending jolts of excitement up his arm. He kept thinking that the night couldn't get any better, but when they reached her porch, Gail had—

"Have a nice evening?"

Heart somersaulting, Jeff stumbled to a halt at the foot of his own front steps. Dad stood on the porch, leaning against the door, his arms crossed over his chest. He was staring at the sky.

"Uh—yeah," Jeff mumbled. Inside his head, he scrambled to

pick up the pieces of his sock-hop alibi. He should have rehearsed it on the way home.

"Son?"

Jeff opened his mouth, then sighed. "I went to Big Bopper after the game," he said.

Dad nodded slowly at the stars.

Words began to spew out of Jeff like water from a hose: "Mike invited me. A bunch of the guys were going, and I knew you and Mom were playing cards and I didn't want to call and bother you, so I thought it would be okay . . ." He bit it off. This wouldn't work, and he knew it. He was in trouble, honesty or no honesty. Which wasn't fair. Jeez, it wasn't like going to Big Bopper made him a Jerry Wagner or something.

Then he realized something else: in his heart, he didn't much care what punishment might be coming. Nothing could damage the glory of this night. Nothing. On Gail's porch, with shadows all around and the sound of a TV coming through the open window from the living room, he had kissed his girlfriend for the first time. He could still taste her lips. Feel the firm-soft contours of her body pressed against his.

Dad finally looked down, the lenses of his glasses comets of reflected streetlight. "Since when," he said stonily, "is it Mike's job to give you permission to go places?"

Jeff was yanked back to the present. "I—" He shut himself up again.

"You know you're not supposed to go to Big Bopper by yourself," Dad said. "Least of all at night. How did you get there?"

"Walked."

A pause. "You didn't ride with Mike's brother?"

Jeff shook his head.

"Well, at least you have that much sense." Another pause. "What about coming home?"

"I walked Gail home first." Jeff wasn't sure why he said it; it seemed like a detail that might count for something. But a very long pause followed, and Jeff's imagination filled it with dire scenarios: Dad was going to call Mr. Rohr, or make Jeff himself call and apologize for endangering Gail on that deadly highway. Or Dad was going to demand to know what Jeff thought he was doing, getting other kids involved in his illicit activities. Or, worst of all, Dad was going to forbid Jeff to ever see Gail Rohr again . . .

Instead, Jeff heard an unexpected sound—a soft chuckle.

Jeff looked up to his father, whose face was turned toward the sky again; the Milky Way gleamed softly on his glasses. He murmured, "I was about your age when I had my first love."

Jeff gaped. He'd never imagined that Dad could have *ever* loved someone besides Mom—the idea made him feel suddenly unstable, loose inside, as if he'd caught the stomach flu. Did *Mom* know? Then he realized something else: Dad had shared this personal fact with *him*. This man-to-man kind of fact. The sense of instability was replaced by warm, swelling pride.

"You'll have greater loves in the future," Dad told the stars in a wistful tone nothing at all like his usual no-nonsense cadence. "Like your mom and I have. But you'll never have another love like your first one. I'm excited for you, Jeff."

Jeff felt his face reddening, but blurted a secret of his own: "I like Gail a lot."

"She's a terrific girl." Abruptly, Dad detached himself from the wall. "Okay. Now we have to decide what to do about your little trick tonight."

Jeff swallowed. He should have known. Dad's two favorite words were *responsibility* and *pay*.

"I should ground you for a week or so," Dad said. "And I would, except you were man enough to admit what you did and not try to lie your way out of it. I know you thought about that. So here's the deal: Tomorrow, you mow the lawn and wash all the windows, then help your mother dig up her flower bulbs before you go anywhere. Deal?"

Jeff raised his head. "Really? I'm not grounded?"

"This time. Next time you'll grow roots."

"There won't be a next time," Jeff said earnestly.

A dry grunt. "Well, you'd better get inside and apologize to your mother for worrying her half to death, then get to bed and—"

An eerie wailing sound cut through his words. Jeff whirled toward the street, the hairs standing up on the back of his neck. For a moment he thought he was hearing the Middlefield air-raid siren, which at this hour and in this weather could only mean the Russians were attacking. Then he realized the noise was coming from the corner across the street from Fred's house, and his eyes found the exact source: a ghost. A squat and billowy apparition gliding across the Mean Lady's front yard, turning slow circles on the grass. And *wailing.* Jeff stumbled back against the bottom step of the porch, almost fell over. He was glad Dad was here to witness it.

"There she goes again," Dad sighed. *She.* Instantly Jeff realized the ghost was not a ghost at all. It was the Mean Lady herself, dressed in an enormous nightgown and keening a single word into the night: *"LIIIIIIIIIIIIIIIIINNNNNNNNNNNNDDDD-EEEEEEEEEEEEEEE!"*

Lindy.

"That's the third time tonight," Dad said, an odd mix of compassion and disapproval in his voice. "Your mother went over to talk to her earlier, but she just refuses to calm down."

"What's wrong?" Jeff asked.

"Evidently her dog ran away." Dad hesitated. "She's pretty frantic; just so you know, she accused you and your friends of stealing him."

"Us?"

"You, the Wagners, every kid on the block. Don't worry, son, I don't suspect you. It was an old dog; it probably wandered off into the gullies to die in peace."

CHAPTER SIXTEEN

THE DAYS AFTER

I opened my eyes, saw gloom and unfamiliar shadows, realized everything in my bedroom had changed locations. I clutched at the sheets.

Then I remembered. Motel. Middlefield, Indiana.

The Middlefield Motor Lodge had changed names and owner-ship since I was a horny teenager, but the place still wasn't going to turn up in the Triple-A guidebook anytime soon. Since there were no other guests, I'd chosen the room farthest from the office. It was clean enough, but smelled stale. There was a queen-sized bed, a bathroom with a lime-stained toilet, a small desk. Outside, cultivated fields extended in three directions. All in all, the place was quiet, cheap, and close to town—perfect living arrangements for as long as I'd be here.

And how long will that be?

I still wasn't sure. At least until I'd visited Mike, though.

And Gail again.

Gail. So much about her had changed. Gone was the brash, spontaneous laugh, the quick temper . . . the *fire.*

My husband . . . my children . . . they've passed.

When I dropped her off at her house, she had allowed me a brief hug. At first her body felt still and cool in my arms, then she relaxed a bit and hugged me back quickly. As I drove away, she watched from the front porch, her hands folded in front of her. Later I discovered her McDonald's milkshake cup lying on the floor of the car with white goop spilled all around it. She couldn't possibly have drunk more than a sip or two. Gail, who used to be able to eat Bopper Burgers with the best of them.

I looked at the motel clock. Just past midnight, local time. Still early for me. Through the open windows poured a thunderous crackle, the massed voices of insects and frogs. The cacophony was so outrageous that at first I'd debated closing the windows and switching on the air conditioning. But I'd gotten used to it. Sitting up slowly, I looked around the room. Old shadows everywhere, even *worse* than in California.

I lay back again, sighing. Suddenly I wanted to hear my mother's voice. Maybe because of my dreams, to feel closer to home. I should call her anyway to let her know I wouldn't be in L.A. for the next few days, just in case she tried to get hold of me. I wouldn't tell her where I was. How could I explain it?

I picked up the phone and dialed. As usual, Mom answered after the second ring.

The connection wasn't the greatest, full of hisses and crackling, but Mom sounded good, if a bit surprised to hear from me again so soon. But she talked cheerfully about the red-tailed hawk that liked to perch on the telephone pole across the street, and the new swimming pool the neighbors were putting in, and how she read to Dad from a Tom Clancy novel every night and he seemed to really enjoy that. Then came the dreaded question: "Would you like to talk to him?"

"Sure."

The breathing. The flat, pointless breathing audible even over the interference. I thought about how not five miles from where I lay now was the house on Oak Lane where Dad had listened to me admit I'd gone to Big Bopper after the game; where in earlier years he'd chased me laughing around the yard, and pushed me on the swingset, and carried me piggyback through the summer air. Love and anger tightened my heart into a flaming Gordian knot. "Hi, Dad," I said, swallowing painfully. "Listen, I'm in Middlefield right now. I didn't want to tell Mom because . . . let's just keep it between us, okay?"

I actually paused, as if expecting to hear something besides the breathing, the breathing. Then I said, "I love you, Dad," in a voice I barely understood myself.

"*Crrrrrrrrrrrrrr* . . ." A dry, faint growl.

I stiffened. "Dad?"

"*Crrrrrrrooooooooooohhhhh* . . ."

"*Dad?*"

Suddenly Mom's voice was on the phone. "Jeff? Are you shouting? Are you all right?"

My heart and lungs battled for space in my chest. "Did Dad just say something?"

"Say—no, honey, of course not . . ." Her voice frayed. Sometimes I forgot just how close to breaking she must constantly be.

"Must have been something on the line," I said. "It's long distance; I'm on a business trip."

"Oh, you are? Where?"

"The Midwest. That's what I wanted to let you know. I told Dad. I'm not sure when I'll be home, actually."

"Well, you know how much we love to hear from you. We really love you, Jeff, your father and I. Are you sleeping better, honey?"

"Oh, much better," I said, sinking back onto the pillow. "Thank you, Mother, much better."

Jeff wondered if Mom was deliberately taking forever to dig up her flower beds. Maybe she and Dad had worked out this exquisite torture to make Jeff pay for his illicit activities the night before. As Mom scraped gently away at the hardened earth, Jeff hacked at it wildly with his trowel. He'd already finished his other chores; now he had to get in the shower and hurry over to Gail's before noon. Last night they'd agreed to go to the Saturday matinee at Topp's Theater. He didn't even know what was showing. Didn't care.

"Are you all right, honey?" Mom asked him. "You don't seem to be all here this morning."

Was she being funny? Probably not. Jeff smiled at her. The truth was, he didn't *feel* all there. Part of his mind was straining forward to Topp's, of course; to that flickering darkness with the close-set seats . . . but another part kept mulling over the dream he'd had last night. The nightmare, more accurately—one as disturbing as any that had tormented him in his childhood.

It hadn't started out so bad. It was dark and he was walking through the cornfield . . . well, not so much walking as *floating*, passing through the dry sheaves without sound or resistance. That strange quality had given away that this was a dream, and he'd reveled in the fact that he *knew* it was a dream but wasn't waking up. He also knew where he was going—out to the Big Tree, to try to talk Timmy into attending the next Fall Festival. A hopeless quest, of course, but dreams have their own logic.

Ahead, above the corn, the Big Tree was visible only as an expanding absence of stars, a void. As it grew larger, Jeff began to hear a voice, speaking quietly and earnestly. Then he noticed a dim, reddish flicker of light at the far end of the corn row.

He kept wafting forward. The voice became clearer, until he recognized it as Timmy's: ". . . need their help, Abe. We can do it by ourselves. We just have to want it bad enough, that's all. We just have to concentrate. Are you done down there? Good. That's good. Don't cry, you know we had to do it. It'll be okay. Hey. It'll be okay."

Suddenly Jeff wasn't sure he wanted this dream to go on. He slowed down. Ahead, the source of the red glow became visible: dying remnants of a fire built in the clearing beneath the Big Tree. Its sullen coals cast a blush against the canopy of leaves and the trunk of the tree. Abe sat on one of the roots, forearms draped slackly across his knees, head hanging between them. A spade leaned against the trunk behind him, as did a long, slender object that looked almost like a sword. But where would Abe have gotten a sword? Between the nearest roots, a section of ground looked churned, as if that was where the spade had been used.

Without warning a shower of leaves and acorns fell out of the Big Tree, followed by Timmy. He landed solidly on both feet but remained in a half-crouching posture, his hands braced against his knees. A violent shudder ran through him, as if he were about to puke. Then he straightened, shook his head and walked toward Abe. Jeff noticed a shiny dark stain all over the front of his shirt; in the dim light it was impossible to guess what color it might be. "Okay," Timmy said in an unusually thick voice, "that's taken care of. Let's do the rest."

Slowly, Abe raised his head. Tears gleamed in orange ribbons on his cheeks. For the first time in Jeff's memory, Abe's glasses were hazed with dust.

"This is what the Indians did," Timmy said. "It makes the difference between crossing over in your mind or with your whole body. The Nodkin *told* me."

Abe's chin quivered.

"Besides," Timmy said, his voice suddenly harder than concrete, "it's done now. Hey—we couldn't undo it even if we wanted to. Right?"

Abe swallowed twice, then nodded. Taking off his glasses, he wiped them with his hanky, which was stained brownish. His clothes were filthy, too. Jeff was more surprised by that than anything else; the poor kid would catch hell when he got home, especially at this hour. Or rather, he'd catch hell if this was *real* life, Jeff told himself.

"Okay, Abe-o" Timmy said. "Close your eyes and think about where you want to go. Think about it real hard."

"What if I can't do it?" Abe asked.

"Of course you can do it," Timmy said angrily. "Don't think that way. We both gotta concentrate on where we're going. *Concentrate.*"

"Okay," Abe said, eyes clenched tight. "I'm concentrating."

"Good." Turning away from the tree, Timmy closed his eyes, too. From his back pocket he extracted the bull-roarer. It dropped to the end of its string, and Timmy raised his hand overhead and started to swing it in a circle. But before completing a single revolution, he halted. His eyes opened again and he craned forward, squinting into the corn. "Jeff?" he called.

Jeff felt his skin tighten. He was in plain sight at the edge of the clearing—or maybe not. Timmy's eyes were aimed right at him, but kept blinking, squinting.

That's because this is a dream, Jeff reminded himself. But the idea was getting harder to accept. Everything seemed so real; the sky, the corn, the fire. Also, in the past, the mere realization he was dreaming always woke him up. Either way, he felt no desire to speak, to risk drawing attention to himself.

Timmy shook his head, closed his eyes and began to swing the bull-roarer in a circle overhead, like a lariat. "CROATOAN!" he shouted, arm cranking harder. "Come on, Abe, say it with me! CROATOAN!"

The sonorous note of the bull-roarer rose into the night. "CRO-AH-TOAN!" Timmy cried. "CRO . . . AHH . . . TOH . . . AAA . . . *Come on, Abe!*"

Abe's mouth finally opened, lips moving, matching Timmy's cadence.   "CROOO . . . AHHHH . . . TOHHHHH . . . AAAAN . . ."

The song of the bull-roarer grew louder and stronger, pulling the

chant with it: *"CROOOOOOOO . . . AAAAAAAAAA . . .
TOOOOOOOOOO . . . AAAAAAAAAAANNNNN . . ."*

Overhead, the leaves of the Big Tree began to stir.

*"OOOOOOOOOOOAAAAAAAAAAOOOOOOOOOOOAAAA-
AAAAAAANNNNN . . ."* Bull-roarer and voices mingled, merging into a single smooth chord that made Jeff's ears hum. Up in the tree, something in the moving leaves caught Jeff's eye—the body of a little beige dog, suspended from a piece of rope. Where the neck should have been was a flat, glistening stump that drizzled blood onto the surrounding leaves. Then it was gone again, swallowed up by the Big Tree.

*"AAAAAAAAAAAAAAAAOOOOOOOOOOOOOOAAAAAAAA-
AAAAAAAAAAAA . . ."*

Shock and disgust flooded through Jeff. Dream or no dream, he couldn't put up with *this*. "Timmy!" he shouted. But either his dream-self had no voice or his words were absorbed by the chant, because he heard only the faintest whisper in the air.

Now the limbs of the Big Tree were moving as well, surging up and down as if heaved by a mighty storm. They seemed jointed, flexible. They lunged toward Jeff, leaves whirling into the air, acorns rumbling down like hail.

"Concentrate, Abe!" Timmy shouted from somewhere inside the blur of leaves and shadows. He sounded simultaneously frightened and ecstatic, and Jeff noticed that even while he was speaking, the chant went on unabated. "Help me! Hey! You gotta help me!"

The Big Tree writhed, crackled. Again it seemed to stretch out; a supple limb whipped over Jeff's head with a roar like a hard-swung baseball bat. He ducked.

"We're so close, Abe!"

The limb swung by again, even lower, stirring Jeff's hair. *I want out of here!* Jeff thought wildly. *Wood and leaves and bark! Wood and leaves and bark I want out of here I want to WAKE UP WAKE UP WAKE UP!*

Abruptly he found himself back in his bed, jouncing on groaning springs as if he'd just slammed all his weight onto the mattress. He sat up. Timmy stood outside the open window, staring at him, clutching a bloody sword in one hand. Jeff bit off a shout just in time as he realized it wasn't Timmy at all. It was nothing but the silhouette of the Big Tree. Part of the dream. The nightmare.

Now, digging up flower bulbs in the full light of day, he couldn't help but remember that filled-in hole by Abe's feet. Hadn't Timmy once said something about Indians burying things under the Big Tree—sacrifices? And putting other things up amongst the limbs? Sometimes Jeff wished he could stop dreaming altogether.

Finally, to his relief, Mom stood, gazed with satisfaction at the mounds of fat tubers in the wheelbarrow, and said, "Well, that's it for this year." She smiled at him. "You can go if you want to. By the way, your father said Gail called about an hour ago."

Jeff showered and dressed in ten minutes flat, ran outside, leaped off the porch and waved at Dad, who was washing the car. As he was charging across Oak Lane, he glanced over at Abe's house. Abe's round, melancholy face stared from his bedroom window. Jeff's footsteps faltered. He waved.

Abe stared at him for a moment, then turned and disappeared back into the house. Grounded, all right. Must have gotten home really late last night; and worse, covered with all that mud and . . .

No, that had been part of the dream.

Jeff sprinted all the way to Gail's house, the wind drying his hair, and was excited to see her sitting on the porch swing as if watching for him. But the face that met him at the top of the steps was tense, disturbed.

"It's okay," he said as he bounded up to her. "I got in a little trouble last night, but—"

"Shh—my father." Grabbing his hand, she turned him right around and led him back to the sidewalk. "Come with me." She headed west along School Street, hauling him by his fingers. Baffled, Jeff went along without a word.

When they reached the junior high campus, Gail took him around back and under one of the maple trees, out of view of passersby on either School Street or Farr Way. Then she whirled, put both arms around Jeff's waist and pulled him hard against her. He was shocked by both her strength and the tension in her body. "What's the matter?" he asked, clutching her in return. "Gail? What's wrong?"

"Last night. I was so scared." Her mouth vibrated against his shoulder. "I wish I could have talked to you right away, but I— we—"

"It's okay, it's okay." Cripes, she was *shaking*. When had he ever before seen Gail Rohr, horseback rider and eye-blackener of Wagner boys, actually *frightened?* "What happened?"

"Timmy . . . Timmy was in my room last night."

"What?"

She sucked in a deep, trembling breath. "I couldn't sleep after . . . you know, after I got home, so I was just lying in bed thinking about our date. Then I heard something. This weird noise, like a moan. But I didn't see anything. Then I saw something in my mirror, you know, the big one on my closet door? Something moving. A shadow. And all of a sudden, there he was."

Jeff said nothing. Felt his breath halt in his chest.

"At first I thought I was dreaming," Gail went on. "He was looking at me like . . . I don't know, like he wanted to kill me or something. He comes walking toward me. I thought I was asleep, but I just started screaming anyway. He jumps back and yells, 'It's not my *fault!*' Then he runs over to the window, jerks out the screen, and jumps onto the roof. By the time I get over there, he's running across the backyard."

Jeff's arms drew tighter and tighter. Gail had never been like this with him before, all needy and shaky and clingy. That made him feel crazy inside, as if part of him was struggling to break free and do something *fearful.* "Then what happened?" he asked.

"Nothing. Mom and Dad came upstairs, but by then I was thinking maybe I just dreamt the whole thing. I thought maybe I even pulled the screen out myself in my sleep, you know?"

He nodded, rubbing a palm over her back. Despite his anger, he was acutely aware of the bump under her blouse where her bra fastened. A mystical place. He kept his hand there, and wondered if it was true that unfastening those hooks was like breaking into a combination lock.

Gail eased away from him. Reluctantly, he let her go. Reaching into the front pocket of her jeans, she pulled something out, clutching it out of sight in her palm. "This morning," she said, "I found this on the floor by the mirror." She opened her hand. In it lay two items: a crushed red leaf, and a single autumn-browned acorn.

Staring at them, Jeff first thought about his dream from last night . . . but that memory was instantly overwhelmed by the recollection of Timmy predicting what Gail would be wearing on the first day of school. Now Jeff pictured Timmy climbing onto the roof outside her bedroom window, night after night, peering in at her while she undressed. Getting more and more excited, until finally he grabbed the screen and . . .

"When I see him again," Jeff said in a voice he didn't recognize, "I'll kill him."

CHAPTER SEVENTEEN

PUT 'EM UP

When I was a kid, the Norris farm had been located well outside the town line. Now, as I drove down the highway, I couldn't even *find* the town line. I cruised past a shopping center, clumps of houses, a small industrial park, the place where Big Bopper used to be—a gas station now. It was a while before I realized I had already missed the turnoff to Mike's house. Turning, I drove back more slowly, searching for familiar landmarks. In the days of my youth, the Norris's driveway had consisted of a pair of ruts with a lush beanfield on one side and a thick stand of woods on the other. The entrance had been marked by a pair of stunted sassafras trees and a battered mailbox.

Finally I spotted what had to be the place—but there were no sassafras trees, no mailbox; instead, a pair of low stone walls flanked a paved lane. One of the walls was decorated with an embossed sign: BELLE FOREST ESTATES. Ironic name, I thought, considering that the woods looked to have been replaced with ranch-style homes. Still, I pulled in. Was it possible Mike lived here?

The development wasn't nearly as extensive as it appeared from the highway. A hundred yards in, the street ended abruptly at a steel-bar gate. Beyond, the pavement dissolved into rutted dirt and gravel. To the left was the old beanfield, except now it contained masses of weeds: goldenrod, Queen Anne's lace, milkweed dangling brownish pods like mummified mice. Some distance to the right, the woods reappeared: old oaks and maples, thorny locust trees, dense second-growth saplings.

From the gate hung a ladder of metal signs:

POSTED
PRIVATE PROPERTY
NO TRESPASSING
NO HUNTING
KEEP OUT

And hand-painted in red on the steel bar itself:

THIS MEANS YOU!!!!

I hesitated, staring at the gate, beyond it, back again.
I'm not sure he'd welcome visitors.
THIS MEANS YOU!!!!
Maybe I should take the hint. Maybe I didn't really need to visit
Mike after all.

But what if I *did* need to? My dreams hadn't stopped, after all.
What if seeing Mike was an essential part of this? I parked the car
and climbed out.

Although there was no visible lock on the gate, it wouldn't
budge when I pushed, pulled or lifted. Maybe it was remote controlled exclusively. *Paranoid, really.*

I had no choice but to duck under the bar, hoping no one was
watching from a house behind me. On the far side, the lane was
pocketed with glistening blotches of mud, indicators of a fairly
recent rainfall. I noticed there were no tire tread-marks in them, so
Mike must be home.

As I walked along the road, keeping to the gravel mounded in
the center, I felt sweat migrating steadily down my face. Everything around me was wet and lush, growing wildly. I'd forgotten
how life proliferates in humid environments. The green of the
trees and bushes was so vivid it looked fake. The air throbbed with
the massed voices of insects and birds. Grasshoppers arced out of
my path in such hordes they looked like the bow wave of a boat;
above the fields, white butterflies danced in lascivious pairs.

Bit by bit, the woods to my right came closer, intersecting the
lane up ahead. My memory took me beyond that spot, up a slight
incline to the Norris farm. I recalled the farm buildings. There was
the house, of course, a big, traditional wooden structure of two
stories, with an attic and a wide veranda. The barnyard was domi-
nated by an enormous hay barn and assorted other buildings, in-

cluding an outhouse. Mike's dad had kept the last structure intact mostly to buttress his endless "When I was a boy" stories. The north side of the property had been shielded from winter winds by a half-dozen old walnut trees.

At the spot where the road cut through the woods it also sank a few feet, the low spot webbed with connected puddles of brown water. I leaped gingerly from high spot to high spot, trying to keep my discount-store shoes dry. On the other side, I looked up.

—And staggered back into a pool of muddy water.

The house stood in the center of a flat, barren plain. The walnut trees were gone; so were the barns, the tractors, the farm implements, even the infamous privy. There were no bushes, no flowers, no rocks. Just patchy grass extending in every direction to the surrounding fields. The scene was like something from a surrealist painting—"Farmhouse on the Moon."

Then I noticed something equally strange: the perimeter of this wasteland was marked by a chain of utility poles. Atop each pole perched a glittering cluster of football-stadium-style floodlights, all pointing into the yard.

I looked more closely at the house. Mike's mother had always taken good care of the place, keeping the white paint fresh and the masses of flowers edging the veranda vibrant. During the spring and summer, sitting on that porch had been like climbing inside a perfume bottle. But now the house was an uneven gray color, paint peeling scabbily along the eaves, gutters sagging like garlands left over from a long-ago party. The veranda roof was swaybacked.

On the highest peak of the roofline perched a double cluster of floodlights. From what I could see, half the lamps pointed into the front yard, half into the back.

Slowly, I walked toward the house. A pickup truck with bulbous 1950s contours sat at the top of the driveway. As I got closer I saw that it, too, was festooned with spotlights—on a high roll bar, on the front bumper, even clinging like barnacles to the fenders. They aimed in every direction, including straight up.

At the top of the driveway, I stopped again. Utter stillness. Only four things prevented me from believing the place was abandoned: the truck; the grass-stained John Deere lawn tractor parked beside the house; the mown grass itself; and Gail's assurance that Mike still lived here.

Behind every window hung stained, torn lace curtains. They were drawn, giving the windows the aura of cataract-filled eyes.

The room on the nearest corner of the second story had been Mike's. I remembered the time he'd sprained his ankle trying to clamber down the drainpipe to rendezvous with Timmy and me for a night of UFO watching. It had never occurred to me before, but maybe that incident explained his fear of climbing the Big Tree.

So many windows. Someone could be standing behind any one of them, watching me through the dirty lace.

I shook myself. So what? It would just be Mike. Mike Norris, my one-time best friend. I had nothing to fear from my one-time best friend, had I?

The last time I visited him, he acted . . . strange. Paranoid, really.

Taking a deep breath, I mounted the steps onto the veranda. The clunk of my heels on the boards sounded as loud as empty fifty-gallon barrels tumbling into a canyon. The veranda smelled of mildew instead of flowers.

Gooseflesh prickled up my arms, and an odd thought struck me: I was the only object in the vicinity even *capable* of moving.

When I pushed the doorbell, I didn't hear anything. After a moment's hesitation, I opened the screen door and peeked through the stained curtain covering the inner window. I saw the staircase straight ahead, the living room to the right, the kitchen doorway to the left. I frowned. The only furnishings in sight were a few floor lamps. Nothing else; not even a chair. I remembered that Mrs. Norris had been a knick-knack lover; you could scarcely turn around in this house without knocking over a porcelain dog or blown-glass tall ship.

Still, I rang the bell again, then rapped loudly on the door. Echoes chased each other through rooms where we kids had once run.

No response.

All right, then. I'd tried. I turned and was just heading down the steps when I heard a soft click behind me.

I spun. A man stood on the other side of the screen door, filling the door frame from side to side. He was goat bellied, with shoulders that sloped right up to his ears. I was reminded of Dick the Bruiser, a professional wrestler from the pre-steroid era whom I had watched on TV when I was a kid. This guy wore bulging overalls and a dirty T-shirt that ballooned with fat on the sides. Cellulite saddlebags hung from the backs of his arms. On his head sat a greasy Cincinnati Reds baseball cap, from beneath which spewed a haystack of brown and white hair. He wore a beard, enormous but scraggly, and crystal white everywhere except around his mouth, where it was stained a noxious yellow brown.

Glaring at me through narrowed eyes, he growled, "Who the fuck are you?" in a voice like millstones grinding together.

I swallowed. "E-excuse me. I was looking for Mike Norris. I'm an old friend of his. He used—"

The man's beard flattened against the screen. "Oh, Christ. Jeff Dittimore."

I blinked. *"Mike?"* The unmistakable scent of burnt marijuana rolled over me, so strong it made me cough.

He sighed. Didn't open the screen door. "Bummer, Jeff. But I should have known. I should have known you'd show up sooner or later. I guess no one gets away from *him*, not even you."

I took a step forward. "Hey, Mike, it's . . . it's great to see you." And in a way, it was. He looked horrible.

Taking a jerky half-step back, he raised one hand and extended it toward the screen. All the fingers were curled under except the pinky, which stood up like a post. I stared. He was flashing the Indian sign of protection at me. "He figures I can't stay stoned all the time, right?" he growled. Even through the rusty haze of the screen, I could see that his eyes were lined in bright, almost fluorescent red. "That's the plan, right? You're just going to keep at me and keep at me until I give in, aren't you?"

"Listen, Mike—"

"Or maybe it's just that you used to be my best friend, huh, Jeff? Maybe he thinks you can get closer to me than the others. Is that right?"

"Listen, can't I just come in and talk to you? We *were* best friends, after all."

He swelled even larger; I was reminded of a grizzly bear guarding the door of its den. His extended hand trembled. "You think you're so smart. You were always able to push me around, get me to do what you wanted. Well, fuck you. We ain't got nothing to talk about anymore."

I took another step toward him. I was suddenly *desperate* to talk to him. What had gone wrong here?

"Don't come any closer," he said. "Last warning. Go back where
you belong, man."

I took another step. "Let's talk, Mike."

His hand swung out of sight, then reappeared holding the biggest, blackest revolver I'd ever seen. But even as my bladder loos-
ened in shock, Mike bent his elbow, raised the gun and pushed the
muzzle under his own chin.

"I'll do it," he said. "I know what Timmy wants, and he won't
like it if I use this." The sound of the hammer locking back was
like a finger bone breaking. "But I swear I'll do it. I'll do it if you
don't get the fuck out of here *right now.*"

The moment I climbed back into my car, my knees started quivering like hardware store paint shakers, and I had to pin them together with my hands.

I know what Timmy wants. He won't like it if I use this.

The pistol rising, sinking into whiskers and fat.

I'd almost run to the car, not looking back, half-certain Mike
would change his mind about which way to point the gun.

I know what Timmy wants.

My knees finally settled down to vibrator speed. I started the
engine and drove quickly back to the highway.

I know what Timmy wants. The words kept rolling through my
mind . . . *what Timmy wants. Timmy . . .*

Part of me felt compelled to go back to Mike's house, *insisted* I
go back and demand to know what he had meant by those words.
Was he talking about Timmy Kegler? Timmy was gone. Dead,
probably. Or was he?

I shook my head violently. *Stop thinking crazy.*

I stopped by Gail's house, but she wasn't there. Where would
she have gone? None of my business. After a moment's hesitation,
I pulled out of her driveway and turned north. I still had places to
visit.

"Maybe Timmy ain't even at school today," Mike said, shifting
his feet. Jeff had noticed before that whenever Mike got nervous or
worried, he started talking like his father, who had never finished
high school.

"He'll be here," Jeff said. They stood together on the playground, watching the cafeteria door.

Timmy hadn't shown up for the morning walk to school, but of course that wasn't unusual lately. On the other hand Abe was there, waiting on the sidewalk with Marla. He was staring at the toes of his shoes. "Abe got in trouble," Marla had said smugly. "Mom says he can't play with Timmy Kegler anymore."

"What happened, Abe?" Jeff asked, hoping for some detail about what had gone on Friday night, and further confirmation that Timmy had sneaked over to Gail's.

"He left without me," Abe told the curb. "I couldn't keep up, and he went to Nod without me."

Jeff's jaw tightened. "Right. I've got news for you, Abe—Timmy's gonna *wish* he was in Nod before the day's over."

Now Jeff and Mike stood in the shade of a maple tree, watching the black rectangle of the cafeteria door. Fred wasn't with them; he'd chosen to play touch football at the far end of the grounds. Gail was in study hall because Jeff had suggested she ought to stay out of the picture. "What for?" she'd demanded, her hands defiantly on her hips, but her eyes wary. "What are you going to do?"

"I'm not sure yet," he'd said. "But he's my friend—was—so this is up to me."

Actually, Jeff still wasn't sure what he intended to do. But the wild thing inside him had been growing hungrier and hungrier since Gail had told him her story on Saturday, and now it strained steadily at its chain.

"Might be a storm tonight," Mike said. "Thunderheads over the fields, see? Ever notice how it almost always storms at night? Wonder why that is."

Jeff just grunted. He didn't look at the sky. Who cared if it stormed tonight?

"Are you sure he even came to school?" Mike asked. "Maybe he stayed home. Maybe he's sick." His constant chatter was irritating. Mike could tackle a charging fullback with the best of them—but he didn't like real conflict, not even arguments. He was the only person with whom Jeff had shared Gail's story.

"Timmy complains about school all the time," Jeff said, "but he never misses a day. It's just something else he likes to pretend about."

Mike shifted his feet. His hands were stuck in the pockets of his jeans as if welded there. "But what if he don't show up, though?"

"Then I'll get him tomorrow."

"No, I mean . . . what if he's *gone?*"

"Gone where?"

"Friday night . . ." Mike shuffled his feet in the pea gravel. "I know it sounds weird, but Friday night I had a dream that Timmy and Abe went out to the Big Tree, and Timmy . . . disappeared. Just like—"

His words dropped off. Jeff had turned to see Timmy standing just outside the cafeteria door, gazing around in that disdainful way he had. Abe appeared behind him, blinking in the sunlight like an unearthed mole. Evidently, Jeff thought, Mrs. Perry's "no Timmy" edict didn't extend to the schoolyard.

Just then, Timmy's gaze snapped across the playground and met Jeff's.

In his reading about space travel, Jeff had learned about something called the Theory of Relativity. Relativity was supposedly the reason nobody could travel faster than light. Among other things, relativity stated that time and velocity were connected. The closer a spaceship came to flying at the speed of light, the more time would slow down for the astronauts inside. So when the astronauts came back to earth, only a few months might have passed for them—but they'd be greeted by their own great-great-great-great-grandchildren. Something like that. Time as Silly Putty, stretching and compressing.

Right now, Jeff felt relativity surround him. It seemed like everything in the playground accelerated to the speed of light. Moving so fast nothing seemed to move at all. Frozen in time.

Except Timmy and him.

Then Timmy shook his head with a disgusted expression on his face, and time snapped back into place. Timmy. Timmy, turning and strolling toward the most remote corner of the playground. Abe following like a well-trained puppy. They stopped where a tree leaned over the fence and tufts of crabgrass snarled the pea gravel. The usual lunchtime hangout spot of Captain Strange and Mr. Weird.

"Come on," Jeff said to Mike, and went crunching across the playground. He heard Mike following, and thought about the knights of old England going out to joust, their squires tagging along. He wondered if anybody was watching this.

Timmy saw him coming, crossed his arms and smiled.

Somehow, the smile did it. When Jeff was only a few feet away, the chain holding the wild thing inside him snapped. Jeff had a vague impression of knobby shoulders in the palms of his hands, the smug smile hovering in the air like a ghost . . . and then Timmy was sprawling on his back near the fence.

Abe gasped. Mike gasped.

Jeff stood over his old friend, feeling satisfied and horrified and slightly nauseous. How many times over the years had he tackled Timmy, wrestled with him, knocked him down? Thousands. But only when he was playing a tiger and Timmy a lion, or he a triceratops and Timmy a tyrannosaurus rex. Never before like this. Timmy looked up, face knotted in disbelief and anger. Somehow that only infuriated Jeff more. "I bet you think you're funny," he snarled.

Timmy scrambled to his feet. The back of his greased hair stood out as if his brains had exploded, and his narrow face was as red as cayenne pepper. "What's your problem, man?"

"You know what my problem is. Friday night's my problem."

Timmy seemed to relax. He brushed a hand over his hair. "Hey, that was your own fault. I invited you to go along. If you'd come out to the Big Tree and helped us like I asked, we'd all be in the land of Nod right now, not at this stupid school. I *asked* you."

This was so outrageous Jeff was stunned. "What are you *talking* about?"

"I was *this* close, Jeff." Timmy seemed to have forgotten being pushed; he leaned forward eagerly, thumb and forefinger extended, almost touching. "I was right *there,* on the doorstep . . . but I couldn't quite make it. I needed more help. I ended up . . . someplace else for a second. But I was *so close.*"

The wild thing inside Jeff strained ahead again. He took a step forward, bumping Timmy with his chest. Timmy looked surprised, then angry; he didn't retreat. "Don't give me this land of Nod crap, Kegler," Jeff said, swelling to his full height, half a head greater than Timmy's. "I *know* where you went Friday night."

For the first time, Timmy's gaze faltered. "What are you talking about?"

Jeff couldn't believe the denial. Before he knew it, Timmy was landing on his butt with a grunt, eyes jittering like they were mounted on springs.

"*Stop* it!" Abe screamed, but didn't move.

Jeff pointed a rigid finger at Timmy. "Don't you *ever* go near Gail again. Don't you *ever*, or you'll get a lot worse than that. Believe me."

Timmy stared back, eyes compressing to the thinnest of lines. "I'll go wherever I want, *Kemo Sabe.*"

"I'll break your neck if you do."

"I'll send the Nodkin after you." Almost a whisper, but intense. "They're my friends. They know who I am, and who *you* are. They'll rip you to pieces."

This was such a pathetic comment, Jeff's anger dropped away like a dud bomb. "Timmy, you're such an asshole loser."

"That," said an adult voice behind him, "will be enough of that."

CHAPTER EIGHTEEN

MARKERS

The memory faded as I drove into downtown Middlefield. It almost made me smile, even. Mrs. Edelstein had been the one to hear my cursing, and had given me my first and only detention. And this time Dad *had* grounded me for a week—except for football practice and that weekend's game.

Grounded. Now there was an ironic word, under the present circumstances. *Go back where you belong, man.*

Instead, I drove to Shady Acres Cemetery. Oddly, once I actually pulled through the arch-topped gate, the place didn't seem at all menacing. Old maple trees and bright fresh grass, rows of headstones and monuments, flowers and the drying stems of flowers. The trees were widely spaced, but so big and old their branches formed a continuous lacy canopy overhead. Dots of light dappled the ground like strategic spotlights pointing out graves of interest.

The lane serpentined through the cemetery, the grass on either side so closely cropped it looked like green tile. The headstones came in all different styles, from simple rectangular slabs to winged marble statues twelve feet tall. The older stones were weather softened like old bars of soap, their inscriptions blurred. I assumed that Fred's grave would be marked by a fairly conspicuous monument worthy of a local war hero. I drove deeper and deeper into the grounds, checking out dates on the stones visible from the road. When I started seeing graves of late 1960s vintage, I parked the car and climbed out.

It was pleasant back here. The air was almost cool in the freckled shade, plush with scents of grass, pollen and a whiff of water from White Lick Creek somewhere in the near distance.

I wasn't really sure why I was doing this. Although Fred had remained an acquaintance right up until I moved away from Middlefield, we'd stopped being really close by the end of the eighth grade. Just gone different directions, the way teenagers do. Still, he *had* been one of my best buddies during the years I kept dreaming about; maybe that was all that mattered. Or maybe I just wanted to spend time here because none of Shady Acres' residents were likely to wave a loaded revolver around.

I walked slowly across the grounds, scanning headstones, noticing that most of the graves were arranged in groups—family plots. It hadn't occurred to me that this might be the case, and I found the custom both quaint and absurd. Janice and I had always intended to be cremated and have our ashes spread at sea.

Now that I thought about it, a cemetery seemed an apt metaphor for human ambivalence about death. Timmy had once told me that the original purpose of headstones was to keep the dead from sitting up. Now they were more like anchors left by the dead in the world of the living. *Here I am.* I wondered if anyone, however pious, *really* believed in an afterlife.

The shade suddenly seemed less comforting, too cool. I thought I could hear White Lick Creek bubbling over its rocky bed; looking up, I saw a wall of trees not far away. The end of the cemetery.

Still walking, I almost tripped over a row of six identical markers. When I looked down, my gaze fell directly on the third one, and I blinked.

CHRIS WAGNER

1949–1970

The eldest son of the feared Wagner clan—dead at twenty-one. I wondered if he had been a Vietnam War casualty, too. Then I looked at the next stone:

VINCENT WAGNER

1951–1970

Vince had been the worst. One time he'd caught Timmy riding his bike by the railroad tracks, knocked him down and held his head against one of the rails as a freight train screamed closer . . .

The next day Vince had told everyone at school that Timmy had peed his pants like a baby.

The next headstone was Jerry Wagner's. He'd been my age, a genuine psycho-in-training. I remembered one time I was watching a toad hop down the sidewalk. Jerry ran up and stomped on it, scuffing its body into a bloody smear while he guffawed and pointed at my stricken face. According to the headstone, Jerry had also died in 1970.

So had the youngest boy, Steve.

And so had Mr. and Mrs. Wagner.

Wow, there must have been an accident, a major piece of bad luck for the Wagner clan. I couldn't conjure up much sympathy, though. Fate was rarely so fair.

Moving on, I found Fred's monument.

It wasn't nearly as grand as those of the victims of earlier wars, but it did have an emblem of two crossed rifles etched into its polished face, and the motto HE DIED THAT WE MIGHT LIVE MORE FREELY, and someone had planted a miniature American flag on the gravestone.

As I stood there, I thought again how little good reason there was for my being here. Certainly I didn't believe Fred was capable of observing me through some celestial telescope. The poor guy was dead. Gone, except as a memory. There was nothing I could do for him, nothing he could do for me.

But maybe now I'll stop hallucinating him.

The cemetery extended for another fifty yards before reaching the wall of trees. It wouldn't take me long to wander back there and see what was to be seen. For example, the graves of Gail's family. Assuming they were buried here. I still couldn't remember Gail's married name and had forgotten to ask her, but the grim truth was that it shouldn't be hard to find another family plot where all the dates of death were the same. Not that it was any of my business. Still, it wouldn't hurt to—

"Liiiiiiiiiiindyyyyyyyy. . ."

The voice, rolling unexpectedly through the quiet shadows, grabbed me like a hand and whirled me around.

"Liiiiiiiiindyyyyyyy . . . Heeeeeeere, Liiiiindyyyyy . . ."

The voice faded away. I couldn't see anybody. Well, what did I expect? The Mean Lady would be pushing eighty by now if she were still alive, and of course she could hardly still be trying to find her missing dog.

"Hey, you! Little boy!"

I whirled. Striding toward me out of the shadows was the woman I'd seen yesterday on Oak Lane: tight patterned pants, square-necked baggy blouse, dated hairstyle. She still carried the pink leash, dragging it over the ground as if it were itself some kind of pet. "Where's my dog?" she cried shrilly. In her left hand she clutched a gardening trowel, waving it like a weapon. "I know you know where my Lindy went, you bad little boy."

My mind reeled forward and back like a broken videotape player. Now I recognized her, sure I did. It was the Mean Lady herself, not pushing eighty at all but frozen in time, looking little different than she had in the 1960s. Or yesterday on Oak Lane. "You did something to my Lindy, didn't you?" she shouted. "You and your horrible friends." Striding through the headstones. Striding *through* the headstones. "You think I'm stupid? Well, I'll teach you. I'll teach you—" She slashed the air with the trowel.

I turned my back on her, closed my eyes. "You're not real," I said out loud in a steady voice. "You're not real. You're not real."

"Teach you . . ."

The skin on my back writhed, awaiting the agonizing arrival of the trowel. But nothing happened. I opened my eyes. Nobody there. Turned. Nobody there. Sunlight jingled gold coins across the grass.

"Well, well," I murmured. I felt like laughing. Dancing.

Maybe I should have tried telling Mike he wasn't real, either.

"Do you think it's going to rain tonight?" I asked.

"Hm?" Gail looked at me. We were parked at McDonald's again as the sun sank behind a distant ridge of clouds. Gail sat with her hands folded in her lap; this evening she hadn't even pretended to want a milkshake. Maybe her lack of appetite was why she'd turned down my offer to go into Indianapolis for a nice dinner.

She hadn't said much since we got here, just sat watching the passing teenagers. Still, I was happy to be with her. She looked very pretty in a loose white blouse and khaki shorts. The curves of her calves hadn't changed at all over the years.

I pointed at the distant clouds, a ragged purple wall low on the horizon. "Look at those thunderheads. Think we'll have a storm?"

She looked in the direction I was pointing, and the muscles of her face constricted briefly. "You never know around here . . . but probably not tonight."

"I'd kind of like to see a real thunderstorm again. It's been a long time."

"Not long enough," Gail murmured.

I was surprised. As I recalled, she'd loved the gaudy display of lightning and thunder; we used to cuddle together on the porch swing in front of her house, laughing and cringing.

"Anyway," Gail said, "if you really want a storm, all you have to do is wait awhile." She looked at me. "How long *are* you planning to stay, Jeff? Have you decided yet?"

"It depends . . . Today I took care of a couple of things I wanted to do, like visiting Mike Norris."

A beat passed. "How was he?"

I shrugged, answered obliquely: "What did he look like the last time you saw him?"

"About eighty pounds overweight. Big white beard. Dirty. Like a biker or something."

"He hasn't changed."

She shook her head sadly. "Did he even talk to you?"

"Sort of. Until he pulled a gun."

She stiffened violently. "A *gun?*"

"Yeah, but he aimed it at *himself*; threatened to blow his own brains out if I didn't leave."

"He was going to *kill* himself?"

"Yeah. I think he meant it, too."

"But—he can't *do* that!"

Her vehemence surprised me; I realized she hadn't shown this much emotion about anything since I'd been here. "It's okay," I said. "He didn't actually *do* it. But . . . you were right about the paranoia. Did you know he's got floodlights set up all over the place? It looks like a prison compound out there." I took a sip of Coke, then added in a perfectly even tone, "He even acted like Timmy Kegler was back in town, like he was tormenting him."

Over by the drive-through lane, two teenaged girls scampered up to the passenger side of a waiting car and leaned through the window, their pert backsides waving to the parking lot. Gail said,

"You don't suppose . . . you don't suppose Mike feels guilty about the way we treated Timmy back in the old days, do you? Maybe that's why he's seeing things now."

I almost laughed, even though I'd often entertained the same thought about myself in the past few days. Hearing it uttered out loud made it seem blissfully cockeyed. "Junior high was a long time ago, Gail," I said. "And none of us did anything bad to Timmy. We just grew apart. It happens."

"But Timmy blamed all of us. Remember that night at the Fall Festival?"

"Yeah," I said uncomfortably. "Well, to Timmy we were all like actors in his personal fantasy. His problem was he didn't want to grow up."

The two girls by the car started laughing, heads tossing artfully. They looked marvelously happy, flawlessly *alive.*

Gail was watching them, too. "Sometimes I think growing up is very overrated," she said softly.

Although Jeff always showered in the locker room after football practice, he liked to take a second shower at home before going to bed. It was an opportunity to relax and think. Tonight, as the hot spray beat on him, he thought about Timmy and the confrontation in the playground. *I'll send the Nodkin after you. They know who you are. They'll rip you to pieces.*

Jesus. How could that little freak have ever been a *friend?*

Jeff squirted an emerald lump of Prell into his hand. He'd been letting his hair grow longer since summer. Nothing as extreme as the way the Beatles wore theirs—Mom and Dad would flip out if he tried that—but it had gotten long enough to part on the side and let hang halfway to his eyebrows in front. "Lather, rinse, and repeat," were the instructions on the shampoo tube, and that's what he did, religiously. He was in the middle of the second lathering when he realized someone was watching him.

He froze, fingers buried in his hair, lather streaming over his closed eyelids. He couldn't see anything, or hear over the rumble of water. Still, that feeling . . . maybe he'd felt an unusual vibration, or a shift in the air temperature. Sure, that was it; Mom must have entered the bathroom to put some clean towels in the closet or something.

Except she wouldn't do that. And besides, he had locked the door.

So why was he certain someone had pulled the shower curtain aside and was staring at him from inches away?

He forced himself to keep scrubbing his hair. Talk about stupid feelings. This was what he got for listening to Les Williams tell all about the shower scene in that old movie *Psycho*, which Jeff had wanted to see when it came out but Mom and Dad wouldn't let him. Les Williams claimed to have seen it, though, naked lady in the shower and all. He'd described how the knife plunged down again and again, and the blood spiraled into the drain . . .

Jeff refused to open his eyes, refused to look. But he couldn't help remembering what Gail had told him last Saturday, on the playground, as she clutched him so tightly: . . . *I saw something in my mirror. Something moving. A shadow. And all of a sudden, there was Timmy* . . .

In the darkness behind his eyelids, Jeff pictured Timmy's face thrust toward him, greasy hair glittering with a dew of thrown-off water. And a big knife—no, a sword—rising high . . .

You can't let your imagination run away with you, he told himself sternly. *What do you think, Timmy sneaked in at dinnertime and spent all evening hiding in the linen closet, waiting for you? Besides, he's too much of a chicken to stab anyone. So stop thinking about it. Think about good things.*

So of course he thought about Gail. Remembered the way she had felt pressed up against him in the playground. He shifted his body slightly, letting the water strike his penis more directly. His mouth hung open, his head drooped. Streams of water rattled and drummed against the backs of his ears.

Through the racket, he heard a knowing giggle.

Choking, he whirled, wiping water out of his eyes with one arm. Something moved beyond the shower curtain.

He jerked the curtain aside. The air swirled with steam. As he stumbled out of the tub, he glimpsed movement to one side and whirled toward it, fists half-raised.

A leering face hung in the mist. He started to punch it, but caught himself just before his fist connected. Almost slipped and fell.

It was his own face. His own face reflected in the bathroom mirror.

A knock at the door. "Jeff?" his mother called. "Jeff, are you alright, honey?"

I blinked, focused my attention on the telephone. "Yeah, Mom, I'm fine. This is a lousy connection, that's all." The one with my wife's home in California hadn't been much better, not that it mattered. I'd hung up on a strange male voice.

"Goodness, it's even worse than last night," Mom said. "Like you're fading away. Are you still in Chicago?"

I'd only told her I was in the Midwest; Chicago was an assumption on her part. "Still out here," I said. "Working away."

"How's it going?"

I thought about Gail. This evening when I'd said good night to her on her front porch, she'd hugged me back with some real force and said, "I'll be here tomorrow evening, if you want to come by." Which made me wonder what she did with her mornings.

"Everything's going fine," I told Mom. "How about there?"

"Great, just great. The Farleys are going to have a party to . . . their . . . wee . . ." Static rose up like fire, consuming half her words.

"Mom?" I cried.

". . . ly hear . . . be a storm . . . your way."

"Probably," I shouted over the raspy crackling. I remembered the masses of clouds that had blotted out the sunset earlier. Obviously, even with modern fiber optics and satellite linkups, thunderheads could play hell with telephone reception. "Well, I'll let you go, then."

". . . ear."

I hung up and leaned back on the bed, feeling vaguely guilty about my sense of relief that I hadn't had to listen to Dad inhale and exhale over the phone.

Think good thoughts.

So I did. I started thinking about Terri, wondering how she was doing, and I fell asleep thinking about Gail's smooth hips, her smiling eyes.

CHAPTER NINETEEN

PORCH SWING

Her lips were soft, her tongue strong and probing, rough and slick at the same time. Her body felt hot even through two sets of clothes. The porch swing grunted and groaned.

Second base, Jeff thought for the hundredth time. *Tonight I try for second base.*

He'd contemplated the possibility all day at school, even thought about it at odd moments during the football game with Pittsboro, which the Wolfpack almost lost. Jeff, distracted, hadn't played his best. First base was kissing, especially French kissing. He'd reached that base long ago. But second base . . .

An October wind bustled around the porch, first balmy, then chilly, then balmy again, rattling with the scent of dry leaves and moonlight. The wind made him feel itchy inside.

Second base . . .

Earlier, Gail had modeled her Halloween costume for him, the Maid Marian outfit with its long skirt and tight bodice. Hint of cleavage. A spray of freckles there. Beautiful cleft . . .

The chains holding the swing chirped like lazy crickets. Jeff and Gail had made out a lot here, but despite what Jeff hinted to the guys in the locker room, he had never tried to get to second base, never even dared leave first. He'd been too horrified that Gail would slap him, scream for her dad, hate him forever.

But tonight he had to try. Just had to. Maybe it was the wild autumn wind. Or the memory of that glimpse of cleavage. Or maybe it was just that he *had to do it;* his hands demanded it, his dreams demanded it, his whole body *screamed* that he try.

He'd heard how to get to second base from Mike's big brother

Joe, who was sixteen and might even have spoken from experience. The trick, according to Joe, was to make it all seem accidental: "Like, you're making out and you've got your hand on the girl's back, see. You kind of let your palm slide around in a circle. Girls love that. Then you let the circle get bigger until your hand is kind of on her side, under her arm. You're halfway to second base."

Well, Jeff's hand had begun the spiral around Gail's back an eternity ago. Now it was moving along her side, feeling the faint ripples of her ribs under the blouse, the taut side panel of her bra. She pulled herself even closer to him, her tongue probing his, her hot breath snagging his out of his nostrils.

Still, he hesitated on the cusp of stealing second, burning inside, dizzy with desire, absolutely terrified. An inch below ecstasy or disaster, his hand. One inch. Now, according to Joe, you just let your thumb kind of wander up. Let it nudge . . . let it . . .

. . . oh, softness, firmness, wonderful resilience. He couldn't breathe at all. Gail was gasping through her nose, blowing her sweet exhalations into his nostrils as if to breathe for them both. From the living room on the other side of the wall came the tinny sound of voices—Mr. and Mrs. Rohr were watching *That Was the Week That Was* on TV. Jeff heard Mr. Rohr's throaty chuckle, seemingly inches away.

It didn't matter. At this point, Jeff couldn't have stopped himself if Mr. Rohr had come out to sit on the porch and clean a shotgun. Jeff's hand moved up, cupping full wonder.

Never had he felt anything like it. Not like a water balloon, as Joe had described it. Lighter than that. And not like Silly Putty, which was kind of what the exposed bulges in the Sears catalog brassiere ads reminded him of. This was unique. Firm, springy, *alive.* His nerves tingled with the secret miracle of it. He wondered what would happen if he slipped his hand under her blouse, got that much closer to—

Gail gasped in shock and clawed at his hand, pushing it away while simultaneously hauling herself closer to him. Jeff's body went watery with terror. Had her father stepped onto the porch? Was her mother peeking through the window? Was—

Then he realized Gail was looking into the yard. He did, too. Timmy stood beside the porch, glaring at them.

Jeff started to leap up, awkward on the rocking, twisting swing,

Gail clinging to him, before he realized it wasn't Timmy at all. It was a long frond on one of Mrs. Rohr's shrubs, which she refused to "torture into geometric shapes." Something about the way the moonlight hit the frond had made it look like Timmy for a second. Exactly like Timmy.

Gail made a ragged giggling sound and slumped back. She must have figured the truth out at the same moment Jeff did. He sat down again, but he didn't laugh. He was quivering all over.

"I'm sorry," Gail whispered, straightening her sweater. "I thought I saw Timmy watching us."

"Me, too." Jeff kicked at the shrub, but it was too far away. For a moment he wondered if Timmy was at home right now, sleeping, or appearing to sleep. Pushing the thought away, he turned back to Gail and started to kiss her again. She turned her face to the side. "I can't, Jeff. I'm sorry."

"I think it's finally going to rain tonight."

"Huh?" I started, interrupting the smooth rhythm of the porch swing. Gail and I had been sitting here for about an hour, talking a little, being quiet a lot. Evening shadows stretched across the front yard, blotting up the last of the sunlight. Gail's profile was framed by the smooth curtain of her hair. I hoped she didn't turn to look in my direction for a moment; my face felt far too hot.

This porch. This swing. The firmness of her young breast . . .

But her attention seemed focused on the house across the street. Or rather, on the sky above the house. Looking closely, I saw a wall of clouds rising up, a shade or two darker than the violet evening sky. "That storm you were wondering about," Gail said. "It looks like you're going to get your wish tonight."

I peered more closely at the clouds. They seemed so pale and pretty . . . yet now I noticed their edges, curdled like cottage cheese. They meant that, deep inside, cauldrons of heat and humidity were boiling mightily. "Think it's going to be a big one?" I asked.

"Yes." She shivered and crossed her arms as if hugging herself.

"What's wrong?"

"Nothing. I just . . . I don't like thunderstorms anymore."

Her profile was turning two-dimensional against the dimming

sky. Something in its chiseled reserve kept me from asking the obvious question.

"So," she said after a minute. "What did you do in cosmopolitan Middlefield today?"

"Well . . . for one thing, I tried to go to the library. I used to love that place. I can't believe they're moving it into a new building."

"It won't change that much," Gail said. "Nothing around here ever does, believe me."

"You seem awfully bitter about Middlefield," I said. "If you don't like it, why do you stay?"

She hesitated, then swung toward me, mouth open, as if about to say something crucial. Then she hesitated again, shivered, and turned her attention back toward the clouds. "Sometimes," she sighed, "you just do what you have to do."

I hated to see her sinking toward melancholy again. "Speaking of change," I said, "after the library I went over to Railroad Street to look at Timmy's place. Did you know they tore out the whole street?"

"Those old houses were a fire hazard. And after what happened to the Wagners—"

"The Wagners? What happened?" I asked, remembering the family plot.

"Oh, their house burned down in 1970. Evidently the gas stove was left on, and it blew up. The place was gone in an hour; fire trucks came from all over the county to keep the whole town from burning down."

"Wow," I said. "Well, leave it to the Wagners to endanger every—"

"They deserved it." She paused. "Look at the clouds."

The storm had piled itself higher in the last few minutes, or moved closer, or both. It looked much more three-dimensional now, all knots and outcroppings. A craggy purple mountain with sunbeams streaming over its shoulder. Swallows careened through the air like boomerangs.

"Beautiful," I said, although I was no longer so sure I wanted this storm to come any closer. The air felt thick as broth.

"Remember how we used to try to see things in the clouds?" Gail asked.

"Yeah."

"You and Timmy were always the best at it."

I snorted. "That's because we'd pretend we saw things even if we didn't."

"Really?"

"I know I did. Every game we played was a competition."

Her face was a perfect silhouette now, but I thought I saw her smile. "I remember those games. Monsters and wild animals and all. You guys had quite an imagination."

"It was mostly Timmy. He always came up with the weirdest—"

"That's not how I remember it. You did your share of playacting, too."

"Well . . . maybe. But the difference is, I grew out of it and Timmy didn't."

"What about ghost stories? You guys were really into ghosts, too, I remember."

"I grew out of that, too."

"You used to think *this* house was haunted. Remember?"

I glanced behind us, at the windows, at the blackness behind the windows. "Gee, I can't imagine why."

She giggled. The sound made me feel good; I'd begun to think she'd lost her laugh forever. "Remember," she said, "you'd go, 'Aren't you afraid to sleep in that place?' "

"—And you'd go, 'Why, do you want to spend the night?' " I finished, surprised she'd brought that up. She was facing me now, her knee almost touching mine, but with the twilight behind her, her features were a blur onto which any expression could be sculpted. I chose contentment.

Unfortunately her next words didn't go with the face I'd selected: "I've been thinking about Mike."

At that moment, the last speck of sunlight died from the battlements of the storm front. Not a puff of wind stirred the air. "What about him?" I asked.

"Do you think *he* believes in ghosts?"

"You mean . . . like in Timmy coming back to haunt him?"

"Yes."

"Well . . . it occurred to me."

"But you don't think it's possible."

"*Possible?*" A vivid memory arose in my mind: Gail and me in Topp's Theater, watching some cheesy horror movie. While shrieks arise from adjoining seats, Gail giggles helplessly and says over and over, "That's so *fake.*"

"Are you saying *you* think it's possible Timmy's a ghost?" I asked.

She didn't reply for a moment. "Let's just say . . . I've come to believe in life after death."

I had to laugh. "We've really reversed roles, haven't we?"

"I've learned a few things since I was young," she said.

"Well, so have I." Now there was anger in my voice. I couldn't help it.

The swing creaked as she leaned toward me. "What happened to you, Jeff? Why don't you believe in anything anymore?"

"I do believe in things. I believe in life, and work, and my daughter. *Real* things, not superstitions."

She said nothing.

I sighed. Waited for the storm to arrive. Then the words came pouring out: "For years I went through all the usual motions—church, saying grace at dinner, all that. I sort of vaguely believed there was a God, and he'd take care of you if you were good. Then, a few years ago, my father had a stroke—you remember my dad, a truly good guy, always active, always helping out. I prayed for the stroke to not be too bad. That's not much of a request as prayers go, right? But Dad ended up . . . very bad. Most of his brain died, in fact. In fact, he's a vegetable. He sits in a wheelchair. When I asked his doctor how long he might go on like that, the guy smiled and said, 'He should enjoy a full and natural lifespan.' A full and natural lifespan!" Thunder rolled in the distance. "Dad would *hate* to be like he is now, you know. But of course now he has no choice. And of course Mom insists on taking care of him herself, as if he might recover someday. That's *two* lives ruined, and for what? So she can read him Bible bedtime stories?" Taking a deep breath, I said, "Anyway, I don't believe in ghosts, an afterlife, any of that. In my opinion, all that stuff is just wishful thinking from people who can't accept there's no good reason for anything."

"Life's not fair, eh?" Gail asked softly.

"Obviously not."

Out in the distant gloom, a frog chirped. Then another. The sound was oddly comforting; I could almost believe the marshy wasteland behind Fred's house was still there. In the indigo sky, the thunderheads continued their growth, obliterating the first evening stars. The storm's face was dull pewter, its flat belly as black as an old griddle. The silence made me nervous. "See?" I asked shakily. "If there was a God, he would have just sent a lightning bolt to strike some humility in me."

Gail's hand wafted down on top of mine, warm as day. "I'm sorry about your father," she said. "And that I upset you." She smiled. "But this is more like the old you. You used to be so passionate about everything."

"I could say the same thing about you." I looked into her eyes and turned my palm up to meet hers. She didn't pull away.

Janice and I had built our patio and swimming pool to provide an environment like this. There had been none.

A dull flicker of light danced at the horizon. I looked closer. It happened again—lightning playing tag deep inside the thunderheads. *That's really dragons fighting*—Timmy's words.

Fuck Timmy. Forget Timmy.

No more thunder, though. The air remained thick and motionless, as if the whole world was holding its breath.

"Maybe you're right about religion," Gail said softly. "But that doesn't mean there's no life after death. Just because we don't understand how something works, that doesn't mean it's not real."

"I guess that's true," I said. Poor Gail. She had every reason to insist on an afterlife, some place where her family had gone to wait for her. I couldn't blame her.

The lightning finally broke out of the clouds, chasing itself back and forth across the face of the storm. A few seconds later a soft rumble riffled the air. "Listen," I said.

More lightning plucked at the clouds. I tried to remember the formula for calculating the distance of a lightning strike by timing its thunder, but couldn't. Like so many childhood skills, it was gone.

But when the thunder did come, it sounded stronger than before, more insistent. "Well," I said, "you were right. We're going to get stormed on for sure." Her palm felt slightly moist in mine.

As we sat watching, a thick crutch of lightning jabbed down into a distant field. Gail shuddered so violently the swing's chains squealed. Her fingers clamped on mine with painful force.

"Gail?" I turned toward her as thunder shook the air around us.

She didn't look away from the clouds. "My family died in a storm."

I swallowed. Didn't speak. Didn't move.

Despite the rigidity of her body, her voice was unemotional. "We were driving down from Fishers to visit my parents. All of us —Bob, our son and daughter, and their spouses. Bette was pregnant; two months. Can you believe that? I was going to be a grandmother. It was storming really bad, lightning and thunder and so much rain you could barely see the road. All of a sudden, there was a car in front of us, on the wrong side of the road. I was driving. I . . . we . . ."

In my mind, I pictured it—*A car and a minivan lie in the ditch in steaming embrace. A man collapses in a bloody heap on the highway* . . . The swing was shaking, rocking. I squeezed Gail's hand, although whether to comfort her or myself, I wasn't certain. *That was just an hallucination.*

She squeezed back. "I can't remember everything. I just remember finding out I was the only one. The only one." She turned her face to me. You can call what happened an *accident,* but it wasn't. There's a reason I'm still here, Jeff. Maybe . . ."

"What?"

"Look. Here we are, you and me. We wouldn't be together again if my family was still alive. Did you ever think of that?"

I was stunned. Surely she didn't consider this a fair trade—her entire family in exchange for an old boyfriend who had dumped her like an old sock when she wouldn't put out for him? "How long ago was the accident?" I asked.

"Last March. The middle of March. The ides of March . . ."

Now I understood. The crash had happened only a few months ago; her wounds were still fresh, and she was searching for any emotional bandage flexible enough to fit over the horrible wound. I felt sad for her, but honored she'd chosen me for the purpose. I squeezed her hand again, felt the texture and shape of the years in it. So much had changed since we were young. And yet she was right—here we were again, just the two of us, sitting on the porch swing and holding hands. As if it had always been meant to be.

Lightning ripped up and down the length of the storm front in a bright, childish scribble. I cringed in anticipation of the thunder, and felt Gail's shoulder press against mine.

"Jeff, can I make a confession? Even with Bob and a wonderful marriage, from time to time I've wondered what would have happened if I'd said 'yes' to you that night."

I started to put my arm around her before I realized what I was doing and halted. God, how long had I wanted this night to happen, wanted it deep inside, in that hidden place that forgets nothing?

For the first time, I felt a puff of air roam onto the porch. It smelled of cold water—a scout of stronger winds and wetness to come.

"Jeff," Gail said as the thunder passed, "will you stay?"

It took my breath away, but not as much as the sudden press of her lips against mine. The old taste hit me, and the warmth, and a wild feeling I hadn't felt since the first few years of my marriage. I threw my arms around her, pulled her close. The swing pitched, yawed, rolled. I realized Gail was wearing her old perfume. It filled my head, swirled into my brain.

Somewhere beyond the porch, the clouds kept expanding. More lightning. More thunder. Gail's body felt soft and fiery in my arms. *Second base!* a voice far down inside me yodeled. *Go for second!*

"Gail," I whispered.

Her lips crushed against mine. Then, suddenly, she was standing beside the swing, one hand stretched toward me. Beyond her, raindrops began to spatter onto the road and lawn. Dizzy and disoriented, I almost toppled off the swing onto my knees.

"Come inside," Gail murmured. "It's about time, don't you think?"

STEALING HOME

CHAPTER TWENTY

UNDER COVER

"I can't believe it." Mike Norris glared at the corkboard wall at the rear of the booth, where balloons hung in clusters like huge glossy beetles. Three plastic-shafted darts protruded from narrow gaps between balloons. "I missed *every time!* I can't believe it!"

Jeff laughed. He had to laugh pretty loudly just to hear himself over the noise of the crowd. It seemed like everyone in Middlefield had come to the Fall Festival this year. The junior high gymnasium, which had less than half the capacity of the new high school facility, was jammed. The tile walls and vaulted metal roof reflected every sound back into an almost solid block. To make matters worse, the PA system was playing music at such a tinny volume you couldn't tell one song from another.

The crowd oozed in a vaguely clockwise flow around a horseshoe-shaped queue of booths set up on the basketball court. Hand-lettered signs proclaimed: KISSES 25¢; BOB FOR APPLES; WIN A GOLDFISH; RING TOSS. At one end of the room, a row of tables displayed baked goods and craft items. Overhead, suspended paper bats and witches twirled slowly on updrafts of human heat.

Only half the gym's lights were on, providing just enough illumination to prevent necking while preserving the gloomy atmosphere that made even bad Halloween costumes look passable. Mike had used the poor lighting as an excuse for missing the first two balloons, and Jeff had laughed at him then, too. It didn't help that Mike's costume alone was pretty silly—a pair of faded blue jeans, a green shirt, a trident made out of an old broom handle and cardboard, and a paper crown. He was supposed to be Neptune.

Now Mike tried a different tack. "It's these darts! They're so cheap, they don't even fly straight!"

"Then how come *I* hit three balloons?" Jeff asked.

"Because you're lucky."

Jeff just laughed again. It was true; he *was* lucky. After all, he was here with Gail, and the two of them were the best-looking couple in the place.

Mom had done a great job on his Robin Hood costume, complete down to the felt hat and the curly-toed shoes. Actually these were just felt coverings over his sneakers, but on Halloween night, looks were everything. The tunic, belted at the waist, made his shoulders appear six inches wider than normal. Instead of tights— which he wouldn't be caught dead in—he wore green sweatpants. His longbow was fiberglass rather than wood, but the arrows were real, even if they had no points and were glued into the quiver. He'd painted a thin, Errol Flynn-style moustache on his upper lip with Mom's eyebrow liner.

And Gail . . . Gail wore her Maid Marian dress with its cleavage-forming bodice. She had woven her hair into a thick braid that curved down one side of her neck. A tall conical hat trailed a gauzy train. Somebody was bound to yank that off before the night was over, Jeff thought regretfully.

"Mikey . . ." Mike's girlfriend, Amy Tucker, tugged at Neptune's sleeve. Although the top of her head barely reached his shoulder, she looked dazzlingly mature in a sequined leotard, its fake fish tail dangling to her heels. Jeff had spent quite a bit of time glancing between her and Gail, and had to admit Amy's tits were bigger. But that was okay. Gail had other special qualities.

"Come on, Mikey," Amy whined. "Buy me some caramel corn."

Mike's shoulders rose and fell in what had to be a sigh, although it was inaudible. "Okay, okay." He glowered at the balloons again, then turned to Jeff. "See you at the costume contest?"

"You bet." Jeff leaned toward Gail. "Well, what do you want to do next?"

"How about you win me a goldfish?"

"Piece of cake."

"Wait. Earth. Ling." The voice, a harsh mechanical rasp, was so unexpected it made Jeff jump. He turned and found himself facing a robot. His eyes widened. Ever since the TV show *Lost in Space* had debuted last month, robots had been all the rage. Already to-

night he'd seen a dozen off-the-shelf mechanical-man costumes
. . . but this one was different, this one was *great*. Aluminum-
foil-covered cardboard boxes for head and body; some kind of sil-
ver-painted corrugated tubing for arms; cardboard cylinders, also
painted silver, encasing the legs. The eyes were dark glass circles,
the mouth a small speaker grille. The best touch was a row of
flashing lights across the chest. A real work of art.

Timmy? Jeff wondered. No, Timmy would never come to the
Fall Festival. It could be anybody under there. Even the voice, elec-
tronically modified, was impossible to identify. There went first
prize in the costume contest.

Gail leaned down to peer into the sunglass-lens eyes. "Who is
that?"

"*Rob. Bee. The. Ro. Bot.*"

She laughed. "No, I mean who's *in* there?"

"*Rob. Bee. The. Ro. Bot.*"

"Okay, okay. Great costume, Robby."

The robot bowed slowly at the waist. Jeff had the feeling that
whoever was in there was peering down the top of Gail's dress.
"Come on, Gail," Jeff said, "let's get out of here."

"*Wait.*" The robot straightened again. One of its arms, which
terminated in a black glove, moved jerkily to point at the wall of
balloons. "*I. Challenge. Robin. Hood. To. A. Contest.*"

Jeff's eyebrows rose. The guy looked like he could barely move,
let alone throw a dart. "What kind of contest?"

"*Best. Five. Out. Of. Seven. Rounds. The. Winner. Gives. Her.
The. Prize.*" He pointed at Gail.

Jeff grinned again. "In other words, I can't lose. You first."

The robot turned and paid for his darts. Actually, money was
not exchanged at the Fall Festival; everything was bought with
strips of tickets, four for a quarter, which were purchased at the
entrance. At the darts booth, you got three throws per ticket. If
you popped a balloon on all three tries, you won a wooden toy
clown strung between two rods. When the rods were flexed, the
clown spun around and around like a high-bar acrobat. Jeff had
already gotten one of those for Gail. Six burst balloons in a row
won you a small stuffed animal; nine balloons won a big stuffed
bear. Jeff wouldn't mind getting one of those for Gail, too.

The booth attendant was Mrs. Trevor, a stout red-haired
woman, wife of the high school shop teacher. She was dressed as a

gypsy in long skirts, with a bandanna tied around her head. "Tell you what, boys," she said. "Whoever wins gets *two* big bears. Would you like a pair of them, honey?" This was directed at Gail.

Gail shrugged, but Jeff could tell she was excited. "Sure."

The robot clumsily gripped a dart in its left hand, then leaned back, arm rising stiffly as if making a Nazi salute.

Timmy's left-handed, Jeff thought. But so were lots of people. Even Abe.

The robot hesitated, then its entire torso flexed forward in an aborted bow. The arm followed. The dart wobbled through the air.

Bang! A yellow balloon fell limp.

"Pretty good," Jeff grunted. Talk about lucky; how could the guy even see?

"Thank. You." The robot clutched its second dart and reared back again. Threw.

Bang.

Jeff's eyebrows rose. Very lucky.

The third dart reeled through the air.

Pop!

"Ooooh," Mrs. Trevor said. "Nice throwing."

Gail batted her lashes at Jeff. "Well? Are you going to let this tin can beat you?"

"Tin. Can? Watch. It. Maid. Marian."

Gail laughed, gray-green eyes sparkling.

"Stand aside." Jeff handed over a ticket. As he weighed one of the darts in his hand, he became acutely conscious of the eager stares of Gail, Mrs. Trevor, the robot and a few passersby.

A shocking thought struck him: *What if I lose?* He shrugged it off. Ten feet. Who couldn't hit a balloon with a dart at ten feet? Except for Mike, that was.

He took a deep breath, then leaned forward and tossed the dart.

Pop!

And the next. *Bang!*

Grinning at Gail, he lobbed the third dart.

Thump. It landed squarely between the two balloons.

"Nice. Try. Earthling," said the robot.

Gail paused at the front door. "Do you remember where the key is?" she asked. I blinked, then smiled and fished a key out from under the doormat. Only in a small town like Middlefield would somebody actually leave a spare key so poorly concealed.

We entered the foyer, where the air smelled stuffy and dense, as if under pressure. Up the stairs we went. Into Gail's room. Not the master bedroom, but *her* room, the one she had used as a girl. She turned on no lights. Lightning burst outside one window, then the other, making shadows flee back and forth. The room hadn't changed much in twenty-five years. There was the double bed with the daisies stenciled across the headboard; the dresser; the vanity; the desk. Shelves exhibiting blown-glass birds and plastic horses. Gail's parents must have kept the room this way. Why not? Gail was an only child, like me.

I found myself staring at the desk. Once upon a time, a picture of me had stood there. It was gone now, of course. I could imagine her slamming it into a trash can, the way I had Janice's.

Gail turned toward me in the leaping semidarkness. So slim and smooth, she could have been sixteen years old.

"I hope your parents don't catch us," I whispered, barely forcing my voice past the throbbing lump in my throat.

I couldn't tell if she heard me or not. Her fingers moved down the front of her blouse. It fell open, revealing a bra so white it seemed almost fluorescent. Then the bra, too, was gone, and I saw the nipples I had once touched as if they were gems. Her slacks collapsed to the floor.

A moment later she was lying on the bed. The window above the headboard stood open; the curtains soared like angels, and rain-smell poured in along with blinding pulses of light. It occurred to me that I'd never seen Gail naked all at once before. A breast, a thigh, stomach—but never the entirety. Her body formed a long flowing ridge on the bed. She lay motionless while I took off my clothes. Was she watching me? What did she think?

When I touched her shoulder, she gasped. Her skin felt hot and tight under my hand. I lay beside her. Saw her eyes in a flash of lightning; they were wide and glistening, overflowing with some emotion—joy, I hoped.

"Did you ever think," she whispered, "that this *had* to be? Did you ever think that?"

"I'm beginning to," I said, and realized I meant it completely. I touched her where she was softest. She clutched my hand with hers, trembling.

I was too. This felt like my first time in bed with a woman. This felt like the most important time.

"Jeff—" she said, but I covered her mouth with mine.

"Come on, Jeff," Gail said. The group of spectators around the booth had grown appreciably larger in the last few minutes. "Let's go. I don't want a stupid stuffed animal, anyway."

Jeff scowled, a dart clutched between his fingers. This was the seventh and final match, and he was down by two balloons. If he missed this time, the contest was over.

"Please, Jeff. Let's go."

It occurred to him that Gail was trying to help him save face. That infuriated him. Didn't she think he could win? Didn't she have *faith* in him?

He glanced sidelong at Robby the Robot. *Was* it Timmy in there? He still wasn't sure.

"I'm not finished yet," he said to Gail, and concentrated on the balloons. There were a lot fewer of them now, more gaps. He aimed at a red balloon, forcing himself not to think about Gail, or the spectators, or even his opponent. Just that single balloon. Big and ripe, transparent. His arm came back, then forward. Wrist snapping. Dart flying.

Thump. The red balloon danced to one side without popping.

Jeff barely held back a curse. The audience sighed and murmured, except for one vampire couple who tittered.

Jeff whirled toward the robot, wishing he could wrench its head off, see who was under there. "Best seven out of nine," he said. "Come on. Winner gets all the other guy's tickets."

A long pause. The lights on the robot's chest cycled in smooth, regular pulses, left to right. Jeff saw his own reflection, shrunken and warped, in the eye lenses.

Gail tugged on his sleeve. "Come on, Jeff. It's just a game. Let him give me the bears and we'll go."

Jeff didn't look at her. "Come on," he said to the robot. "Seven out of nine. Come on." *Come on, Timmy.*

"*All. Right,*" the robot intoned. "*Best. Seven. Out. Of. Nine. Winner. Takes. All.*"

"Me first this time," Jeff said, and ripped off a ticket. He only had about a dozen left, anyway.

"This is fun," Mrs. Trevor said as she handed over the three darts. "A real duel."

Gail jerked on Jeff's sleeve. "I want a goldfish, Jeff. Come on, let's go over there before they're all gone."

"Just a minute." She *was* trying to help him save face. He'd show her. All of them. He raised his first dart.

She made an exasperated sound. "Well, *I'm* going. See you when you're finished." In a swirl of satin, she turned and pushed through the spectators.

Jeff hesitated, then decided he could always make up with her later, win her a hundred goldfish if she wanted them. But right now . . .

He threw. Threw. And threw.

Pop. Pop. Pop.

The crowd applauded.

Moving jerkily, the robot collected a new clutch of darts, chose one, took aim. Jeff struggled with the urge to scream, to jump up and down, to do anything distracting. He just held his breath.

Pop!

Bang!

Pop!

The spectators applauded again, even more loudly. *Damn!* Jeff thought. The guy *was* a robot. This wasn't fair. In that costume, nobody could see his face, read his reactions, observe his uncertainty. No wonder he was so calm. Confident. *Arrogant.*

It had to be Timmy.

Concentrate.

Jeff tossed a dart. *Bang.*

Another. *Bang.*

Carefully, carefully, a third: *Bang.*

He leaned back, nodding slightly at the applause of the crowd. Sweat darkened the band of his jaunty cap.

The robot flexed its fingers before laying down a ticket for three more darts, and Jeff smiled to himself. Nerves. Nerves at last. Too bad Gail wasn't here to see what was about to happen.

He glanced over at the Fish Toss game, which consisted of a wide table crowded with little globes of water, each containing a single goldfish. The contestants tossed ping-pong balls at the globes. If one landed in the water, the winner took that particular fish home in a waterproof cardboard box. It was a simple game, almost a sure thing.

Bang. He started as the robot threw his first dart. Turned back in time to see the second one fly.

Bang.

And then the third.

Thump. A balloon quivered, settled.

The crowd went "Oooooooooh" in disappointment. Jeff couldn't suppress a grin. "One more round," he said.

"*May. Be,*" the robot droned. "*I'll. Go. First. This. Time.*"

"Be my guest." Jeff glanced back toward the Fish Toss game. Gail stood at the barrier, taking careful underhand aim with a ping-pong ball. The tip of her tongue poked out from the corner of her mouth.

Her arm had just started its forward swing when the gymnasium went black.

CHAPTER TWENTY-ONE

LIGHTS OUT

Third base! a voice shouted inside me as I kissed my way down Gail's body. She gasped, arched her back. My mouth found the softness between her legs, like pudding. She writhed, legs flopping back and forth the way I'd imagined they would even before I'd known of lips and lips, tongue and clitoris.

Somehow we reversed positions and the outlines of my adolescent fantasies were colored in by her mouth, soft, and her teeth, gently harsh. At last I pulled her up and rolled her onto her back, poised above her. Her mouth hung half-open, her eyes glimmered. "Please," she whispered, and I slipped inside her just as the house shook to a tremendous blast of thunder. I almost laughed in shock and joy.

The shaking went on, and the thunder, and the lightning. When Gail cried out, I could barely hear her. Or myself. But I could feel us. I could feel everything at a level I hadn't dreamt of for years. Decades.

We lay together in a blanket of our own heat, the dying thunder of our hearts melding with the real thunder, which was rolling away now, fading.

"Jeff . . ." Gail said. "How long do you plan to stay in Middlefield?"

I stared at the ceiling and the afterglow of lightning throbbing there. Smiled a little. "Longer than I'd expected to, that's for sure."

"Could I ask you a question?"

"Sure."

"If you found out you had to stay forever . . . if you could never go back to your old life . . . would you mind?"

On the ceiling, barely visible, a waterstain formed a shape like the faces on Mount Rushmore, minus George Washington. "That's a tough one," I said. "I mean, my daughter's in California . . . my job . . . my whole life, really." I rolled toward her. "What about you? Would you consider coming to California? I mean, you don't—" I caught my words. Saying *You don't have anything keeping you here* was too blunt, too crude. "You should try it," I finished lamely. "It might be good for you to get away from here, you know?"

Her hands closed tightly over mine. "When the time is right," she said, "we *will* get out of here. And we'll never look back."

We, I thought. *We'll* get out of here.

"But for now," she said, "I can't leave. I just can't."

"Then I'll stay, too." The words leaped out on their own, and made me feel almost giddy. Such a reckless, adolescent idea. Such a perfect idea. "I'll stay until you're ready to go."

"You will? . . . Really?"

"Yes. And I'll tell you why."

"Why?"

"Because I love you, and I always have."

Her eyes widened. She hurled herself at me, covered my body with hers. Sobbing.

I held her tighter than I'd held anything else in my life.

For a minute or two Jeff couldn't see a thing. There were only sounds—shouts of surprise and excitement which quickly transformed into nervous laughter and uneasy chattering. Standing in the black crush of bodies, Jeff wondered what could have put the electricity out. Lightning? The sky had been completely clear just an hour ago. Wind? Not unless a tornado had sprung up since they'd been here.

As his eyes adjusted, he noticed a dim ring far overhead, where a strip of narrow windows encircled the gym. A second later, the moon peeked in on one side like hope. But a significant glow also came through the windows on the other side of the building, which meant the streetlights in Middlefield were still on. Only the gym itself was dark. Somebody must be playing a prank.

"Everybody stay calm," a half-dozen adult voices shouted from all parts of the gym. "We'll get this taken care of . . . find out what's wrong . . ."

But the darkness remained. As invisible bodies pressed into Jeff on all sides, he began to think about the La Brea tar pits out in California. Thousands and thousands of animals piled together, sealed for millennia in a tomb of opaque asphalt. Sweat trickled into his eyes. Where was Gail?

"Quit pinching me, you beast!" some guy squealed in falsetto, and there was laughter. Jeff wondered if Gail was getting knocked around as badly as he was. "Gail!" he shouted. "Gail!" His voice sank in the surrounding chaos.

"Jeff." The voice, not Gail's, came from behind him. He turned. All he saw was Robby the Robot's stream of lights, a foot or two away. "Jeff," the voice said again. It seemed to come from Robby, except it lacked the electronic overtones. And it sounded familiar. "Listen to me."

"*Abe?*" Jeff cried, astonished. It didn't seem possible—Abe Perry, wearing that terrific costume, and challenging him, Jeff, to a *dart-throwing* contest? And almost *winning?*

"I've got to tell you something," the voice said urgently. "Timmy's gonna do something to Gail. He told me if I helped him, I . . . but I can't . . . listen, he's going out to the Big Tree."

"The Big Tree? Abe, is that you?"

"I've got to go." The line of blinking lights shrank, vanished.

"Abe!" Jeff pawed through the darkness, got bumped by somebody. His fingertips brushed aluminum foil, clutched air. "Come back here!"

Without warning, the gymnasium lights flared on again. All faces rose, as if in awe. Paper witches and bats spun against dangling bulbs. At the same moment the PA system fired up, Mick Jagger's voice first moaning, then wailing, "I can't get no . . . sat-is*faction* . . ." The gym echoed to applause and cheers, nervous laughter, and a few exaggerated moans of disappointment.

Jeff looked down and saw the robot's gleaming back lurching away through the crowd. He started to follow, then remembered Gail and turned the other way. The crowd had rearranged itself during the blackout; nothing looked the same now. He couldn't see—

Then he glimpsed the gossamer train of the Maid Marian hat

floating toward the back doors. But Gail wasn't alone. Somebody hurried along beside and slightly behind her, resting a hand on her back as he pushed one of the doors open with the other. He wore green sweatpants, a belted vest and a green felt hat with a pointed bill and jaunty feather. A quiver of arrows bounced against his back.

Jeff blinked.

Gail slipped through the doorway into darkness, and a moment later, so did the other Robin Hood. But first he turned and looked back into the gym, directly into Jeff's eyes. And smiled.

"Timmy!" Jeff bellowed.

My eyes snapped open. Above, the three Presidents stared down through the gloom. But now the one on the left looked like Fred McMillan instead of Thomas Jefferson, and the one in the middle resembled Abe Perry more than Teddy Roosevelt, and the one on the right was not Lincoln, but Timmy Kegler. When distant lightning flashed, their lips began to move . . .

I stared at them harder. And harder, until they turned into stains again. It took such a long time I began to sweat.

I rolled onto my side, half-expecting Gail to be gone. But she lay there, turned away from me, her hair puddled on the pillow. Warmth radiated from her. *Sweetheart.* I hoped her dreams were more peaceful than mine.

Pulling myself against her, I closed my eyes and inhaled the tangy heat of her skin. My dreams might be real in their own way, but not like this. Nothing had ever been more real than this.

For a moment, Jeff couldn't move. His first feeling was amazement: Timmy, wearing a *Robin Hood* costume? Whatever happened to three-eyed aliens, and vampires with blood trickling out of their mouths, and werewolves with long, clicking talons?

Then came the anger. Obviously, Timmy had tricked Gail. He must have crept up to her during the power failure, said he was Jeff, and started leading her toward the door. Kept himself a little behind her, just in case the lights came on too soon. Now, out there in the moonlight, Gail would notice only the Robin Hood outfit, and never guess . . .

Timmy made the lights go out.

Jeff was absolutely sure it was true. His feet propelled him toward the back doors. He caromed off witches and pirates, mummies and princesses. The felt sheaths covering his shoes ripped loose and flapped absurdly from side to side. He slammed into the doors and burst outside, startling the man standing guard there. "Hey!" the guard shouted. "You kids better slow down!"

Jeff bolted across the playground. Bright autumn air whistled through his hair, between his teeth, under the soles of his shoes, through the string of the longbow he had slung around him. His shadow stretched ahead, bounding over the gravel on legs grown much too long. Back when the gang used to play Animals, Jeff was always the cheetah even if that was what Timmy wanted to be, because he, Jeff, was fastest.

He was faster now.

He skidded around the corner of the building just as two figures were about to enter the alley across the street. They were holding hands.

"*Stop!*" Jeff bellowed, accelerating. His cap flew off.

The figures turned. In the moonlight Jeff saw Gail's face, an inverted triangle of surprised "O's" beneath the conical hat. Then he saw Timmy's face . . . except that for an instant, it didn't look like Timmy at all. Jeff had the weird impression he was looking at *himself.* Then Timmy's head tilted, and the black shadow of the cap swung around like an eraser, revealing the sharp Kegler features.

Jeff flew across the last stretch of the playground. From playing Animals, and later as a linebacker, he'd developed an instinct for how many steps away a target was. In this case, in eleven strides he'd be on top of Timmy. Then it would all be over.

One—

Gail turned toward Timmy, obviously confused. Then she recoiled with a startled cry.

Two—

Timmy grabbed Gail's left wrist with both hands.

Three—

Planting her feet, Gail yanked back, and Timmy's feet skidded. *Yes, Gail!* Jeff thought. If she could blacken a Wagner's eye, she could get away from Timmy Kegler.

Four—

Timmy shouted something. To Jeff, half-deafened by the rumbling wind of his own passage, it sounded like *Help.*

Five—

Timmy released Gail with one hand, and extended his free hand toward the alley as if reaching for a safety line. Gail yanked him a half step farther into the street. She was yelling something, too; it sounded angry, but now a real wind had come up, whipping past Jeff with a smell of burnt pumpkin and fallen leaves, almost knocking him off his stride.

Six—

The trees overhanging the alley had long ago lost their leaves. As the wind hit them, they flung bony shadows into the street.

Seven—

The shadows touched Timmy's outstretched hand, twirled around his wrist like tentacles.

Eight—

Abruptly, Gail skidded toward Timmy, her shoes sliding. The shadows scrabbled up Timmy's arm to his shoulder, across his chest, onto his other arm. Gail's shoes slipped some more. "Jeff!" she screamed; this time he heard her clearly.

Nine—

Jeff's right foot hit the street, grabbed, accelerated him into the beginning of the tackle. At the same moment, the tree shadows swarmed onto Gail's wrist. Jeff was close enough to see her eyes fly wide, and her mouth yawn as if in pain or shock.

Ten—

This step was more of a lunge, committing him to a definite point of impact. Simultaneously the shadows engulfed Gail and retreated toward the alley. Amazingly, Gail vanished with them. Jeff had time for one thought: *How did Timmy—*

Eleven—

—do that? Then he was diving, body fully extended, arms reaching toward the precise spot where Timmy would be. As the shadows of the alley rolled over him, his arms snapped triumphantly closed around—

Nothing.

CHAPTER TWENTY-TWO

SHORTCUT

Jeff hit the ground on his solar plexus, a bundle of nerves he'd read about in health class but had never expected to identify in such a personal manner. Agony blasted his limbs to tapioca, emptied his lungs, filled his head with fire. He writhed on the hard-packed earth, wanting to vomit, unable to do so, wanting to inhale, unable to do so.

Across this vacuum of agony, he heard Timmy's laughter, receding. Nothing from Gail.

Jeff was baffled. He knew Gail was far stronger than Timmy; she'd even been pulling away from him before suddenly vanishing into the alley. There was only one explanation—Timmy had gotten help. But from whom? Abe? That didn't make sense. Abe was the one who warned Jeff in the first place.

Jeff staggered to his feet. The alleyway reminded him of a long, tapering basket woven of ink-black wicker; trees and shadows seamlessly joined. As the wind blew, fragments of moonlight swirled around the basket like silverfish, making distances and angles difficult to perceive. Still, Jeff glimpsed something large moving away through that uncertain light, toward the dim oval gleam that was the far end of the alley.

"Gail," he shouted, or tried to. It came out a trembling wheeze. He ordered his legs to move forward. "Gail!" This time it was almost a real shout. He realized his chin was bleeding, and allowed this indignity to fuel his anger and energy. "Timmy! You better let her go!"

Laughter, much farther away. But Jeff wasn't worried. He was accelerating now, feet flying like wings over the hard-packed earth. He could always outrun Timmy.

Ahead he saw the irregular oval of light that marked the far end of the alley. Against it moved a large, amoeba-shaped cluster of shadows. Jesus, it almost spanned the width of the alley—three people at least, maybe more. Where had Timmy gotten so many friends? It didn't matter. Jeff could take on a dozen Captain Stranges any day. "I'm gonna kill you, Kegler!" he bellowed.

He thought he heard a gasp from ahead. A moment later the amoeba shivered, broke apart. Suddenly, through the thundering wind of his own speed, Jeff heard a new sound:

Vvvvvvp-vvvvvvp-vvvvvvp . . .

His feet missed a beat, and he almost fell. Three tall shapes materialized in the chaotic gloom before him, jogging in his direction.

Jeff realized he'd stopped running. Why? Those three shadows couldn't possibly be seniors—no senior would be caught dead hanging around with Timmy Kegler.

"I told you the Nodkin would get you, Jeff!" Timmy shouted. He sounded a hundred miles away now.

Fragments of moonlight flashed over the figures, illuminating an eye here, a nose there, a mouth . . .

Vvvvveeeeep-vvvvveeeeep-vvvveeeeeep . . .

Black holes for eyes. Knife blades for noses. Mouths lopsided and grinning. Teeth glinting—

Jeff found himself backing up. Suddenly he wasn't thinking about Gail, or Timmy, or anything except, *The Bikkids are gonna get me! The Bikkids are gonna get me!*

VVVVVEEEEEP-VVVVVVEEEEEP-VVVVVVEEEEEP . . .

The three shapes rushed toward him. He started to turn and run from their jack-o'-lantern grins.

Jack-o'-lanterns. Halloween.

Masks!

Halting, wheeling back, Jeff shrugged his longbow off his back. With his free hand he reached over his shoulder and grabbed the feathered shaft of an arrow. Whoever these assholes were, he'd threaten to shoot them if they gave him trouble. He'd drive them off, then get back on the tail of—

Ahead of him in the alley was only a swirl of moonlight. No masks, no looming figures. The wind made the only whistling sound. Jeff was filled with self-disgust. He'd imagined the whole thing! Panicked, let Timmy get to him with that crap about Nodkin!

In the distance, the amoeba lurched toward the end of the alley. The amoeba looked much narrower now. From it trailed a long, faint smudge that had to be the gauzy train of Gail's hat.

Jeff hesitated. He couldn't catch up now; the moment Timmy left the alley he could disappear with Gail in any direction.

He's going out to the Big Tree. Abe's words. Unless it was a lie to make Jeff search in the wrong direction.

He had only seconds to act. He reached back and grabbed another arrow, pulled. It didn't budge. Damn! Glued in! He yanked harder, then twisted. With a snap, the arrow popped free. It had no point. Never mind. It was his only option.

He nocked the arrow, drew it back to his ear. Suddenly the amoeba looked impossibly tiny, impossibly distant. Jeff's arms trembled. The string bit into his unprotected fingertips. What if he hit Gail instead of Timmy? What damage would a headless arrow do to her?

Filling his lungs with air, he bellowed, "Gail! Fall down! Fall *now!*"

He wasn't sure she could obey even if she heard him, but suddenly half the amoeba vanished. Jeff released the arrow.

Although he could see nothing in the darkness, he had the feeling the arrow looped wildly. But a moment later a shrill cry echoed through the alley—Timmy's voice. He sounded surprised rather than hurt, and Jeff started running again, twisting at another arrow. "Here comes another one, Timmy! Here comes another one!" He fired the second arrow on the run, aiming lower, hoping to keep Timmy dodging. This time he distinctly heard the arrow click off the floor of the alley. An instant later there was a cry of outrage from the end of the alley.

Jeff almost tripped over Gail, who was sprawled in the moonlight at the mouth of the alley, her skirt coiled around her. Her conical hat had flown another ten feet and landed improbably upright, its plume twitching in the breeze. Both arrows lay out in the parking lot.

Jeff glanced around and spotted a lone figure in the distance, flitting into the shadows near the football field. Timmy. He didn't seem injured.

No time to think about him now. Jeff crouched beside Gail. "Gail? Gail . . . are you all right?" He touched her shoulder.

She snapped erect, wild-eyed, screaming, batting at his hand.

"Whoa!" he cried, trying to grab her arms. "Whoa, whoa, Gail, it's me!"

Still she struggled, scooting backward on the pavement, catching one foot in her long skirt. The fabric tore with a hoarse hawking sound.

"Gail!" Jeff almost tackled her, then dragged her to her feet. Her eyes gleamed like wet stones in the moonlight. Strands of hair had fallen from her elaborate coif to snake across her shoulders. She blinked, blinked, then hurled herself against him.

"They were *pulling* me!" she cried. "They were *pulling* me!"

"Shhhhh." Jeff smoothed her hair, kissed her forehead. "Who? Who was it? Timmy and who else? Was it Abe?"

"I—I couldn't see. But I felt their *hands* . . ."

"It's okay," Jeff said. "It's okay."

"But . . ."

"It's okay. They ran off."

After a moment, her body relaxed in his arms. Then she pulled free and peered down at herself. "Look at my dress! I spent a week sewing this dress!"

Jeff was relieved to see anger replacing the hysteria. "Come on, I'll take you home."

He helped her to her feet and they moved slowly across the parking lot, Gail leaning on him, limping. "My dad can call the police," she said shakily. "Get Timmy arrested. He's crazy! I told you he was crazy!"

Going to her father was the right thing to do, Jeff knew. Timmy had stepped over some kind of line tonight, crossed out of the realm of childish mischief. He'd tried to *kidnap* somebody, an act not even a Wagner would have attempted. This was an adult thing now. Yet Jeff felt a fiery, lunging need to do something more immediate than run to Gail's parents or his own. He'd panicked back in the alley. He'd acted like a *baby*. "No, Gail," he said. "You let *me* handle this. It's my fault Timmy did this. I should have taught him a better lesson last time."

"But there were a *bunch* of them, Jeff. You can't—"

"Whoever the other ones were, they took off. I'm not worried about them. I saw Timmy running away on his own."

"What are you going to do if you catch him?"

"For one thing, make sure he never tries to bother you again. I can handle Timmy. He used to be my best friend, remember?"

To his relief she didn't argue anymore, or, worse, ask to go along. She was obviously in quite a bit of pain, each step a wincing effort.

Jeff glanced over his shoulder. Gazed past the parking lot, past the football field, across the moon-frosted cornfield. His gaze stopped where a dark blob rose against the sky. The Big Tree, still clinging greedily to its autumn foliage. In the moonlight it looked more than ever like a great, gnarled head glaring over the corn. Its eyes seemed to open and close in time to the fury pounding through Jeff's head.

He used to be my best friend, remember!

CHAPTER TWENTY-THREE

GONE BUT NOT FORGOTTEN

Back when the Middlefield gravel pit was still in business, my friends and I sometimes rode our bikes out there on Sunday afternoons when no one was working. It was a cool place, with the scarred yellow hopper of the stone-crushing machine standing like an alien spaceship in a wasteland of conical hills. Each hill was composed of a different weight and texture of stone—split rock, crushed stone, gravel, pea gravel, sand. Dropping our bikes, we'd charge like commandos onto the sandpile, trying to scramble to the top while the granules poured away from our clawing hands and feet, gradually building into slides that carried us down faster than we could climb.

I scaled my dream the same way. Fought toward the surface, toward wakefulness, toward the light, thrashing at sweaty sheets.

Finally the dream poured away and I found myself sitting up, breathing hard. I was alone in bed. For a terrible moment I expected to find myself surrounded by the motel room; the entire experience with Gail a dream . . . But no. I was in her room.

Sweat trickled down the crease of my lower back. It took me a moment to realize the sunlight wasn't falling through the window over the bed, but slantwise through the window by the desk—which meant it must be late afternoon. My body felt heavy. I shook my head to clear it, and listened for sounds in the house—footsteps, running water, a voice. There was nothing. Even the birdsong outside sounded dull and remote. "Gail?" I called. No reply.

Pulling on my pants, I walked stiffly into the hallway. The air smelled musty. No one answered my shout down the stairs. I was halfway down the stairs when it came to me, and I bolted back up into Gail's room.

The closet was empty.

I stared at the void for a moment, then rushed to the dresser and yanked out drawers. Empty. Empty. Empty. I looked under the bed. No suitcases.

Crossing the hall, I checked the master bedroom, just in case. Nothing. In the bathroom cabinet I found a ceramic toothbrush holder—no toothbrush—and a bottle of aspirin. She hand't fled in panic, then? No, she had taken care. For what?

Tell me something—what are the odds you and I would both happen to be here in Middlefield, together, after all these years?

I glanced into the mirror above the sink. At first I was startled by the grim, stricken expression on my face—then I saw Timmy Kegler, wearing his Robin Hood outfit, sitting on the edge of the bathtub behind me. He still looked thirteen years old. He smiled. "Hi, Jeff," he said, his voice faint and flat, as if coming around many corners. "Allee-allee-in-free."

I whirled. The bathroom rug screwed around my foot, stealing my balance; I toppled awkwardly onto the toilet seat. There was no one else in the room. My heart banged inside my chest like a bird in a glass room. "Shit!"

From somewhere came faint, metallic laughter.

I fled the bathroom, stood helplessly in the hall. I had to find Gail. I needed her, her help, her balance, her *presence*. And she needed me, wanted me to stay with her. Maybe she'd gone back to her home in Fishers. If I could remember her married name, I could look the address up in the phone book. But I couldn't remember . . .

There *was* one place I could go to check for those names, a place where, if the information was available, it would literally be written in stone.

Throwing on the rest of my clothes, I ran for my car.

Running through the autumn corn wasn't easy. The interlaced leaves, dry and stiff, left burning cuts all over his wrists, cheeks and forehead. The air was getting distinctly cool, but Jeff's skin streamed with sweat.

Overhead, the full moon gleamed like a tarnished clockface that told no time. The night seemed to have dragged to a halt. Jeff remembered the dream he'd had where he'd floated through this field in the darkness, untouched. If only he were dreaming now, too . . .

I shook my head. I wasn't dreaming. And this was not the time to think about the past. This was the time to think about the future, the future I would share with Gail.

As soon as I found her.

As I drove under the arch at Shady Acres, clouds of midges were dancing in bands of antique gold sunlight. The walnut trees stood like palace guards in the rear of the graveyard. If Gail's husband and children were buried in this cemetery, their graves would be back here. Finding a brand-new family plot shouldn't be too difficult. From the stones I could learn Gail's married name and use it to track her down.

As I started to climb out of the car, I heard a sound and glanced into the rear-view mirror. Timmy Kegler sat in the back seat, arms stretched across the backrest. He smiled. "Cool wheels," he said. At least, his lips formed those words; his voice was as tenuous as rustling leaves. I whirled. The back seat was empty.

The next thing I knew, I was standing next to the car, shuddering, wanting to throw up. The only sound besides my gasping was the hiss and burble of invisible White Lick Creek, swollen from the storm. It sounded like throaty laughter.

Turning, I hurried toward the outer limits of the graveyard. Past Fred's headstone, around a particularly huge walnut tree. Then I froze.

A woman stood a few yards away, head bent over a row of gravestones. She wore a long, stained raincoat. Her hair hung in wet fingers across her face, as if she'd just climbed out of the creek. I was about to turn and move away when something about her half-hidden profile stopped me. I looked closer.

Gail.

After a moment's hesitation, I walked toward her and read the stone at her feet. ROBERT JOHNSON. Just visible beyond the hem of her raincoat was a stone inscribed CHARLES JOHNSON. That would be her son, and the next one, CAROL MCNAULTY-JOHNSON, her daughter-in-law. Her own daughter, the one with the unborn child, must have been buried in her husband's family plot.

"Gail?" I murmured.

She turned her head slowly. Her skin was paler than I'd ever seen it, the negative of her Arizona tan. "Hello."

"Gail . . . are you all right? What happened to you?"

Raising one hand, she wiped her eyes. "I'm sorry, Jeff. I had to make you to want to stay. But I didn't expect you to fall in love with me. And I . . . I didn't think I'd want you to."

"Gail . . ."

"I'm still married, you see. Happily married." She looked down again. "I want to be with my family again."

I also glanced at the headstones. "Listen, Gail . . ."

"I know what you're thinking. But I'm not crazy, Jeff. And I'm not suicidal." A slight smile curled her lips. "It's too late for that."

"I don't understand."

She sighed. "Let me show you." Stepping to the side, she revealed a marker previously hidden by her raincoat. I stared at its inscription:

GAIL JOHNSON

1952–1994

I raised my head. "What is this, a joke?"

"Poor Jeff," she said softly. "Still pretending you don't believe."

"Believe what? That you're *dead*?"

Whirling toward me, she raised her arms. The front of her raincoat opened, revealing gray slacks and a beige sweater. The two were connected by a glistening maroon stain that extended like a beauty queen's sash from one shoulder to the opposite hip. "Come here, Jeff," she said. "Hold me. Hold me like you did last night."

I hesitated, then strode up the slight incline of the grave. My arms opened wide. Gail waited, her eyes fixed on mine.

"I love you," I said, and put my arms around her. I felt something strange—a moment of resistance as ephemeral as a bursting soap bubble—and then my hands touched one another. Each felt cold to the other.

Startled, I stared into Gail's eyes. Saw trees in them. Behind them. Saw trees through them.

With a strangled cry, I leaped away. Gail looked at me sadly.

Then she began to smile, her teeth showing. Her mouth opened wide, then wider, then yawned hugely as the flesh of her cheeks dissolved backward. Her lips split and curled away, revealing blue-black gums. The skin grew taut across her cheekbones and forehead, ripping into shreds backed by yellow-white bone. Her beautiful eyes retreated into their sockets like trapdoor spiders. Blurring and shimmering, her sweater and slacks merged into a simple white dress. As her hands extended toward me, stumps of bone burst through the retreating flesh of her fingertips, and her nails erupted outward, corkscrewing in all directions like confetti streamers. Her wedding ring spun upside down.

"See?" she said in a gargling voice. "You do believe. Welcome to reality, Jeff . . ."

I staggered back, stumbled on the slope of the grave, and fell. The darkening sky arced into view, swept with leafy limbs, then burst into a kaleidoscope of stars . . .

CHAPTER TWENTY-FOUR

HARVEST TIME

Someone was following him through the corn. Jeff noticed only when he stopped to catch his breath and realized that the crackling sound of passage continued anyway. It came from behind him, growing louder. He listened a moment, not breathing at all, then eased sideways through the cornstalks as quietly as he could. He crossed several rows, then squatted and peered back. Something moved past, not quite visible, a strangely bright flicker in the corn. It couldn't be a pursuer, though; whoever it was didn't seem concerned with stealth. Abe? Abe in his Robby the Robot costume? Jeff waited a few heartbeats, then fell in behind.

Gradually the black brow of the Big Tree rose overhead, and the corn began to grow shorter. Jeff was forced to walk in a crouch, then get onto his hands and knees and crawl. He didn't want to be seen until he knew exactly who was out here and what was going on. Finally he slithered forward on his belly like a soldier, stopping only when the corn had shrunk to the top of his head. He was almost at the edge of the clearing.

The Big Tree rose like a sooty cloud of smoke before him. Abe stood under it. He wasn't wearing his robot helmet, and reminded Jeff of a spaceman as he stood looking around. Near Abe's feet was a black rectanglar hole about four feet long and half as wide. Abe stepped around it carefully. "Timmy?" he called in a low voice. "You here?"

An angular silhouette flung itself from behind the tree. Abe cried out and almost fell into the hole.

"I had her," Timmy said. "But I lost her."

"So . . . the joke's off?"

"No." Timmy jumped onto one of the exposed roots of the tree. "Jeff will be here anyway. I know him. I just need someone to take Gail's place."

There was a pause, then Abe squeaked, *"Me?"*

"Yeah. You get in the grave, and I'll climb in the tree. When Jeff shows up, we both jump out and scare the heck out of him. It'll be great. Like Halloween's supposed to be."

"But . . ."

"Come on, Abe-O. Gail would have been better, but this will work. Hurry up, he could be here any second."

Abe sighed, then knelt and eased himself into the hole. When he stood, the lip came up to his armpits.

"Now turn around," Timmy said. "You gotta be able to see him coming."

Abe sighed again, then turned. Jeff saw the faint gleam of his glasses. Behind him, Timmy leaned down and lifted something from among the roots. "It's nice of you to help me out, Abe," he said. "I'll make sure you have a good time in the land of Nod."

"I wish we could go there," Abe said wistfully. "I wish we didn't have to just *pretend* all the time."

"We won't," Timmy said, and raised his hand. Jeff blinked. From Timmy's hand extended a long, gleaming sword. The sword from Jeff's dream? No—it wasn't a sword at all. It was just a corn knife, a common tool for chopping down weeds.

"Gail would have been best," Timmy said, his voice trembling and wet. "Then you and I could have gone to Nod together, Abe. But I can't wait anymore."

He swung the corn knife. Jeff heard a wet thumping sound as Abe leaned forward, slowly at first, then faster. As his body vanished into the hole, his head rolled across the clearing.

Jeff heard a shrill cry. It seemed very loud.

Timmy's head snapped up. "Jeff?"

Jeff locked his throat, flattened himself further in the corn, imagined himself a shadow, a shadow.

Timmy walked around the grave, the corn knife gleaming darkly in his hand. Overhead, the branches of the Big Tree began to stir.

"Jeff?" Timmy called. "I know you're out there. I knew you'd come. Abe wouldn't mind if you went to the land of Nod with me. Come on, please?"

Jeff began to creep backward on his elbows and hips, keeping flat, trying not to disturb a single leaf. Trying not to scream.

Timmy dropped the corn knife, then bent down and picked up Abe's head. "You never believed me about going to Nod, did you, Jeff?" he shouted. "Well, watch this!" With a grunt, he hurled Abe's head straight up into the lightless heart of the Big Tree. Jeff waited for it to drop back like a terrible ripe fruit, but it didn't. Instead, the tree's branches began to stir faster and harder, as if something were crawling through them.

"It's time, Jeff!" Timmy yelled, excitement spiking his voice. He reached into his pocket, then raised his arm and began to swing it in a circle over his head. The sonorous note of the bull-roarer rose into the air. "I'm going places you've only dreamed of, man! Croatoan! *Crooooaaaaaaatooooooaaaaaannnnnn . . .*"

The bull-roarer's hum thickened into a bellow that merged with Timmy's voice. Jeff clambered to his hands and knees and scuttled backward that way, no longer caring about making noise.

The Big Tree's limbs lashed violently up and down, and a hailstorm of acorns clattered through the corn. Near the trunk of the tree, ridges of earth began to heave up.

"It's working, Jeff!" Timmy shouted, although the mixed-together chant and drone continued at the same time. "I'm on my way to Nod! You can still come with me if you hurry!"

The earth behind him erupted with thick roots that coiled up, groping, swarming into Abe's grave, collapsing it. "Last chance, Jeff!" Timmy cried. "Last chance!"

Stumbling to his feet, Jeff turned and ran as fast as he could down the cornrow. But even the crackle of dry vegetation and the thunder of his own breathing didn't drown out the unholy voice of the bull-roarer: "*AAAAAAAAAAAAAA . . .*"

Jeff ran and ran, until his ankle turned on a dirt clod and he fell at an angle through the corn, shattering stalks, flattening them. He rolled, somersaulted, skidded to a halt on his back. Overhead hung a circle of sky.

Only then did he realize the droning had stopped.

He must have gotten turned around during the fall. From here he could see the top of a nearby tree—but it couldn't be the Big Tree. The Big Tree had been covered with leaves; this one was a naked net of branches. But what other tree would be visible from the middle of the cornfield?

A single cloud hung above the leafless tree. The only cloud in the sky, it was not white or silver but smudgy brown, like smoke. Its surface pulsed in and out. As Jeff watched, hollows formed here, a protruding triangle there, a long slit below that. The cloud became a head. A giant head hanging in the sky like a Macy's parade balloon.

It had Timmy Kegler's face.

The mouth curled up. *I see you* . . . Jeff wasn't sure if he actually heard the voice, or only thought it. It seemed to come from the corn, the cloud, everywhere. *I can see* . . . *I can see* . . .

The cloud began to drift toward Jeff, grinning, trailing dark vapor behind it. *I'll bet I can see a hundred miles* . . .

Whimpering, Jeff tried to squirm away, shoes skidding on the smooth cornstalks, kernels scooping down the back of his pants. The cloud loomed closer, its dark tail stretching behind it. Then its features began to lose their shape and clarity. The cloud dissolved, turning into a fine, descending haze, like ashes falling from a column of smoke. Jeff watched the particles sift slowly earthward in all directions, growing steadily larger. One of them danced directly overhead, spun down, landed on his chest. It was a big dry leaf.

Collapsing back on the corn again, Jeff stared up at the sky. Now that it was empty, it was a nice thing to look at. Pretty. Pretty.

He didn't notice the dew collecting on his cheeks like tears.

CHAPTER TWENTY-FIVE

SHINE YOUR LIGHT ON ME

I stared at the sky until the fireworks show ended, leaving only a throbbing pain in my head that matched the one in my heart. For all these years I'd buried the memories of that night under the Big Tree. Convinced myself that I'd imagined them, dreamt them. Buried them. Poor Abe. Poor Abe.

The grass felt cool beneath me. The air smelled of creek water and mown lawns. A bullfrog pounded out its bass note.

I sat up slowly, looking for Gail. She was still there, no longer a desiccated corpse but a sad woman dressed in a dripping raincoat. "Why?" I asked.

She said nothing. I got slowly to my feet, waited for my equilibrium to catch up. "Why did you do this to me, Gail? Do you hate me that much?"

She closed her eyes. "I don't hate you at all. I did what I had to do. Timmy won't let me cross the land of Nod until he gets what he wants. And if I can't cross Nod, I can't join my family."

"What does Timmy want?"

"Out. Out of the land of Nod."

"*Out?* Why?"

"I don't know."

I hesitated. The tree-shadows were growing very long around us, standing like walls of smoked glass in the mote-filled air. "Fred and Abe are trapped too, aren't they?" I asked.

"Not just them. Please help us, Jeff. You're the only one who can."

"Why me?"

"Because Timmy knows you. And because you're alive."

Shine Your Light On Me

I swallowed. "What am I supposed to do?"

"Wait until dark, that's all. Timmy will tell you then."

I looked around. The sun was a flattened tangerine just above the horizon. I felt its dying warmth on my face. "Dark?" I said. "I don't understand. Timmy hated the dark."

"You have to do this Timmy's way, Jeff. Nod's way."

"But something's wrong. I don't think—"

"Selfish."

I turned. Gail resembled an old-fashioned marble grave marker, a pale and glistening angel, only her lips moving. "You're the same old Jeff Dittimore after all, aren't you? Everything has to be the way you want it. Nobody gets the better of Jeff Dittimore, right?"

"You did," I said harshly, and turned away. On the ground, the shadows interconnected in a rough plaid pattern. Without looking back, I headed toward my car. I didn't look back.

The sun had reached the stage where its movement was visible. It extended a molten toe toward the horizon, then an entire foot. Around me, the shadows began to blur together. *Walk right through them*, I told myself. *They can't hurt you.*

The moment I stepped out of the sunlight, I heard a sound that iced my blood: *Vvvvvvvvp-vvvvvvvvp-vvvvvvvp.* Across the clearing, a tall figure rushed toward me, pantlegs whistling together. Then another figure appeared, and another. They wore Senior cords, Lettermen jackets and jagged grins. I knew them for what they were—Bikkids. The things that had lurked in my closet when I was a kid. That had waited under the bed, in the dark hallway. That had come from the Big Tree.

Bikkids.

Shadow people.

Nodkin.

VVVVEEEEEP-VVVVEEEEEP-VVVEEEEEP . . .

Not real, I thought. *Not even as real as ghosts. Just ignore them and they can't hurt you.* But I couldn't ignore them. I was too frightened to even run. I had regressed into my childhood beliefs. *Childhood beliefs . . .*

The first Bikkid was almost upon me. As it extended its bony hands I did the same with one of my own, fingers curled into a fist except for the pinky, which was outstretched. I thrust it into the Bikkid's face. "Remember this?" I cried.

The Bikkid looked at the Indian sign of protection for a moment, then recoiled with a shrill scream and dissolved into the shadows. Its companions vanished as well. I strode toward my car, grinning, fist extended like a battering ram.

The sun was half-eaten by the horizon now. Only an island or two of sunlight remained in the clearing, but I wasn't worried about that anymore. I was armed now.

Without warning, a new figure lunged up in front of me, a shadow among shadows, white fangs flashing. It was the shadow beast, the shadow beast itself, Timmy's favorite. Choking back a scream, I shoved the Indian sign of protection at it. It grinned. A taloned hand swung back, claws like miniature corn knives, gleaming. As they swept forward I resisted the overwhelming instinct to duck, and smiled instead. *Can't hurt me. I have to face my—*

Scalding pain ripped across my ear. A hot cascade poured down the side of my neck. I gasped.

"Give up yet?" the shadow beast asked in a thick, slobbering voice. I waved the Indian sign at it wildly, like a cop trying to stop a bullet with a search warrant. At the same moment, the last spark of the sun burned out on the horizon.

The shadow beast began to change shape. It shrank in stature, its teeth withdrew, its talons folded away. One by one its features compressed, sharpened, became increasingly familiar. Timmy Kegler's face. Somehow this was the most horrifying thing of all. Timmy, coming into his own again. Standing here with me in the darkness. Grinning at me.

"Welcome home, Jeff," he said in a half-finished voice. "It's time to—"

Without warning the sun leaped above the western horizon and blazed across the graveyard with a thundering roar and a dozen swords of light. One of the beams pierced Timmy, who shrieked and broke into a whirl of fleeing shadows.

As the sun grew larger I realized it was not one big light but many small ones hurtling along in formation. And its roar was the aggressive bellow of a V-8 engine. The apparition lunged past my rental car, spewing ribbons of turf behind it. It looked like a giant sea urchin bristling with lights instead of spines; beams shot forward, backward, straight up, to both sides, down onto the grass. Beyond the glare I saw the primer-gray body of a pickup truck. It skidded to a halt only a yard away, bathing me in the living stench of hot oil and rubber.

The driver's door flew open. "Get your ass in here!" Mike Norris bellowed.

I stared at him like a rabbit frozen by headlights.

"Come on!"

My paralysis broke and I staggered forward, jerked open the passenger door and leaped in. The cab was as brilliantly lit as a surgical theater. As I slammed the door, I noticed the side window was rolled down. I groped wildly for the handle, only to discover it was missing; there was nothing in its place, not even a hole. Then I realized there was no glass on Mike's side, either; nor behind me, nor even where the windshield should be.

"Got tired of seeing Timmy in every fucking reflection," Mike muttered, slamming the transmission into gear. I rocked back as the truck lunged forward, rapping into at least one of the Johnson family's headstones. The truck made a broad turn, spotlights slicing across trees and grass, chasing shadows. Shadows with arms, legs . . .

I turned my head.

Mike was dressed exactly the way he'd been the other day at his house, in filthy overalls and an even filthier T-shirt, the Cincinnati Reds ballcap pulled low over his haystack of white hair. Although the truck's cab was roomy, his corpulence filled it by more than half; his gut swallowed the bottom of the steering wheel. He smelled of sweat, marijuana and motor oil.

"Thanks for . . ." I began, my voice quivering on the edge of hysteria.

"No problem," he said. "Always glad to help another living, breathing human being." He paused. "Especially my all-time best friend."

I slumped back in the seat, blinking at hot tears. This truck might look like a "piecer," as my daughter would have put it, but it ran like a bull. Mike pushed it hard, sticking to the pavement now, tires screeching on turns designed for more sedate speeds. Overhead, the sky was purple plunging into indigo. I tried not to watch the shadows leaping behind trees and headstones. "How can you stand it here?" I asked. "Why are you still—"

"Hang on a sec."

We were approaching the gate. Mike flicked switches, and some of the truck's sidelights and all the overhead spots went out. I stiffened.

"Don't worry," Mike said. "We got streetlights to protect us now, and I don't want to get pulled over by the cops. They don't like my truck much." He turned toward downtown Middlefield.

I bolted upright. "We can't go this way!"

"Relax."

"But—"

Without warning he yanked the big truck into a U-turn, tires smoking, lights flashing in every direction. "Okay, you want to call the shots? Where would you like to go? The freeway? The airport?"

I looked at him warily in the dazzle of the interior lights. "Anywhere. Just . . . out of here."

"You got it."

He put his foot down. Soon the arch of branches that marked Middlefield's town line appeared. I held my breath as we passed under it, but nothing jumped out of the trees, nothing tried to stop us.

I leaned back with a sigh and glanced at Mike. He said nothing, switched on the full array of lights again. Bushes and fence posts leaped into lurid relief alongside the road. Beyond them there was pure darkness punctuated by the occasional mercury-vapor light in a distant barnyard. Segments of white line on the road flick-flick-flicked toward us like tracer shells. Warm wind whipped through the empty windshield frame, pushing Mike's beard and hair back, outlining a profile that was familiar if I used my imagination.

"When I came to your house a few days ago," I said, "you thought I was a ghost, didn't you?"

"Yeah. Sorry about that. But the Indian sign of protection didn't bother you, and that bothered *me*. So pretty soon I checked around and found out you'd moved into that motel." He paused. "After that, it wasn't hard to find you. All the dark things were heading for Shady Acres, so I did too."

All the dark things. I shuddered, gingerly touched my ear. To my surprise, the pain was gone. I looked at my fingertips. No blood. "They attacked," I said, rubbing my ear. No blood. No blood. "One of them *cut* me. I was bleeding. I swear I was *bleeding.*"

"Reality is kind of twisted around here," Mike said blandly.

"That's more or less what Gail told me." I swallowed hard.

"You saw Gail? Christ, that must have been a shock." Mike's tongue came out, fished into his mouth the tuft of beard that grew under his lower lip. He chewed it a moment, watching me carefully from the corner of his eye. Then he said, "Don't worry, ghosts are only as real as you expect them to be. They can't really hurt you, just wear you down. It's the dark things you have to worry about."

"The Nodkin," I said.

He jerked toward me. "Don't ever say that in my truck."

I recoiled. "I didn't think you even knew—"

"Timmy told me about the dark things before I learned how to shut him out." He shook his head angrily. "Shit, fuck, never mind. That's what all these lights are for. The—the *Nodkin*, okay?—they can't stand light, just like when we were kids. Remember?"

"Yeah. They don't like the Indian sign of protection, either."

For the first time he smiled, revealing teeth the color of his T-shirt. Then it faded. "You can fight the things, but be careful, man. They use your own fears against you. And they never stop trying."

I touched my ear again. "You're saying I only *believed* I was cut? But I was *bleeding.*"

"You thought you were bleeding, so you were bleeding. This light makes you feel safe, so now you're safe."

I thought about my encounter with the shadow beast . . . Timmy. The Indian sign had been useless against him. But then, the Indian sign had never been the most effective tool in the arsenal, had it?

Ahead, low to the ground, two eyes flared red by the side of the road, and a possum started to step out of the bushes. It hesitated, glaring, then turned and slipped back into the ditch with a whiplash of naked tail. In the distance, the lights of a town twinkled against the darkness.

"Has Timmy been after you to help him, too?" I asked.

"Yeah. Timmy, Abe, Fred, Gail . . . all of them. But I'm scared. Remember, Timmy used to think the shadow people were monsters? Now they're on his side. Something's wrong with that."

"I agree," I said.

"Besides, he's not like the others," Mike went on, chewing furiously at the tuft of beard. "He's not even dead. He's just sort of . . ."

"He's in the land of Nod," I said.

A wide-eyed look. "You know about that?"

"I know what Timmy told me when we were kids." I paused. "And what I saw the night he went there."

"What do you mean?"

"Halloween night, 1965. Remember that night?"

"The night Timmy and Abe disappeared . . ."

"Remember how you and Mike found me in the cornfield?"

"Gail called and told us you were going out there. She said you were after Timmy. Jesus, when Fred and I found you we thought you were dead."

I nodded. "I'd already been out at the Big Tree. I saw Timmy kill Abe."

The truck swerved, came back to the middle of the road. *"What?"*

"Chopped his head off with a corn knife. It was a sacrifice. Remember how he used to talk about the Indians making sacrifices? That's how he got into the land of Nod. The Big Tree sort of . . . took him."

"The Big Tree. Jesus. No wonder you blacked out."

"That's why I've got to get out of here, Mike. I can't deal with this. I'm surprised you can."

He nodded. "Memory check. What town is coming up?"

Ahead, cozy lines of lit windows extended into the darkness on either side of the road. We were going north, and we hadn't made any turns.

"Pittsboro?" I asked.

"Close." Mike pointed as a big white sign, half-buried in weeds, swept into the headlights:

WELCOME TO MIDDLEFIELD
A GREAT PLACE TO PLANT YOUR ROOTS!

CHAPTER TWENTY-SIX

SIGNS OF THE TIMES

As we drove under the tree arch, Mike switched some of the exterior lights off again. "When I was in Vietnam," he said into my silence, "I told this one guy where I was from, and he said, 'I drove through Indiana one time. Every town looked the same to me.' Maybe he had a point."

We passed the modern housing developments. "Does this happen every time you try to leave?" I asked in a voice so weak the wind carried most of it away.

But Mike heard. "All roads lead home for me, buddy. And now for you, too."

"But . . ." I looked at passing traffic. "What about these other people? Can *they* leave? Or is this some kind of show?"

"They're real, but they didn't know Timmy. They can come and go. But you and me . . . remember the games we used to play when we were kids? Spaceman, Army, all those? Timmy made up the rules and set the boundaries, right? And we always went along with him. Right? I think this is the same thing. Timmy's boundaries. They work on us because we know they're here."

I tried to think it through. "If that's true," I said, "couldn't we just get on a bus or hitch a ride out of town with someone who *didn't* know Timmy? Wouldn't that work?"

"I tried taking a bus once. Every town we came to was Middlefield, or looked like it to me. Other people got on and off; maybe they were seeing other towns. Or maybe I wasn't really on a bus at all, and just thought I was. Doesn't matter. After a while I couldn't stand it anymore and I got off, too. Never tried again."

We were passing the McDonald's now. Faces gaped at our weird vehicle. From a convertible came a shout: "Get a real car, Mr. Sunshine!"

"The kids these days," Mike said with a brown grin.

Next we passed Shady Acres. Fred stood under the arch, still cradling Abe's head in his arms. Despite myself I looked for Gail. She wasn't there.

"Don't let them get to you," Mike said. "It's pretty sad, but they only have themselves to blame for being dead."

I shivered. "I thought Timmy was to blame."

"Well, yes and no. Fred and Gail both died because they freaked out when Timmy sent a ghost to talk to them. But the others . . . he drove them all nuts, made them kill themselves or each other, just to get even with them. Even his own father."

A block away, a woman stood on a street corner. As we drew closer I saw it was Gail, dressed in her burial gown. Her eyes were socketed black by the lamplight. Her head turned slowly as we passed. "How can you *not* let it get to you?" I whispered.

"Easy. I stay stoned as much as I can. Around here, your mind is your own worst enemy."

We stopped at the traffic signal downtown, then turned left onto Main Street. "See," Mike said, "some ideas get planted early in life, so deep you never get rid of them. That's why Catholics still cross themselves even if they don't go to church anymore. Know what I'm talking about?"

I sat up straighter. "If this is just our minds working against us, then all we have to do is control what we think. Maybe we can find a way to—"

My voice cut off as Mike made an abrupt right-hand turn onto Landrus Avenue. "You still don't get it," he snapped. "The part of our minds I'm talking about doesn't *want* to be controlled, see? It *wants* to believe in Santa Claus and the boogeyman, it *wants* to believe in the land of Nod, just like we did back then." Now we were on School Street. As we passed Gail's house, I stared at it. Black windows, sagging porch, overgrown lawn. It looked so *haunted*. How could I have ever thought otherwise?

"Where are we going?" I asked.

"You'll see."

A minute later, the truck rumbled to a halt at the intersection of Lincoln Avenue and Oak Lane. Mike pointed across the street. "Look."

I raised my head, expecting to see the new housing development. It wasn't there. There were no houses at all beyond Fred's,
just weeds, then a cornfield. And above the corn, rearing black
against the stars, the shadow of the Big Tree.

On past Halloween nights, Jeff had always had trouble falling
asleep because his belly was churning with Snickers bars, Milky
Ways, Necco Wafers, Milk Duds. He couldn't sleep tonight, either,
but the reasons were different. He'd lain in the dew-soaked cornfield until Mike and Fred found him and carried him shaking into
his house. Mom stuck a thermometer in his mouth, gasped, buried
him in blankets.

Now he lay sweating and shivering in his bed, visions looping
through his mind. Timmy. The alley. Gail. The Big Tree. Abe in
his robot suit. Abe . . .

Slowly his eyes opened. He looked out the window. The Big
Tree, naked and grim, the moon sinking behind it. What had happened to all the Big Tree's leaves?

"*Jeff.*" The whisper was soft but very clear. Jeff lay motionless,
sweat beading on his brow.

"*Over here.*"

He looked to his left. The closet. Door open slightly. Timmy in
there, staring out. A shadow shaped like Timmy.

"I made it," the shadow said. Its voice was faint and flat, as if
squeezing through a mole's tunnel. But Jeff heard the excitement
in it. "I made it, Jeff. I brought you a going-away present to thank
you for all your help." A shadow hand moved, rolling something
out of the closet like a bowling ball. Not quite round, the object
didn't get far before it stopped, wobbling, moonlight enfolding it.

Abe Perry's head. Somehow the glasses had stayed on.

"Don't forget us, Jeff," Timmy said.

Abe's eyes blinked open, luminous behind thick lenses. His
mouth opened. "Help me," he whispered. "Oh, help me, Jeff."

Jeff screamed. From the closet came a chuckle. Jeff screamed.

The bedroom door flew open. The light exploded on. Mom and
Dad ran to him. Held him. "Oh, Jeff," Mom said. "You're all right
now, Jeff." Over Dad's shoulder, Jeff saw there was nothing in his
closet but clothes on hangers, piles of shoes, discarded socks. And
closer, lying in the middle of the floor, the football he'd received

for his thirteenth birthday. Closing his eyes, he fell again into a fitful sleep.

"How could it happen?" I asked after we'd driven for a minute, putting a few blocks between the truck and the Big Tree.

Mike glanced at me. "You're on Timmy's playground now, ol' buddy."

"But . . ."

"But what?"

"I *know* the Big Tree is gone. I'm the one who burned it down." The truck weaved slightly. "What?"

"I went out and set it on fire, the year after Timmy and Abe disappeared."

Mike stared at me wide-eyed, then threw back his head and laughed, revealing a lot of brownish teeth. "Jesus Christ, you're full of surprises all of a sudden. We watched that fire together, and you never said shit! You pretended to be sick!"

"I was embarrassed. I burned it down because it kept giving me nightmares, just like when I was a kid."

Mike sobered instantly.

"After I torched it," I said, "the nightmares stopped."

"Or got buried," he said. "Until now."

The truck turned off the highway and rumbled between the decorative walls labeled Belle Forest Estates. "We'll feel a lot safer in a minute," Mike said.

As I'd guessed, the security gate responded to a remote-control button. We bumped down the lane, through the band of trees, up Mike's driveway.

"My God," I said. Even though I'd had a pretty good idea what to expect, I still had to gape. The front and back yards, unbroken wastelands, shone like porcelain under the combined glare of the field lights. Inside the house, every window blazed.

"The locals call this the Field of Dreams," Mike said wryly. "Everything's on timers. I've got a backup generator in case of a power failure, too." He stopped at the top of the drive.

I was reluctant to leave the truck. "If Middlefield is Timmy's playground, why doesn't he just shut all these lights off?"

"I'm sure he would if he could. But remember, we grew up thinking light was more powerful than anything."

"You must have quite an electric bill," I said.

"Why do you think I sold so much of the land?"

"Because you hate farming."

He chuckled. "That, too." Looking straight at me, he said, "Man, it's good to have you back. Come on inside."

The interior of the house was decorated as I recalled from my brief glimpse the other day: Neo-monastic. No furniture, no knick-knacks, no pictures on the walls, almost no anything. Mrs. Norris's floral wallpaper had been covered with flat off-white paint. In what used to be the living room, the only decorations were floor lamps in each corner, a mattress lying flat on the floor, and an ashtray, also sitting directly on the floor. Now, of course, I understood the rationale behind Mike's two-dimensional esthetics: the desire to eliminate shadows.

"Home sweet home," he grunted. "Hey—want a beer?"

"Or two."

"Have a seat. I'll be right back."

I looked at the stained mattress, then lowered myself onto a corner of it. The pungent burnt-rope smell of pot billowed up around me. I noticed that despite Mike's best efforts, I still threw a shadow—five of them, actually, one for each lamp and the ceiling fixture. They were faint but quite real, extending from my body like the petals of a flower. I realized they didn't move quite the same way I did. I tried not to look at them.

"The decor isn't much," Mike said, walking back in with two cans, "but it lets me sleep at night. At least I know there's nothing under the bed." He lowered his enormous bulk to the mattress in wheezy intervals and handed me a beer. "Keep your hand around the can so you don't see any reflections. Unless you want Timmy peeking at you."

I shuddered. "I've been wondering about that. I saw him in a mirror twice today, and then at Shady Acres, but before that I never saw him at all. How come?"

"Because he didn't *want* you to see him too soon; he wanted to soften you up first. That's what Abe and Fred were for. With me, Timmy didn't show up in person until after Mom and Dad died and I was all alone." He popped the tab on the beer and took three long swallows. "Thank God my folks both passed away in the hospital. If they were trapped in Middlefield, too, and kept coming to visit me, I'd go fucking nuts for sure."

I sat up straighter. "Are you saying people who don't die in Middlefield are free?"

"Well . . . I never see any of them."

"That's got to be important," I said. "Why do you suppose that is?"

"You're not gonna quit on this, are you? I should have left you in that graveyard. Okay, okay." From one of the many pockets on his overalls he extracted a plastic bag full of twisted cigarettes. From another pocket came a Bic lighter. A moment later, a cloud of marijuana smoke poured into the room. "Okay . . . The thing is, I don't think Timmy's powers reach very far. Just around here, around Middlefield. Not that that's a big help to us, since this is where *we* are."

"But Fred and Abe came clear out to *California* after me."

"They're ghosts. They can go as far as Timmy will let them; he's in control of the . . . doorways . . . they need. I'm saying *Timmy's* stuck here."

I thought about that. "No, he knew about Mars. I mean, he knew there weren't canals, just canyons. And remember when he told Mrs. Edelstein dinosaurs were warm-blooded? That's what scientists think now, but back then . . . how could he have known those things unless he *saw* them?"

"Maybe he did see them. Maybe he just can't *do* anything outside of Middlefield." He inhaled more smoke. "No wonder he wants to come back."

I hesitated. As far as I knew, the Big Tree was the farthest Timmy had ever gotten from town—except through the two-dimensional media of books and TV.

"What do you think would happen if he *did* come back?" I asked.

Mike snorted smoke. "Do you really think Timmy would come back here if he wasn't sure he'd be King of the Hill?"

I started to retort, couldn't. "I still say there has to be *some* way out of this."

"You know what your problem is?" Mike took a long drink of beer, followed by another hit on the nub of the joint. "You always have to win. It's not enough just to keep somebody else from winning, *you* have to win. You're the same as Timmy that way."

Same old Jeff Dittimore. Nobody gets the better of him.

"Maybe," I said. "But that's better than doing nothing. I can't live like this, Mike. I have a daughter, a career, a life back in—"

"Not anymore. You're part of this world now."

"Damn it!" Leaping to my feet, I began to pace. It was what I did at the office when I needed to work through a particularly thorny problem. There was something else I used to do at work, too, when the problem would not relent. All those leather-bound books in my office were not just for show. "What we need is more information. If all Timmy wanted was a favor from us, he wouldn't be so threatening. There's something else going on, and if we could find out what it is, we might be able to use it against him."

Mike grunted, tossed the final ember into his mouth and swallowed. He winced. "That's you, Jeff, always talking."

Looking at him sitting there, swigging beer, obese and doing *nothing*, I was too disgusted to reply.

After a moment he focused on me again. "You *really* want to know what's going on in Timmy's head?"

"Come on, Mike."

"Fine. You got it. Wait right here." Hoisting himself off the mattress in a series of cumbersome phases, like a hot air balloon inflating, he turned and slouched off down the hall.

Standing alone in the middle of that vacant room, I suddenly became nervous. I had the feeling that if I turned my head, I'd see Gail staring at me through the lacy curtains on the window. Maybe I'd been too hard on Mike. Merely surviving in this place, enduring this atmosphere night after night, took more guts than I probably had. Perhaps what Mike thought of as my aggression was really panic, the frenzied need to get things resolved, one way or the other. It felt like panic to me. Without looking at the window, I walked back to the mattress and sat down.

A moment later there was a rumbling sound, and Mike reappeared pushing something draped in a floor-length sheet. The object was tall and flat and apparently mounted on casters. He parked it in front of me and lit a joint. "I'm gonna stand right back here," he said. "When you've had enough, I'll put the cover back on and we'll get blitzed together. Okay?"

Then, like a magician, Mike swept the sheet off the wheeled object. Beneath was a full-length, antique mirror in a wheeled hardwood frame. "I couldn't throw it out," Mike said. "It was Mom's favorite."

I looked at myself in the beveled glass.

Timmy Kegler stood beside me.

CHAPTER TWENTY-SEVEN

OUT OF THE FRYING PAN

He wore his favorite outfit—Red Ball Fliers, rolled-up jeans, stained, baggy T-shirt with sleeves that hung past his elbows. His hair was greased back, his narrow face deeply tanned.

Despite myself, I twisted around so fast the air squeezed out of my lungs in a bark—*"Huh!"*

There was no one beside me, of course.

Slowly, I turned back toward the mirror. Timmy still stood there, arms crossed, hips cocked, mouth slanted in a sardonic, but nevertheless genuine, smile. "Greetings, Earthling," he said. His voice sounded like it came from some other room.

I opened my mouth, but made no sound.

Mike stood next to the mirror, eyes closed, the joint locked between his lips and hissing steadily like a tiny oxygen tank.

"Hello, Timmy," I said.

"Welcome home, *Kemo Sabe.*"

"This isn't my home anymore."

"That's not what you told Gail."

I felt my face tighten. "Forget about Gail. What do you want? I mean, what do you *really* want?"

His smile slipped. "Don't talk to me like that. 'What do you want?' Like some big kid. You're not the boss around here."

"So sue me."

He blinked, then laughed. "Still think you're pretty tough, don't you? Okay, that's cool. What I want is for you to quit playing hide-and-seek, and come help me get out of here."

I couldn't resist turning around again. For the first time, I no-

214

ticed a skinny shadow on the wall behind me. Faint, washed out by the lamps, but clearly not my own. And not Mike's.

"Well?" Timmy said.

"Why do you want to come back, anyway?" I asked his reflection. "Isn't the land of Nod where you always wanted to be?"

He shrugged. "Let's just say it's time for a change."

"Why do you need our help?"

He sighed, then stepped around and sat on the mattress beside me. Although I could see nothing from the corner of my eye, I thought I felt something as his shadow brushed against me—a soft crackle as if my shoulder had passed through a skein of cobwebs. I held in a shudder.

"I need someone to push the door to Nod open from your side. You guys are my buddies, or at least you were until that *girl* came along. You've got the belief to make it happen. Wynken, Blynken and Nod."

"And if we do help you, then what? When you're on this side again . . . what are you going to do?"

He shrugged. "What I always did. Explore. Play. Go places. Do things."

"Will you still be thirteen years old?"

"Why?" He grinned.

"I'm just curious how you're planning to survive over here."

The grin faded, and he eyed me carefully, first in the mirror, then directly. The thought that he was separated from me by nothing but some invisible curtain gave me a sensation like ants teeming across my body. Then he said, "Don't worry, I'll get along fine, *Kemo Sabe*. Your job is just to bring me back."

"Not so fast. What about Fred and Gail and the others? What will happen to them?"

"I already told them—as soon as I'm out of here, they'll be free. That's what you want, isn't it?"

"What about Mike and me? Will we be free to leave, too?"

"Sure, why not?"

Something was wrong. After all Timmy had put us through so far, his requests were far too simple. "Exactly how are we supposed to open the door for you?" I asked. "I'm not going to sacrifice anybody, if that's what it takes."

"You won't have to do that," he said seriously. "I'll be pulling from this side. All you have to do is go to the Big Tree and I'll show you the rest."

"Why don't you just tell me now?"

His eyes narrowed. "I guess I'm better at showing than telling."

"And I'm better at not going than going."

"Fine." He clapped me on the shoulder—at least his hand came down in the mirror, although all I felt was what might have been a spray of morning mist—and shot to his feet. "You know, I think I might send Fred on another little trip to California. Or maybe Arizona. He loves to travel."

I found myself standing, too. Head and shoulders above Timmy in the mirror. "Don't."

He grinned. "Or what?" Out of his back pocket came one of the acrobat-clown toys given as prizes at the Fall Festival. Except this clown wore black tights and had Terri's face. Timmy squeezed the uprights, and the figure jigged and whirled. "Or what, Jeff?"

"Okay," I said, fists clenched at my sides. "I'll think about it."

"You do that. But think fast. I'll see you at the Big Tree, old buddy." I watched him wander toward the foyer, his hand still squeezing the acrobat toy. In the doorway, he paused and turned. "Don't let me down this time," he said. His hand clenched hard, and the clown shattered, dismembering pieces flying everywhere.

Then Timmy was gone.

I stood silently, waiting for something—a flashback, a memory, a message from the past—to tell me what to do next. There was nothing. Mike covered the mirror and wheeled it out of the room. When he came back, he stood directly in front of me and stared into my eyes. "You get what you wanted?"

I started to answer, then hesitated. "Can he hear us?"

"I don't think so. Not in all this light, with the mirror in the other room. But keep your voice down just to be safe."

I met Mike's gaze. "You heard him. He'll hurt my family."

"But you can't just *help* him."

"I don't plan to. But I have to do *something* to keep him off-balance until I can figure a way out of this."

"Keep him off-balance? How?"

"I guess . . . for starters, I'll have to go to the Big Tree."

He threw his arms over his head as if pumping up a bellow, then glanced down the hall and visibly calmed himself. "That's suicide."

"You don't have to go along," I said.

"Oh, no-no-no-no-no you don't. You ain't pulling that shit on me."

"I'm not trying to pull any shit on you. I'm just tel—"

"Because it won't work. I ain't going with you. No way. In fact, if I had half a brain, I'd stop *you* from going." He reached inside the front of his overalls and came out clutching the same pistol he'd pointed at his own head the first time I'd visited him.

But this time, it was pointed at *me.*

"Jesus, Mike!" I screamed, holding up a hand as if that would stop a bullet. My scalp seemed to flee to the back of my skull.

"You always bossed me around," he said. "But not anymore. Not this time." The gun pitched and rolled like a rowboat in the ocean. I felt my heart trying to stop itself before the bullet had a chance. Then Mike's eyes filled with tears and his arm dropped heavily to his side. "Fuck. *Fuck.* Get out of here. Leave me alone, I'm used to it. I saved your ass for nothing, you son of a bitch."

I backed away slowly, surprised my legs would move. At the foyer I paused. Mike stood in an unchanged position, arms dangling, face lowered, hair spraying in all directions.

Turning, I let myself out onto the veranda. For a moment I leaned on the rail, spirals of color blooming in front of my face like the sparks of a toy ray gun. Eventually they dissolved into the bright, even glare of the field lights. To the right, the driveway led into the woods and from there to the highway. To the left, a half-mile or so away as I recalled, Mike's property was crossed by a set of railroad tracks that also ran past Middlefield. Both routes would take me in the direction I needed to go.

But they would also take me into darkness—the place where the land of Nod overlapped the world as I knew it.

I tried to lick my lips, but my tongue was as dry as an autumn leaf.

Behind me, the door opened. "Jeff."

Mike was leaning out, right hand raised as if to shake mine. I responded automatically, tears of relief flooding my eyes, but an instant before my palm met his, it encountered a flat, hard chunk of metal.

"It's only .25 caliber," Mike murmured, "so you have to use it up close."

"I don't—"

"Just in case," he said.

"Mike . . ."

"I can't go, man," he whispered. "After all these years . . . I just . . . can't."

"I understand." I'd had a client once who was a gun nut; I'd learned just enough about firearms to know, from the feel, that this was a semiautomatic pistol. It was very small, and fit in the front pocket of my pants. I'd fired a semiautomatic at my client's gun club. And hated it. Real firearms were much louder and smellier than the toy ones I'd loved as a child.

"Good luck," Mike said, and closed the door.

I hesitated a moment longer, then turned and walked into the yard. Found myself veering to the left, toward the railroad tracks.

As I moved across the white plain of Mike's front yard, I felt certain I was being watched. Not by just one pair of eyes but by myriads, from all directions including the shadows under my own feet.

At the edge of the yard, I didn't give myself the chance to think. I strode straight into the gloom.

The railroad tracks rested on an eight-foot-tall berm designed to keep them above even the highest floodwaters. For central Indiana, that elevation was the equivalent of a mountain ridge. On all sides, fields of corn, beans and alfalfa rippled like rectangular oceans under a starlit sky. The highway lay far to my right, marked by the occasional set of passing headlights. Straight ahead, twin steel rails extended in blue-gray lines to the horizon, where they appeared to touch. Elementary geometry: *Parallel lines meet at infinity.* But I wasn't going that far. I hoped.

No Nodkin approached me. No ghosts. But then, why should they? I was going to their turf, and willingly.

My shoes alternately crunched on cinders and thumped on wooden cross ties, stirring up the acrid fumes of creosote. Overhead, a nighthawk circled invisibly, traceable only by its keening cry.

After perhaps ten minutes, I realized I was actually enjoying myself. Walking along here reminded me of the nights when the gang slept over at Timmy's house. Halfway to dawn we'd scale his back fence, scramble onto the railroad tracks and run until all the houses were out of sight. Then we'd sit down and scan the sky for airplanes, meteorites—and above all, flying saucers. Timmy would aim a flashlight toward the stars and blink it on and off, describing to us how the beam was darting into space at 186,000 miles per second. Someone was sure to see it, and then, if we were patient enough and *worthy* enough, a UFO would drop out of the sky and whisk us away.

The Milky Way reached the horizon at the same time I reached Middlefield. I left the tracks, wincing at the aching muscles in my legs as I slipped down the embankment to the streets. The town was silent, every window dark, no traffic anywhere. Moths swirled like snowflakes under the streetlights. I looked at my watch, but the liquid crystal display seemed to have failed; all it showed was a string of dashes. I shivered, convinced that the problem wasn't in the watch but in time itself. It had stopped, or was moving in a direction my watch could not register. It seemed to me there were far more 1960s-vintage cars parked along the curbs than there should have been.

By the time I reached Lincoln Avenue, morning birds were beginning to sing, and so were the muscles in my legs. I trudged along, head down, until the pavement ended. Beyond was dirt and weeds.

I looked up. Ahead lay an expanse of terrain as tumbled and uneven as a discarded blanket, then a field where corn raised pale tassels toward the fading stars. And beyond that, rearing high into the sky, the Big Tree. It was autumn red.

I hesitated a few seconds more, breathing hard. Then I trudged through the gullies to the edge of the cornfield and chose a gap between two furrows. Before stepping into its dull-toothed mouth, I raised one hand in the Indian sign of protection.

Despite the height and coverage of the corn, the rising sun was soon scalding the back of my head, and sweat dribbled steadily down my sides. I was tempted to strip off my shirt, but resisted the urge. The edges of the leaves clung to one another like Velcro fabric, then sawed at me when I pushed them apart. The effect grew worse and worse as I proceeded, because the corn gradually transformed from the supple green of late summer to the rigid gold of autumn. Once again I consulted my watch, this time to check the date; the face remained blank except for the meaningless dashes.

Had the hike to the Big Tree always taken so long? As I trudged forward, head down, arms raised to knock aside corn leaves, I began to wonder how much of this trek was really taking place inside my mind. In some other reality, was I was plodding down the middle of a suburban Middlefield street, arms slapping away invisible obstacles while kids circled me on their bikes and laughed?

I tried not to think about that.

As usual, I *heard* the Big Tree first. But I kept going without raising my head until the corn had shrunk to the level of my knees. Then I looked up.

The Big Tree was everything I remembered. Scarlet foliage billowing up in a mass so dense it looked far too heavy for any trunk to support, and on the ground, a shadow like a dark lake.

I approached the edge of that lake, but didn't step in. Not yet. As long as I was still in sunlight, I could always turn and run. In the light, I had a modicum of negotiating power.

"Okay, Timmy!" I shouted. "I'm here."

The only answer was the rush of the wind, the short-circuited buzz of cicadas.

"I don't have all day!" I bellowed.

A voice swooped like a bird from the heights of the Big Tree: "Hold your horses, *Kemo Sabe!*"

Despite myself, I took a step back. "Timmy?"

"I'm a mandrill baboon, the toughest animal in the jungle! *EEEEEEEEEEEE-YAAAAAAAAAA!*"

"Why don't you come down?"

"I wish I could, but it's not that easy, Mr. Wizard. The door to Nod is hard to find. You've got to really *want* to find it. You've got to prove how much you want it."

"Sorry, I left my corn knife at home."

He laughed quietly. "All you have to do is come up here and get me, Jeff. That will be good enough."

I felt my jaw drop. "You expect me to *climb?*"

"Hey—you did it before, remember? You and me—the only people to ever reach the top of the Big Tree!"

Of all the bizarre and terrifying things that had happened to me in the last week, this was somehow the worst. "Timmy," I said, "I can't climb trees anymore. I'm forty-one years old."

"You're too *mature* to climb now?"

"No, you idiot, I'm too fucking *old!*"

"Hey, man, watch your language." A pause. "You're not trying to back out on me, are you, *Kemo Sabe?*"

"No—"

A gust of wind roared through the clearing, making the tree's foliage pitch and roll like a storm cloud. From behind me came a rippling crash. I whirled. The wind died away, and everything became still. No—not quite. Out in the field, in one small area, the corn was moving, swaying and crackling as if something were swimming through it. Something large.

Coming this way.

CHAPTER TWENTY-EIGHT

END OF THE ROW

"Timmy . . ." I said.

There was no answer. The disturbance in the corn drew steadily closer.

"Timmy!"

No reply. It was like watching an earthquake fissure approach. I looked around, spotted a decent-sized rock and clawed it out of the turf. It wasn't much of a weapon, but I felt better with it in my hand.

Now I could glimpse something dark bludgeoning its way through the corn. I raised the stone over my head. And waited.

The ripple had nearly reached the clearing when there was a loud, thumping crash, and a fan of corn plants cascaded toward me. Dust billowed up. A voice roared, "Fucking goddamn corn!"

Mike Norris got to his feet, brushing chaff out of his beard. He glared at me. "What's the matter, Dittimore? See something green?"

I just gaped.

"You alive or dead?" he demanded, face serious. He stood waist-deep in the corn, poised as if about to run or fight.

Curling my hand into the Indian sign of protection, I placed it against the side of my head.

He visibly relaxed. "So the Nodkin didn't grab you last night after all."

"Like you said, they didn't need to."

He waded the rest of the way out of the field. His sweaty T-shirt was flesh colored where it stuck to the skin bulging from the sides

222

of his overalls. Yellow corn beetles dotted his beard. He ignored the Big Tree as if it weren't there. "So now what?"

"Depends. Did you come out here to help me or shoot me?"

"To help. I'm sure this is a mistake, but . . ." He shrugged. "Hell, it's pathetic, but you're the best friend I ever had."

"That is pathetic."

He laughed, but sobered instantly and cast a sidelong glance at the Big Tree. "Yeah . . . well, like I said, now what?"

I hesitated. "I just talked to Timmy. He's way up in the tree. You won't believe this, but he wants me to climb up and get him."

"Climb up *there?*"

"Yeah. But since you're here, maybe things have changed." I turned back toward the tree. "Hey, Timmy! Mike's here! Now there are *two* of us who want you to come down, so why don't you just do it?"

No reply. Far overhead, a couple of purple martins wheeled against the sky like boomerangs. I tried again. "Wynken, Blynken and Nod, traveling the universe! Remember?"

No reply.

"Damn it." I lowered my gaze to the tree trunk; thick and wrinkled, it reminded me of the leg of a brontosaur. "Well, I guess there's no choice."

"Think about this, Jeff," Mike said earnestly. "Even if you manage not to fall and break your neck, then what? What are you gonna do once you're up there? What's *he* gonna do?"

"How would I know?" I asked irritably.

"Well, it's guaranteed you won't like it, whatever it is."

"Unless I think of something *he* won't like. I have to try."

"Then I'm going, too."

I blinked at him. "Thanks, but . . . you . . ."

"I know, I know. I'm a big fat whale, right? And big fat whales can't climb trees."

"That's not it," I said, although it certainly was part of it. "Remember that time we climbed the tree when we were kids? You couldn't make it even then."

"Maybe that's why I have to do it now."

I started to object some more, then gave up. Why bother? There was no chance Mike would get as far as the fork of the tree, much less all the way to the top. For that matter, there wasn't much chance *I'd* make it.

He stepped closer. "Still have the gun?"

I caught myself just before I reached for it. "Yeah."

"Good. Remember to take the safety off if you have to use it."

"And get real close to the target," I said woodenly, trying to picture myself shooting a thirteen-year-old kid in the head.

"Yeah," Mike said, "but don't worry." He smiled his brown smile. "I've got the Magnum on me."

If anyone had been watching, what happened next would have looked like a Laurel and Hardy routine. Mike insisted that I boost him up first, rather than trying to haul him into the tree from above, against gravity. Or perhaps he was afraid I'd just abandon him. Rightfully so.

As it was, I didn't have the strength to keep my fingers laced together when he leaned on them. They popped apart, but not before I lost my balance and crashed face-first into the heavy bark of the tree.

Whirling constellations filled my head, like something from a cartoon. Bugs Bunny. The Road Runner. I heard myself laughing. I couldn't help it.

"Asshole," Mike said, but he was laughing, too.

"Okay." After my head cleared, I got down on my hands and knees. "Climb on my back."

"You're gonna regret this, old man," he said, and put one of his size twelves between my shoulders. I heard him grunt, and suddenly an almost unbearable pressure crushed down on my spine. But I managed to keep my quivering arms locked, and after a moment most of the weight receded. Grunts, curses and bark fragments showered down around me, and then the rest of the pressure vanished.

I stumbled to my feet. Mike's shoulders and upper rib cage were wedged into the fork of the tree, legs kicking ineffectually below. His denim-encased backside looked as big as Hawaii. It should have been funny, this enormous ass protruding out of the tree, but it wasn't funny at all. It was pathetic and frightening. Why were we out here, anyway? You can't send a man to do a boy's job.

But I didn't say anything, just braced one of Mike's feet so he could wriggle his way up into a seated position. His face was almost purple, and he rubbed his hairy chin. "Christ, I think I ripped out half my beard." He turned his cap around backward on his head, and I had a weird flash of the long-ago Mike. One of his hands extended down. "You ready?"

"Sure." I reached up and took his hand, and the next thing I knew I was hurtling upward, gasping, astonished by the power hidden under all that flab. I grabbed one of the trunks and scrambled onto it, clinging just above Mike.

God, the ground looked far away.

"You better take the lead from here on out," Mike said. The color had left what was visible of his face—not just the flush, *all* the color. Skin and white beard seemed to blend together seamlessly. "If I fall, I don't wanna take you with me."

"That's real encouraging." I raised my head. The tree looked just like it had in my memories: two major forks, both seemingly infinite in length and offering no real handholds for far too great a distance.

"Timmy!" I shouted at the top of my lungs. "Come on, man! Do we have to do this?"

The canopy seemed to absorb my voice, giving nothing back.

"Maybe he's pissed off that I'm with you," Mike said grimly.

"Maybe. Or maybe he's been waiting for you, too."

"That's what I'm afraid of."

"Yeah," I said. "Well . . . we've come this far. Might as well finish."

I reached up and got a grip on the bark.

Almost immediately, I knew this was a big mistake. I weighed two and a half times as much as I had the last time I'd climbed this tree, but I was far from two and a half times as strong. My shoes didn't help, either—the soles were pliable enough but provided very little traction. As for my hands, they were the soft, uncalloused tools of the professional paper pusher. The rest of my skin was softer yet. As a result, the bark of the tree felt like bundles of dull saw blades dragging across my body. To make matters worse, the unyielding lump of the pistol in my pocket ground against my hipbone. Why had I kept the damn thing, anyway? To use on myself, maybe.

If it weren't for the fact that my arms and legs were now far longer than they'd been in the old days, I would have fallen out of the tree in half a minute. But as it was, I was able to maintain enough of a grip around the trunk to keep myself attached, and moving.

I had no idea how Mike was faring, but didn't make the mistake of looking down to find out. I didn't look up, either. I kept my left cheek pressed firmly against the bark of the tree and my eyes fixed on the leaves to one side as I inched along.

And I thought good thoughts. Of all things, driving across the Sonoran Desert with Mom and Dad during our move west, all three of us bellowing out traveling songs—"B.I.N.G.O." and "The Witchdoctor" and "She'll Be Coming 'Round the Mountain."

The insides of my shoulders suddenly filled with fire, locking as solid as overheated pistons. I halted, face twisted in agony as I clung desperately to scales of bark and trembled all over. I could feel the subtle wagging of the truck under me. Could imagine the acceleration of my incipient fall; the brief flash of agony at the bottom—

Then I heard a growl: *Grrrrrrrrrrrrrmph.* A pause. *Grrrrrrrrrrrrrmph.* A pause. *Grrrrrrrrrrrrrmph.* My skin started contracting in fear before I realized the sound came from Mike. Each grunt represented the gain of a foot, or perhaps an inch, of altitude. Mike, despite his ponderous weight and his acrophobia, was still climbing the Big Tree behind me. And he sounded close.

"Hey, you bozos!" Timmy shouted abruptly, his voice so loud I almost lost my grip. "Get the lead out! And Mike, see if you can make it a little farther this time, okay?"

Mike said nothing. The growling continued.

Despite myself, I looked up. The first branch hung only ten or fifteen feet away. *Only.* It might as well have been ten or fifteen miles. When I tried to move again I discovered I simply had nothing left. My fingers, so numb I couldn't feel them, began to slip. My shoes scraped ineffectually at the bark. I slid down an inch, two inches . . .

Gail's image leaped into my mind. Gail, thirteen years old, Arizona tanned, clinging for her life on the branch above me. *Help me, Jeff. I'm scared. Help me!*

My fingers tightened on the bark. I scrambled with my toes, yanked with my arms. Jerked my body up a few inches. Did it again. Again. *I'm coming, Gail. I'll help you. I'll save you.* It was working.

An eternity later, I slung an arm over the limb. Hung there for a moment, eyes closed, lungs heaving at maximum capacity, then hauled my body up. Hugged the tree desperately, as if I'd always felt pure love and respect for it. I wanted to pray. I wanted to throw up. I did neither. I'd made it. Made it. Made—

"Jeff." Mike's choked voice came from just below. "Help me, Jeff. God . . . help me, I'm slipping . . ."

I leaned over. He was in about the same place I'd been when I started to lose it. His eyelids were sphinctered closed. "Come on, Mike," I said. "You're almost there. You can make it."

"I can't. I can't."

"Can you go down, then? Can you just slide back down?"

"No. No. I'm *slipping* . . ."

"Look at me, Mike! Look up!"

With a rasping sound, one of his feet skidded down the trunk. He scrambled madly with both legs, like a man running on ice.

"Mike! *Look at me!*"

He finally opened his eyes. They were so wide and bloodshot I half expected them to burst like overripe pomegranates. "Come on," I said, and slid my hips off my perch, hooking the branch under one knee and dangling the other leg as far as it would go. "Grab my foot. Come on. Climb up and grab my foot. You can do it."

I couldn't see him around my own body now, but I heard him grunting again. I strained my leg down until I started to lose my own grip. A minute later there was a snarl so loud it was nearly a scream, and suddenly something hauled down on my leg with such force I screamed.

For several long seconds we stayed in that position. My groin muscles trembled. Mike's breathing was a symphony of panicky whistles. I gritted my teeth.

"Okay," Mike said just when I was beginning to think he was going to rip me in half. "Okay, I can make it now." The weight released my foot.

With difficulty, I hauled myself back onto my branch, rested a moment, then clambered up to the next higher branch. I didn't sit down; my crotch felt like the inside of a catcher's mitt after a tough game. Below me, Mike's baseball cap appeared. Then his flabby arm as he hurled it over the lower branch. He rested again, and I heard him sobbing softly. Finally he managed to haul himself the rest of the way onto the branch, where he hugged the trunk as if it were his first lover.

When I was sure he was safe, I scanned the canopy overhead. "Timmy?" I called. "You satisfied yet?"

From far above came the ape scream followed by a laugh, but no movement except that of leaves and light.

"Shit," I muttered, and looked back down. "You okay, Mike?"

"Told you I'd make it. Told you."

"We're not finished yet. You ready to keep going? It's easier from here on."

"I'll bet." He looked up. One of his cheeks was scraped raw, but now his eyes contained more anger than fear. "Okay. Let's go. When we find Timmy, I'm going to personally pitch him out of this tree."

We moved up through swaying leafy spaces, taking our time, testing each handhold, each foothold. Watching for Timmy.

Up and up. Larger shreds of sky began to appear overhead. At the same time, the trunk of the tree narrowed until I could encircle it with both hands. Under my feet, the branches became so skinny they bent under my weight with every step. I stopped and looked down. Mike had fallen behind, wedging his feet against the thickest part of each branch and transferring his weight carefully. Something was wrong with my perspective, though . . . I realized I could see his sweat-soaked back. A chill showered through me. The trunk was bowing outward under our weight.

"Hold on, Mike," I said. "Stop."

He looked up; his face was almost as green as the tree should have been. "What?"

"That's far enough."

"Okay. Okay." He enfolded the trunk in his arms and found a resting spot for each shoe. "Now what?"

"I guess we wait."

"Not for long, I hope. This is killing my feet." He closed his eyes again.

I looked around. Still no sign of Timmy. I watched a black and orange woolly worm creep tentatively along a twig. Beyond that, sunlight flashed like fireworks through a mass of leaves. Spurred by my memory of the aerial view of Middlefield, I leaned out to push the leaves aside.

As I touched them they exploded toward me, disgorging a roaring, fanged face.

I knew what it was. Even as I screamed and threw up my hands, I knew. Even as I recoiled, I knew. Part of my mind, calm and cynical, acknowledged that I'd been fooled again.

My body was already beyond the balancing point. The tree trunk was out of reach. I rotated helplessly over the fulcrum of my feet. Looking down, I saw the top of Mike's Reds cap.

I screamed. Something.

Acceleration. Twigs shattered around me; leaves fled like shoals of frightened fish. A dull roar began to build in my ears. My scream grew—

—and ended in an agonized grunt as I struck Mike. For a moment I stopped falling. A branch hovered directly in front of me; I clutched it with both hands. I hung there, eyes closed, listening in anguish for the sounds of Mike's fall. Instead, from somewhere came a deep, resonant hum. And then a voice: *"CROOOOOOOOOO-AAAAAAAAAAA-TOOOOOOOOOOOO-AAAAAAAAAAAA-HHHHHHHHHHNNNNNNNNN . . ."*

I opened my eyes. Below me I saw Mike, also clinging to a branch, but positioned much farther away from the trunk of the tree. As I watched, his branch sagged an inch, four inches, a foot. Mike stared up at me, teeth bared in a rigid, bitten-off scream.

"Hang on," I said, and started swinging hand-over-hand toward the trunk. "Hang—"

There was a crackling sound, and the whole tree jolted. Mike let out a wail. I halted, looked down. Mike's branch now slanted down at a thirty-degree angle. "Oh, God," Mike said. "Oh, God, Jeff . . ."

Crack!

The report was so loud that for an irrational moment I thought Mike had fired his pistol. Then he began to fall, still clutching the broken branch. The expression on his face was more of surprise than fear, as if he couldn't believe, after all this time, that he was really going to die.

His descent developed with nightmarish slowness. He rotated backward, arms flailing for branches that seemed to deliberately pull out of his reach. I doubt he even glimpsed the first limb that didn't move, a fat branch that smashed into the back of his head with a meaty *crack* I heard plainly. His body spun forward, arms and legs flopping. Seconds later another branch shattered his legs with a sharper *snap*, whirling him the other way in a shower of his own blood before he was swallowed by the leaves of the Big Tree.

I couldn't hear my own weeping over the throbbing note of the bull-roarer.

Raising my head, I saw Timmy crouched on a limb above me, swinging the bull-roarer in a tilted arc that avoided the surrounding branches. He was dressed in his tree-climbing uniform of cut-off shorts and sneakers, and his greasy hair erupted from his pate in dark, glossy blades. "AAAAAAAAAAAAAAAAAAAAAAAAA-AAAAAAAAAAAAAAAA . . ." he droned.

"You—you—"

". . . AAAAAAAAAAAAAAAAAAAAAAAAAAAAAAAAAAA-AAAAA . . ."

Without warning, the branch to which I clung broke free. Screaming, I grabbed at everything around me, just as Mike had done. Nothing held. Branches whacked my hands, my legs. I began to spin through a scarlet tornado.

". . . AAAAAAAAAAAAAAAAAAAAAAAAAAAAAAAAAAA-AAAA . . ."

Spinning. Just like in my falling dreams.

". . . AAAAAAAAAAAAAAAAAAAAAAAAAAAAAAAAAAA-AAAA . . ."

Any moment now I'd feel the same terrible impact that had killed Mike. No! That never happened in my falling dreams. In those, I always awakened before it was too late.

Spinning.

". . . AAAAAAAAAAAAAAAAAAAAAAAAAAAAAAAAAAA-AAA . . ."

". . . AAAAAAAA . . ."

Wake up!

Spinning . . .

Wait.

Motionless.

Eyes closed, I felt the texture of cotton sheets beneath me—and under that, the dense resistance of a mattress.

I relaxed. A falling dream, just a falling dream. But what about the rest of it? Timmy . . . Mike . . . the Big Tree . . .

Opening my eyes, I blinked at the dim daylight spilling through the window. Which day, though? Which window?

I sat up. Small rectangular room. The window was situated across from the foot of the bed. Closet on one long wall. Near the head of the bed, a door, closed. The floor was mostly hidden by a swath of homely flotsam: clothing, books, parts of a plastic airplane.

The bed itself was very narrow, and too short for me. The sheets featured a design of donut-shaped space stations, spacewalking astronauts, and rocket ships with big fins. On the wall next to the bed hung posters depicting the Andromeda Galaxy and Earth's solar system.

Near the window stood a dresser with a mirror above it. On top of the dresser sat a model of a Gemini 4 space capsule. Even from here I could see globs of poorly applied glue along its seams. I'd never had much patience with models.

Suddenly I was on my feet. *My* feet, my adult feet clad in the cheap shoes I'd bought the day I got off the plane in Indianapolis. My pantlegs were torn and stained in streaks of ocher, as if I'd worn them while . . . well, while climbing a tree.

Now I was sitting on the bed again, trembling all over. Cold to the core. The undersides of my arms abraded red, my fingers stiff and weak.

Almost against my will, I turned my head and looked through the window. Outside, the air was gloomy yet curiously luminescent, as if a storm was approaching. The cornfield was colored the warm golden brown of autumn. In the distance stood the Big Tree, red as a blot of blood.

I turned away and slowly got to my feet again. Walked to the mirror.

When I peered into it I saw a twelve-year-old boy, his hair clipped into a Hollywood Burr. I recoiled violently. Then I realized the boy wasn't moving the way I was. He was rummaging in one of the dresser drawers, stirring through wads of mismatched socks.

Behind this young Jeff, the bedroom door opened. A youthful Dad leaned in, all flat-top haircut and horn-rimmed glasses. "Oh, good, you're up," he said in a faint, metallic voice. "Wouldn't want you to sleep away a beautiful fall day like this."

I spun around. My elbow struck the Gemini capsule, propelling it into an unsuccessful orbit and ruinous landing.

The door was closed. No Dad. No one in the room but me.

Back in the mirror, the Gemini model stood intact on the dresser. Jeff had lifted his head to look at Dad in dismay. "We're not gonna rake leaves, are we?" he asked in his own distant voice.

"Well, you could help your mom do laundry if you'd prefer."

Jeff's mouth twisted in disgust. Laughing, Dad closed the door. Young Jeff returned to his excavation, finally found a pair of matching socks and flopped down on the bed to pull them on.

I turned away from the mirror again. No one on the bed. No one in the room. I looked down at myself. *I* was in the room, wasn't I? *Wasn't I?*

"Christ." My knees weakened, and I slid down the front of the dresser until I was kneeling. "Oh, Christ."

After a while I was able to get up again. Without looking back into the mirror, I walked across the room and opened the door. Peeked into the hall. Empty. Everything looked exactly as I remembered from the old days, except the proportions were wrong. The bathroom was only a few feet away, not the hundred miles or so it had seemed when I was a child. To the right were the master bedroom and the spare room where Mom had kept her sewing stuff. In the other direction was the living room, furnished with a recliner and couch with flat 1950s contours, a console TV, a paramecium-shaped coffee table. A *Life* magazine lay atop the table. Young Liz Taylor on the cover.

I walked into the living room. It was gloomy, the curtains drawn. Although there was no one there, I sensed movement just beyond my perception. I felt sure that if I had a mirror, I'd see Mom walking past with a cup of coffee in one hand while she used the other to scruff the hair of a drowsy Jeff Dittimore who was on his way to the kitchen for a bowl of Honeycombs cereal . . .

The doorbell rang. It was quite loud, perfectly clear. I hesitated, then strode over and pulled the door open.

Timmy Kegler stood on the front porch, wearing sneakers, jeans with rolled-up cuffs, an oversized T-shirt. "Can you come out and play?" he asked, and grinned.

SNIPS AND SNAILS

CHAPTER TWENTY-NINE

DON'T FORGET TO CLOSE THE DOOR BEHIND YOU

Looking past Timmy again, I saw an autumn day. But this wasn't the Middlefield of 1994, with its mature trees and refurbished houses; this was the town where I'd grown up. In each front yard stood a spindly tree fluttering with golden leaves. The houses were all shoeboxes with small concrete porches and asphalt-shingle roofs. Here and there rakes stood upright from piles of leaves that might have just been scraped together. Overhead, the sky was filled with the kind of dark, roiling clouds that look more like smoke than water vapor—the kind of clouds I remembered from late autumn days in Indiana. The air held just a snap of coolness, and was tinted with the spice of burning leaves. In the distance, a crow unwound its rattling cry. I inhaled deeply. I'd forgotten about days like this. It had been so long . . .

How long?

A chill rippled through me. Looking down, I saw the same paunchy waistline I'd been threatening to whip into shape for years, still dressed in the sweat-and-bark-stained clothes I'd had on when I climbed the Big Tree. *It is me,* I thought.

When I raised my head again, I noticed I wasn't the only anomaly. Despite the autumn-painted trees and cool, spicy air, the grass was the bright Kelly green of springtime. Also, none of the houses seemed to need their paint touched up, or their windows washed. The sidewalks were free of dog turds and the flattened pink disks of bubble gum. Strangest of all, there were no cars. Not in the driveways, not parked at the curbs, not cruising down the street. I couldn't even hear the drone of wheels in the distance.

I raised my eyes. As always, the water tower stood sentinel above the downtown district—but now the name painted on the side of the storage tank was TIMFIELD.

"Welcome to the land of Nod," Timmy said.

My knees felt as if they'd come unhinged. "This can't be right," I said, leaning against the door frame. Gray amoebas swarmed across my vision. "You were supposed to *leave* the land of Nod. That was why we went through all this."

Timmy sucked in his lips. "Yeah, but Mike messed it up. When he fell, he died, and that was like a sacrifice. The door opened. You were falling, too, so I had to make a choice—come to Earth or bring you to Nod. You would have died, too, if—"

"Mike . . ." I swallowed. "You're sure . . ."

"You saw him hit that branch. Splatto."

I blinked, made my eyes focus. Now I was squatting on my heels, my head lower than Timmy's. I realized I was making a terrible mistake. No matter what, Timmy mustn't feed off my fear. Rising back to my full height, I looked around again and said, "So, we're really in the land of Nod?"

Timmy smiled smugly. "And you thought I just made it up."

I glanced again at the water tower. TIMFIELD. "Okay, I believe you. The land of Nod is real. Now let's leave."

The corners of his mouth sank, making a straight line. "You don't even want to look around?"

"No. I want to get back to my own life. Right now."

"But it's—"

"*Right now*, Timmy."

He crossed his arms. "There you go, talking like a grownup again. 'Right now, Timmy.' I thought you'd at least want to see what Nod's like. The Jeff *I* knew would want to see."

"I'm not the Jeff you knew. I *am* a grownup. And I want to go back to the other side, the real world, whatever you call it." I paused, frowned. "I thought that's what *you* wanted, too."

His huffiness dissolved. Scuffing a toe briskly over the surface of the porch, he said, "Well, that's the thing."

"What do you mean?"

"We can't go back."

"*What?*"

"I thought you understood how this works. With you here and Mike dead, there's no one left on the other side to open the door." He looked up. "We're stuck in Nod forever now, *Kemo Sabe.* Both of us."

"That can't . . ."

"It won't be so bad; you'll *like* it once you get used to it, believe me. Anyway, we don't have a choice. Might as well make the best of it. Come on, I'll show you around." Turning, he marched down the steps toward the street.

But I stayed where I was. Maybe if I hurried back into the house, into my bedroom, I could undo this nightmare. Maybe if I fell asleep in that narrow little bed, I'd wake up in California, listening to the Santa Anas blow and being relieved I'd just had a vivid dream. Maybe—

Behind me, the door slammed shut. I jumped.

"Coming?" Timmy asked. He was standing at the curb.

On legs as stiff and heavy as bags of cement, I walked toward him. At the same time, he stuffed a couple of fingers into his mouth and let out a painfully loud whistle. He'd always wanted to be able to do that, but never could. Not in the real world.

From the direction of Lincoln Avenue came a cadenced, clomping sound, like double-time marching. As I watched, an open carriage rolled around the corner at Oak Lane and turned toward us. It was pulled not by horses but by four young men in denim and leather, their bodies straining against the traces, their boots stomping in rhythm. The driver was a portly woman dressed in bright colors. As the vehicle drew closer, I recognized her: the Mean Lady.

The carriage angled over and stopped in front of Timmy. Leaning down from the driver's seat, the Mean Lady threw open a small door. "Hop in, gentlemen!" she cried, grinning.

As Timmy complied, I stared at the four youths attached to the traces. They wore black leather jackets and square-toed engineer's boots. Reins hung from the metal bits which stretched their mouths into drooling rectangles. They stared back at me silently, their eyes caves of hatred.

"Hurry up, Jeff," Timmy said.

The passenger seat of the carriage was upholstered in tuck-and-roll leather. As I settled next to Timmy, I cleared my throat. "Are those really the Wagners?"

He smiled, wobbled a hand back and forth. "Well, sort of. They're ghosts, they're not like you and me. The cool thing is, over here ghosts are like Play-Doh; you can shape them any way you want, make them do things."

"Who made you God, Timmy?"

He scowled. "I'm not God, I'm the king of Nod. Without me, there's no kingdom. Nobody wants that. Nod is the best place ever."

"Who says?"

"Everyone who matters. I'll show you." Leaning forward, he tapped the Mean Lady's broad hip and said, "Driver, take us to Finney's."

"Yes, your lordship." The Mean Lady raised the reins and snapped them. Instantly the Wagners pulled against the traces. The buggy rolled forward, made an impossibly tight U-turn and headed back toward Lincoln Avenue.

I glanced at my house as we passed. It had the brown and beige paint job I remembered. Behind it, the Big Tree looked three or four times bigger than it should be, towering into the sky, a strident red smear.

"Pretty scary, huh?" Timmy asked softly, not looking at the tree. "We were right about it in the first place, you know."

"What do you mean?"

In his lap, he made the Indian sign of protection with both hands. "It doesn't like kids very much."

"But I thought—"

"Hey, do you want to go flying later?"

"Flying?"

"You haven't forgotten how, have you? You used to dream about flying all the time, remember? Just raise your arms and *go!*"

"I haven't dreamt that . . . for years."

He shook his head. "You'll have to practice, then. But I know you can do it, or you would never have made it over here in the first place."

I said nothing, just lowered my eyes. The canopy of clouds pressed down like a cast-iron lid. I wondered if the sky was always this gloomy here. Probably. This *shadowy.*

The carriage turned onto Lincoln Avenue, and I glanced over at the high school. CROATOAN HIGH, proclaimed the letters above the entrance. Spanning the breezeway was a hand-lettered banner: CLOSED UNTIL HELL FREEZES OVER.

"You don't look very happy," Timmy said petulantly. "Would you have liked it better if I let you fall and break your neck?"

"I'd like it better if I were back home."

"You are home."

"You know what I mean. I've got a family, Timmy. There has to be some way for me to get back to them. My daughter will be worried sick. She—"

Timmy grunted. Without warning, the surrounding street and buildings vanished, as did the clouds. Bright sunlight blasted down on us. To the left, the high school campus melted into a blue ocean, surf heaving itself against a beach. The image was perfect, although the rumble of waves sounded oddly soft and muffled. There were people all over the beach, some lying on towels, others wading in the shallows. No one seemed to notice the carriage rolling past.

Ahead, a volleyball game was in progress, teenagers of both sexes jumping up and down. Slim, tanned legs and flat bellies.

And Terri. She stood on the sidelines with some other kids. Her slender body was barely covered by a couple of strips of cloth; I doubted her mother knew she owned such a swimsuit. She also held a burning cigarette between her fingers. A boy's hand was planted on her back, well below the waist. His head was shaved except for a couple of arbitrarily placed braids. He wore a silver loop through one nostril. As the carriage drew closer, he kissed Terri, pulling her close, rubbing his crotch against hers. She reciprocated.

"Like mother, like daughter," Timmy said.

I was out of the carriage before I knew it, charging across the sand, barely aware that the surface under my shoes didn't *feel* like sand, it felt like pavement. When I reached Braid-head, I reached out and grabbed his arm.

Tried to grab his arm. My hands passed right through it without any resistance at all. He went on kissing my daughter, my underaged daughter, with plenty of tongue. Now he had a thumb hooked in the back of her bikini bottoms, all but exposing her to the world.

I started to reach for him again, caught myself, trembling.

The carriage had stopped. Timmy stood beside me, staring

scornfully at the clinching couple. "She doesn't look worried about anything if you ask me, *Kemo Sabe.*"

I clenched my fists. "Is this *real?*"

He hesitated. "It's like watching Ed Sullivan on TV. I mean, it's really *happening,* but we can't touch anybody or anything; they can't even see us. Come on, let's get back to Timfield."

I looked at Terri one more time, then followed Timmy back to the buggy. As I dropped onto the seat, I felt the gray amoebas closing in on me again.

"Your life kind of stinks, doesn't it?" Timmy asked. The buggy lurched forward and the scenery blurred, darkened; a moment later we were back on Lincoln Avenue, still heading toward School Street.

"Everybody has problems," I muttered.

He smiled. "Not me. Not in the land of Nod."

"Then why were you so eager to leave?"

For a moment he looked puzzled, as if he didn't understand the question. Then he said, "Oh," and gestured at the passing scenery. "Look. Here in Timfield I can *do* stuff; play games, move things around, even mess with stuff on the other side. But if I get very far away, everything turns to pictures like we just saw. That gets boring after a while."

"Poor Mike," I muttered.

"Huh?"

"He guessed that's why you wanted to come back to earth. Because you're stuck here."

"What a smart guy. It's amazing he's dead and you're still alive, huh?"

I ignored that. "What's the boundary?"

"What do you mean?"

"You can't go any farther than the Big Tree, can you?"

He winced, glanced over his shoulder. So did I. The crown of the Big Tree was still visible above all the rooftops that lay between us and Oak Lane; red and gnarled, it looked like a bloody brain. Timmy turned back. His cockiness was gone. "The Big Tree . . . won't let me go."

"Won't *let* you go? But I thought it was just a doorway."

"It's more like . . . a mouth. It swallows things."

I looked at him, at his pale face, and had a revelation. "That's not it. You're scared, that's all. Scared to go back."

Color returned instantly, flushing his cheeks. "I am not."

"Sure you are. You were always afraid of unfamiliar things unless you made them up yourself."

"You're full of it." Leaning forward, he tapped the Mean Lady's shoulder. "Slave, let's pick up the pace a little."

"Yes, your worship." From a holder at her side the Mean Lady pulled a long whip, which she raised high over her head. Its supple braid curled back, coiled into a figure eight, snapped forward too quickly to see. *Crack!* Jerry Wagner's left ear ripped in half in a flash of blood. Jerry screamed.

"Earsplitting," Timmy murmured, smiling.

The carriage sped up. I felt slightly nauseous from the movement, not to mention Timmy's casual barbarity. I remembered how, when we were kids, he and I used to run around after rainstorms, scooping earthworms out of puddles so the worms wouldn't drown.

What was the old saying? *Absolute power corrupts absolutely . . .*

I turned toward Timmy. Took in the smug, relaxed expression on his face. What had I said to him a minute ago? *Everybody has problems.*

Not me, he'd replied. *Not in the land of Nod.*

My spine stiffened, as if receiving a charge of electricity. "You son of a bitch," I said.

Timmy's smile slowly inverted. "What?"

"You never even *intended* to go back to the other side. Did you?"

"What are—"

"You only wanted to bring one of us, one of your old friends, *here.* Isn't that right? One of *us* could make the land of Nod bigger for you just be being here. Isn't that right?"

He scowled. "You don't know what you're talking about."

"Sure I do. Mike and I were your last hope . . . you set us up, didn't you, you murdering little son of a bitch?"

His eyes narrowed to black slits. "Stop calling me names."

"Asshole. Motherfucker. Dickhead." I rose taller and taller in the seat, until I was almost standing. "I ought to beat the shit out of you. I could do it when we were kids, and now I'm twice your—"

My voice broke like a dry twig as the light abruptly failed. The sky darkened until it was almost black, then lit up with tangles of violet lightning. Timmy no longer sat beside me. Instead, a shadow beast stood there, rearing against the clouds, fangs shining. Before I could react, taloned hands snapped around my upper arms with agonizing strength. My feet left the floor. The shadow beast grinned into my face. "What were you saying, *Kemo Sabe?*" Its breath reeked of maggot-swarming flesh. Thunder roared.

I couldn't reply.

"That's what I thought." My soles contacted the floorboards again and I collapsed onto the seat. The sky lightened to its previous gloomy level. Timmy sat down beside me and sighed. "You're wrong," he said. "I mean, yeah, you might be able to help me make the land of Nod bigger. But maybe not. The Big Tree used to scare *you*, too, remember?"

"I got over it."

"Sure you did. But there's another reason I brought you here, anyway." He paused, stared at his feet. For the first time since I'd arrived, he seemed unable to look at me. "Jeff . . . I got *lonely.*"

CHAPTER THIRTY

SEE YOU NEXT FALL

The carriage made a left turn onto School Street.

"Lonely?" I said. My biceps felt bruised, but I resisted the urge to rub them. "You always said you wanted to be a mountain man, live by yourself in the Rockies."

He was still looking down. "Yeah, but this isn't the Rockies. See, I already know what everything's like here; I know all the hiding places and I know how everybody's going to act. After a while . . . I kept remembering the old days when you and I were best friends. Remember, we always came up with the best games? And sometimes you could almost beat me when we played. Mike would have been okay to have here, too, but I really wanted *you.*" He glanced back at me. "And here you are."

I could hear the grainy hiss of blood pulsing through my veins. *And here you are.*

"See," Timmy said, "even if we can't make the land of Nod bigger, together we can have a lot of fun. It won't be so bad, will it?"

I turned away from him. Just up School Street was Gail's house, purple irises blooming in brilliant swaths along the driveway. What had she told me, back at Shady Acres? *You're the one he wanted all along, you know. Not Fred or Mike or me. You.*

Someone was sitting on the porch swing. As we drew closer I saw it was an adolescent girl dressed in a cheerleader's sweater and pleated skirt. Although the colors of the uniform were Middlefield's, the big letter sewn on the front of the sweater was a т instead of an м. The girl waved. I automatically started to wave

243

back, caught myself. It was Gail, Gail as she had looked in eighth grade. She was smiling broadly.

"I thought you were going to let her go," I said without looking at Timmy. "You said you'd let her join her husband and kids if I helped you."

"I said I'd let her go if I went back to Earth, which I didn't. Besides, she doesn't really want to leave. Look how happy she is."

Gail turned to follow us. Her grin never wavered. Neither did the frenzied motion of her hand.

"Oh, by the way," Timmy said, "I hate to tell you this, but she likes *me* better than you now. That's what you get for moving to California."

I said nothing, faced straight ahead. Here came the old junior high school building. Its windows were festooned with construction-paper cutouts in the shapes of Halloween jack-o'-lanterns, Thanksgiving turkeys, Christmas trees, St. Valentine's Day hearts, Easter bunnies. A sign on the front lawn proclaimed HAPPY TIMDAY! There were no kids in sight. No people at all.

The buggy turned right onto Landrus Avenue, then left onto Main Street. The trees growing on either side of the road here were so large their branches arched overhead in a canopy of red and gold. Timmy's buggy was the only vehicle of any description to be seen. It rolled down the middle of the street to the *clomp, clomp, clomp* of Wagner boots.

"Fall was always your favorite season, right?" Timmy asked.

I nodded.

"Mine, too." Leaves began to shower from the trees by the thousands; a dazzling storm of red, orange and gold. They spun and swooped around the buggy, gathered in hissing drifts around the wheels.

"Here in the land of Nod," Timmy said, "we can have any season we want whenever we want it. We can build snow forts later on, or go swimming out by the gravel pit, or whatever you want to do."

I said nothing. Now we were passing the Timfield Public Library. A sign on the front lawn proclaimed, TODAY ONLY—ETERNAL LOAN OF "THE WONDERFUL FLIGHT TO THE MUSHROOM PLANET."

"That's your favorite, right?" Timmy asked.

"I prefer the *Wall Street Journal*."

He snorted. "Yeah, sure."

Just beyond the library were several blocks of big wooden houses, the oldest homes in Middlefield. As we approached the nearest one, its front door flew open and a little girl leaped out, shouting, "It's them! It's them!" She vaulted down the steps and ran toward the street with a strange, lurching gait, waving wildly. Behind her, a woman wearing a flower-print dress and white apron stepped out of the house. In her hand she held a wooden spoon slathered in chocolate. Her face lit up, and she hurried after her daughter with a similar rigid stride, brandishing the spoon like a flag. The pair reached the curb just as the buggy was passing. Did I know them? There was a vague sense of familiarity; perhaps they had once been people I'd passed on the street as a child. As they stared at me, their faces ignited with a degree of happiness bordering on ecstasy. "Jeff!" they shouted. "Welcome home, Jeff! Welcome home!" When I got a better look at their faces, I recoiled. Their mouths weren't really smiling, they were stretched up at the corners as if yanked by invisible fingers. Above that, their eyes were even worse—the eyes of starving children.

The front door of the next house on the street flew open and a middle-aged man ran out, limbs as stiff as those of a poorly constructed marionette. I recognized him as the guy who used to put out produce at the IGA. He, too, waved and grinned and called greetings to me as he lurched down to the street.

Someone ran out of the next house, too.

And the next.

And the next.

Before long, Main Street was lined on both sides with a cheering, waving crowd. Here and there I recognized a face—Mrs. Edelstein the science teacher; Mr. Perkins, who had taught seventh-grade PE and who used to make Timmy display a damp towel to prove he'd taken a shower after class. Jerry Wagner. Even Mr. Kegler. All of them grinning madly beneath agonized or furious eyes. I'd never even seen Mr. Kegler smile before.

And they chanted: "Jeff! Jeff! Jeff!" while the trees released leaves like butterflies.

"Isn't this great?" Timmy said.

Looking up the street, I saw that the crowd extended clear to the edge of the business district. Which was impossible; there was no way this many people had died inside the Middlefield town limits during the last twenty-five years, not even with Timmy helping things along. I scanned the surrounding faces again. Suddenly I realized there was a similarity about many of them, almost a family resemblance—mismatched features, lopsided grins, deep-set eyes. Then, with a chill, I realized they *were* a family, in a way. They were the children of Timmy's imagination. They were Nodkin. I wondered—had they always existed here in this shadowy place beyond the Big Tree, waiting for Timmy to come to them, or were they merely the products of his greedy imagination? Did it make any difference?

We had almost reached the business district. Ahead, a banner hung above the main intersection: WELCOME HOME JEFF!!! The sound of cheering abruptly ceased. I glanced around. The sidewalks were deserted.

The buggy passed Vanover's Emporium, the five-and-dime store we boys had loved so much, then Manson's Bakery, then Freeman's Boutique. Pulling to the curb in front of Finney's Pharmacy, it stopped.

"Thanks, driver," Timmy said. "Maybe I'll let you have your dog back someday."

The Mean Lady grinned, gums blood red, eyes darting in their sockets like flies trapped between two panes of glass. "Thank you, your lordship. Thank you."

Jumping out of the buggy, Timmy scampered into Finney's. I followed, walking almost as stiffly as the ghosts had done. Above the door, a bell jingled.

The drugstore looked like I remembered—four narrow aisles, shelves piled with pills and salves, shampoos and soaps, pens and notebooks, candy and notions. Mr. Finney must still be alive, or else he died somewhere other than Middlefield, because he was not behind the elevated pharmacy counter. Instead Mrs. Edelstein stood there, wearing a green smock and a puppet smile. "Dinosaurs were warm-blooded!" she chirped. "Did you know that, boys? They sure were! I'm glad I got corrected on that one!"

Timmy ignored her and led me to the soda fountain in the back of the store. Its long counter was topped in Formica with a swirling pattern of gray and white with gold flecks. On the near side stood a row of swiveling stools; on the far side were the stainless-steel freezers and spigots and dispensers. From chrome tubes on the wall hung the cylindrical bases of sugar cones. The rest of the wall was taken up by an enormous mirror that revealed the aisles behind us, reversed. Timmy and I weren't reflected at all . . .

But other people were. I stared into the glass. The pharmacy was crowded. There were women wearing clunky shoes and cat's-eye glasses; men whose short haircuts revealed the pink gleam of scalp; kids in plaid Bermuda shorts, canvas sneakers and button-down shirts. I heard faint sounds of voices and laughter, passing cars.

"Can *they* see us?" I asked as I sank slowly onto a stool.

Timmy shrugged. "Since we're in Middlefield, some of them could if they tried, or if *we* tried. But don't worry about them right now. I've got a surprise for you. Look."

I turned. To Timmy's right sat three young boys. Short haircuts, canvas sneakers, sun-browned skin.

Timmy beamed. "Hail, hail, the gang's all here."

Mike, Fred, Abe, all looking the way they had in my dreams— skinny and innocent, all their lives before them. Their faces were stamped with identical grins.

Fred saluted me. "Hey, Jeff, it's about time you showed up!"

Abe nodded enthusiastically. I half-expected to see Franken-stein's-monster stitches around his neck, but the flesh was un-marked. "Good to see you again, Jeff."

Mike held his arms up and flexed them, muscle-man style. "I can't believe I was afraid to come here," he said. "This is the best place in the universe."

I stared at them, one after another. The rubbery grins. The haunted eyes. I whirled toward Timmy. "Cut it out."

"Cut what out?"

"You're making them act this way. Stop it."

Timmy's own smile faded. "You don't get it, do you? I'm the *boss* here. I can make them do whatever I want."

I started to retort, caught myself. Arguing had never been the way to persuade Timmy. I managed an indifferent shrug. "I thought you wanted this to be like old times. Doing *that* isn't like old times. It's . . . boring."

Timmy eyed me narrowly. "Well, sometimes they've got big mouths."

"So? Are you afraid of them or what?"

"Afraid of *them?* Ha!"

"Then let them be themselves."

He sighed, rolled his eyes. "Okay, okay. Just because this is your holiday." He waved his hand and all three grins vanished, replaced by expressions of wary relief.

"How do you guys feel?" I asked, leaning forward to look past Timmy.

Fred and Abe exchanged glances and said nothing. But Mike scowled, looked me straight in the eye and said, "How do I feel? If I had a gun, I'd blow Timmy's head right off his shoulders."

Timmy sighed. "See what I mean?"

Mike ignored him, kept staring at me. "I'm not kidding. If I had a gun—"

"Oh, shut up," Timmy snapped. The lower half of Mike's face shifted, and his mouth folded down and away like sand under surf. Between chin and nose, nothing was left but smooth skin.

"That's better," Timmy said.

"Timmy . . ." I began. Mike's hands pawed at the bottom of his face; his eyes were lenses of horror.

"Hey, I'm not telling him what to say, am I? Too bad he can't eat any ice cream now, unless he wants to suck it through his nose." Laughing, Timmy turned toward the counter. "Slave! Bring me a root beer float!"

Gail rose from behind the counter. This time she looked about sixteen years old, her hair parted in the middle and falling straight to her shoulders where it curled like foaming water. She wore a white polyester waitress's dress that was far too short, its hem reaching just below the width of her smooth hips. The front was unbuttoned to her navel. She wasn't wearing a bra, and the inside curves of her fresh breasts rolled toward one another as she leaned forward. "And what would *you* like, sir?" she asked me. Above her rictus smile, her eyes shimmered with tears.

I couldn't help it; I glanced down, saw the pink bud of one of her nipples. Closed my eyes. "Root beer," I muttered.

"Root beer *float*," Timmy said. "He wants a root beer *float*. See, Jeff, being able to make everybody do whatever you want isn't so bad, is it?"

My eyes were still closed. In the darkness I heard shuffling sounds, the thump of a freezer door opening. What if I didn't ever open my eyes again? If a tree falls in the forest and no one is there, is it visible?

"Do you want your eyes to get stuck that way?" Timmy asked with sinister nonchalance.

My eyes snapped open. Gail, her back to me, was leaning deep inside the ice cream freezer. The hem of her dress had ridden up over her little butt, almost to her waist. She wore no panties. Timmy stared at her with an uneasy expression composed of equal parts lust and revulsion.

"Goddamn it, that's enough!" I shot to my feet. "What's the matter with you, you sick little bastard?"

"Take it easy, *Kemo Sabe*," Timmy said softly, without looking at me. Gail straightened stiffly, the scoop in her hand, and stood facing the mirror. She wasn't reflected, either. In the glass, the shoppers of 1965 moved about busily.

Fred and Abe watched me, faces rigid. Mike, mouthless, rolled his eyes and bobbed his head at me in some incomprehensible code.

No. Not incomprehensible. Shocked at my own stupidity, I whirled toward Timmy. "Don't tell me to take it easy," I said. "And don't ever call me *Kemo Sabe* again."

Seen from the side, his ears rose a bit as he smiled. "Who's gonna stop me, *Kemo Sabe?*"

"I am."

"You don't learn very fast, d—" He swiveled toward me, and his eyes widened. In my hand was the little pistol Mike had given me, the one he'd been trying to remind me about. I thumbed back the hammer. Despite the diminutive size of the gun, the clacking sound was suitably nasty.

Timmy's face went as white as the ice cream dripping off Gail's scoop. "Where did you get that?"

"From Mike." Suddenly our surroundings, the counter and stools and spigot handles, made me feel like we were enacting a parody of a Western movie. But that was all right; that was appropriate. I knew who was wearing the white hat here.

Mike nodded wildly. Fred, Abe and Gail stood very still, watching with stiff faces.

"What did you tell me before?" I asked Timmy. "There's no land of Nod without you? Does that mean we all go free if I kill you? I'll bet it does. And will you turn into a ghost? I'll bet these guys would love to have a crack at you then."

His gaze flicked from my hand to my face and back. He smiled uneasily. "I'll bet that's not even a real gun."

Rotating my arm to the side, I pulled the trigger. I'll admit I half-expected nothing to happen, but there was a high-pitched *crack*, and the mirror shattered into several large fragments. They clung in their places, bending 1965 reflections into odd perspectives.

I was pretty sure about what was going to come next, and in a way it was a relief when it happened. Although I wasn't sure I could shoot Timmy Kegler, the shadow beast was a different matter.

Still, the creature moved so fast it almost caught me before I could swing my arm back around. The barrel of the pistol was actually touching its smooth black flesh when I pulled the trigger. This time a horrible scream almost drowned out the *crack*. My arm was slammed aside hard enough to spin me halfway around as the creature stumbled past, colliding with a rack of comic books. Archie, Sergeant Fury and the Howling Commandoes, Richie Rich, all fluttered to the floor. The shadow beast kept its feet and whirled toward me, its half-Timmy face startled and furious. From a small hole in the center of its torso pumped thick black fluid, like melted tar.

Aiming, I pulled the trigger again.

And again.

And again.

Againagainagainagainagain.

The shadow beast stumbled backward, arms flailing, viscous blood spewing from its wounds like motor oil from a cracked engine block. Stumbling over the wreckage of the comic rack, it crashed into the wall, then slid to the floor in a shower of Band-Aids and gauze. There it stayed, body tilted to one side, eyes fluttering, lips twitching up and down over its rows of fangs. A moment later its form melted and shifted, became Timmy Kegler. The black blood turned to bright red, glaring from walls and floor.

Timmy raised his head, blinked at me sadly. "You . . . best . . . friend," he whispered. His hands quivered, and then, with a single hacking cough that sprayed blood almost to my feet, he sagged and was still.

*   *   *

After half a minute, I turned slowly toward my friends.

They were all staring fixedly at Timmy's body. Mike had a mouth again. On the other side of the counter, Gail clutched the front of her uniform closed.

"Is he . . . dead?" Abe whispered. "Really, really dead?"

"What's it look like to you?" I demanded, and was shocked by the quaver in my voice. The stench of burned cordite made me want to retch.

Fred looked warily around the room. "If he's dead, then how come nothing's changed?"

I looked around, too. He was right. "Maybe it takes a while," I said uncertainly, but glanced back at Timmy. He looked dead to me. Very dead. And I'd done it. I'd shot and killed someone . . .

"I don't even *feel* any different," Fred said.

There was only one way to be sure. Slowly, I walked over to Timmy, then bent down to check the pulse in his throat. As I reached out, I was certain he would lunge up and grab me. But he didn't move. When I touched his neck, I felt no throbbing at all.

I relaxed. "Dead," I said, and started to straighten up. "I'm sure he—"

Timmy's left hand whipped up and clutched my wrist. I screamed and tried to wrench away; instead, I hauled Timmy to his feet.

He let go of me and laughed. Looked at all of us, threw back his head and howled. "You should see your faces! That was great!"

Stumbling away, I stared at the bloody holes in his T-shirt. He waved a hand over them, and they disappeared. *"Voilà,"* he said, snapping his fingers.

I glanced at the little pistol, still in my hand. Checked the register. Empty.

"You dummy," Timmy said, shaking his head. "How many times do I have to tell you, this is *my* place? That gun's from the *other* side; it's no good here." He walked up and punched my arm playfully. "Hey, don't feel bad, *Kemo Sabe.* That was really cool— Bam! Bam! Bam! You always did like to play Army."

"You're not going to punish him?" Abe blurted. "You always punish—" He cut himself off, cringing.

But Timmy just smiled. "Naw, no way. Jeff's trying to be a

tough guy, but he forgot: I always win our games. He needed a reminder."

I started to object, then shut my mouth. So he was lying—what difference did it make? Why did I even care?

"So, Jeff," Timmy said, "you wanna play Army? I mean *really* play, like in the old days?"

"No." I dropped the pistol onto the counter.

"No?" Timmy glanced at Gail and frowned. Instantly her arms flew wide, as did the front of her uniform. Her breasts were exposed. She grinned, licked her lips.

"Stop it," I said. "All right, stop it."

"You'll play?" he asked. Gail's hands cupped her breasts, squeezed them, pinched the nipples.

"Yes, I'll play Army. Stop it."

Timmy nodded. Gail yanked the dress closed and whirled around, head bowed.

"On one condition," I said.

Timmy eyed me warily. "What?"

"If I win, Gail goes free."

"Why would I do that?"

"Because if you don't, I won't play any more games with you, ever. I mean it. I ought to make you set *all* these guys free."

Timmy scowled. "I remember when you used to play just for fun."

"I remember when you didn't force me to play." I leaned toward him. "What's the matter, are you *afraid* to bet? Afraid you might *lose?*"

He laughed. "No way. Okay, you want to bet on Gail, we'll bet on Gail. I don't care."

"Do you swear on your honor that you'll let her go if I win?"

His face sobered, and he placed both hands over his heart. "On my honor, I swear it." Corny as the words sounded, it was a solemn oath; I'd never known him not to do anything he'd *sworn* to do. He lowered his hands. "But if I win, I get a prize, too."

"What's that?"

"First, Gail stays here. Second, after that you'll play games whenever I want, and you won't gripe about it."

"That's two prizes. That's not fair."

"What's the matter, afraid of losing?"

I took a deep breath. "All right. Deal."

We shook on it.

"Cool!" Timmy said. "Let's go get our weapons."

As he marched toward the door, the other guys hung back a moment. "You know you can't beat him, Jeff," Abe murmured.

"I'll think of something."

Fred shook his head. "You don't know what you're doing, man. This isn't like the old days, no matter what *he* says."

"I'll think of something."

Fred looked like he was going to retort, then glanced at Timmy's retreating back and just shook his head. He and Abe walked away. Mike stepped toward me, shrugged ruefully. "I really thought the gun would work."

"Me, too. Mike . . . I'm sorry I got you into all this. You were right about everything."

He shrugged. "What the hell, I was bound to end up here sooner or later, even if it wasn't until I died of old age. At least you're keeping Timmy distracted. I guess he was *really* nasty before you showed up."

"Terrific," I said.

"You guys coming or not?" Timmy shouted from the front of the store.

I glanced back at the soda fountain. Gail still stood behind the counter, gripping her dress closed. Tears glittered in her eyes. "Thank you," she whispered. "But . . . why are you trying to help me? It's my fault you're here. I can't . . . I don't . . ."

"Don't blame yourself," I said, half-strangled by love and anger. "Maybe *this* is the way things were meant to be."

The bell on the front door jingled. "Have fun, boys!" Mrs. Edelstein crowed. "Watch out for those warm-blooded dinosaurs!"

CHAPTER THIRTY-ONE

COUNTDOWN

Outside, the town looked deserted. Although a carpet of leaves turned Main Street into a golden river, the trees were still coated, too. Higher still, the grim drapery of clouds pressed down on everything. The top of the Big Tree was just visible in the distance.

Turning left, Timmy marched down the sidewalk with the rest of us tagging behind. We entered Vanover's Emporium. Inside, the store looked pretty much as I remembered—a cavernous main room with ceiling fans whisking brown shadows high above, surrounded by smaller rooms full of tools, hardware, gardening supplies, pet supplies.

But Timmy wasn't interested in the adjacent rooms. The main room was what mattered, because it was devoted entirely to toys —shelf after shelf after shelf of them.

"Pick your weapon!" Timmy cried. "Everything's free!"

We began to walk up and down the aisles. Despite myself, I found distinct pleasure in the surroundings. Although I'd visited plenty of modern toy stores as Terri grew up, even the biggest of them had never impressed me the way Vanover's always had. There were squirt guns in a dozen colors; string-wound plastic bugs that climbed the wall on suction-cup feet; pistols that fired spring-wound plastic propellers; rubber spiders and snakes; stuffed animals; cap guns; BB rifles; beanbags; toy soldiers; models of airplanes and spacecraft and submarines. Nothing here was sophisticated by modern standards, but that was part of the allure. Prominently absent were basketballs and baseballs and footballs, the accoutrements of organized sports.

I picked toys up, put them down. Most of them conjured up

some memory—a birthday, a Christmas. Everything was marked with tags reading: FREE. TAKE TOO THEIR SMALL.

I turned a corner, halted, went back. From a shelf I lifted a plastic rifle. It was almost a yard long, with a wood-grained stock in back and a pistol grip in front. The color was camouflage green, except for the spring-loaded knob on one side, which was bright, warning red. Stamped on the opposite side were the words MP-80 HIGH-POWER SUBMACHINE GUN.

"Remember?" Timmy asked from beside me.

I realized I was caressing the stock of the gun. I scowled. "I guess I'll use this."

"I thought you would. Let's go."

Near the door waited the other members of the gang, each armed with one of the realistic-looking plastic weapons that many cities back in the world of teenage drug lords and prepubescent gang-bangers had banned. Maybe, I thought, there were worse places to be than the land of Nod. All things considered . . .

I reeled the thought in quickly. All things considered, this was a game preserve and Timmy was the warden.

Outside, our group collected on the sidewalk. "Okay," I said. "What are the rules?" I remembered that this was an important part of the ritual. Timmy's games were so varied, it was critical everyone agreed up front on the parameters.

Timmy didn't even have to think about it. "Your front porch is base, Jeff; that's where Gail will be. We all start here and try to get to her. First one there wins. But there will be other soldiers trying to stop us along the way, plus we have to fight each other, too."

"What do you mean, 'other soldiers'?" I asked.

"You know, enemies. Don't worry, you'll be able to see them and everything."

"And they'll be fighting *all* of us?" I asked pointedly.

"Yes, all of us." He squinted at me. "You don't think I'd *cheat*, do you?"

No more than gambling casinos cheat people by setting the odds astronomically in the house's favor. "I just want this to be fair," I said. "That means no changing into animals or monsters, no flying, no teleporting. All right?"

"Like I need to do any of that."

Raising the MP-80, I said, "No surprise weapons, either. You can't, like, whip out a hand grenade or knife later. What we've got right now is *all* we've got."

"Okay, okay. Jeez."

Mike stepped forward. "And no using other ghosts, either."

"Hey, who asked *you* to—"

"That's a good point," I said, imagining Mr. Kegler leaning out of a house and pointing me out to Timmy. "Keep the other ghosts out of this. Just us and the other soldiers."

"Okay, okay, okay. Let's just *play.*"

I was sure there were more angles to cover, important angles. I thought back, tried to remember all the permutations of Army. "How many lives do we get?"

"Let's say three. Third time you get killed, you're out of the game. Anything else?"

I hesitated. "I don't think so."

"You guys?" Timmy turned toward the others. They said nothing. I realized that they were all now wearing uniforms in military green. Mike's engineer's cap had turned into an American GI helmet, circa World War II. I felt a fuzzy tickling sensation all over my body, and when I glanced down, my department-store garments had transformed into Army fatigues, too.

"Then we're ready," Timmy said, his voice tense with excitement. His jacket had three stripes on the shoulder. Sergeant Kegler of the Army of Nod. "Okay. When I start to count, everybody scatter. Get out of sight and get ready to fight. But you can't head for Jeff's house until I get to thirty and say 'go.' Okay?"

I nodded. No one else reacted at all. "*Okay?*" Timmy snapped. "You guys can *talk* now, you know."

There was a chorus of agreement.

"Okay. Now remember, the first man to reach Jeff's porch wins. But if you die three times, you're out." He looked at me. "Oh— remember how we always used to argue about whether somebody missed or not? Remember, we wished we had guns that could hit you so you'd feel it, but not really hurt you?"

I nodded.

"Well, these guns do that. You can feel it when you get shot. It hurts a little, but not too bad. Okay?"

"What about when you get killed?" I asked uneasily.

"Well, that hurts worse. But not as bad as *really* getting shot to death . . . right, Fred?"

Fred's eyes twitched. "Right."

Taking a step back, Timmy looked us all over. "Okay, guys, just like the old days. Every man for himself. Ready?" He closed his eyes. "Go! One . . . two . . . three . . ."

We scattered.

". . . twenty-eight . . . twenty-nine . . . *thirty!* Okay, men! You can head out now!"

I heard the command clearly, but didn't obey. I liked it where I was, stuffed inside a window well in front of the first house on Main Street. Thick shrubs provided even more cover. I'd almost forgotten about window wells; they don't exist in your average basementless Southern California house. This one was full of daddy-longlegs spiders, which climbed all over me with their tickling, harmless legs. I could put up with that. The window well made an outstanding foxhole. True, the surrounding bushes reduced my own line of sight to a few degrees straight ahead, but that meant nobody could see me, either, unless they fell into my lap. This was a good place to wait.

I was no fool; I knew better than to play this game the way I would have when I was a kid. For one thing, I was out of practice at prowling and sniping; also, I was physically bulkier and slower than I used to be. And finally, although in theory the entire gang was supposed to fight their way to Oak Lane, in practice things would probably be different. Abe and Fred were unlikely to truly struggle against Timmy; they were too afraid of him. Mike might also realize at any moment that the quality of his future depended on not pissing Timmy off.

My game plan was therefore unique. Rather than stalking enemies and gunning them down, I'd sneak through the fray without shooting at all if I could help it. That way, no one would know where I was until I showed up on the front porch of my house on Oak Lane and freed Gail.

Then I'd savor the look of surprise and fury on Timmy's face.

The neighborhood was very quiet. From my low perspective I heard the rustling of dry leaves in the grass, the singing of birds, and that was all. No gunfire yet, no voices. Was everybody doing the same thing I was—hiding out, waiting? I shifted uncomfortably in the close embrace of the window well. If only I could see something besides evergreen needles and dead leaves. What if I'd misjudged Timmy, and he was already on his way to Gail? What if he reached my front porch while I was still crouching here like an idiot?

I couldn't take it any longer. I started to rise, wincing at the crackling in my knees—then froze. A foot had just appeared in the gap in front of me.

Legs half-bent, I held my breath and waited. The foot was clad in a black Converse basketball shoe. Above that was a tan corduroy pantleg slathered with inked inscriptions: TIMMY RULES. CROATOAN FOREVER. DEATH TO ORGANIZED SPORTS. Farther up still I saw the leather sleeve of a Middlefield lettermens' jacket. It moved, revealing the barrel of a submachine gun.

My heart pounded. This must be one of Timmy's "other soldiers"—a Senior. Yet Timmy had promised not to use ghosts . . . Just then the soldier turned a little more, revealing the angular, lopsided visage of a Nodkin. Not a ghost at all, then. Bikkids as enemy soldiers; it figured.

My thighs were trembling, threatening to cramp. But I didn't want to start shooting and attract all kinds of attention to myself. That wasn't my plan at all.

Please go away, you ugly son of a bitch. Hurry; I can't hold this position much longer . . .

But the Nodkin just kept standing there, scanning the street. If he happened to glance over his shoulder . . .

Do it!

Kneecaps popping like cap guns, I sprang erect, jerked the MP-80 into firing position and squeezed the trigger.

Nothing. I hadn't cocked the goddamned gun.

The Nodkin swung around, blinked, grinned a snaggle-toothed grin. *"You."*

At the same moment, I remembered that as a boy, I'd never used the mechanical noisemaker on my weapons.

"Bang!" I shouted.

The Nodkin started, then grinned even wider. Its pupils glowed red. *"Bang!"*

Of course. I'd never said "bang" when I was a kid, either. None of us had. We'd preferred to produce more realistic sound effects with lips and tongue, going *Kshooo-kshooo-kshooo* for pistols and *K-cheeeeoooom* for rifles. Automatic gunfire had been the hardest to imitate; the proper noise was a many-textured blend of deep-throated chuffing, rattling hiss and booming echo: *KAKAAKAKAKAKAKAKAKAKAKAKKKKK!*

The Nodkin's rifle swung toward me, bore changing from a narrow ellipse into a perfect circle.

To my horror, although I could remember how gunfire *sounded*, I couldn't recall how to *make* it. So I just stood there silently, pointing the MP-80 at the Nodkin's chest, my finger hauling back on the trigger. The Nodkin's gun steadied on my face. "I've always wanted to kill you, Jeffy," he growled. "Eat your heart out."

"K-*cheeooooom!*" The sound erupted from my throat before I thought about it. To my shock, the MP-80's stock butted hard against my shoulder and a lance of flame shot from the barrel. Grunting, the Nodkin staggered back a step, a bright red medallion appearing on the front of his uniform shirt. "Hey," the Nodkin said. "That—"

"K-*cheeeooooom!*" I bellowed. "K-*cheeeeooooom! K-cheeeee-oooom!*" The Nodkin reeled back with each shot, blood flying from his chest. Finally he crashed onto his back and lay twitching spasmodically in the leaves.

I gasped at the scorched air, my heart galloping until the Nodkin became completely still. His chest was a crater of gore. "Eat *your* heart out," I said. Timmy must love this—enemy soldiers who *really* died, or at least gave a realistic facsimile of it.

Unfortunately, the apparent victory was a setback for my plan. Now every enemy within earshot knew where I was.

I clambered stiffly out of the window well, wincing as my shins dragged across the edge of the sheet-metal lining. Every joint in my body ached. I poked my head above the bushes. To the right lay the business district, mostly cut off from my view. To the left, east, were the residences of Main Street. I needed to go southeast. Main Street was a possible route for the first part of the trip, of course. It offered plenty of cover—trees, shrubbery, lawn ornaments, garages, sheds, porches. Unfortunately I wasn't familiar enough with this neighborhood to know what the safest routes through it were. Which gave my enemies, with the exception of Mike, the advantage—because they'd dwelt here for decades now.

K-cheooom, k-cheooom, k-cheooom . . . KAKAKAKAKAKK-KKK . . . K-cheooom . . . I ducked as gunfire erupted somewhere nearby. In a moment it became clear none of the shots were directed at me, and I relaxed. A moment later I heard a scream that sounded like Abe Perry's. Then silence. The skirmish had taken place somewhere east of my position, farther down Main Street—which meant that Abe, the worst Army player in the world, had nevertheless sneaked past me while I hid in my window well. The rest of the gang must be even closer to Oak Lane. Jesus, I was *way* behind.

Still, I didn't panic. If Main Street was too hazardous, then I'd head south to School Street before turning east. School Street was more familiar to me.

Directly across Main Street stood a house with a big juniper bush growing at one corner; good cover. But to reach it I'd have to cross two lawns and Main Street itself, with only a couple of trees along the way to hide behind.

I could see no decent alternative. Taking a deep breath, I shouldered out of the bushes and started running. God, I felt clumsy and slow, not to mention *exposed*. But there was no gunfire during the seconds it took me to reach one of the maple trees that grew alongside Main Street. I flattened myself against it, rifle pressed vertically to my chest in a pose familiar to anyone who had watched *Combat* as a kid. From here my back was covered, and although I was exposed from every other angle, I also had a clear field of fire.

I realized I was breathing too fast, making myself dizzy. Had to take it easy. Had to keep cool.

Once again the rattle of gunfire made me cringe. As I watched, a Nodkin soldier toppled dramatically off a porch a few houses away and fell into the yard. The shots themselves seemed to have come from my side of the street. A moment later Mike Norris appeared, glanced around without seeing me, and headed across the street at a lope. He vanished between houses half a block away.

Before I could move, a second Nodkin soldier appeared on my side of the street, running after Mike. But to my surprise, the Nodkin halted at the far sidewalk, then turned and moved east along Main Street. Once it was out of sight I sprinted with all my might across the street, leaves spraying up around my ankles. I had almost reached the juniper bush when Timmy leaped out from behind it, rifle raised, face alight with joy: *"KAKAKAKAKAKAKAKAKKAKAKAKAKAKAKKKKKKKKK!"*

*   *   *

I felt as if I were being punched to pieces by fists of rough glass. Sky and grass traded places as I collapsed, ending up facedown with my nose buried in rich mulch. I wanted to squirm and weep in pain but was unable to do either. I remembered Halloween night in 1965, that time in the alley when I'd fallen on my solar plexus. Then I remembered the Nodkin I'd just shot, its insides splattered everywhere. Did I look like that now?

"Don't worry," came Timmy's voice. He appeared in my limited wedge of vision, kneeling. "You're not really hurt, it just keeps you down for a minute or two."

I groaned. Felt myself drooling into the dead leaves.

"I knew you'd come this way," Timmy went on. "I was always able to figure you out, remember? Well, you've only got two lives left now, so you'd better wise up." Laughing, he ran away.

After a full minute, the bruising ache in my stomach began to fade, and my limbs abruptly relaxed. Still, I didn't move, reveling in the bliss. According to standard Army protocol, a dead man had a minute or so of grace time before he could be killed again. Soon I felt as if nothing at all had happened. When I looked tentatively down at myself, I saw no pulverized flesh, no wound at all. There was blood all over the surrounding grass, though. Mine? Must be. Artificial, land of Nod blood.

Only when I sat all the way up did I become aware of a symphony of minor pains: skinned knees and elbows, abraded face, bruised ribs—the aches and twinges of a middle-aged man who got carried away playing touch football at the company picnic.

But this was no picnic. Obviously Timmy intended to hunt me all over Middlefield, "killing" me at his leisure. It wasn't fair. I was no longer a twelve-year-old boy. I didn't even *want* to play Army.

Then why did you have to challenge him?

Well, because . . . because . . .

The MP-80 lay nearby. Grabbing it, I got to my feet and limped behind the juniper bush, where I crouched and tried to calm myself. My despair was already fleeing; into the void swept anger.

I was always able to figure you out, remember?

Bullshit. In the old days, Timmy and I had split the victories in our games pretty much fifty-fifty. Just because he'd chosen to for-

get that fact didn't mean *I* had to forget it. Least of all here and
now, with the stakes so high.

*You know what your problem is? You always have to win.
You're the same as Timmy that way.*

Maybe so. And maybe that was what was needed around here
right now. So think, Dittimore. Take advantage of your age, your
experience. Surely you can outsmart a twelve-year-old kid.

I did have a few factors in my favor. First, Timmy would have to
spend at least some of his time dodging his own Nodkin soldiers.
He'd also be trying to hunt down the other members of the gang,
to show us he was still the best. Every time he fired his gun, he'd
give away his position. So if I stuck to my original plan and kept a
low profile—and was *very* careful—sooner or later I'd be in the
right place to slip past him and run for it . . .

I spotted a Nodkin soldier walking down the sidewalk alongside
Main Street, scanning the houses. I held perfectly still until he
was out of sight, then slipped away from the juniper bush and
started moving southward again. Slowly, stealthily.

A man with a mission.

CHAPTER THIRTY-TWO

BATTLEFIELD OF DREAMS

In this part of town, the backyards were broad and unfenced. The result was a kind of elongated park strewn with shrubbery, trees, gardens, flower beds, swingsets, doghouses, laundry lines. The park extended east and west for many blocks, broken only by occasional cross streets.

I debated logistics. Timmy probably expected me to head directly for School Street, which lay just beyond the houses to the south. Admittedly, that had been my original plan—so now it was out. Instead, I'd take advantage of the ample cover in the connected backyards and head east until it was time to turn toward Oak Lane.

Keeping low, I kept moving. Bush to tree to birdbath, knees popping like corn, back aching hideously. I saw no one. Every now and then the rattle of gunfire would come from somewhere, and I'd freeze until it was over. After a few such exchanges, I began to recognize who was shooting by the sound of his weapon—his voice. Timmy was involved in most of the battles, and he always got off the final shot. Big surprise. Unfortunately, with all the houses around here, I had no clear fix on where the gunmen were located. So I just kept moving, being as careful as possible.

At the first cross street I stopped, looked both ways carefully, then scampered onto the open pavement.

"*KAKAKAKAKAKAKAKAKAKAKAKKKK!*" The gunfire erupted from the direction of Main Street. I broke into a sprint, glancing over to see a Nodkin soldier, his machine gun blazing. Chunks of asphalt erupted into the air at my heels. Jesus! I lost my balance, tripped over the far curb and belly-flopped onto the grass. My breath kept going. Blue and red lights sparkled before my eyes. At the same time, flakes of bark showered down as the Nodkin's next blast cut across a tree at the height where by body should have been. Half-panting, half-screaming, I crawled behind the tree.

Sitting on the ground, I clutched the MP-80 to my chest and tried not to panic. The Nodkin was probably sprinting toward me right now, his submachine gun pointed at my hiding place. The moment I showed my face, blammo. One more life gone.

I listened, but heard no footsteps. After a moment, I peeked warily around the tree.

The Nodkin was still standing down by Main Street. I had plenty of time to duck back before slugs ripped into the tree where my face had been. What was going on? Why was he holding back?

Never mind. I had to get out of here before someone else came along to investigate the gunfire. I could almost hear Timmy now: *You didn't used to be this careless, Jeff. Now you only have one life left.*

Clambering to my feet, keeping my body squarely behind the tree trunk, I took a deep breath and launched myself toward the next yard. Again the Nodkin opened fire, but he was too far away and I just kept running until I was out of his sight. Then I flopped down behind a hedge and tried to catch my breath.

Other battles were going on nearby, their constituencies and locations changing from minute to minute. Peering around the base of the hedge, I spotted Fred clear down by Landrus Avenue, diving into cover like the real soldier he had once been. I waited until he'd crawled out of sight before I set off again, keeping my eyes and ears on full alert. At the next cross street I spotted not one but two Nodkin, both standing near Main Street and looking in my general direction. It occurred to me that they were behaving more like sentries than like combat soldiers.

Still, they posed a problem. I didn't want to shoot at them and give my position away, but I didn't want them gunning me down when I tried to cross the street, either. How could I—

Just then, from nearby came Abe's high-pitched gunfire: "K-*cheeowww*! K-*cheeowww*!" One of the Nodkin went down. The other dropped to its stomach and started firing at a point somewhere behind me. I twisted around to see if I could spot Abe, but he was hidden from my view. Still, he'd accidentally done me a favor. Folding myself almost double, I scurried across the street.

If either Abe or the Nodkin saw me, they didn't bother to do anything about it.

As I took cover again, I began to feel almost optimistic. I'd managed to get ahead of one of my opponents without giving my own
position away. Not even Timmy had taken a shot at me since that
first one. *So you can always figure me out, eh, you little jerk?*

Half a block later I heard Mike shooting, followed by Fred, then
Mike again. I dove behind a child's sandbox and peered over it just
as Fred sprinted into sight around the corner of a nearby garage. He
slammed against the wall, rifle clutched vertically against his
body, face turned back the way he had come. The pose of an ambush.

My optimism flared into elation. This was perfect; my chance to
slip past two enemies at the same time. All I had to do was circle
south while Fred and Mike shot it out. After that, I'd have only
Timmy and the Nodkin to worry about.

Fred didn't notice as I crawled to my right for a dozen feet, putting the northwest corner of the garage between us. Then I got up
and slipped behind a redbud tree barely wide enough to hide my
body. I was tempted to bolt for home immediately, but restrained
myself. Not until I knew where Mike was.

No sooner had I thought this than Mike tiptoed around the
southwest corner of the garage, obviously intending to flank Fred
and shoot him from behind. He was only twenty feet away from
me. I tried to suck in my gut.

Mike was concentrating on stepping between patches of dry
leaves. In fact, he was so absorbed in his own stealth that he didn't
notice Timmy come around the corner of the garage behind *him*.

But I noticed, and couldn't believe my good fortune. Timmy was
obviously planning a double ambush. He'd let Mike shoot Fred,
and then he'd shoot Mike. Two birds with one bullet.

And then *I'd* shoot *him*.

Doing so would be a departure from my basic game plan, of
course, but a wise one. Aside from the revenge factor, killing
Timmy would guarantee me a minute or two of relatively unob-
structed time to rush toward Oak Lane.

I waited, not breathing, amazed no one else could hear the jun-
gle-drumming of my heart. Finally Mike reached the corner,
peered around it, stepped out. "K-*cheeeowwwww*! K-*cheeeeowww*!"

he shouted. Fred rolled into sight, limp and bloody. Smiling, Mike started to turn back the way he had come. His face dropped when he saw Timmy.

"*KAKAKAKAKAKAKAKAKAKAKAKAKAKAKAKAKAKAKAKK-KKKKKK!*" Timmy didn't just shoot Mike, he annihilated him, firing and firing until he was out of breath. Blood and flesh erupted into the air. From the expression on Mike's face, being a ghost did not protect him from pain. He finally collapsed like a pile of blocks.

Grinning, Timmy walked up to his shredded body and prodded it with the barrel of his gun. "I thought you used to be a real soldier, Mr. Dopehead," he said. "But that was pretty—"

"Timmy," I said. The MP-80 was already braced against the tree.

He swung around, placing his chest squarely in my sights. The expression of disbelief on his face did my heart good. "K-*cheeeowwww!*" I roared. He slammed backward into the garage. "K-*cheeeowww!* K-*cheeeowww!* K-*cheeeowww!*" Holes exploded open in his shirt. He dropped to his knees, then his face, and his limp body rolled over and over and over, finally stopping in the bottom of a shallow depression. Perfect. I remembered that when Timmy got killed in our games, he always perished spectacularly. If he had to die, he wanted to do *that* better than anyone else, too.

Stepping away from the redbud tree, I walked toward him. Before I headed for home, I just had to say something. I deserved a moment to gloat.

To my surprise, there was no blood on Timmy's body or the surrounding grass. I hadn't expected him to stint on the red stuff, even his own. Kneeling beside him, I said, "How does it feel to get nailed by a grownup, Timmy? I'll bet you're—"

Suddenly he was moving, rolling onto his side. I jerked back, yelling, "That's not fair!" as I fumbled with the MP-80. But Timmy fired first, three bursts in rapid succession.

I felt no pain, no sensation of impact. I realized Timmy was looking beyond me. Whirling, I saw Abe slump to the ground not fifteen feet away.

I turned back toward Timmy.

"Nobody said we couldn't wear bulletproof vests," he said. Then he shot me in the heart.

*   *   *

I lay curled in an agonized spasm, my visible world reduced to a forest of grass and leaves. Heard a crunching noise, then Timmy's voice: "This makes it too easy. From now on, no more bulletproof vests for anybody. Okay? Okay."

I tried to tell him he was a coward and a sneak, but managed only an anguished moan.

"I knew you were there all along," he said. "But it was a good try. You're doing better. Don't worry, I won't finish you off too soon." Leaves crackled as he departed.

By the time I was able to sit up, Fred and Mike were both gone, too. I glanced at Abe. He lay a couple of feet away, not moving at all. I didn't think he was going to. Half his head was blown off. Evidently he'd died his third and last death, in which case he wouldn't be able to move again until the game was over. Those were always the rules.

Nobody said we couldn't wear bulletproof vests.

What an asshole. Timmy used to pull tricks like that all the time—bend the rules as far as possible, then make the exception illegal so no one else could try it.

I knew you were there all along.

Bullshit again. Yes, Timmy used to sometimes let people kill him during a multiple-life game like this one. That was Timmy's way of throwing Abe, Fred and occasionally even Mike a bone so they wouldn't get too discouraged. But he'd never done it with me. Never had to.

Whenever I'd killed Timmy, I'd earned it.

So, how did you used to kill him?

That didn't matter. It was irrelevant. My purpose here was to save Gail, not to fight Timmy.

Especially since I was now on my last life.

I climbed slowly to my feet. I'd been dead long enough for someone to come back and bushwhack me if they wanted to. Gathering up the MP-80, I staggered behind the garage, then made my way along the back wall. To the east were four or five more houses, then Landrus Avenue. I was almost halfway home.

But now I'd have to be careful to the point of paranoia. Although Abe was out of the picture, everyone else knew approximately where I was. I crept past the next house, and the one after that. I heard no gunfire, saw no soldiers of any kind. The tranquility made me nervous.

Finally I reached the last house on the block. It was a big place, half its backyard taken up by a vegetable garden and the rest shaded by an enormous walnut tree. Close to the house, a rake stood upright from a small pile of leaves, as if someone had started the thankless job of cleaning up under the walnut tree, then given up. I focused on the tree itself, with its broad trunk. From behind there I should be able to observe the junior high campus and decide what route to take past it. Sucking in a deep breath, I sprinted toward the tree as fast as my aching legs would carry me.

I'm not sure exactly what happened next—if I heard something, or just had a feeling. But five yards from the tree I dropped to the ground, twisting, rolling onto my back, firing into the branches overhead: *"KAKAKAKAKAKAKAKAKAKKKKKK!"*

Chips of bark hurtled upward; walnuts still wrapped in their soft, aromatic outer covers dropped like hand grenades. Fred fell too, in a cascade of leaves and blood. He landed with a snapping thud on his head and left shoulder.

I rolled onto my stomach. Fred's body was almost cut in half. "Sorry, Fred," I whispered. But I wasn't, really. He had been waiting in the tree to steal my final life, after all. Instead, *I* was still in the game. Now I just had to—

Something very hard touched the back of my head. "Don't move," Mike said.

I didn't move.

"Stand up," Mike said.

I did as he asked, leaving the MP-80 on the ground. Mike backed away, peering at me through the sights of his rifle. "Pick up your gun and follow me."

"Fol—"

"Quick. Before Timmy shows up."

I grabbed the MP-80. When I straightened, Mike was already running toward the vegetable garden—the wrong direction. Still, I followed him. He hadn't shot me. I had an idea what he was up to.

Four rows of sweet corn grew in the garden, and Mike and I slipped into their embrace. There was something wonderfully ironic about crouching out of sight in a cornfield, even a miniature one. Even better, we could see in every direction without being visible ourselves.

"Is this a truce?" I asked.

He nodded. "I heard what Timmy said to you about the bullet-proof vest. What a bunch of crap. So I thought to myself, hey, nobody said we couldn't have teams, either."

I grinned. "That's right. That's right . . ."

"Gotta fight fire with fire, man." He peered through the corn-stalks. "I think Fred's out of it. We'll know pretty soon if Timmy's going to come and check out your shooting. If he does . . ." He patted his rifle.

"Mike?"

He looked at me. His plain, suntanned face.

"Mike . . . is it really *you?*"

"What do you mean?"

"I mean . . . you're not something Timmy made up, are you? Like the Nodkin? It's really *you?*"

"If you mean am I really a ghost, the answer is yes. Jesus, you're hardheaded. Get with the program."

"I just . . . never mind, you're right. How many lives do you have left?"

"Just one."

"Yeah, me too."

"With Timmy chasing after you—and *cheating*—I'd say that's pretty good."

I shrugged. "I've tried to stick to the backyards where there's plenty of cover."

"Good thinking. We should probably keep doing that, because Timmy hangs around School Street most of the time. And we can't take Main Street because it's crawling with Nodkin."

"Yeah, I noticed. Why don't they come after us?"

"I think they're trying to keep us from sneaking around the long way."

"In other words, we're being herded . . . right past the junior high."

"Where there's not much cover." Mike peeked through the corn again. "Yeah, Fred's out of it all right. That was cool shooting, man."

I surprised myself by grinning. "Thanks."

"Now it's just you and me against Timmy. Still want to try and save Gail?"

"Bet your ass."

"Good. We ought to move in relays from here on out, one guy covering the other. You know what I'm talking about?"

"Like on *Combat.*"

He smiled. "You got it."

"You're kind of enjoying this, aren't you?"

His smile faded. "Aren't you? Just a little? I mean, except for getting shot; that hurts like a mother."

"I'm just in this to help Gail. Help her and make Timmy . . . uh-oh. Look." I pointed across Landrus Street. A block or so to the east, Nodkin soldiers were swarming through the corridor of back-yards. There were at least a dozen of them, walking back and forth, checking out every bush and rock. Moving slowly our way.

"Goddammit," Mike said, "they're closing us off, all right. That's not fair—I thought the Nodkin were supposed to be after Timmy, too. He *swore* it."

"He swore they'd be hunting him. I'm sure they are. But in the meantime, they're just sort of *accidentally* helping him out. You know how Timmy works things."

Mike grunted. "Well, we'd better get moving if we don't want to be spotted."

"I don't like it. We'd be doing exactly what Timmy wants."

"I know, but what else can we—"

I put a hand on his shoulder. "Hang on. I've got an idea."

Cpl. Jeffry Dittimore knew his stuff. He lay very still in the darkness, clutching the still-hot MP-80 to his chest. The last of the gunfire had ended only a few seconds ago; as he and Private Norris had agreed, Dittimore had fired the last burst. To a listener, the conclusion would be inescapable: Norris and Dittimore had had a massive firefight, and Dittimore had won.

Now, if only the right fish was attracted by the bait.

Dittimore waited, breathing very shallowly. The darkness was prickly and aromatic; to sneeze right now would be disastrous. Also, he didn't want any noise to interfere with his hearing.

A few seconds later, he heard what he'd been waiting for: the softest crunching of dry leaves. Then again. And again.

Now!

The pile of leaves spewed in all directions as Dittimore sat up, leveling the MP-80. To his joy, the commander of the enemy forces was bending over Norris. Dittimore pulled the trigger: *"KAKAKAKAKAKAKAKAKAKAKAKAKAKKKKK!"*

This time I hadn't given Timmy a chance to think up some tricky ploy. His expression of surprise was wiped out by pain. Blood flew from the holes in his chest. Hurtling backward, he stumbled over Mike before sprawling onto the grass.

Mike sat up and rubbed his ribs. "What a klutz. Good shooting, Jeff."

Laughing, I leaped to my feet and shook leaves off myself. Again, I couldn't help running over to Timmy. "How do you like it, Mr. Cheater?" I crowed, touching the hot muzzle of the MP-80 to his temple. "I outsmarted you, and now Mike and I have a head start. How do you like that?" I turned toward Mike. "Let's go."

A peek down the park strip revealed that the Nodkin soldiers were still milling around a hundred yards away, craning their heads in our direction. Evidently they weren't trained to automatically investigate the sounds of battle. Good. Keeping out of sight, Mike and I proceeded south in cycles, covering each other as we'd agreed. When we reached School Street we leapfrogged east as fast as we dared, moving-moving-moving. We both knew one thing: the instant Timmy came back to life, he'd be after us with a vengeance.

Nevertheless, I felt optimistic again. Even with an old man like me slowing us down, Mike and I had enough of a head start that Timmy himself would never be able to catch us.

We had almost reached the junior high gymnasium when the air-raid siren began to howl.

CHAPTER THIRTY-THREE

THINK SMALL

When I was a kid, that siren had wailed every day at noon; a familiar, comforting sound meaning "all's well." But if it went off at any other time of day, you knew it meant trouble—a tornado, a bad fire. Or, of course, the ultimate threat—the start of World War III.

Duck and cover, we'd been taught. Without thinking, I dove over the bushes growing alongside the gym, Mike right behind me, and burrowed down to the ground. Only then did I take the time to notice that the siren sounded odd—not the oscillating shriek I remembered, but a deep, steady drone. It was the sound of the bull-roarer, vastly amplified; I found its din more frightening than any air-raid siren.

"*Now* what?" I shouted.

Mike just shook his head.

Peering through the bushes, I saw nothing. The bone-shaking howl continued for half a minute, then faded. I found the resulting silence even more ominous. Looking at Mike, I said, "I don't—"

"Shh!"

From somewhere, faintly, came the crackle of gunfire. First just a couple of weapons, then six or eight. A dozen. Two dozen. The noise swiftly grew both louder and closer; it sounded like a full battle on the move.

"What?" Mike cried.

"I don't know," I said, "but I doubt it's the cavalry coming to our rescue. Let's get out of here."

Since most of the shooting seemed to come from the north, I crawled in the other direction, to the rear corner of the building.

Peering around, I examined the wide pea-gravel yard that consti-
tuted the playground and parking area for the gym. The back side
of the buildings rose in a long, red-brick cliff. There was no cover
anywhere except for the occasional tree trunk and a few pieces of
playground equipment.

But at least no one was shooting here yet.

"Whatever's happening," Mike said nervously, "it's getting
closer."

I nodded. "Let's make a break for it."

Scrambling around the corner, we jumped to our feet and started
running.

We'd gone only twenty yards when a handful of Nodkin soldiers
appeared at the far end of the building. They were moving backward, firing their guns steadily in the direction of School Street,
but when they saw us they immediately turned our way.

Skidding to a halt, I looked around frantically. It was no good
going back; the approaching battle sounded especially loud in that
direction. God, the game was up. We'd lost. We—

The locker rooms!

I spun toward the gym. Centered along its back wall was a deep
trench with steps going down on either end. These led to a pair of
doors, one marked VISITORS, the other, WOLFPACK.

"Come on!" I shouted, and lunged toward the steps just as gunfire erupted from both ends of the playground. Shattered gravel
flew through the air like snow as Mike and I half-leaped, half-
tumbled into the trench.

It was cool down there, and smelled of mildew and body odor. I
yanked on each of the doors. Locked. "I'll get us in, you keep those
assholes back!" I shouted.

Mike scurried to the top of the steps and peered over, then
started shooting, first one way, then the other. Return fire gouged
at the bricks on the side of the gym.

Pointing the MP-80 at the WOLFPACK door where the knob met the
jamb, I pulled the trigger.

When we were kids, ricochets were never a danger; luckily that
seemed to still hold true. Although shell fragments whined all
around me as the doorknob and part of the adjacent wall dissolved,
nothing hit me. I crashed shoulder-first into the door, glad for once
for my adult bulk and strength. The door flew open so fast I almost
fell into the room beyond.

The BO stench was much worse in here, and the acrid odor of cordite didn't help. But at least the room was deserted. Mike stumbled in behind me, blood running down his face. "It's just a nick," he said when he saw my expression. "But they'll be here any second. What are we gonna do, man? We're trapped!"

"Go through the school building," I gasped. "Try to get out at the other end."

"But they'll think of that, too! They'll head us off and—"

"You got a better idea?" I shouted into his face. He recoiled, then shook his head. We ran down the long, narrow room, skirting the wooden benches and lockers, the tile-walled showers and stained urinals, the sinks, the mirrors reflecting teenaged boys snapping wet towels at one another.

I didn't even pause at the inside door, although there could easily be an ambush waiting on the other side. That risk was problematic; the threat from behind was unquestionable. Kicking the door open, I leaped through.

The gymnasium was dark and empty. Enough light fell through the high windows to reveal the basketball goals at either end, the wooden bleachers, the polished surface of the court. Paper cutouts of witches and bats twirled on strings from the rafters.

Side by side, Mike and I sprinted toward the main doors. I had a few seconds to search my memory for the layout of the adjacent buildings. As I recalled, just beyond the gym doors was a crosswise hallway, one end of which led outside and the other end of which went into the school building. It was the perfect place to get caught in a crossfire.

Nudging open the gym doors, I peered out carefully. The hallway looked as I recalled—long and narrow, built below ground level. To the left, steps led up to the front doors; to the right, the hall ended at a pair of wide portals. One of those opened into the cafeteria; the other led to a staircase that went up into the school building proper.

The battle was deafening now, much of it taking place just outside the exterior doors. Mike and I ran in the other direction; I felt my back tensing in expectation of final agony.

But we reached the end of the hall without being fired at. I glanced quickly into the cafeteria. The rows of long tables were there, and the metal chairs. But the only other way out of that room was onto the playground, which of course belonged to the Nodkin. The stairs were the only other option.

The staircase was wood, darkly varnished except where worn down by stamping feet and dragging hands. As Mike and I started up it, the sounds of battle outside began to subside; by the time we reached the ground floor, silence ruled again. I didn't like that any better than the gunfire.

Halting, I peered into the school's foyer. It was a broad open area, high ceilinged, with the principal's office on one side and a display case full of sports trophies on the other. The air smelled of floor wax and book bindings. Across the way, light spilled through two sets of glass doors. The gap between the doors was where students paused to stomp the snow or mud off their shoes and boots. Beyond the outer doors lay the steps down to School Street. Rising onto my toes, I looked into the street, then ducked back.

"What's wrong?" Mike asked.

"There're dead soldiers all over the place—and new soldiers, alive."

"New soldiers? What do you mean?"

"Guys in black berets, with different kinds of rifles. You should see their faces. I don't—"

The rest of my words were trampled by an amplified voice slamming out of wall-mounted speakers: "ATTENTION INVADERS! THIS IS GENERAL KEGLER OF THE TIMFIELD ARMY! WE KNOW YOU'RE TRESPASSING IN THIS BUILDING, AND WE'RE GOING TO HUNT YOU DOWN LIKE DOGS! REMEMBER—WE NEVER SAID I COULDN'T CREATE ANOTHER ARMY."

"What the *fuck?*" Mike cried.

I slumped against the wall. "The little asshole made a new army to wipe out the one he said could hunt *him*. Now he's free to go wherever he wants."

"Shit!"

"Yeah. Well, all we can do now is keep making our way through the building and hope we find a way out."

Sweat beaded Mike's forehead. "Maybe we should split up."

"Why?"

"Because now we have to be sneaky, and it's easier to sneak on your own. Plus it doubles the chances one of us will get away."

He was right, but I didn't like the idea. His companionship had become a comfort as well as a benefit. "Okay," I said reluctantly. "If you get out, what are you going to do?"

"Head for the alley. Take the shortcut to your place."

I nodded. "Maybe I'll see you there."

"You want the high road or the low?" he asked, nodding at the staircase.

"Rock-scissors-paper," I said.

We each raised a fist to waist level, then pumped them up and down as I counted, "One, two, three." On "three," I flattened my hand into the semblance of a sheet of paper, and he extended two fingers. "Scissors cut paper," he said. "I'll take the low road."

I knew he was surrendering to me the safer route, but there was no time to argue. From downstairs came the shuffling clatter of feet and metal equipment. Mike thrust out his hand, and I shook it. "Hey," he said, "don't look so glum. Even if we die, we'll just have to put up with Timmy's gloating, that's all. There will always be another game."

. . . *and you won't gripe about it.*

"It can't be that easy," I said, and started running up the stairs.

In planform, the junior high building was shaped like a capital I. Classrooms lined the perimeter; the center section was given over to windowless storerooms. In between were wide hallways. I took the hallway on the south side of the building, running at top speed over the black and brown linoleum floor. On my left, tall metal lockers filled the walls. On the right were the classrooms, doors open. The only light came from there.

As I ran past the classrooms, from the corner of my eye I glimpsed the ranks of old-fashioned desks, the kind with flip-up wooden tops, heavy metal frames, even holes for inkwells. The underside of the lid on one of them would be marked with the letters JD + GR, scratched in with the point of a paper clip.

I was halfway down the hall when I heard gunfire break out downstairs, raucous, echoing. I skidded to a halt. From the sound, the first weapon to fire was Mike's; then came a barrage of other guns—Timmy's among them. There was a moment of silence, then more gunfire. Mike let out a scream that made my skin tighten. Finally, silence returned.

"ATTENTION INVADER!" the PA system blared. "YOUR

PARTNER IS DEAD. WE KNOW YOU'RE UPSTAIRS; THERE'S NO WAY OUT. PREPARE TO DIE FOR YOUR CRIMES."

I didn't know what to do. Timmy was right—if his new army had taken the first floor, then both staircases were now death traps. And there was no other way out, no other way down.

From behind me came the sound of tramping footsteps; then similar noises from the front. The enemy was closing in. I sprinted into the nearest room, which happened to be the science room.

It was twice as long as the other classrooms. Most of the space was given over to square-topped tables equipped with sinks, electrical outlets and brass connectors for Bunsen burners. Windows stretched across one wall, with storage cabinets beneath. What if I could find some rope or cable? Would it be possible to slide out a window and down into the playground?

I ran to the windows, peered out warily. As I'd feared, five or six black-bereted soldiers stood guard amongst the dead. From what I could see of their long, sharkish faces, they made the original Nodkin look attractive.

From the hallway came the sound of scraping boots, then a familiar voice: "Check every room, men. Remember to cover each other. He's even sneakier than Mike." Timmy didn't sound angry —he sounded excited. Enjoying himself.

Desperate, I looked around. There was a storeroom on one side, where expensive items like mercury and microscopes were kept. I checked the door. Locked.

Out in the hall, footsteps drew nearer.

I ran along the row of cabinets, yanking them open, looking inside. Each cabinet was only a couple of feet deep, maybe four feet wide, with eighteen inches of space between shelves. Some of the shelves were empty, but there was so little room . . .

The scrambling footsteps in the hallway were getting much closer. "Check the storerooms, too!" Timmy shouted.

Squatting behind one of the science tables, I tried to think. What was I going to do? Through the open doorway, shapes moved in the hall. I had only seconds, seconds.

I looked at the nearest cabinet again. As a kid I would have been able to squeeze myself in there. If only I weren't so big now. Still . . . maybe I could conceal most of myself inside, survive a cursory inspection of the room. It was better than nothing.

Lying on my side, I slid my feet into the opening and started cramming the rest of myself in, trying to fold myself up like the handkerchief a magician pokes into his closed fist, and from which it will disappear.

Think small, I told myself, squirming, pushing. *Think small . . .*

Think small, Corporal Dittimore thought as he wriggled desperately, forcing his body into the tiny storm drain in the curb of the Parisian street. It didn't seem possible he could get all of himself in there, but the Nazis were about to goose-step around the corner, and if they found any part of him exposed . . . well, everybody knew what happened to captive American GIs.

Think small. He managed to bend his knees a little more, pulling them up against his chest. *You can do it.* Surprisingly, his hips made it through the narrow gap with only a little scraping. Squirming, he got in up to his shoulders. For a moment he was certain that would be the end of it, the Nazis would find him sprawled half-in and half-out of the hole like a rat too large for the python to swallow, but he exhaled and thought small and managed to squeeze his shoulders in, too.

Heavy footsteps approached the end of the alley. Dittimore twisted his head into the darkness, wincing at the pulling on his scalp, then reached out, grabbed his MP-80 and pulled it in with him. He was even able to scoop some rubble over the mouth of the hole before the first hobnailed boot entered the alley . . .

I lay perfectly still—not a difficult trick in that tight space—without even breathing. My heart hammered deafeningly in my ears. How I managed to fit myself in here, I wasn't sure; I'd even closed the cabinet door most of the way before having to slip my fingers in. Now I could only hope the gap wasn't glaringly obvious from the outside.

I heard scuffling footsteps, the squealing of desks being pushed around—and then, to my dismay, the thump of cabinet doors opening and closing. Closer, closer . . .

. . . my hiding place was now a trap . . .

. . . closer . . .

. . . I couldn't even bring my gun into firing position . . .

Something moved across the gap of light. The gap began to widen. I held my breath.

"What's the matter with you?" Timmy's voice barked. The streak of light stopped growing. "He's a big fat grownup, you know, not a midget. Go check that storeroom over there. The rest of you look under the teacher's desk and in the closets. Hurry up."

A shadow briefly obliterated my slice of daylight as a soldier hustled past. I bit the inside of my cheeks, certain I was going to burst out in hysterical laughter.

"Nothing here, sir," growled a coarse Nodkin voice after a moment.

"All right, men, let's move out. He must be down in social studies."

A few seconds later, the room became silent. I heard Timmy's voice shouting orders out in the hall, followed by receding footsteps. Still I waited. Timmy's voice came again, fainter, then faded again. He and his soldiers were working their way down the hall, room by room.

Still I remained motionless. The trick now was to be very patient. Patient and small, small and patient.

The air in the cabinet smelled of chemicals and varnish. My neck felt like it was about to break, and the back of my right calf had developed an intolerable itch. If only I could reach them; if only I could move more than my fingers. My hipbone and right elbow ground painfully into the bottom of the cabinet. *Think small. Stay still. Think small.*

After an eternity, the noise from the hallways ceased entirely. Still I remained where I was, half certain Timmy was waiting in the doorway of the science room, his gun aimed casually at this cabinet, a smile on his face. When I crawled out, he'd say, "I could always figure you out," and blast me.

After the silence had stretched on for five more minutes, I couldn't take it anymore. I inched the cabinet door open, saw nothing but table legs and rubber hoses leading up to the Bunsen burners. No voices challenged me, no footsteps approached. I slipped the MP-80 through the opening, then my shoulders, sliding out onto the floor. Huge relief.

I climbed to my feet with gingerly care, waiting for the agony to erupt from my tortured joints . . . but it didn't happen. I felt a little stiff, that was all.

The room looked funny, the angles wrong. When I turned toward the windows, I could see only the most distant portion of the playground. What—

I raised my hands. Blinked. They were smooth and almost hairless, devoid of wrinkles, bulging veins, blemishes. I turned them one way, then the other. Brought them up and touched my face. Felt no rasp of whiskers, no loose skin. Higher, I ran my palms over the stiff bristles of a crew cut, except in front where there was a soft tuft of hair.

My arms fell of their own accord, and I leaned against a nearby table to hold myself up.

Think small! I thought giddily. *Yeah—yeah, it's what you believe that's real, not the oth—*

"ATTENTION INTRUDER!" Timmy bellowed over the PA system. Now he did sound angry. "I KNOW YOU'RE STILL IN THERE, JEFF! YOU'RE CHEATING, HIDING ALL THE TIME! THIS ISN'T A HIDING GAME! SO IF THAT'S THE WAY YOU WANT TO PLAY IT, I GUESS I'LL JUST GO TO YOUR HOUSE AND GET GAIL! SEE YOU LATER, LOSER!"

CHAPTER THIRTY-FOUR

PICTURE THIS

Corporal Dittimore was a changed man. War did that to a person, of course; you either accepted the change and used it, or you went crazy.

Dittimore would use it.

My first instinct was to take off running on my strong young legs, sprint down the stairs and out the doors as fast as I could. Try to head Timmy off, do *something*.

But I realized panic was just what Timmy expected of me, so I made myself calm down. Although I now had the body of a thirteen-year-old, I also had the life experience of an adult. I should use that. Be smart. Creeping to the windows, I rose onto my tiptoes and peeked out.

Down in the playground, the Black Berets were on the move, disappearing around the corner of the building. Were they getting ready to set up an ambush? How many of their buddies were still *inside* the building? Did Timmy honestly know I was in here myself, or was he just blowing smoke with all his threats?

Flexing my limbs, I paced up and down the room. Maybe Timmy had told the truth; maybe he really *was* heading for my house.

No. I knew him; he wanted to kill me again. Take my last life. He'd do that before ending the game.

My body felt terribly restless; it wanted to *move*.

Be careful, man.

I peered into the hall. Deserted. Listening, I heard only the hollow silence of an abandoned building. Despite that, I worked my way down the hall with care, checking each room before I passed it. I did the same with the staircase, creeping down silently, a step at a time. One riser creaked. I froze, my heart drumming in my ears, but no gunshots followed. Timmy really *had* cleared the building.

Still, when I reached the landing between floors, I peered down carefully.

And saw Mike. What was left of him.

He'd obviously been caught from both directions. His body looked like something from one of the old EC horror comics, the ones right-minded adults had blamed for all juvenile delinquency in the 1950s. An arm here, a leg there, loops of pink-gray intestine strewn between. Blood dripping from the ceiling. The top half of his head had been placed on the newel post at the foot of the stairs, eyes staring fixedly up at me.

I remembered how Mike had screamed. This death was only temporary, of course. With Timmy running the show, Mike had an infinite number of such deaths to look forward to . . .

Carefully, I made my way through the gore without looking at Mike's face again, turned a corner and leaned against the wall. Then I began to shake with anger. I'd escaped from Timmy here in the school, but so what? He'd only put himself between me and the goal again. Taken the initiative again. He'd also destroyed my partner while furnishing himself with an elite army of supporters. All so he could turn me into an EC Comics victim, too, and be a big man.

And it was my fault.

The truth was I'd been doing this all wrong, from the moment Timmy started counting down from thirty. Trying to outsmart Timmy, trying to outfox and outmaneuver him. You didn't beat Timmy Kegler that way—you beat him by *outplaying* him.

And outplaying him didn't mean running away, avoiding contact, hiding. It meant remembering the real purpose of the game. What was the real purpose? To rescue Gail Rohr? No. The real purpose of this game, of *all* games, was to destroy the enemy.

The way I used to.

The nearest exit was just around the corner, but that door was sure to be under observation. Turning, I made my way back to the main entrance of the school, checked the foyer carefully, then approached the double glass doors. No movement on the street, just dead Nodkin. I pushed through the first set of doors, then the second, opening them just enough to emit my slender young self. No shots rang out. Quickly, I climbed over one of the concrete lions and dropped down between the hedges and the front of the building. I was easily small enough to fit into the narrow space, and I made good time on my hands and knees through the dirt and discarded bubble-gum wrappers.

When I neared the eastern end of the building, I slowed down, slithering forward on my belly until I could see the doors I was probably expected to exit through. Oddly, no enemies lay in wait. There was no ambush. No—

Then I spotted the sentries.

There were two of them, one beside a house near the alley, the other crouching behind a bush on School Street. I watched them for a minute. Both carried walkie-talkies. They weren't sentries at all—they were *scouts.*

At once everything became clear. Timmy *wanted* me to get away from the school, where I'd had such success avoiding him. But he didn't intend to risk my actually beating him to Oak Lane, so he'd left a couple of men behind to report which direction I took. Then Timmy could pick up the trail himself and kill me at his leisure—probably just before I reached Gail, at the moment of my victory. Timmy Kegler triumphant once again, and never mind that he'd had to stretch the rules of the game entirely out of shape to win.

I could picture him right now, waiting somewhere . . . most likely Lincoln Avenue, from where he could move quickly toward either the alley or School Street, depending on the direction I chose. Timmy, feeling no concern for his own safety, knowing he was dealing with a cowardly adult who had only one life left anyway. .

Well, he was half-right.

I looked at the scouts again. Between me and them stretched quite a bit of open space, more than I could sneak across undetected, even in my new body. Nor could I shoot both soldiers from here—one, yes, but the second would have plenty of time to take cover and report in on his radio.

If only the MP-80 wasn't so damned noisy. If only . . .

. . . only . . .

I hesitated, then reached into one of the breast pockets of my fatigues. Groped for a moment, then touched a smooth, perforated cylinder and pulled it out. Sure enough, it screwed neatly onto the MP-80's barrel.

Just as I had imagined it would.

I smiled. "Nobody said we couldn't use silencers," I murmured.

Corporal Dittimore covered the last dozen feet to his goal slowly, flat on his belly. He knew the enemy command post was behind this house on Lincoln Avenue; he'd seen at least six Black Berets run out from here in the last five minutes, heading west. That was okay. When they got to the school, they'd find nothing. No scouts, no radios, no blood. Dittimore had covered his tracks thoroughly.

During the trip here from the school he'd encountered no scouts after the first two, and only one roving sentry. Timmy was over-confident. As usual.

As Dittimore crawled, he pushed the MP-80 silently ahead of himself. More than once he had considered abandoning this mission, and just proceeding on to Oak Lane. He didn't *need* to be doing what he was doing now. But he ignored that voice. It came from some half-remembered life. The life of a sissy.

Static crackled around the corner, followed by a harsh voice: "Give me that mike. Sergeant? Sergeant, this is Commander Kegler . . . What do you mean they're not there? They've got to be there!"

Dittimore crept forward, totally silent. The shrubs ended at the rear corner of the house, so he took special care covering the last couple of feet. Then he peeked around the corner.

The command post consisted of an open-sided tent sheltering a radio transceiver, a table, a couple of chairs, a pitcher of Kool-Aid. A dozen Black Berets stood at attention around the tent, obviously awaiting orders. Commander Kegler, six stars on his uniform shirt, was pacing in front of the radio, clutching the microphone. "No, don't go inside the school. Post two guards and the rest of you sweep back this way. Look for him; he's got to be out there somewhere. Radio when you have his position." He slammed the mike down.

Dittimore leaped to his feet. Kegler spun around, and his jaw dropped.

"Here's my position," Dittimore said. Then, "*Thmp-thmp-thmp-thmp-thmp-thmp-thmp,*" the silenced gun. A shooting gallery.

When it was over Dittimore lowered the smoking MP-80. Blood and bodies everywhere. Sparks spat from the wreckage of the radio. Walking up to Timmy's shredded remains, he bent down and said, "That's for Mike. And now you and I are even, too. One life each. See you at my house, loser." He ran away.

But not far. Hunkering behind a mailbox in front of the high school, he waited, listening for the sound of pursuit. In a minute it would come—the pounding footsteps of soldiers, Kegler no doubt in the lead. His narrow face contorted in fury.

Grinning, Dittimore unscrewed the silencer from the barrel of the MP-80. Shooting on full automatic was easier without it; besides, this time around a little extra noise wouldn't matter.

From his current position he could see part of Oak Lane. When Kegler arrived he would be looking in that direction, too. Paying no attention to the mailbox.

Dittimore listened. There. Yes. Footsteps, running. He waited . . . waited . . .

Sprang up.

Again, Kegler's eyes flew wide in shock. The Black Berets snarled, started to swing their weapons around.

"*KAKAKAKAKAKAKAKAKAKAKAKAKAKAKAKAKAKAKAKA-KAKKKKKKKKK!*" Dittimore used all the slugs he had in his lungs, sweeping the MP-80 back and forth in a tight arc.

Crows called wildly in the distance. Blood flowed into the gutter. Echoes faded.

Stillness.

Clothed in cordite fumes, I walked up to Timmy's body yet again. His shocked face was intact, staring up at the cloudy sky. The rest of him was quite a mess. Worse than Mike.

"You lose," I said.

No response. Even Timmy had to obey some of his own rules.

On feet as light as sunbeams I ran down Lincoln Avenue, then slowed as I came around the corner at Oak Lane. There, across the street, was my house. Gail sat alone on the porch. Almost thirteen years old, long brown hair, dark Arizona suntan. White blouse and blue skirt. Blue ribbon in her hair. She looked exactly the way she had on the first day of school in 1965, and my heart yanked at its tether like a hunting dog.

When she saw me walking toward her, she rose to her feet, mouth dropping open.

"What's the matter?" I called, grinning. "You look like you've seen a ghost."

"Look out!"

The warning was a surprise, but not as much as having a half-dozen Black Berets leap out of the bushes behind me. I whirled, but they were already on me, pinning my arms, ripping the MP-80 away. Then they released me. I stood in the center of a ring of leveled guns.

"Why don't you shoot me, you ugly freaks?" I shouted, cursing myself. Why had I assumed there would be no more resistance just because Timmy was dead?

The Nodkin glanced at one another. Finally one of them said, "Orders. Killing you is for the commander to do."

I laughed. "Sorry, the commander's already dead. I killed *him*— three times. The war's over."

Another exchange of looks. "It's never over," the same Nodkin growled. "There's always a commander."

Gail watched in silence from across the street. Again I cursed myself. I'd failed her. In my zeal to play this game the old-fashioned way, I'd forgotten that there really *was* a higher goal.

"How long are we going to stand here?" I asked the leader of the Nodkin. "Timmy's—"

"Right here," Timmy said, and I turned as he walked around the corner of the Mean Lady's house. His uniform was clean, without bloodstains, bullet holes or even wrinkles. The six stars gleamed on his shirt.

The cordon of Black Berets parted to let him through and he parked himself in front of me, arms crossed. "Happy, you big cheater?"

"*Me? You're* the one with a whole army helping you!"

"That's only because you had Mike helping *you*."

"Oh, *that's* real fair! I have one, so you have a million! Besides, Mike and I only joined up because of your bulletproof vest trick."

"That wasn't a trick. It was totally legal. And you wouldn't have gotten away at the school if you didn't change into your old self."

"What's wrong with that?" I leaned toward him. "You're just mad because you lost the war."

"No I'm not. Because I didn't lose."

"What are you talking about? I killed you three times!"

"Yeah, but you didn't save Gail."

"I can't believe you're such a *cheater.*"

He wiped his brow with his sleeve. "Tell you what. We'll call it a draw."

"A *draw?* No way! I killed you three times!"

"All I have to do is let these soldiers shoot, and then you'll be dead three times, too. Do you want that, or do you want to just call it a draw and play something else?"

I looked at him for a long moment. Then at the Nodkin. Facing the one that held my weapon, I said, "They won't shoot me."

"They will if I tell them to."

"Will not." I held a hand toward the Nodkin. "Give me that."

He hesitated. Then passed me the MP-80.

Timmy's eyes widened. Stepping back two paces, he cried, "Okay, you asked for it! Men—shoot him!"

A heartbeat passed. Then, one by one, the Nodkin lowered their guns until every muzzle pointed at the ground. Timmy gaped.

"They won't shoot me, Timmy," I said. "Because I don't want them to."

"Shoot him!" Timmy screamed. "I'm your commander! I made you; you have to do what I say! Shoot him shoot him *shoot him!*"

They stared blankly at Timmy, not moving.

"Hey," I said, "it's your own fault. You made me remember something—I used to be as good at this as you were. Maybe even better." Shoving past him, I strode between two of the Nodkin and into the street.

"No!" he screamed from the curb. "You don't understand, Jeff! You can't let her go! Remember the Big Tree! The *Big Tree won't let anyone go!*"

I halted, spun toward him. "The Big Tree? Let me tell you something. It's not the Big Tree that's the problem around here, it's *you. You're* the one who's afraid to let anyone go. *You're* the one who's got to control everything. I'm going to set Gail free, and you're not going to interfere, because you *swore on your honor* that she could go!"

"Only if you won the game," he said, face scarlet, sweat gleaming on the sides of his nose. "But you didn't; it was a *draw.*"

"Keep talking, Timmy." Turning away again, I walked across the street. Gail stood on the porch. The expression on her face, a combination of disbelief and hope, almost made me smile. This could have been the last chapter of one of the space-opera novels I'd so adored as a kid. *I'm here to free you, my princess.*

"Noooooooooorrrrrrrrrrrgggggghhh!" Behind me, Timmy's voice disintegrated into a horrible roar. I heard the clatter of claws on asphalt. I could have run, and might have even reached the porch first. Instead, I whirled around, MP-80 leveled. The shadow beast was already halfway across the street.

"*KAKAKAKAKAKAKAKAKAKAKAKAKAKAKAKKKKKKK!*" The rifle bucked in my hands while I silently counted, *One-Mississippi, two-Mississippi, three-Mississippi . . .*

I released the trigger. The shadow beast stood right in front of me, unmarked, grinning a fang-studded grin.

"Three seconds," I said. "I shot for three seconds."

The shadow beast curled a lip. "Doesn't matter. This time I mean it for real, Jeff. You'll be a ghost, which isn't great, but at least you—"

"*Three seconds,*" I said, poking him in the chest with the muzzle of the MP-80. "Those have always been the rules. And Timmy, guess what? This time I mean it for real, too. *You're dead.*"

The shadow beast's grin faltered. It stared into my eyes for a moment, then looked down at its own torso. A dozen holes popped open in the slick flesh. Black blood pulsed out. Grunting, the shadow beast staggered back, then looked at me. Timmy's eyes in its head, astonished and hurting.

"I'm sorry, Timmy," I said, meaning it. "But I believe you're going to die this time. *Really* die."

The ebony blood turned brilliant, gushing red. The beast's smooth flesh paled, tightened; its body withered into the shape of Timmy Kegler standing there in his blue jeans and T-shirt. The T-shirt was scarlet, stitched with holes, dripping. Timmy touched a finger to one of the holes. "This—" Blood sprayed from between his lips. He gulped. "This can't—"

"Anything's possible in the land of Nod," I said. "You said so yourself."

He looked up at me, eyes questioning, then his eyelids flickered and he simply fell, an angular pile of flesh and clothing in the street.

He didn't move. Behind me, Gail made a sound that was half whimper and half gasp.

Leaning down, I poked Timmy warily with the barrel of the MP-80. No response. I wondered if his ghost would appear. I hoped not.

Straightening, I looked around one more time. The iron-gray sky, the bright little houses, the Nodkin soldiers standing uncertainly on the far side of the street, staring at me as if awaiting orders.

CHAPTER THIRTY-FIVE

HIDE AND NO SEEK

I turned around. Gail still stood on the porch, still looked thirteen, still stared at me. But now she wasn't alone—Mike, Fred and Abe had also appeared, as soldiers always do at the end of a war. Still adolescents, but now wearing their civilian clothes and showing no visible wounds.

"Seems like we've been in this situation before," Fred said.

I turned back toward the street. Timmy's body hadn't moved; tentacles of blood spread from it toward the gutter. Still, just to be sure, I raised the MP-80 and fired a burst. His limbs jerked from the impact, but that was the only response. "He's dead," I said. "He's *dead* this time, you can see that . . . so why haven't things changed?"

"One thing has," Mike said. "Look at yourself."

I did. "You mean you think *I'm* holding all this together?"

He crossed his arms over his chest. "You've gotten pretty . . . involved."

"Yeah, but . . . I'm not like *Timmy.*"

No one replied.

I stared down at myself again, then at them. "What should I do?"

"You could try killing yourself," Fred said.

Gail turned on him. "Now who sounds like Timmy?"

"Sorry." He looked at his feet. "Just kidding."

"Wait a second," I said. "I think I've got it." Striding up the walkway, I planted a foot on the bottom step leading onto the porch and announced in a loud voice, "Okay, this makes it official. I win. I win the war. It's all over."

A handful of leaves blew down the street. One of them got stuck in the blood surrounding Timmy.

Nothing else changed.

I looked at the stricken faces of my friends, then walked to the porch and sat down on the top step. A moment later, Gail sat beside me and slipped her arm around my shoulders. I inhaled the dandelion scent of her, and sighed.

Fred's voice rang out in a giggling singsong: "Jeff and Gay-ayl sitting in a tree!" He bounded into the yard and did a bump-and-grind with his hips. "K-I-S-S-I-N-G!"

Mike jumped out to join him. "First comes love, then comes marriage—"

Abe leaped down, too, adding his voice to the chorus: "Then comes Junior in a baby carriage!"

I stared at them in astonishment, then started to grin. Aimed my MP-80 at them. "Shut up or I'll blow you all away."

"Sure, tough guy!" Fred cried. "I'm so *scaaaaaared*! Think your sweetie will let you do it?"

"Come on, Jeff," Mike said, "let's go play some more Army. Just the four of us. It will be *fun* this time."

"You can be commander!" Abe said, eyes bright behind his glasses. "You were always the best commander. Not like Timmy."

"Yeah! Not like Timmy." Fred turned and pointed his finger at the body in the street. Instantly a Luger pistol appeared in his fist. He pulled the trigger, putting a new hole in the motionless corpse. The report of the gun echoed out to the water tower. Maybe farther.

I leaped to my feet. "Hey, I just thought of something. We can play Army all over the place now. We can go clear to California if we want to!"

"Yeah!" The guys jumped up and down, slapped hands. Fred fired the Luger into the sky.

Something tugged urgently at my shirt. I pulled away in irritation. The tugging resumed, even harder, and I glared down at Gail.

"Jeff," she said, "isn't California where your daughter lives?"

"My . . . what?"

"Your *daughter*. Remember, you told me about her?"

I miss you. Can I come and visit you sometimes?

"Oh my God," I said, and sat down again. "Terri."

"What's going on?" Fred demanded. "Aren't we ever going to have any fun around here?"

"She dyed her hair," I said. "She dyed her hair black, and cut it all weird."

Gail squeezed my arm. "She needs her father. She needs him a lot."

"Come *on*, Jeff!" Mike yelled. "Let's play Army!"

I swallowed thickly. "I can't," I said. "I can't play anymore, guys, I have to go back. I'm sorry, but I have to go back."

Suddenly, soft warmth brushed my shoulder. I looked up. A small crack had opened in the clouds, allowing a spear of sunlight to cut the gloom. Across the street, the Nodkin stirred uneasily.

"Oh, man!" Abe wailed. "You're gonna ruin everything!"

Gail clutched my arm. "That's it. Keep going, Jeff. Think about your daughter."

"She's . . . fifteen. She'll need a car pretty soon."

The crack in the clouds widened. Sunlight spilled onto the street.

"Cut it out, Jeff!" Mike cried. "Think! No more house payments! No more insurance! Come on!"

The clouds rippled and closed again, squeezing off the beam of light. From somewhere in the distance came a soft grumbling sound. Thunder.

"Jeff?" Gail said warily.

"I'm not doing it." I rose to my feet. Behind the house, the Big Tree began to sway back and forth. "I . . . I don't *think* I'm doing it."

The light began to fail, the clouds darkening, churning in eddies and whorls. Thunder thumped again, louder.

"Jeff?" Gail cried, backing away from me, out into the yard with the rest of the gang. "What are you doing?"

I winced as lightning jabbed down behind the house, bringing with it a clap of thunder that made the windows buzz.

"It's the Big Tree!" Abe cried, eyes round. "Timmy said it wouldn't let anyone leave!"

"He's right, Jeff!" Fred shouted. "Come on, man! Don't fight it! Stay here!"

Another bolt of lightning ripped down, and I turned to see it strike behind the Big Tree. The wind was rising quickly, heaving the Big Tree's limbs up and down. I spun back. Across the street, the Nodkin sprinted away among the houses.

"You can make it stop, Jeff!" Mike shouted over the gale. "Don't try to leave! Come on, say you'll stay!"

From behind me came a splintering crash. I whirled as the picture window imploded. An instant later the front door burst inward, too. Shingles ripped off the roof in flocks and hurtled out of sight into the black sky. The house groaned, leaned away. With a shriek of nails, the roof bowed up in the center.

"Terri!" I shouted, but the wind drowned it out.

The entire house hurtled away in a wave of wood and masonry, twisting like a cardboard box, rolling and collapsing into the cornfield, disintegrating. I stared across the ragged foundation at the Big Tree. It was embraced in lightning, branches thrashing, foliage contorting. Suddenly a snarling face formed among the leaves. If you used your imagination, it could have been Timmy Kegler's face . . . or someone else's . . . my own . . .

"Jeff!" Gail shrieked. *"Jeff!"*

The Big Tree's mouth stretched wide open, and with a crackling, ripping roar, its enormous roots tore out of the ground and lashed out like tentacles. They clutched at the field and pulled. The Big Tree lurched forward.

I stared, knees locked in place, heart hurtling wildly inside my chest. The Big Tree was *coming.* It would never let me leave. It was coming for me, just as I'd always feared it would.

. . . or as I'd *hoped*?

You can't let your imagination run away with you. Dad's voice was so clear it might have been spoken into my ear. And suddenly I knew exactly what I had to do. Try to do.

With a tremendous effort, I whirled around. My friends still stood in the yard, staring at the Big Tree with expressions of superstitious horror on their faces. "It's okay!" I shouted. "It's part of the game! You've all gotta run and hide now!"

They glanced at one another, then Fred turned and sprinted across Oak Lane, firing his pistol into the air.

"Hey!" Abe cried, running after him. "Wait for me!"

Behind me, a massive grinding, ripping sound grew steadily louder.

Suddenly Gail was bounding up the porch steps, arms extended. I caught her and pulled her tight.

"This isn't a game, is it?" she whispered in my ear.

Tears pushed into my eyes. "If it works, I won't see you any-more. Thanks . . . thanks for letting me love you again."

She kissed my cheek, then whirled and raced away on her long brown legs. In a moment she had vanished among the houses.

Now there was only Mike. He stared at me, squinting against the howling wind. "What are you up to, Jeff?"

"Please, Mike. You've gotta get out of here."

"Are you sure you wanna do this?"

"It's time for all of us to move on." I smiled. "Save a good seat in Heaven for me, man."

He grinned. "Like that's where you're going." The grin faded as his gaze rose to the sky behind me. "Better get busy," he said, and sprinted off after the others.

The splintering crackle in the air had grown almost deafening. Something shot down near my feet and exploded into brown frag-ments. An acorn six inches across. Another blasted a crater in the front yard.

Shivering, I closed my eyes. Pictured Terri. Terri, my sweet child, my lost child. Terri who needed me.

The porch trembled violently under my feet. A vast rending noise bellowed through the air.

I'm coming for you, Terri, I thought. *I'm coming for you.* My heart filled with love and longing for her, but it wasn't good enough. Acorns clapped loudly against the street. Love and longing weren't enough. Thinking good thoughts wasn't enough. Those were the ways children fought their fears—but that wasn't reality, at least not all of it. There was more. For adults, there was far more.

Financial statements, I thought. *Dirty diapers. Tax returns and college tuition and interest rates and cholesterol levels and . . .*

Splintering explosions hammered the air like fireworks. Or like great wooden branches bending, extending themselves . . .

. . . Sinclair Synthetics and starvation in Africa and Rush Limbaugh and global warming and . . .

The explosions became muffled. Softer. Fainter.

. . . the information superhighway and prostate cancer and did I pay last month's water bill and . . .

Fainter. They might have been the pounding of my own heart.

. . . and my god I didn't turn off the electricity in the house

when I left, what if there's a short circuit and the whole place burns down? What if some kid climbs the fence and drowns in the swimming pool? What if . . .

A wash of heat prickled my head, my shoulders.

Slowly, I opened my eyes.

I was standing on the front porch of the little house in Middlefield, summer sunshine washing down on me. Out on Oak Lane, a brand-new Hyundai cruised past. Its driver looked at me with mild suspicion, unaware that he was driving across a faint stain of vaguely human shape.

A block away, the clamor of a bell poured out of the new junior high building. A moment later so did youngsters, rivers of them, their happy laughter rising into the blue air.

Tears stung my eyes, but I didn't wipe them away.

EPILOGUE

"Wow," Terri said, stepping onto my back patio, "this place is *rad!*"

"Glad you like it," I said, smiling. "There's no swimming pool, though."

"Yeah, but . . ." Lost for words, she waved a hand at the backyard.

It was the backyard, rather than the size or quality of the adjacent house, that had sold me on this place. Because of the canyons descending on either side, the rearmost section of the lot had an odd, tapered shape that had baffled the developers and been left appended, at essentially no extra charge, to the property. The previous owner had landscaped it heavily with everything from fragrant bougainvillea to magnolia trees, letting the vegetation spill down into the canyons. Here in the backyard, you heard more birds than cars, and saw more greenery than asphalt. "Think you'll mind visiting here a couple of times a week?" I asked.

"I like to visit you no matter what." She ran her hand along the rim of a ceramic birdbath. "But here . . . can we eat back here? I'll barbecue."

"Sounds great. You can invite friends over if you want to."

She shrugged. "Maybe sometime."

I watched her move across the yard from plant to plant. Her left ear was still triple-pierced, but she'd dyed her hair back almost to its natural color, and most of the shaved parts had grown back in. I hadn't seen her with another cigarette, either.

Best of all, I hadn't asked her to make any of these changes. It was just that the more time we spent together, the more her ap-

296

pearance mellowed. Mine, too. I'd lost almost thirty pounds since returning from Indiana.

One thing I hadn't lost was my job, although I'd looked Mr. Warrick straight in the eye and told him I wouldn't be working so many hours anymore. He'd glared back, then suddenly used those six smile muscles. "Smart man," he'd said, clapping me on the shoulder.

In case I needed more evidence that I'd changed, all I had to do was look at Janice's face whenever I stopped by her place to pick Terri up. My ex-wife always stared at me searchingly, with perhaps a little bit of fear, as if she thought I'd become possessed. That meant a lot to me.

"Hey," Terri said, "what happened over here?" She was standing in one of the few open areas in the yard, staring at something in the grass. Without going over, I knew what it was. A fat stump sheared off at ground level.

"Oh," I said casually, "I had this one old tree cut down."

"How come? Was it sick?"

"No, I just didn't like it."

"Why? What kind was it?"

I smiled. "I don't remember."

CLEMENT   Clements, Mark A.,
        1955-

       The land of nod.

$21.95

DATE			